Dear Reader,

I'm delighted to welcome you to a very special Bestselling Author Collection for 2024! In celebration of Harlequin's 75 years in publishing, this collection features fan-favorite stories from some of our readers' most cherished authors. Each book also includes a free full-length story by an exciting writer from one of our current programs.

Our company has grown and changed since its inception 75 years ago. Today, Harlequin publishes more than 100 titles a month in 30 countries and 15 languages, with stories for a diverse readership across a range of genres and formats, including hardcover, trade paperback, mass market paperback, ebook and audiobook.

But our commitment to you, our romance reader, remains the same: in every Harlequin romance, a guaranteed happily-ever-after!

Thank you for coming on this journey with us. And happy reading as we embark on the next 75 years of bringing joy to readers around the world!

Dianne Moggy

Vice-President, Editorial

Harlequin

Debbie Macomber is a #1 *New York Times* bestselling author and a leading voice in women's fiction worldwide. Her work has appeared on every major bestseller list, with more than a hundred and seventy million copies in print, and she is a multiple-award winner. The Hallmark Channel based a television series on Debbie's popular Cedar Cove books. For more information, visit her website, debbiemacomber.com.

New York Times and *USA TODAY* bestselling author **Lee Tobin McClain** read *Gone with the Wind* in the third grade and has been an incurable romantic ever since. When she's not writing angst-filled love stories with happy endings, she's probably Snapchatting with her college-student daughter, mediating battles between her goofy goldendoodle and her rescue cat, or teaching aspiring writers in Seton Hill University's MFA program. She is probably not cleaning her house. For more about Lee, visit her website at leetobinmcclain.com.

#1 *New York Times* Bestselling Author

DEBBIE MACOMBER

A Little Bit Country

ISBN-13: 978-1-335-00878-7

For questions and comments about the quality of this book, please contact us at CustomerService@Harlequin.com.

Harlequin Enterprises ULC
22 Adelaide St. West, 41st Floor
Toronto, Ontario M5H 4E3, Canada
www.Harlequin.com

Printed in U.S.A.

CONTENTS

A LITTLE BIT COUNTRY 7
Debbie Macomber

HER EASTER PRAYER 195
Lee Tobin McClain

Also by Debbie Macomber

MIRA

Blossom Street

The Shop on Blossom Street
A Good Yarn
Susannah's Garden
Back on Blossom Street
Twenty Wishes
Summer on Blossom Street
Hannah's List
"The Twenty-First Wish" (in *The Knitting Diaries*)
A Turn in the Road

Cedar Cove

16 Lighthouse Road
204 Rosewood Lane
311 Pelican Court
44 Cranberry Point
50 Harbor Street
6 Rainier Drive
74 Seaside Avenue
8 Sandpiper Way
92 Pacific Boulevard
1022 Evergreen Place
Christmas in Cedar Cove (*5-B Poppy Lane*
and *A Cedar Cove Christmas*)
1105 Yakima Street
1225 Christmas Tree Lane

Visit her Author Profile page at Harlequin.com,
or debbiemacomber.com, for more titles!

A LITTLE BIT COUNTRY

Debbie Macomber

One

"Help! Fire!" Rorie Campbell cried as she leaped out of the small foreign car. Smoke billowed from beneath the hood, rising like a burnt offering to a disgruntled god. Rorie ran across the road, and a black-and-white cow ambled through the pasture toward her, stopping at the split-rail fence. Soulful brown eyes studied her, as if the cow wondered what all the commotion was about.

"It's not even my car," Rorie said, pointing in the direction of the vehicle. "All of a sudden smoke started coming out."

The cow regarded her blankly, chewing its cud, then returned lazily to the shade of a huge oak tree.

"I think it's on fire. Dan's going to kill me for this," Rorie muttered as she watched the uninterested animal saunter away. "I don't know what to do." There was no water in sight and even if there had been, Rorie didn't have any way of hauling it to the car. She was so desperate, she was talking to a cow—and she'd almost expected the creature to advise her.

"Howdy."

Rorie whirled around to discover a man astride a

chestnut stallion. Silhouetted against the warm afternoon sun, he looked like an apparition smiling down at her from the side of the hill opposite Dan's car.

"Hello." Rorie's faith in a benign destiny increased tenfold in that moment. "Boy, am I glad to see another human being." She'd been on this road for the past two hours and hadn't encountered another car in either direction.

"What seems to be the problem?" Leather creaked as the man swung out of the saddle with an ease that bespoke years of experience.

"I… I don't know," Rorie said, flapping her hands in frustration. "Everything was going just great when all of a sudden the car started smoking like crazy."

"That's steam."

"Steam! You mean the car isn't on fire?"

The man flipped the reins over his horse's head and walked toward the hood of the sports car. It was then that Rorie realized the man wasn't a man at all, but a boy. Sixteen, or possibly a little older. Not that Rorie was particular. She was just grateful someone had stopped. "A friend of mine insisted I drive his MGB up to Seattle." She sighed. "I should've known that if anything went wrong, I'd be at a total loss about what to do. I should've known…"

The boy whipped a large blue-starred hankie from the hip pocket of his faded jeans and used it to protect his hand while he raised the hood of her car. The instant he did, a great white cloud of steam swirled up like mist from a graveyard in a horror movie.

"I…thought I'd take the scenic route," Rorie explained, frantically waving her hand in front of her face to dispel the vapor. "The man at the gas station a hundred miles back said this is beautiful country. He said I'd miss some of the best scenery in Oregon if I stuck to the freeway." Rorie knew she was chattering, but she'd never experienced this type of situation before or felt quite so helpless.

"It's not only the best scenery in the state, it tops the whole country, if you ask me," the boy murmured absently while he examined several black hoses beneath the raised hood.

Rorie looked at her watch and moaned. If she wasn't in Seattle before six, she'd lose her hotel reservation. This vacation wasn't starting out well—not at all. And she'd had such high expectations for the next two weeks.

"I think you've got a leak in your water pump," the teenager stated, sounding as though he knew what he was talking about. "But it's hard to tell with all that fancy stuff they got in these foreign cars. Clay can tell you for sure."

"Clay?"

"My brother."

"Is he a mechanic?" Rorie's hopes soared.

"He's done his share of working on cars, but he's not a mechanic."

Rorie gnawed on her lower lip as her spirits plummeted again. Her first concern was getting to a phone. She'd make the necessary arrangements to have the car repaired and then call the hotel to ask if they'd hold her room. Depending on how close she was to the nearest town, Rorie figured it would take an hour for a tow truck to arrive and then another for it to get her car to a garage. Once there, the repairs shouldn't take too long. Just how hard could it be to fix a water pump?

"How far is it to a phone?"

The young man grinned and pointed toward his horse. "Just over that ridge…"

Rorie relaxed. At least that part wasn't going to be much of a problem.

"…about ten miles," he finished.

"Ten miles?" Rorie leaned her weight against the side of the car. This was the last time she'd ever take the scenic route and the last time she'd ever let Dan talk her into borrowing his car!

"Don't worry, you won't have to walk. Venture can handle both of us. You don't look like you weigh much."

"Venture?" Rorie was beginning to feel like an echo.

"My horse."

Rorie's gaze shifted to the stallion, who had lowered his head to sample the tall hillside grass. Now that she had a chance to study him, she realized what an extraordinarily large animal he was. Rorie hadn't been on the back of a horse since she was a child. Somehow, the experience of riding a pony in a slow circle with a bunch of other six-year-olds didn't lend her much confidence now.

"You…you want me to ride double with you?" She was wearing a summer dress and mounting a horse might prove…interesting. She eyed the stallion, wondering how she could manage to climb into the saddle and still maintain her dignity.

"You wearing a dress and all could make that difficult." The boy rubbed the side of his jaw, frowning doubtfully.

"I could wait here until someone else comes along," she offered.

He used his index finger to set his snap-brim hat further back on his head. “You might do that,” he drawled, “but it could be another day or so—if you’re lucky.”

“Oh, dear!”

“I suppose I could head back to the house and grab the pickup,” he suggested.

It sounded like a stroke of genius to Rorie. “Would you? Listen, I’d be more than happy to pay you for your time.”

He gave her an odd look. “Why would you want to do that? I’m only doing the neighborly thing.”

Rorie smiled at him. She’d lived in San Francisco most of her life. She loved everything about the City by the Bay, but she couldn’t have named the couple in the apartment next door had her life depended on it. People in the city kept to themselves.

“By the way,” he said, wiping his hands with the bright blue handkerchief, “the name’s Skip. Skip Franklin.”

Rorie eagerly shook his hand, overwhelmingly grateful that he’d happened along when he did. “Rorie Campbell.”

“Pleased to meet you, ma’am.”

“Me too, Skip.”

The teenager grinned. “Now you stay right here and I’ll be back before you know it.” He paused, apparently considering something else. “You’ll be all right by yourself, won’t you?”

“Oh, sure, don’t worry about me.” She braced her feet wide apart and held up her hands in the classic karate position. “I can take care of myself. I’ve had three self-defence lessons.”

Skip chuckled, ambled toward Venture and swung

up into the saddle. Within minutes he'd disappeared over the ridge.

Rorie watched him until he was out of sight, then walked over to the grassy hillside and sat down, arranging her dress carefully around her knees. The cow she'd been conversing with earlier glanced in her direction and Rorie felt obliged to explain. "He's gone for help," she called out. "Said it was the neighborly thing to do."

The animal mooed loudly.

Rorie smiled. "I thought so, too."

An hour passed, and it seemed the longest of Rorie's life. With the sun out in full force now, she felt as if she was wilting more by the minute. Just when she began to suspect that Skip Franklin had been a figment of her overwrought imagination, she heard a loud chugging sound. She leaped to her feet and, shading her eyes with her hand, looked down the road. It was Skip, sitting on a huge piece of farm equipment, heading straight toward her.

Rorie gulped. Her gallant rescuer had come to get her on a tractor!

Skip removed his hat and waved it. Even from this distance, she could see his grin.

Rorie feebly returned the gesture, but her smile felt brittle. Of the two modes of transportation, she would have preferred the stallion. Good grief, there was only one seat on the tractor. Where exactly did Skip plan for her to sit? On the engine?

Once he'd reached the car, he parked the tractor directly in front of it. "Clay said we should tow the car to our place instead of leaving it on the road. You don't mind, do you?"

"Whatever he thinks is best."

"He'll be along any minute," Skip explained, jumping down from his perch. He used a hook and chain to connect the sports car to the tractor. "Clay had a couple of things he needed to do first."

Rorie nodded, grateful her options weren't so limited, after all.

A few minutes later, she heard the sound of another vehicle. This time it was a late-model truck in critical need of a paint job. Rust showed through on the left front fender, which had been badly dented.

"That's Clay now," Skip announced, nodding toward the winding road.

Rorie busied herself brushing bits of grass from the skirt of her dress. When she'd finished, she looked up to see a tall muscular man sliding from the driver's side of the pickup. He was dressed in jeans and a denim shirt, and his hat was pulled low over his forehead, shading his eyes. Rorie's breath caught in her throat as she noticed his grace of movement—a thoroughly masculine grace. Something about Clay Franklin grabbed her imagination. He embodied everything she'd ever linked with the idea of an outdoorsman, a man's man. She could imagine him taming a wilderness or forging an empire. In his clearly defined features she sensed a strength that reminded her of the land itself. The spellbinding quality of his steel-gray eyes drew her own and held them for a long moment. His nose had a slight curve, as though it had been broken once. He smiled, and a tingling sensation Rorie couldn't explain skittered down her spine.

His eyes still looked straight into hers and his hands rested on his lean hips. "Looks as if you've got yourself into a predicament here." His voice was low, husky—and slightly amused.

His words seemed to wrap themselves around Rorie's throat, choking off any intelligent reply. Her lips parted, but to her embarrassment nothing came out.

Clay smiled and the fine lines that fanned out from the corners of his eyes crinkled appealingly.

"Skip thinks it might be the water pump," she said, pointing at the MGB. The words came out weak and rusty and Rorie felt even more foolish. She'd never had a man affect her this way. He wasn't really even handsome. Not like Dan Rogers. No, Clay wasn't the least bit like Dan, who was urbane and polished—and very proud of his little MGB.

"From the sounds of it, Skip's probably right." Clay walked over to the car, which his brother had connected to the tractor. He twisted the same black hose Skip had earlier and shook his head. Next he checked to see that the bumper of Dan's car was securely fastened to the chain. He nodded, lightly slapping his brother's back in approval. "Nice work."

Skip beamed under his praise.

"I assume you're interested in finding a phone. There's one at the house you're welcome to use," Clay said, looking at Rorie.

"Thank you." Her heart pounded in her ears and her stomach felt queasy. This reaction was so unusual for her. Normally she was a calm, levelheaded twenty-four-year-old, not a flighty teenager who didn't know how to act when an attractive male happened to glance in her direction.

Clay walked around to the passenger side of the pickup and held open the door. He waited for Rorie, then gave her his hand to help her climb inside. The simple action touched her; it had been a long time since anyone had shown her such unselfconscious courtesy.

Then Clay walked to the driver's side and hoisted himself in. He started the engine, which roared to life immediately, and shifted gears.

"I apologize for any inconvenience I've caused you," Rorie said stiffly, after several moments of silence.

"It's no problem," Clay murmured, concentrating on his driving, doing just the speed limit and not a fraction more.

They'd been driving for about ten minutes when Clay turned off the road and through a huge log archway with ELK RUN lettered across the top. Lush green pastures flanked the private road, and several horses were grazing calmly in one of them. Rorie knew next to nothing about horse breeds, but whatever these were revealed a grace and beauty that was apparent even to her untrained eye.

The next thing Rorie noticed was the large two-story house with a wide wraparound veranda on which a white wicker swing swayed gently. Budding rosebushes lined the meandering brick walkway.

"It's beautiful," she said softly. Rorie would have expected something like this in the bluegrass hills of Kentucky, not on the back roads of Oregon.

Clay made no comment.

He drove past the house and around the back toward the largest stable Rorie had ever seen. The sprawling wood structure must have had room for thirty or more horses.

"You raise horses?" she said.

A smile moved through his eyes like distant light. "That's one way of putting it. Elk Run is a stud farm."

"Quarter horses?"

That was the only breed that came to mind.

"No. American Saddlebreds."

"I don't think I've ever heard of them before."

"Probably not," Clay said, not unkindly.

He parked the truck, helped Rorie down and led her toward the back of the house.

"Mary," he called, holding the screen door for Rorie to precede him into the large country kitchen. She was met with the smell of cinnamon and apples. The delectable aroma came from a freshly baked pie, cooling on the counter. A black Labrador retriever slept on a braided rug. He raised his head and thumped his tail gently when Clay stepped over to him and bent down to scratch the dog's ears. "This is Blue."

"Hi, Blue," Rorie said, realizing the dog had probably been a childhood pet. He looked well advanced in years.

"Mary doesn't seem to be around."

"Mary's your wife?"

"Housekeeper," Clay informed her. "I'm not married."

That small piece of information gladdened Rorie's heart and she instantly felt foolish. Okay, so she was attracted to this man with eyes as gray as a San Francisco sky, but that didn't change a thing. If her plans went according to schedule, she'd be in and out of his life within hours.

"Mary's probably upstairs," Clay said when the housekeeper didn't answer. "There's a phone on the wall." He pointed to the other side of the kitchen.

While Rorie retrieved her AT&T card from her eelskin wallet, Clay crossed to the refrigerator and took out a brightly colored ceramic pitcher.

"Iced tea?" he asked.

"Please." Her throat felt parched. She had to swallow several times before she could make her call.

As she spoke on the phone, Clay took two tall glasses from a cupboard and half filled them with ice cubes. He poured in the tea, then added thin slices of lemon.

Rorie finished her conversation and walked over to the table. Sitting opposite Clay, she reached for the drink he'd prepared. "That was my hotel in Seattle. They won't be able to hold the room past six."

"I'm sure there'll be space in another," he said confidently.

Rorie nodded, although she thought that was unlikely. She was on her way to a writers' conference, one for which she'd paid a hefty fee, and she hated to miss one minute of it. Every hotel in the city was said to be filled.

"I'll call the garage in Nightingale for you," Clay offered.

"Is that close by?"

"About five miles down the road."

Rorie was relieved. She'd never heard of Nightingale and was grateful to learn it had a garage. After all, the place was barely large enough to rate a mention on the road map.

"Old Joe's been working on cars most of his life. He'll do a good job for you."

Rorie nodded again, not knowing how else to respond.

Clay quickly strode to the phone, punched out the number and talked for a few minutes. He was frowning when he replaced the receiver. Rorie wanted to question him, but before she could, he grabbed an impossibly thin phone book and dialed a second number. His frown was deeper by the time he'd completed the call.

"I've got more bad news for you."

"Oh?" Rorie's heart had planted itself somewhere between her chest and her throat. She didn't like the way Clay was frowning, or the concern she heard in his voice. "What's wrong now?"

"Old Joe's gone fishing and isn't expected back this month. The mechanic in Riversdale, which is about sixty miles south of here, says that if it is your pump it'll take at least four days to ship a replacement."

Two

"Four days!" Rorie felt the color drain from her face. "But that's impossible! I can't possibly wait that long."

"Seems to me," Clay said in his smooth drawl, "you don't have much choice. George tells me he could have the water pump within a day if you weren't driving a foreign job."

"Surely there's someone else I could call."

Clay seemed to mull that over; then he shrugged. "Go ahead and give it a try if you like, but it isn't going to do you any good. If the shop in Riversdale can't get the part until Saturday, what makes you think someone else can do it any faster?"

Clay's calm acceptance of the situation infuriated Rorie. If she stayed here four days, in the middle of nowhere, she'd completely miss the writers' conference, which she'd been planning to attend for months. She'd scheduled her entire vacation around it. She'd made arrangements to travel to Victoria on British Columbia's Vancouver Island after the conference and on the way home take a leisurely trip down the coast.

Clay handed her the phone book, and feeling defeated Rorie thumbed through the brief yellow pages until she came to the section headed Automobile Repair. Only a handful were listed and none of them promised quick service, she noted.

"Yes, well," she muttered, expelling her breath, "there doesn't seem to be any other option." Discouraged, she set the directory back on the counter. "You and your brother have been most helpful and I want you to know how much I appreciate everything you've done. Now if you could recommend a hotel in…what was the name of the town again?"

"Nightingale."

"Right," she said, with a wobbly smile, which was the best she could do at the moment. "Actually, anyplace that's clean will be fine."

Clay rubbed the side of his jaw. "I'm afraid that's going to present another problem."

"Now what? Has the manager gone fishing with Old Joe?" Rorie did her best to keep the sarcasm out of her voice, but it was difficult. Obviously the people in the community of… Nightingale didn't take their responsibilities too seriously. If they were on the job when someone happened to need them, it was probably by coincidence.

"A fishing trip isn't the problem this time," Clay explained, his expression thoughtful. "Nightingale doesn't have a hotel."

"What?" Rorie exploded. "No hotel…but there must be."

"We don't get much traffic through here. People usually stick to the freeway."

If he was implying that *she* should have done so, Rorie couldn't have agreed with him more. She might have seen some lovely scenery, but look where this little side trip had taken her! Her entire vacation was about to be ruined. She slowly released her breath, trying hard to maintain her composure, which was cracking more with every passing minute.

"What about Riversdale? Surely they have a hotel?"

Clay nodded. "They do. It's a real nice one, but I suspect it's full."

"Full? I thought you just told me people don't often take this route."

"Tourists don't."

"Then how could the hotel possibly be full?"

"The Jerome family."

"I beg your pardon?"

"The Jerome family is having a big reunion. People are coming from all over the country. Jed was telling me the other day that a cousin of his is driving out from Boston. The overflow will more than likely fill up Riversdale's only hotel."

One phone call confirmed Clay's suspicion.

"Terrific," Rorie murmured, her hand still on the receiver. The way things were beginning to look, she'd end up sleeping on a park bench—if Nightingale even had a park.

The back door opened and Skip wandered in, obviously pleased about something. He poured himself a glass of iced tea and leaned against the counter, glancing from Rorie to Clay and then back again.

"What's happening?" he asked, when no one volunteered any information.

"Nothing much," Rorie said. "Getting the water pump for my car is going to take four days and it seems the only hotel within a sixty-mile radius is booked full for the next two weeks and—"

"That's no problem. You can stay here," Skip inserted quickly, his blue eyes flashing with eagerness. "We'd love to have you, wouldn't we, Clay?"

Rorie spoke before the elder Franklin had an opportunity to answer. "No, really, I appreciate the offer, but I can't inconvenience you any more than I already have."

"She wouldn't be an inconvenience, would she?" Once more Skip directed the question to his older brother. "Tell her she wouldn't, Clay."

"I can't stay here," she returned, without giving Clay the chance to echo his brother's invitation. She didn't know these people. And, more important, they didn't know her and Rorie refused to impose on them further.

Clay gazed into her eyes and a slow smile turned up the edges of his mouth. "It's up to you, Rorie. You're welcome on Elk Run if you want to stay."

"But you've done so much. I really couldn't—"

"There's plenty of room," Skip announced ardently.

Those baby-blue eyes of his would melt the strongest resolve, Rorie mused.

"There's three bedrooms upstairs that are sitting empty. And you wouldn't need to worry about staying with two bachelors, because Mary's here—she has a cottage across the way."

It seemed inconceivable to Rorie that this family would take her in just like that. But, given her options, her arguments for refusing their offer were weak, to say the least. "You don't even know me."

"We know all we need to, don't we, Clay?" Skip glanced at his older brother, seeking his support.

"You're welcome to stay here, if you like," Clay repeated, his gaze continuing to hold Rorie's.

Again she was struck by the compelling quality of this man. He had a stubborn jaw and she doubted there were many confrontations where he walked away a loser. She'd always prided herself on her ability to read people. And her instincts told her firmly that Clay Franklin could be trusted. She sensed he was scrupulously honest, utterly dependable—and she already knew he was generous to a fault.

"I'd be most grateful," she said, swallowing a surge of tears at the Franklins' uncomplicated kindness to a complete stranger. "But, please, let me do something to make up for all the trouble I've caused you."

"It's no trouble," Skip said, looking as if he wanted to jump up and click his heels in jubilation.

Clay frowned as he watched his younger brother.

"Really," Rorie stressed. "If there's anything I can do, I'd be more than happy to lend a hand."

"Do you know anything about computers?"

"A little," she said. "We use them at the library."

"You're a librarian?"

Rorie nodded and brushed a stray dark curl from her forehead. "I specialize in children's literature." Someday she hoped to have her own work published. That had been her reason for attending the conference in Seattle. Three of the top children's authors in the country were slated to speak. "If you have a computer system, I'd be happy to do whatever I can..."

"Clay bought a new one last winter," Skip informed her proudly. "He has a program that records horse breeding and pedigrees up to the fourth and fifth generation."

A heavyset woman Rorie assumed was the housekeeper entered the kitchen, hauling a mop and bucket. She inspected Rorie with a measuring glance and seemed to find her lacking. She grumbled something about city girls as she sidled past Skip.

"Didn't know you'd decided to hold a convention right in the middle of my kitchen."

"Mary," Clay said, "this is Rorie Campbell, from San Francisco. Her car broke down, so she'll be staying with us for the next few days. Could you see that a bed is made up for her?"

The older woman's wide face broke into a network of frown lines.

"Oh, please, I can do that myself," Rorie said quickly.

Mary nodded. "Sheets are in the closet at the top of the stairs."

"Rorie is our guest." Clay didn't raise his voice, but his displeasure was evident in every syllable.

Mary shrugged, muttering, "I got my own things to do. If the girl claims she can make a bed, then let her."

Rorie couldn't contain her smile.

"You want to invite some city slicker to stay, then fine, but I got more important matters to attend to before I make up a bed for her." With that, Mary marched out of the kitchen.

"Mary's like family," Skip explained. "It's just her way to be sassy. She doesn't mean anything by it."

"I'm sure she doesn't," Rorie said, smiling so Clay and Skip would know she wasn't offended. She gathered that the Franklins' housekeeper didn't hold a high opinion of anyone from the city and briefly wondered why.

"I'll get your suitcase from the car," Skip said, heading for the door.

Clay finished his drink and set the glass on the counter. "I've got to get back to work," he told her, pausing for a moment before he added, "You won't be bored by yourself, will you?"

"Not at all. Don't worry about me."

Clay nodded. "Dinner's at six."

"I'll be ready."

Rorie picked up the empty glasses and put them by the sink. While she waited for Skip to carry in her luggage, she phoned Dan. Unfortunately he was in a meeting and couldn't be reached, so she left a message, explaining that she'd been delayed and would call again. She felt strangely reluctant to give him the Franklins' phone number, but decided there was no reason not to do so. She also decided not to examine that feeling too closely.

Skip had returned by the time she'd hung up. "Clay says you can have Mom and Dad's old room," the teenager announced on his way through the door. He hauled her large suitcase in one hand and her flight bag was slung over his shoulder. "Their room's at the other end of the house. They were killed in an accident five years ago."

"But—"

"Their room's got the best view."

"Skip, really, any bedroom will do… I don't want your parents' room."

"But that's the one Clay wants for you." He bounded up the curving stairway with the energy reserved for the young.

Rorie followed him more slowly. She slid her hand along the polished banister and glanced into the living room. A large natural-rock fireplace dominated one wall. The furniture was built of solid oak, made comfortable with thick chintz-covered cushions. Several braided rugs were placed here and there on the polished wood floor. A piano with well-worn ivory keys stood to one side. The collection of family photographs displayed on top of it immediately caught her eye. She recognized a much younger Clay in what had to be his high-school graduation photo. The largest picture in an ornate brass frame was of a middle-aged couple, obviously Clay and Skip's parents.

Skip paused at the top of the stairway and looked over his shoulder. "My grandfather built this house more than fifty years ago."

"It's magnificent."

"We think so," he admitted, eyes shining with pride.

The master bedroom, which was at the end of the hallway, opened onto a balcony that presented an unobstructed panorama of the entire valley. Rolling green pastures stretched as far as the eye could see. Rorie felt instantly drawn to this unfamiliar rural beauty. She drew a deep breath, and the thought flashed through her mind that it must be comforting to wake up to this serene landscape day after day.

"Everyone loves it here," Skip said from behind her.

"I can understand why."

"Well, I suppose I should get back to work," he said regretfully, setting her suitcases on the double bed. A colorful quilt lay folded at its foot.

Rorie turned toward him, smiling. "Thank you, Skip. I hate to think what would've happened to me if you hadn't come along when you did."

He blushed and started backing out of the room, taking small steps as though he was loath to leave her. "I'll see you at dinner, okay?"

Rorie smiled again. "I'll look forward to it."

"Bye for now." He raised his right hand in a farewell gesture, then whirled around and dashed down the hallway. She could hear his feet pounding on the stairs.

It took Rorie only a few minutes to hang her things in the bare closet. When she'd finished, she went back to the kitchen, where Mary was busy peeling potatoes at the stainless steel sink.

"I'd like to help, if I could."

"Fine," the housekeeper answered gruffly. She took another potato peeler out of a nearby drawer, slapping it down on the counter. "I suppose that's your fancy sports car in the yard."

"The water pump has to be replaced… I think," Rorie answered, not bothering to mention that the MGB wasn't actually hers.

"Humph," was Mary's only response.

Rorie sighed and reached for a large potato. "The mechanic in Riversdale said it would take until Saturday to get a replacement part."

For the second time, Mary answered her with a gruff-sounding *humph.* "If then! Saturday or next Thursday or a month from now, it's all the same to George. Fact is, you could end up staying here all summer."

Three

Mary's words echoed in Rorie's head as she joined Clay and Skip at the dinner table that evening. She stood just inside the dining room, dressed in a summer skirt and a cotton-knit cream-colored sweater, and announced, "I can't stay any longer than four days."

Clay regarded her blankly. "I have no intention of holding you prisoner, Rorie."

"I know, but Mary told me that if I'm counting on George what's-his-name to fix the MG, I could end up spending the summer here. I've got to get back to San Francisco—I have a job there." She realized how nonsensical her little speech sounded, as if that last bit about having a job explained everything.

"If you want, I'll keep after George to make sure he doesn't forget about it."

"Please." Rorie felt a little better for having spoken her mind.

"And the Greyhound bus comes through on Mondays," Skip said reassuringly. "If you had to, you could take that back to California and return later for your friend's car."

"The bus," she repeated. "I *could* take the bus." As

it was, the first half of her vacation was ruined, but it'd be nice to salvage what she could of the rest.

Both men were seated, but as Rorie approached the table Skip rose noisily to his feet, rushed around to the opposite side and pulled out a chair for her.

"Thank you," she said, smiling up at him. His dark hair was wet and slicked down close to his head. He'd changed out of his work clothes and into what appeared to be his Sunday best—a dress shirt, tie and pearl-gray slacks. With a good deal of ceremony, he pushed in her chair. As he leaned toward her, it was all Rorie could do to keep from grimacing at the overpowering scent of his spicy aftershave. He must have drenched himself in the stuff.

Clay's gaze seemed to tug at hers and when Rorie glanced in his direction, she saw that he was doing his utmost not to laugh. He clearly found his brother's antics amusing, though he took pains not to hurt Skip's feelings, but Rorie wasn't sure how she should react. Skip was only in his teens, and she didn't want to encourage any romantic fantasies he might have.

"I hope you're hungry," Skip said, once he'd reclaimed his chair. "Mary puts on a good feed."

"I'm starved," Rorie admitted, eyeing the numerous serving dishes spread out on the table.

Clay handed her a large platter of fried chicken. That was followed by mashed potatoes, gravy, rolls, fresh green beans, a mixed green salad, milk and a variety of preserves. By the time they'd finished passing around the food, there wasn't any space left on Rorie's oversize plate.

"Don't forget to leave room for dessert," Clay commented, again with that slow, easy drawl of his. Here

Skip was practically doing cartwheels to attract her attention and all Clay needed to do was look at her and she became light-headed. Rorie couldn't understand it. From the moment Clay Franklin had stepped down from his pickup, she hadn't been the same.

"After dinner I thought I'd take you up to the stable and introduce you to King Genius," Skip said, waving a chicken leg.

"I'd be happy to meet him."

"Once you do, you'll feel like you did when you stood on the balcony in the big bedroom and looked at the valley."

Obviously this King wasn't a foreman, as Rorie had first assumed. More than likely, he was one of the horses she'd seen earlier grazing on the pasture in front of the house.

"I don't think it would be a good idea to take Rorie around Hercules," Clay warned his younger brother.

"Of course not." But it looked as if Skip wanted to argue.

"Who's Hercules?"

"Clay's stallion," Skip explained. "He has a tendency to act up if Clay isn't around."

Rorie could only guess what "act up" meant, but even if Skip didn't intend to heed Clay's advice, she gladly would. Other than that pony ride when she was six, Rorie hadn't been near a horse. One thing was certain; she planned to steer a wide path around the creature, no matter how much Skip encouraged her. The largest pet she'd ever owned had been a guinea pig.

"When Hercules first came to Elk Run, the man who brought him said he was mean-spirited and untrainable.

He wanted him destroyed, but Clay insisted on working with the stallion."

"Now he's your own personal horse?" Rorie asked Clay.

He nodded. "We've got an understanding."

"But it's only between them," Skip added. "Hercules doesn't like anyone else getting close."

"He doesn't have anything to worry about as far as I'm concerned," Rorie was quick to assure both brothers. "I'll give him as much space as he needs."

Clay grinned, and once again she felt her heart turn over. This strange affinity with Clay was affirmed in the look he gave her. Unexpected thoughts of Dan Rogers sprang to mind. Dan was a divorced stockbroker she'd been seeing steadily for the past few months. Rorie enjoyed Dan's company and had recently come to believe she was falling in love with him. Now she knew differently. She couldn't be this powerfully drawn to Clay Franklin if Dan was anything more than a good friend. One of the reasons Rorie had decided on this vacation was to test her feelings for Dan. Two days out of San Francisco, and she had her answer.

Deliberately Rorie pulled her gaze from Clay, wanting to attribute everything she was experiencing to the clean scent of country air.

Skip's deep blue eyes sparkled with pride as he started to tell Rorie about Elk Run's other champion horses. "But you'll love the King best. He was the five-gaited world champion four years running. Clay put him out to stud four years ago. National Show Horses are commanding top dollar and we've produced three of the best. King's the sire, naturally."

"Do all the horses I saw in the pasture belong to you?"

"We board several," Skip answered. "Some of the others are brought here from around the country for Clay to break and train."

"You break horses?" She couldn't conceal her sudden alarm. The image of Clay sitting on a wild bronco that bucked and heaved in a furious effort to unseat him did funny things to Rorie's stomach.

"Breaking horses isn't exactly the way Hollywood pictures show it," Clay explained.

Rorie was about to ask him more when Skip planted his elbows on the table and leaned forward. Once again Rorie was assaulted by the overpowering scent of his aftershave. She did her best to smile, but if he remained in that position much longer, her eyes would start watering. Already she could feel a sneeze tickling her nose.

"How old are you, Rorie?" he asked.

The question was so unexpected that she was too surprised to answer immediately. Then she said, "Twenty-four."

"And you live in San Francisco. Is your family there, too?"

"No. My parents moved to Arizona and my brother's going to school back east."

"And you're not engaged or anything?"

As Rorie shook her head, Clay shot his brother an exasperated look. "Are you interviewing Rorie for the *Independent?*"

"No. I was just curious."

"She's too old for you, little brother."

"I don't know about that," Skip returned fervently. "I've always liked my women more mature. Besides, Rorie's kind of cute."

"Kind of?"

Skip shrugged. "You know what I mean. She doesn't act like a city girl…much."

Rorie's eyes flew from one brother to the next. They were talking as if she wasn't even in the room, and that annoyed her—especially since she was the main topic of conversation.

Unaware of her reaction, Skip helped himself to another roll. "Actually, I thought she might be closer to twenty. With some women it's hard to tell."

"I'll take that as a compliment," Rorie muttered to no one in particular.

"My apologies, Rorie," Clay said contritely. "We were being rude."

She took time buttering her biscuit. "Apology accepted."

"How old do you think I am?" Skip asked her, his eyes wide and hopeful.

It was Rorie's nature to be kind, and besides, Skip had saved her from an unknown fate. "Twenty," she answered with barely a pause.

The younger Franklin straightened and sent his brother a smirk. "I was seventeen last week."

"That surprises me," Rorie continued, setting aside her butter knife and swallowing a smile. "I could've sworn you were much older."

Looking even more pleased with himself, Skip cleared his throat. "Lots of girls think that."

"Don't I remember you telling me you're helping Luke Rivers tonight?" Clay reminded his brother.

Skip's face fell. "I guess I did."

"If Rorie doesn't mind, I'll introduce her to King."

Clay's offer appeared to surprise Skip, and Rorie studied the boy, a little worried now about causing problems between the two brothers. Nor did she want to disappoint Skip, who had offered first.

"But I thought..." Skip began, then swallowed. "You want to take Rorie?"

Clay's eyes narrowed, and when he spoke, his voice was cool. "That's what I just said. Is there a problem?"

"No...of course not." Skip stuffed half a biscuit in his mouth and shook his head vigorously. After a moment of chewing, he said, "Clay will show you around the stable." His words were measured and even, but his gaze held his brother's.

"I heard," Rorie said gently. She could only speculate on what was going on between them, but obviously something was amiss. There'd been more than a hint of surprise in Skip's eyes at Clay's offer. She noticed that the younger Franklin seemed angry. Because his vanity was bruised? Rorie supposed so. "I could wait until tomorrow if you want, Skip," she suggested.

"No, that's all right," he answered, lowering his eyes. "Clay can do it, since that's what he seems to want."

When they finished the meal, Rorie cleared the table, but Mary refused to let her help with cleaning up the kitchen.

"You'd just be in the way," she grumbled, though her eyes weren't unfriendly. "Besides, I heard the boys were showing you the barn."

"I'll do the dishes tomorrow night then."

Mary murmured a response, then asked brusquely, "How was the apple pie?"

"Absolutely delicious."

A satisfied smile touched the edges of the woman's mouth. "Good. I did things a little differently this time, and I was just wondering."

Clay led Rorie out the back door and across the yard toward the barn. The minute Rorie walked through the enormous double doors she felt she'd entered another world. The wonderful smells of leather and liniments and saddle soap mingled with the fragrance of fresh hay and the pungent odor of the horses themselves. Rorie found it surprisingly pleasant. Flashes of bright color from halters and blankets captured her attention, as did the gleam of steel bits against the far wall.

"King's over here," Clay said, guiding her with a firm hand beneath her elbow.

When Clay opened the top of the stall door, the most magnificent creature Rorie had ever seen turned to face them. He was a deep chestnut color, so sleek and powerful it took her breath away. This splendid horse seemed to know he was royalty. He regarded Rorie with a keen eye, as though he expected her to show him the proper respect and curtsy. For a wild moment, Rorie was tempted to do exactly that.

"I brought a young lady for you to impress," Clay told the stallion.

King took a couple of steps back and pawed the ground.

"He really is something," Rorie whispered, once she'd found her voice. "Did you raise him from a colt?"

Clay nodded.

Rorie was about to ask him more when they heard frantic whinnying from the other side of the aisle.

Clay looked almost apologetic. "If you haven't already guessed, that's Hercules. He doesn't like being ignored." He walked to the stall opposite King's and opened the upper half of the door. Instantly the black stallion stuck his head out and complained about the lack of attention in a loud snort, which brought an involuntary smile to Rorie's mouth. "I was bringing Rorie over to meet you, too, so don't get your nose out of joint," Clay chastised.

"Hi," Rorie said, and raised her right hand in a stiff greeting. It amused her that Clay talked to his animals as if he honestly expected them to understand his remarks and join in the conversation. But then who was she to criticize? Only a few hours earlier, she'd been conversing with a cow.

"You don't need to be frightened of him," Clay told her when she stood, unmoving, a good distance from the stall. Taking into consideration what Skip had mentioned earlier about the moody stallion, Rorie decided to stay where she was.

Clay ran his hand down the side of Hercules's neck, and his touch seemed to appease the stallion's obviously delicate ego.

Looking around her, Rorie was impressed by the size of the barn. "How many stalls are there altogether?"

"Thirty-six regular and four foaling. But this is only a small part of Elk Run." He led her outside to a large arena and pointed at a building on the opposite side. "My office is over there, if you'd like to see it."

Rorie nodded, and they crossed to the office. Clay opened the door for her. Inside, the first thing she noticed was the collection of championship ribbons and photographs displayed on the walls. A large trophy case was filled with a variety of awards. When he saw her interest in the computer, Clay explained the system he'd had installed and how it would aid him in the future.

"This looks pretty straightforward," Rorie told him.

"I've been meaning to hire a high-school kid to enter

the data for me so I can get started, but I haven't got around to it yet."

Rorie sorted through the file folders. There were only a few hours of work and her typing skills were good. "There's no need to pay anyone. If I'm going to be imposing on your hospitality, the least I can do is enter this into the computer for you."

"Rorie, that isn't necessary. I don't want you to spend your time stuck here in the office doing all that tedious typing."

"It'll give me something productive to do instead of fretting over how long it's taking to get the MG repaired."

He glanced at her, his expression concerned. "All right, if you insist, but it really isn't necessary, you know."

"I do insist." Rorie clasped her hands behind her back and decided to change the subject. "What's that?" she asked, gesturing toward a large room off the office. Floor-to-ceiling windows looked out over the arena.

"The observation room."

"So you can have your own private shows?"

"In a manner of speaking. Would you like to go down there?"

"Oh, yes!"

Inside the arena, Rorie saw that it was much bigger than it had appeared from above. They'd been walking around for several minutes when Clay checked his watch and frowned. "I hate to cut this short, but I've got a meeting in town. Normally I wouldn't leave company."

"Oh, please," she said hurriedly, "don't worry about it. I mean, it's not as though I was expected or anything. I hardly consider myself company."

Still Clay seemed regretful. "I'll walk you back to the house."

He left in the pickup a couple of minutes later. The place was quiet; Mary had apparently finished in the kitchen and retired to her own quarters, a cottage not far from the main house. Skip, who had returned from helping his friend, was busy talking on the phone. He smiled when he saw Rorie, without interrupting his conversation.

Rorie moved into the living room and idly picked up a magazine, leafing through it. Restless and bored, she read a heated article on the pros and cons of a new medication used for equine worming, although she couldn't have described what it said.

When Skip was finished on the phone, he suggested they play cribbage. Not until after ten did Rorie realize she was unconsciously waiting for Clay's return. But she wasn't quite sure why.

Skip yawned rather pointedly and Rorie took the hint.

"I suppose I should think about heading up to bed," she said, putting down the deck of playing cards.

"Yeah, it seems to be that time," he answered, yawning again.

"I didn't intend to keep you up so late."

"Oh, that's no problem. It's just that we start our days early around here. But you sleep in. We don't expect you to get up before the sun just because we do."

By Rorie's rough calculation, getting up before the sun meant Clay and Skip started their workday between four-thirty and five in the morning.

Skip must have read the look in her eyes, because he chuckled and said, "You get used to it."

Rorie followed him up the stairs, and they said their

good-nights. But even after a warm bath, she couldn't sleep. Wearing her flower-sprigged cotton pajamas, she sat on the bed with the light still on and thought about how different everything was from what she'd planned. She was supposed to be in Seattle now, at a cocktail party arranged for the first night of the conference; she'd hoped to talk to several of the authors there. But she'd missed that, and the likelihood of attending even one workshop was dim. Instead she'd made an unscheduled detour onto a stud farm and stumbled upon a handsome rancher.

She grinned. Things could be worse. Much worse.

An hour later, Rorie heard a noise outside, behind the house. Clay must be home. She smiled, oddly pleased that he was back. Yawning, she reached for the lamp on the bedside table and turned it off.

The discordant noise came again.

Rorie frowned. This time, whatever was making the racket didn't sound the least bit like a pickup truck parking, or anything else she could readily identify. The dog was barking intermittently.

Grabbing her housecoat from the foot of the bed and tucking her feet into fuzzy slippers, Rorie went downstairs to investigate.

As she stood in the kitchen, she could tell that the clamor was coming from the barn. A problem with the horses?

Not knowing what else to do, she scrambled up the stairs and hurried from room to room until she found Skip's bedroom.

The teenager lay sprawled across his bed, snoring loudly.

"Skip," she cried, "something's wrong with the horses!"

He continued to snore.

"Skip," she cried, louder this time. "Wake up!"

He remained deep in sleep.

"Skip, please, oh, please, wake up!" Rorie pleaded, shaking him so hard he'd probably have bruises in the morning. "I'm from the city. Remember? I don't know what to do."

The thumps and bangs coming from the barn were growing fiercer and Blue's barking more frantic. Perhaps there was a fire. Oh, dear Lord, she prayed, not that. Rorie raced halfway down the stairs, paused and then reversed her direction.

"Skip," she yelled. "Skip!" Rorie heard the panic in her own voice. "Someone's got to do something!"

No one else seemed to think so.

Nearly frantic now, Rorie dashed back down the stairs and across the yard. Trembling, she entered the barn. A lone electric light shone from the ceiling, dimly illuminating the area.

Several of the stalls' upper doors were open and Rorie could sense the horses becoming increasingly restless. Walking on tiptoe, she moved slowly toward the source of the noise, somewhere in the middle of the stable. The horses were curious and their cries brought Rorie's heart straight to her throat.

"Nice horsey, nice horsey," she repeated soothingly over and over until she reached the stall those unearthly sounds were coming from.

The upper half of the door was open and Rorie flattened herself against it before daring to peek inside. She saw a speckled gray mare, head thrown back and teeth bared, neighing loudly, ceaselessly. Rorie quickly jerked away and resumed her position against the outside of the door. She didn't know much about horses, but she knew this one was in dire trouble.

Running out of the stable, Rorie picked up the hem of her robe and sprinted toward the house. She'd find a way to wake Skip or die trying.

She was breathless by the time she got to the yard. That was when she saw Clay's battered blue truck.

"Clay," she screamed, halting in the middle of the moonlit yard. "Oh, Clay."

He was at her side instantly, his hands roughly gripping her shoulders. "Rorie, what is it?"

She was so glad to see him, she hugged his waist and only just resisted bursting into tears. Her shoulders were heaving and her voice shook uncontrollably. "There's trouble in the barn...."

Four

Clay ran toward the barn with Rorie right behind him. He paused to flip a switch, flooding the interior with bright light.

The gray mare in the center stall continued to neigh and thrash around. Rorie found it astonishing that the walls had remained intact. The noise of the animal's pain echoed through the stable, reflected by the rising anxiety of the other horses.

Clay took one look at the mare and released a low groan, then muttered something under his breath.

"What's wrong?" Rorie cried.

"It seems Star Bright is about to become a mother."

"But why isn't she in one of the foaling stalls?"

"Because two different vets palpated her and said she wasn't in foal."

"But…"

"She's already had six foals and her stomach's so stretched she looks pregnant even when she isn't." Clay opened the stall door and entered. Rorie's hand flew to her heart. Good grief, he could get killed in there!

"What do you want me to do?" she said.

Clay shook his head. "This is no place for you. Get back to the house and stay there." His brow furrowed, every line a testament to his hard, outdoor life.

"But shouldn't I be phoning a vet?"

"It's too late for that."

"Boiling water—I could get that for you." She wanted to help; she just had no idea how.

"Boiling water?" he repeated. "What the hell would I need that for?"

"I don't know," she confessed with a shrug, "but they always seem to need it in the movies."

Clay gave an exasperated sigh. "Rorie, please, just go to the house."

She made it all the way to the barn door, then abruptly turned back. If anyone had asked why she felt it so necessary to remain with Clay, she wouldn't have been able to answer. But something kept her there, something far stronger than the threat of Clay's temper.

She marched to the center stall, her head and shoulders held stiff and straight. She stood with her feet braced, prepared for an argument.

"Clay," she said, "I'm not leaving."

"Listen, Rorie, you're a city girl. This isn't going to be pretty."

"I'm a woman, too. The sight of a little blood isn't enough to make me faint."

Clay was doing his best to calm the frightened mare, but without much success. The tension in the air seemed to crackle like static electricity.

"I haven't got time to argue with you," he said through clenched teeth.

"Good."

Star Bright heaved her neck backward and gave a

deep groan that seemed to reverberate in the stall like the boom of a cannon.

"Poor little mother," Rorie whispered in a soothing voice. Led by instinct, she carefully unlatched the stall door and slipped inside.

Clay sent her a look hot enough to peel paint. "Get out of here before you get hurt." His voice was low and urgent.

Star Bright reacted to his tension immediately, jerking about, her body twitching convulsively. One of her hooves caught Clay in the forearm and, almost immediately, blood seeped through his sleeve. Rorie bit her lip to suppress a cry of alarm, but if Clay felt any pain he didn't show it.

"Hold her head," Clay said sharply.

Somehow Rorie found the courage to do as he asked. Star Bright groaned once more and her pleading eyes looked directly into Rorie's, seeming to beg for help. The mare's lips pulled back from her teeth as she flailed her head to and fro, shaking Rorie in the process.

"Whoa, girl," Rorie said softly, gaining control. "It's painful, isn't it, but soon you'll have a beautiful baby to show off to the world."

"Foal," Clay corrected from behind the mare.

"A beautiful foal." Rorie stroked the sweat-dampened neck, doing what she could to reassure the frightened horse.

"Keep talking to her," Clay whispered.

Rorie kept up a running dialogue for several tense minutes, but there was only so much she could find to say on such short acquaintance. When she ran out of ideas, she started to sing in a soft, lilting voice. She began with lullabies her mother had once sung to her, then followed those with a few childhood ditties. Her singing lasted only minutes, but Rorie's lungs felt close to collapse.

Suddenly the mare's water broke. Clay wasn't saying much, but he began to work quickly, although she couldn't see what he was doing. Star Bright tossed her neck in the final throes of birth and Rorie watched, fascinated, as two hooves and front legs emerged, followed by a white nose.

The mare lifted her head, eager to see. Clay tugged gently, and within seconds, the foal was free. Rorie's heart pounded like a locomotive struggling up a steep hill as Clay's strong hands completed the task.

"A filly," he announced, a smile lighting his face. He reached for a rag and wiped his hands and arms.

Star Bright turned her head to view her offspring. "See?" Rorie told the mare, her eyes moist with relief. "Didn't I tell you it would all be worth it?"

The mare nickered. Her newborn filly was gray, like her mother, and finely marked with white streaks on her nose, mane and tail. Rorie was touched to her very soul by the sight. Tears blurred her vision and ran down her flushed cheeks. She blotted them with her sleeve so Clay couldn't see them, and silently chided herself for being such a sentimental fool.

It was almost another hour before they left Star Bright's stall. The mare, who stood guard over her long-legged baby, seemed content and utterly pleased with herself. As they prepared to leave, Rorie whispered in her ear.

"What was that all about?" Clay wanted to know, latching the stall door.

"I just told her she'd done a good job."

"That she did," Clay whispered. A moment later, he

added, "And so did you, Rorie. I was grateful for your help."

Once more tears sprang to her eyes. She responded with a nod, unable to trust her voice. Her heart was racing with exhilaration. She couldn't remember a time she'd felt more excited. It was well past midnight, but she'd never felt less sleepy.

"Rorie?" He was staring at her, his eyes bright with concern.

She owed him an explanation, although she couldn't fully explain this sudden burst of emotion. "It was so… beautiful." She brushed the hair from her face and smiled up at him, hoping he wouldn't think she was just a foolish city girl. She wasn't sure why it mattered, but she doubted that any man had seen her looking worse, although Rorie was well aware that she didn't possess a classic beauty. She was usually referred to as cute, with her slightly turned-up nose and dark brown eyes.

"I understand." He walked to the sink against the barn's opposite wall and busily washed his hands, then splashed water on his face. When he'd finished, Rorie handed him a towel hanging on a nearby hook.

"Thanks."

"I don't know how to describe it," she said, after a fruitless effort to find the words to explain all the feeling that had surged up inside her.

"It's the same for me every time I witness a birth," Clay told her. He looked at her then and gently touched her face, letting his finger glide along her jaw. All the world went still as his eyes caressed hers. There was a primitive wonder in the experience of birth, a wonder that struck deep within the soul. For the first time, Rorie understood this. And sharing it with Clay seemed to intensify the attraction she already felt for him. During that brief time in the stall, just before Star Bright delivered her foal, Rorie had felt closer to Clay than she ever had to any other man. It was as though her heart had taken flight and joined his in a moment of sheer challenge and joy. That was a silly romantic thought, she realized. But it seemed so incredible to her that she could feel anything this strong for a man she'd known for mere hours.

"I've got a name for her," Clay said, hanging up the towel. "What do you think of Nightsong?"

"Nightsong," Rorie repeated softly. "I like it."

"In honor of the woman who sang to her mother."

Rorie nodded as emotion clogged her throat. "Does this mean I did all right for a city slicker?"

"You did more than all right."

"Thanks for not sending me away… I probably would've gone if you'd insisted."

They left the barn, and Clay draped his arm across her shoulders as though he'd been doing it for years. Rorie was grateful for his touch because, somehow, it helped ground the unfamiliar feelings and sensations.

As they strolled across the yard, she noticed that the sky was filled with a thousand glittering stars, brighter than any she'd ever seen in the city. She paused midstep to gaze up at them.

Clay's quiet voice didn't dispel the serenity. "It's a lovely night, isn't it?"

Rorie wanted to hold on to each exquisite minute and make it last a lifetime. A nod was all she could manage as she reminded herself that this time with Clay was about to end. They would walk into the house and

Clay would probably thank her again. Then she'd climb the stairs to her room and that would be all there was.

"How about some coffee?" he asked once they'd entered the kitchen. Blue left his rug and wandered over to Clay. "The way I feel now, it would be a waste of time to go to bed."

"Me, too." Rorie leaped at the suggestion, pleased that he wanted to delay their parting, too. And when she did return to her room, she knew the adrenaline in her system would make sleep impossible, anyway.

Clay was reaching up for the canister of coffee, when Rorie suddenly noticed the bloodstain on his sleeve and remembered Star Bright's kick.

"Clay, you need to take care of that cut."

From the surprised way he glanced at his arm, she guessed that he, too, had forgotten about the injury. "Yes, I suppose I should." Then he calmly returned to his task.

"Let me clean it for you," Rorie offered, joining him at the kitchen counter.

"If you like." He led her into the bathroom down the hall and took a variety of medical supplies from the cabinet above the sink. "Do you want to do it here or in the kitchen?"

"Here is fine."

Clay sat on the edge of the bath and unfastened the cuff, then rolled back his sleeve.

"Oh, Clay," Rorie whispered when she saw the angry torn flesh just above his elbow. Gently her fingers tested the edges, wondering if he needed stitches. He winced slightly at her probing fingers.

"Sorry."

"Just put some antiseptic on it and it'll be all right."

"But this is really deep—you should probably have a doctor look at it."

"Rorie, I'm as tough as old leather. This kind of thing happens all the time. I'll recover."

"I don't doubt that," she said primly.

"Then put on a bandage and be done with it."

"But—"

"I've been injured often enough to know when a cut needs a doctor's attention."

She hesitated, then conceded that he was probably right. She filled the sink with warm tap water and took care to clean the wound thoroughly. All the while, Rorie was conscious of Clay's eyes moving over her face, solemnly perusing the chin-length, dark brown hair and the big dark eyes that—judging by a glance in the mirror—still displayed a hint of vulnerability. She was tall, almost five-eight, her figure willowy. But if Clay found anything attractive about her, he didn't mention it. Her throat muscles squeezed shut, and, although she was grateful for the silence between them, it confused her.

"You missed your vocation," he told her as she rinsed the bloody cloth. "You should've been a nurse."

"I toyed with the idea when I was ten, but decided I liked books better."

His shoulders were tense, Rorie noted, and she tried to be as gentle as possible. A muscle leaped in his jaw.

"Am I…hurting you?"

"No," he answered, his voice curt.

After that, he was an excellent patient. He didn't complain when she dabbed on the antiseptic, although she was sure it must have stung like crazy. He cooperated when she wrapped the gauze around his arm, lifting and lowering it when she asked him to. The silence continued as she secured the bandage with adhesive tape. Rorie had the feeling that he wanted to escape the close confines of the bathroom as quickly as possible.

"I hope that stays."

He stood up and flexed his elbow a couple of times. "It's fine. You do good work."

"I'm glad you think so."

"The coffee's probably ready by now." He spoke quickly, as if eager to be gone.

She sighed. "I could use a cup."

She put the medical supplies neatly back inside the cabinet, while Clay returned to the kitchen. Rorie could smell the freshly made coffee even before she entered the room.

He was leaning against the counter, sipping a cup of the fragrant coffee, waiting for her.

"It's been quite a night, hasn't it?" she murmured, adding cream and sugar to the mug he'd poured for her.

A certain tension hung in the air, and Rorie couldn't explain or understand it. Only ten minutes earlier, they'd walked across the yard, spellbound by the stars, and Clay had laid his arm across her shoulders. He'd smiled down on her so tenderly. Now he looked as if he couldn't wait to get away from her.

"Have I done anything wrong?" she asked outright.

"Rorie, no." He set his mug aside and gripped her shoulders with both hands. "There's something so intimate and…earthy in what we shared." His eyes were intense, strangely darker. "Wanting you this way isn't right."

Rorie felt a tremor work through him as he lifted his hands to her face. His callused thumbs lightly caressed her cheeks.

"I feel like I've known you all my life," he whispered hoarsely, his expression uncertain.

"It's…been the same for me, from the moment you stepped out of the truck."

Clay smiled, and Rorie thought her knees would melt. She put her coffee down and as soon as she did Clay eased her into his arms, his hands on her shoulders. Her heart stopped, then jolted back to frenzied life.

"I'm going to kiss you…."

He made the statement almost a question. "Yes," she whispered, letting him know she'd welcome his touch. Her stomach fluttered as he slowly lowered his mouth to hers.

Rorie had never wanted a man's kiss more. His moist lips glided over hers in a series of gentle explorations. He drew her closer until their bodies were pressed tight.

"Oh, Rorie," he breathed, dragging his mouth from hers. "You taste so good… I was afraid of that." His mouth found the pulse in her throat and lingered there.

"This afternoon I thought I'd cry when the car broke down and now…now I'm glad…so glad," she said.

He kissed her again, nibbling on her lower lip, gently drawing it between his teeth. Rorie could hardly breathe, her heart was pounding so hard. She slumped against him, delighting in the rise and fall of his broad chest. His hands moved down her back with slow restraint, but paused when he reached the curve of her hips.

He tensed. "I think we should say good-night."

A protest sprang to her lips, but before she could voice it, Clay said, "Now."

She looked at him, dazed. The last thing she wanted to do was leave him. "What about my coffee?"

"That was just an excuse and we both know it."

Rorie said nothing.

The silence between them seemed to throb for endless minutes.

"Good night, Clay," she finally whispered. She broke away, but his hand caught her fingers, and with a groan he pulled her back into his arms.

"What the hell," he muttered fiercely, "sending you upstairs isn't going to help. Nothing's going to change."

His words brought confusion, but Rorie didn't question him, didn't want to. What she longed for was the warmth and security she'd discovered in his arms.

"Come on," he whispered, after he'd kissed her once more. He led her through the living room and outside to the porch, where the swing moved gently in the night breeze.

Rorie sat beside him and he wrapped his arm around her. She nestled her head against his shoulder, savoring these precious moments.

"I'll never forget this night."

"Neither will I," Clay promised, kissing her again.

Rorie awoke when the sun settled on her face and refused to leave her alone. Keeping her eyes closed, she smiled contentedly, basking in the memory of her night with Clay. They'd sat on the swing and talked for hours. Talked and kissed and laughed and touched…

Sitting up, Rorie raised her hands high above her head and stretched, arching her spine. She looked at her watch on the nightstand and was shocked to see that it was after eleven. By the time she'd climbed the stairs for bed the sky had been dappled with faint shreds of light. She suspected Clay hadn't even bothered to sleep.

Tossing aside the blankets, Rorie slid to the floor, anxious to shower and dress. Anxious to see him again. Fifteen minutes later, she was on her way down the stairs.

Mary, who was dusting in the living room, nodded when she saw Rorie. Then the housekeeper resumed her task, but not before she'd muttered something about how city folks were prone to sleeping their lives away.

"Good morning, Mary," Rorie greeted her cheerfully.

"'Mornin'."

"Where is everyone?"

"Where they ought to be this time of day. Working."

"Yes, I know, but where?"

"Outside."

Rorie had trouble hiding her smile.

"I heard about you helping last night," Mary added gruffly. "Seems you did all right for a city girl."

"Thank you, Mary. You don't do half bad for a country girl, either."

The housekeeper seemed uncomfortable with the praise, despite the lightness of Rorie's tone. "I suppose you want me to cook you some fancy breakfast."

"Good heavens, no, you're busy. I'll just make myself some toast."

"That's hardly enough to fill a growing girl," Mary complained.

"It'll suit me fine."

Once her toast was ready, Rorie carried it outside. If she couldn't find Clay, she wanted to check on Nightsong.

"Rorie."

She turned to discover Skip walking toward her, in animated conversation with a blonde. His girlfriend, she guessed. He waved and Rorie returned the gesture, smiling. The sun was glorious and the day held marvelous promise.

"I didn't think you were ever going to wake up," Skip said.

"I'm sorry—I don't usually sleep this late."

"Clay told me how you helped him deliver Star Bright's filly. You could've knocked me over with a feather when I heard."

Rorie nodded, her heart warming with the memory. "Well, I tried to get you up. It would've been easier to wake a dead man than to get you out of bed last night."

Skip looked slightly embarrassed. "Sorry about that, but I generally don't wake up too easily once I'm asleep." As he spoke, he slipped his arm around the blonde girl's shoulders. "Rorie, I want you to meet Kate Logan."

"Hello, Kate." Rorie held out a hand and Kate shook it politely.

"Hello, Rorie," she said. "Clay and Skip told me about your car troubles. I hope everything turns out all right for you."

"I'm sure it will. Do you live around here?" Rorie already knew she was going to like her. At a closer glance, she saw that Kate was older than she'd first assumed. Maybe her own age, which gave credence to Skip's comment about liking older, more mature women.

"I don't live far," Kate said. "The Circle L is down the road, only a few miles from here."

"She's going to be living *with* us in the near future," Skip put in, gazing fondly at Kate.

The young woman's cheeks reddened and she smiled shyly.

"Oh?" Skip couldn't possibly mean he planned to

marry her, Rorie thought. Good heavens, he was still in high school.

He must have seen Rorie's puzzled frown, and hurried to explain. "Not me," he said with a short laugh. "Kate is Clay's fiancée."

Five

"You and Clay are...engaged," Rorie murmured as shock waves coursed through her blood. They stopped with a thud at her heart and spread out in ripples of dismay.

Somehow Rorie managed a smile, her outward composure unbroken. She was even able to offer her congratulations. To all appearances, nothing was wrong. No one would've known that those few simple words had destroyed a night she'd planned to treasure all her life.

"I hope you and Clay will be very happy," Rorie said—and she meant it. She'd just been introduced to Kate Logan, but already Rorie knew that this sweet, friendly woman was exactly the kind of wife a man like Clay would need.

"Skip's rushing things a little," Kate pointed out, but the glint of love in her eyes contradicted her words. "Clay hasn't even given me an engagement ring yet."

"But you and Clay have been talking about getting married, haven't you?" Skip pressed. "And you're crazy about him."

Kate blushed prettily. "I've loved Clay from the time

I was in fifth grade. I wrote his name all over my books. Of course, Clay wouldn't have anything to do with me, not when he was a big important high-schooler and I was just the pesky little girl next door. It took a while for him to notice me—like ten years." She gave a small laugh. "We've been dating steadily for the past two."

"But you and Clay *are* going to get married, right?" Skip continued, clearly wanting to prove his point.

"Eventually, but we haven't set a date, although I'm sure it'll be soon," Kate answered, casting a sharp look at Rorie.

The tightness that had gripped Rorie's throat eased and she struggled to keep her smile intact. It was impossible not to like Kate, but that didn't lessen the ache in Rorie's heart.

"The wedding's inevitable," Skip said offhandedly, "so I wasn't exaggerating when I said you were Clay's fiancée, now was I?"

Kate smiled. "I suppose not. We love each other, and have for years. We're just waiting for the right time." Her eyes held Rorie's, assessing her, but she didn't seem worried about competition.

Rorie supposed she should be pleased about that, at least.

"I was taking Kate over to see Nightsong," Skip explained to Rorie.

"I actually came to Elk Run to meet you," the other woman said. "Clay stopped by last night and told me about your car. I felt terrible for you. Your whole vacation's been ruined. You must be awfully upset."

"These things happen," Rorie said with a shrug. "Being upset isn't going to ship that part any faster. All I can do is accept the facts."

Kate nodded sympathetically. "Skip was about to show me the filly. You'll come with us, won't you?"

Rorie nodded, unable to excuse herself without sounding rude. If there'd been a way, she would have retreated, wanting only to lick her wounds in private. Instead, hoping she sounded more enthusiastic than she felt, she mumbled, "I was headed in that direction myself."

Skip led the way to the barn, which was alive with activity. Clay had explained that Elk Run employed five men full-time, none of whom lived on the premises. Two men mucking out stalls paused when Skip and the women entered the building. Skip introduced Rorie and they touched the tips of their hats in greeting.

"I don't understand Clay," Skip said as they approached the mare's stall. "When we bought Star Bright a few years back, all Clay could do was complain about that silly name. He even talked about getting her registration changed."

"Star Bright's a perfectly good name," Kate insisted, her sunny blue eyes intent on the newborn foal.

Nightsong was standing now on knobby, skinny legs that threatened to buckle, greedily feasting from her mother.

"Oh, she really is lovely, isn't she?" Kate whispered.

Rorie hadn't been able to stop looking at the filly from the moment they'd reached the stall. Finished with her breakfast, Nightsong gazed around, fascinated by everything she surveyed. She returned Rorie's look, not vacantly, but as though she recognized the woman who'd been there at her birth.

Rorie couldn't even identify all the emotions she suddenly felt. Some of these feelings were so new she couldn't put a name to them, but they gripped her heart and squeezed tight.

"What I can't understand," Skip muttered, "is why Clay would go and call her Nightsong when he hates the name Star Bright. It doesn't sound like anything he'd ever come up with on his own, yet he says he did."

"I know," Kate agreed, "but I'm glad, because the name suits her." She sighed. "Clay's always been so practical when it comes to names for his horses, but Nightsong has such a romantic flavor, don't you think?"

Skip chuckled. "You know what Clay thinks about romance, and that makes it even more confusing. But Nightsong she is, and she's bound to bring us a pretty penny in a year or two. Her father was a Polish Arabian, and with Star Bright's bloodlines Nightsong will command big bucks as a National Show Horse."

"Skip." Clay's curt voice interrupted them. He strode from the arena leading a bay mare. The horse's coat gleamed with sweat, turning its color the shade of an oak leaf in autumn. One of the stablemen approached to take the reins. Then Clay removed his hat, wiping his brow with his forearm, and Rorie noticed the now-grimy bandage she'd applied last night. No, this morning.

She stared hungrily at his sun-bronzed face, a face that revealed more than a hint of impatience. The lines around his mouth were etched deep with poorly disguised regrets. Rorie recognized them, even if the others didn't.

Clay stopped short when he saw Kate, his eyes narrowing.

"'Morning, Kate."

"Hello, Clay."

Then his gaze moved, slowly and reluctantly, to

Rorie. The remorse she'd already sensed in him seemed unmistakable.

"I hope you slept well," was all he said to her.

"Fine." She detected a tautness along his jawline and decided he was probably concerned that she'd say or do something to embarrass him in front of his fiancée. Rorie wouldn't, but not because she was worried about him. Her sense of fair play wouldn't allow her to hurt Kate, who so obviously adored this man.

"We're just admiring Nightsong," Kate explained, her expression tender as she smiled up at him.

"I can't understand why you'd name her that," Skip said, his mouth twitching with barely suppressed laughter. "You always pick names like Brutus and Firepower, but Nightsong? I think you're going soft on us." Considering himself particularly funny, Skip chuckled and added, "I suppose that's what love does to a man."

Kate's lashes brushed against the high arch of her cheek and she smiled, her pleasure so keen it was like a physical touch.

"Didn't I ask you to water the horses several hours ago?" Clay asked in a tone that could have chipped rock.

"Yes, but—"

"Then kindly see to it. The farrier will be here any minute."

The humor left Skip's eyes; he was clearly upset by Clay's anger. He looked from his brother to the two women and then back at Clay again. Hot color rose into his neck and invaded his face. "All right," he muttered. "Excuse me for living." Then he stormed out of the barn, slapping his hat against his thigh in an outburst of anger.

Kate waited until Skip was out of the barn. "Clay, what's wrong?"

"He should've done what I told him long before now. Those horses in the pasture are thirsty because of his neglect."

"I'm the one you should be angry with, not Skip." Kate's voice was contrite. "I should never have stopped in without calling first, but I...wanted to meet Rorie."

"You've only been here a few minutes," Clay insisted, his anger in check now. "Skip had plenty of time to complete his chores before you arrived."

Rorie tossed invisible daggers at Clay, annoyed with him for taking his irritation out on his younger brother. Skip had introduced her to Clay's fiancée. *That* was what really bothered him if he'd been willing to admit it—which he clearly wasn't.

"We came here to see Nightsong," Kate said again. "I'm glad you named her that, no matter what Skip thinks." She wrapped her arm around his waist, and rested her head against his broad chest. "He was just teasing you and you know how he loves to do that."

Clay gave her an absent smile, but his gaze settled with disturbing ease on Rorie. She met his eyes boldly, denying the emotions churning furiously inside her. The plea for patience and understanding he sent her was so obvious that Rorie wondered how anyone seeing it wouldn't know what was happening.

As though she'd suddenly remembered something, Kate dropped her arm and glanced hurriedly at her watch. She groaned. "I promised Dad I'd meet him for lunch today. He's getting together with the other Town Council members in one of those horribly boring meetings. He needs me as an excuse to get away." She stopped abruptly, a chagrined expression on her face.

"I guess that tells you how informal everything is in Nightingale, doesn't it, Rorie?"

"The town seems to be doing very well." She didn't know if that was true or not, but it sounded polite.

"He just hates these things, but he likes the prestige of being a Council member—something I tease him about."

"I'll walk you to your car," Clay offered.

"Oh, there's no need. You're busy. Besides, I wanted to talk to Rorie and arrange to meet her tomorrow and show her around town. I certainly hope you remembered to invite her to the Grange dance tomorrow night. I'm sure Luke would be willing to escort her."

"Oh, I couldn't possibly intrude," Rorie blurted.

"Nonsense, you'd be more than welcome. And don't worry about having the right kind of clothes for a square dance, either, because I've got more outfits than I know what to do with. We're about the same size," Kate said, eyeing her. "Perhaps you're a little taller, but not so much that you couldn't wear my skirts."

Rorie smiled blandly, realizing it wouldn't do any good to decline the invitation. But good heavens, square dancing? Her?

"Knowing you and Skip," Kate chastised Clay, "poor Rorie will be stuck on Elk Run for the next four days bored out of her mind. The least I can do is see that she's entertained."

"That's thoughtful of you," Rorie said. The sooner she got back on the road, the safer her heart would be, and if Kate Logan was willing to help her kill time, then all the better.

"I thought I'd give you a tour of our little town in

the morning," Kate went on. "It's small, but the people are friendly."

"I'd love to see Nightingale."

"Clay." The brusque voice of a farmhand interrupted them. "Could you come here a minute?"

Clay turned to the man and nodded. "I have to find out what Don needs," he said quietly. As he met Rorie's eyes, a speculative look flashed into his own.

She nearly flinched, wondering what emotion her face had betrayed. From the minute Clay had walked into the barn, she'd been careful to school her expression, not wanting him to read anything into her words or actions. She'd tried to look cool and unconcerned, as if the night they'd shared had never happened.

"You two will have to excuse me." Weary amusement turned up the corners of his mouth and Rorie realized he'd readily seen through her guise.

"Of course," Kate said. "I'll see you later, sweetheart."

Clay nodded abruptly and departed with firm purposeful strides.

Kate started walking toward the yard. Rorie followed, eager to escape the barn and all the memories associated with it.

"Clay told us you're a librarian," Kate said when she reached the Ford parked in the curving driveway. "If you want, I can take you to our library. We built a new one last year and we're rather proud of it. I know it's small compared to where you probably work, but I think you'll like what we've done."

"I'd love to see it." Libraries were often the heart of a community, and if the citizens of Nightingale had seen fit to upgrade theirs, it was apparent they shared Rorie's love of books.

"I'll pick you up around ten tomorrow, if that's convenient?"

"That'd be fine."

"Plan on spending the afternoon with me and we'll meet Clay and Skip at the dance later."

Rorie agreed, although her enthusiasm was decidedly low. The last thing she wanted was to be at some social event with Clay. Never mind how Dan would tease her if he ever discovered she'd spent part of her vacation square dancing with the folks at the Grange.

"Bye for now," Kate said.

"Bye," Rorie murmured, waving. She stood in the yard until Kate's car was out of sight. Not sure what else to do, she wandered back into the house, where Mary was busy with preparations for lunch.

"Can I help?" she asked.

In response, Mary scurried to a drawer and once again handed her a peeler. Rorie started carefully whittling away at a firm red apple she'd scooped from a large bowlful of them.

"I don't suppose you know anything about cooking?" Mary demanded, pointing her own peeler at Rorie.

"I've managed to keep from starving for the last few years," she retorted idly.

The merest hint of amusement flashed into the older woman's weathered face. "If I was judging your talents in the kitchen on looks alone, I think you'd starve a man to death within a week."

Despite her glum spirits, Rorie laughed. "If you're telling me you think I'm thin, watch out, Mary, because I'm likely to throw my arms around your neck and kiss you."

The other woman threw her a grin. Several peaceful minutes passed while they peeled apple after apple.

"I got a call from my sister," Mary said hesitantly, her eyes darting to Rorie, then back to her task. "She's coming to Riversdale and wants to know if I can drive over and see her. She's only going to be in Oregon one day."

This was the most Mary had said to Rorie since her arrival. It pleased her that the older woman was lowering her guard and extending a friendly hand.

"I'd like to visit with my sister."

"I certainly think you should." It took Rorie another minute to figure out where Mary was heading with this meandering conversation. Then suddenly she understood. "Oh, you're looking for someone to do the cooking while you're away."

Mary shrugged as if it didn't concern her one way or the other. "Just for the evening meal, two nights from now. I could manage lunch for the hands before I leave. It's supper I'm worried about. There's only Clay and Skip who need to be fed—the other men go home in the evenings."

"Well, relax, because I'm sure I can manage one dinner without killing off the menfolk."

"You're sure?"

Mary was so completely serious that Rorie laughed outright. "Since my abilities do seem to worry you, how would you feel if I invited Kate Logan over to help?"

Mary nodded and sighed. "I'd rest easier."

Rorie stayed in the kitchen until the lunch dishes had been put away. Mary thanked her for helping, then went home to watch her daily soap operas.

Feeling a little lost, Rorie wandered outside and into

the stable. Since Clay had already shown her the computer, she decided to spend the afternoon working in his office.

The area was deserted, which went some distance toward reassuring her—but then, she'd assumed it would be. From what she'd observed, a stud farm was a busy place and Clay was bound to be occupied elsewhere. That suited Rorie just fine. She hoped to avoid him as much as possible. In three days she'd be out of his life, leaving hardly a trace, and that was the way she wanted it.

Rorie sat typing in data for about an hour before her neck and shoulders began to cramp. She paused, flexing her muscles, then rotated her head to relieve the building tightness.

"How long have you been here?"

The rough male voice behind her startled Rorie. Her hand flew to her heart and she expelled a shaky breath. "Clay! You frightened me."

"How long?" he repeated.

"An hour or so." She glanced at her watch and nodded.

Clay advanced a step toward her, his mouth a thin line of impatience. "I suppose you're looking for an apology."

Rorie didn't answer. She'd learned not to expect anything from him.

"I'll tell you right now that you're not going to get one," he finished gruffly.

Six

"You don't owe me anything, Clay," Rorie said, struggling to make her voice light. Clay looked driven to the limits of exhaustion. Dark shadows had formed beneath his eyes and fatigue lines fanned out from their corners. His shoulders sagged slightly, as if the weight he carried was more than he could bear. He studied her wearily, then turned away, stalking to the other side of the office. His shoulders heaved as he drew in a shuddering breath.

"I know I should feel some regrets, but God help me, Rorie, I don't."

"Clay, listen…"

He turned to face her then, and drove his fingers into his hair with such force Rorie winced. "I'd like to explain about Kate and me."

"No." Under no circumstances did Rorie want to listen to his explanations or excuses. She didn't have a lot of room to be judgmental herself. She had, after all, been dating a man steadily for the past few months. "Don't. Please don't say anything. It isn't necessary."

He ignored her request. “Kate and I have known each other all our lives.”

“Clay, stop.” She pushed out the chair and stood up, wanting only to escape.

“For the last two years, it’s been understood by everyone around us that Kate and I would eventually get married. I didn’t even question the right or wrong of it, just calmly accepted the fact. A man needs someone to share his life.”

“Kate will make you a wonderful wife,” she said, feeling both disillusioned and indignant, but she refused to let him know how much his indiscretion had hurt her. “If you owe anyone an apology, it’s Kate, not me.”

His responding frown was brooding and dark. “I know.” He drew his fingers across his eyes, and she could feel his exhaustion. “The last thing in the world I want is to hurt Kate.”

“Then don’t.”

He stared at her, and Rorie made herself send him a smile, although she feared it was more flippant than reassuring. “There’s no reason for Kate to find out. What good would it do? She’d only end up feeling betrayed. Last night was a tiny impropriety and best forgotten, don’t you agree?” Walking seemed to help, and Rorie paced the office, her fingers brushing the stack of books and papers on his cluttered desk.

“I don’t know what’s best anymore,” Clay admitted quietly.

“I do,” Rorie said with unwavering confidence, still struggling to make light of the incident. “Think about it, Clay. We were alone together for hours—we shared something beautiful with Star Bright and…her foal. And we shared a few stolen kisses under the stars. If anything's to blame, it's the moonlight. We're strangers, Clay. You don't know me and I don't know you." Afraid to look him directly in the eye, Rorie lowered her gaze and waited, breathless, for his next words.

"So it was the moonlight?" His voice was hoarse and painfully raw.

"Of course," she lied. "What else could it have been?"

"Yes, what else could it have been?" he echoed, then turned and walked out of the office.

It suddenly seemed as though the room's light had dimmed. Rorie felt so weak, she sank into the chair, shocked by how deeply the encounter had disturbed her.

Typing proved to be a distraction and Rorie left the office a couple of hours later with a feeling of accomplishment. She'd been able to enter several time-consuming pages of data into the computer. The routine work was a relief because it meant she had no time to think.

The kitchen smelled of roasting beef and simmering apple crisp when Rorie let herself in the back door. It was an oddly pleasant combination of scents. Mary was nowhere to be seen.

While she thought of it, Rorie reached for the telephone book and called the number listed for the garage in Riversdale.

"Hello," she said when a gruff male voice answered. "This is Rorie Campbell...the woman with the broken water pump. The one in Nightingale."

"Yeah, Miss Campbell, what can I do for you?"

"I just wanted to be sure there wasn't any problem in ordering the part. I don't know if Clay... Mr. Franklin told you, but I'm more or less stuck here until the car's repaired. I'd like to get back on the road as soon as possible—I'm sure you understand."

"Lady, I can't make that pump come any faster than what it already is."

"Well, I just wanted to check that you'd been able to order one."

"It's on its way, at least that's what the guy in Los Angeles told me. They're shipping it by overnight freight to Portland. I've arranged for a man to pick it up the following day, but it's going to take him some time to get it to me."

"But that's only three days."

"You called too late yesterday for me to phone the order in. Lady, there's only so much I can do."

"I know. I'm sorry if I sound impatient."

"The whole world's impatient. Listen, I'll call you the minute it arrives."

She sighed. "Thanks, I'd appreciate it."

"Clay got your car here without a hitch, so don't worry about that—he saved you a bundle on towing charges. Shipping costs and long-distance phone bills are going to be plenty high, though."

Rorie hadn't even noticed that Dan's shiny sports car wasn't in the yard where Skip had originally left it. "So you'll be calling me within the next day or two?" she asked, trying to hide the anxiety in her voice. And trying not to consider the state of her finances, already depleted by this disastrous vacation.

"Right. I'll call as soon as it comes in."

"Thank you. I appreciate it," she said again.

"No problem," the mechanic muttered, obviously eager to end their conversation.

When the call was finished, Rorie toyed with the

idea of phoning Dan next. She'd been half expecting to hear from him, since she'd left the Franklins' number with his secretary the day before. He hadn't phoned her back. But there was nothing new to tell him, so she decided not to call a second time.

Hesitantly Rorie replaced the telephone receiver, pleased that everything was under control—everything except her heart.

Dinner that evening was a strained affair. If it hadn't been for Skip, who seemed oblivious to the tension between her and Clay, Rorie didn't think she could have endured it. Clay hardly said a word throughout the meal. But Skip seemed more than eager to carry the conversation and Rorie did her best to lighten the mood, wondering all the time whether Clay saw through her facade.

"While you're here, Rorie," Skip said with a sudden burst of enthusiasm, "you should learn how to ride."

"No, thank you," she said pointedly, holding up her hand, as though fending off the suggestion. An introduction to King and Hercules was as far as she was willing to go.

"Rain Magic would suit you nicely."

"Rain Magic?"

"That's a silly name Kate thought up, and Clay went along with it," Skip explained. "He's gentle, but smart—the gelding I mean, not Clay." The younger Franklin laughed heartily at his own attempt at humor.

Clay smiled, but Rorie wasn't fooled; he hadn't been amused by the joke, nor, she suspected, was he pleased by the reference to Kate.

"No, thanks, Skip," she said, hoping to bring the subject to a close. "I'm really not interested." There, that said it plainly enough.

"Are you afraid?"

"A little," she admitted truthfully. "I prefer my horses on a merry-go-round. I'm a city girl, remember?"

"But even girls from San Francisco have been known to climb on the back of a horse. It'll be good for you, Rorie. Trust me—it's time to broaden your horizons."

"Thanks, but no thanks," she told him, emphasizing her point by biting down on a crisp carrot stick with a loud crunch.

"Rorie, I insist. You aren't going to get hurt—I wouldn't let that happen, and Rain Magic is as gentle as they come. In fact—" he wiggled his eyebrows up and down "—if you want, we can ride double until you feel more secure."

Rorie laughed. "Skip, honestly."

"All right, you can ride alone, and I'll lead you around in a circle. For as long as you want."

Rorie shook her head and, amused at the mental picture that scenario presented, laughed again.

"Leave it," Clay said with sudden sharpness. "If Rorie doesn't want to ride, drop it, okay?"

Skip's shocked gaze flew from Rorie to his brother. "I was just having fun, Clay."

His older brother gripped his water goblet so hard Rorie thought the glass might shatter. "Enough is enough. She said she wasn't interested and that should be the end of it."

The astounded look left Skip's features, but his eyes narrowed and he stiffened his shoulders in a display of righteous indignation. "What's with you, Clay?" he shouted. "You've been acting like a wounded bear all day, growling at everyone. Who made *you* king of the universe all of a sudden?"

"If you'll excuse me, I'll bring in the apple crisp," Rorie said, and hurriedly rose to her feet, not wanting to be caught in the cross fire between the two brothers. Whatever they had to say wasn't meant for her ears.

The exchange that followed ended quickly, Rorie noted gratefully from inside the kitchen. Their voices were raised and then there was a hush followed by laughter. Rorie relaxed and picked up the dessert, carrying it into the dining room along with a carton of vanilla ice cream.

"I apologize, Rorie," Clay said soberly when she reentered the room. "Skip's right, I've been cross and unreasonable all day. I hope my sour mood hasn't ruined your dinner."

"Of course not," she murmured, giving him a smile.

Clay stood up to serve the dessert, spooning generous helpings of apple crisp and ice cream into each bowl.

Skip chattered aimlessly, commenting on one subject and then bouncing to another without any logical connection, his thoughts darting this way and that.

"What time are you going over to Kate's tonight?" he casually asked Clay.

"I won't be. She's got some meeting with the women's group from the Grange. They're decorating for the dance tomorrow night."

"Now that you mention it, I seem to remember Kate saying something about being busy tonight." Without a pause he turned to Rorie. "You'll be coming, I hope. The Grange is putting on a square dance—the biggest one of the year, and they usually do it up good."

"Kate already invited me. I'll be going with her," Rorie explained, although she hadn't the slightest idea how to square dance. Generally she enjoyed dancing, although she hadn't gone for several months because Dan wasn't keen on it.

"You could drive there with us if you wanted," Skip offered. "I'd kinda like to walk in there with you on my arm. You'd cause quite a stir with the men, especially Luke Rivers—he's the foreman at the Logan place. Most girls go all goo-goo-eyed over him."

Clay's spoon clanged loudly against the side of his glass dish and he murmured an apology.

"I'm sorry, Skip," Rorie said gently. "I told Kate I'd drive over with her."

"Darn," Skip muttered.

The meal was completed in silence. Once, when Rorie happened to glance up, her eyes met Clay's. Her heart felt as though it might hammer its way out of her chest. She was oppressively aware of the chemistry between them. It simmered in Rorie's veins and she could tell that Clay felt everything she did. Throughout dinner, she'd been all too conscious of the swift stolen glances Clay had sent in her direction. She'd sent a few of her own, though she'd tried hard not to. But it was impossible to be in the same room with this man and not react to him.

A thousand times in the next couple of hours, Rorie told herself that everything would be fine as soon as she could leave. Life would return to normal then.

When the dishes were finished, Skip challenged her to a game of cribbage, and grateful for the escape Rorie accepted. Skip sat with his back to his brother, and every time Rorie played her hand, she found her eyes wandering across the room to where Clay sat reading. To all outward appearances, he was relaxed and comfortable, but she knew he felt as tense as she did. She knew he was equally aware of the electricity that sparked between them.

Rorie's fingers shook as she counted out her cards.

"Fifteen eight," Skip corrected. "You forgot two points."

Her eyes fell to the extra ten, and she blinked. "I guess I did."

Skip heaved a sigh. "I don't think your mind's on the game tonight."

"I guess not," she admitted wryly. "If you'll excuse me, I think I'll go up to bed." She threw him an apologetic smile and reached for her coffee cup. Skip was right; her mind hadn't been on the game at all. Instead, her thoughts had been on a man who owed his loyalties to another woman—a woman whose roots were intricately bound with his. A woman Rorie had liked and respected from the moment they met.

Feeling depressed, she bade the two men good-night and carried her cup to the kitchen. Dutifully, she rinsed it out and set it beside the sink, but when she turned around Clay was standing in the doorway, blocking her exit.

"Where's Skip?" she asked a little breathlessly. Heat seemed to throb between them and she retreated a step in a futile effort to escape.

"He went upstairs."

She blinked and faked a yawn. "I was headed in that direction myself."

Clay buried one hand in his jeans pocket. "Do you know what happened tonight at dinner?"

Not finding her voice, Rorie shook her head.

"I was jealous," he said from between clenched teeth. "You were laughing and joking with Skip and I wanted it to be *me* your eyes were shining for. Me. No one else." He stopped abruptly and shook his head. "Jealous of a seventeen-year-old boy… I can't believe it myself."

Seven

Rorie decided to wear a dress for her outing with Kate Logan. Although she rose early, both Skip and Clay had eaten breakfast and left the house by the time she came downstairs. Which was just as well, Rorie thought.

Mary stood at the stove, frying chunks of beef for a luncheon stew. "I spoke to Clay about your cooking dinner later this week. He says that'll be fine if you're still around, but the way he sees it, you'll be on your way in a day or two."

Rorie poured herself a cup of coffee. "I'll be happy to do it if I'm here. Otherwise, I'm sure Kate Logan would be more than pleased."

Mary turned to face her, mouth open as if to comment. Instead her eyes widened in appreciation. "My, my, you look pretty enough to hog-tie a man's heart."

"Thank you, Mary," Rorie answered, grinning.

"I suppose you got yourself a sweetheart back there in San Francisco?" she asked, watching her closely. "A pretty girl like you is bound to attract plenty of men."

Rorie paused to think about her answer. She briefly considered mentioning Dan, but decided against it.

She'd planned this separation to gain a perspective on their relationship. And within hours of arriving at Elk Run, Rorie had found her answer. Dan would always be a special friend—but nothing more.

"The question shouldn't require a week's thought," Mary grumbled, stirring the large pot of simmering beef.

"Sorry… I was mulling something over."

"Then there is someone?"

She shook her head. "No."

The answer didn't seem to please Mary, because she frowned. "When did you say that fancy car of yours was going to be fixed?"

The abrupt question caught Rorie by surprise. Mary was openly concerned about the attraction between her and Clay. The housekeeper, who probably knew Clay as well as anyone did, clearly wasn't blind to what had been happening—and just as clearly didn't like it.

"The mechanic in Riversdale said it should be finished the day after tomorrow if all goes well."

"Good!" Mary proclaimed with a fierce nod, then turned back to her stew.

Rorie couldn't help smiling at the older woman's astuteness. Mary was telling her that the sooner she was off Elk Run the better for everyone concerned. Rorie had to agree.

Kate Logan arrived promptly at ten. She wore tight-fitting jeans, red checkered western shirt and a white silk scarf knotted at her throat. Her long honey-colored hair was woven into thick braids that fell over her shoulders. At first glance, Kate looked closer to sixteen than the twenty-four Rorie knew her to be.

Kate greeted her with a warm smile. "Rorie, there

wasn't any need to wear something so nice. I should've told you to dress casually."

Rorie's shoulders slumped. "I brought along more dresses than jeans. Am I overdressed? I could change," she said hesitantly.

"Oh, no, you look lovely..." But for the first time, Kate seemed worried. The doubt that played across her features would have been amusing if Rorie hadn't already been suffering from such a potent bout of guilt. It was all too obvious that Kate viewed Rorie as a threat.

If Clay Franklin had chosen that moment to walk into the kitchen, Rorie would've called him every foul name she could think of. She was furious with him for doing this to her—and to Kate.

"I wear a lot of dresses because of my job at the library," Rorie rushed to explain. "I also date quite a bit. I've been seeing someone—Dan Rogers—for a while now. In fact, it's his car I was driving."

"You're dating someone special?" Kate asked, sounding relieved.

"Yes, Dan and I've been going out for several months."

Mary coughed noisily and sent Rorie an accusing glare; Rorie ignored her. "Shouldn't we be leaving?"

"Oh, sure, any time you're ready." When they were outside, Kate turned to face Rorie. Looking uncomfortable, she slipped her hands into the back pockets of her jeans. "I've embarrassed you and I'm sorry. I didn't mean to imply that I didn't trust you and Clay."

"There's no need for an apology. I'm sure I wouldn't react any differently if Clay was *my* fiancé."

Kate shook her head. "But I feel as if I *should* apologize. I'm not going to be the kind of wife Clay wants if I can't trust him around a pretty girl once in a while."

Had the earth cracked open just then, Rorie would gladly have fallen in. That had to be preferable to looking at Kate and feeling the things she did about Clay Franklin.

"Don't have any worries about me," she said, dismissing the issue as nonchalantly as she could. "I'll be out of everyone's hair in a day or two."

"Oh, Rorie, please, I don't want you to rush off because I had a silly attack of jealousy. Now I feel terrible."

"Don't, please. I have to leave… I want to leave. My vacation's on hold until I can get my car repaired and there's so much I'd planned to see and do." She dug in her bag for a brochure. "Have you ever been up to Victoria on Vancouver Island?"

"Once, but I was only five, too young to remember much of anything," Kate told her, scanning the pamphlet. "This does sound like fun. Maybe this is where Clay and I should have our honeymoon."

"It'd be perfect for that," Rorie murmured. Her heart constricted with a sudden flash of pain, but she ruthlessly forced down her emotions, praying Kate hadn't noticed. "I'm looking forward to visiting Canada. By the way, Mary's driving to Riversdale to visit her sister later in the week. She's asked me to take charge of cooking dinner if I'm still here. Would you like to help? We could have a good time and really get to know each other."

"Oh, that would be great." Kate slipped her arm around Rorie's waist and gave her an enthusiastic squeeze. "Thank you, Rorie. I know you're trying to reassure me, and I appreciate it."

That had been exactly Rorie's intent.

"It probably sounds selfish," Kate continued, "but

I'm glad your car broke down when it did. Without any difficulty at all, I can see us becoming the best of friends."

Rorie could, too, but that only added to her growing sense of uneasiness.

Nightingale was a sleepy kind of town. Businesses lined both sides of Main Street, with a beauty shop, an insurance agency, Nellie's Café and a service station on one side, a grocery store, pharmacy and five-and-dime on the other. Rorie had the impression that things happened in their own time in Nightingale, Oregon. Few places could have been more unlike San Francisco, where people always seemed to be rushing. Here, no one seemed to feel any need to hurry. It was as though this town, with its population of fifteen hundred, existed in a time warp. Rorie found the relaxed pace unexpectedly pleasant.

"The library is across from the high school on Maple Street," Kate explained as she parked her Ford on Main. "That way, students have easy access."

Rorie climbed out of the car, automatically pressing down the door lock.

"You don't have to do that here. There hasn't been a vehicle stolen in…oh, at least twenty years."

Rorie's eyes must have revealed her surprise, because Kate went on, "Actually, we had trouble passing our last bond issue for a new patrol car. People couldn't see the need since there hasn't been a felony committed in over two years. About the worst thing that goes on is when Harry Ackerman gets drunk. That happens once or twice a year and he's arrested for disturbing the peace." She grinned sheepishly. "He sings old love songs to Nellie at the top of his lungs in front of the café. They were apparently sweet on each other a long time back. Nellie married someone else and Harry never got over the loss of his one true love."

Looping the strap of her bag over her shoulder, Rorie looked around the quiet streets.

"The fire and police station are in the same building," Kate pointed out next. "And there's a really nice restaurant on Oak. If you want, we could have lunch there."

"Only if you let me treat."

"I wouldn't hear of it," Kate said with a shake of her head that sent her braids flying. "You're my guest."

Rorie decided not to argue, asking another question instead. "Where do the ranchers get their supplies?" It seemed to her that type of store would do a thriving business, yet she hadn't seen one.

"At Garner's Feed and Supply. It's on the outskirts of town—I'll take you past on the way out. In fact, we should take a driving tour so you can see a little more of Nightingale. Main Street is only a small part of it."

By the time Kate and Rorie walked over to Maple and the library, Rorie's head was swimming with the names of all the people Kate had insisted on introducing. It seemed everyone had heard about her car problems and was eager to talk to her. Several mentioned the Grange dance that night and said they'd be looking for her there.

"You're really going to be impressed with the library," Kate promised as they walked the two streets over to Maple. "Dad and the others worked hard to get the levy passed so we could build it. People here tend to be tightfisted. Dad says they squeeze a nickel so hard, the buffalo belches."

Rorie laughed outright at that.

The library was the largest building in town, a sprawling one-story structure with lots of windows. The hours were posted on the double glass doors, and Rorie noted that the library wouldn't open until the middle of the afternoon, still several hours away.

"It doesn't seem to be open," she said, disappointed.

"Oh, don't worry, I've got a key. All the volunteers do." Kate rummaged in her bag and took out a large key ring. She opened the door, pushing it wide for Rorie to enter first.

"Mrs. Halldorfson retired last year, a month after the building was finished," Kate told her, flipping on the lights, "and the town's budget wouldn't stretch to hire a new full-time librarian. So a number of parents and teachers are taking turns volunteering. We've got a workable schedule, unless someone goes on vacation, which, I hate to admit, has been happening all summer."

"You don't have a full-time librarian?" Rorie couldn't disguise her astonishment. "Why go to all the trouble and expense of building a modern facility if you can't afford a librarian?"

"You'll have to ask Town Council that," Kate returned, shrugging. "It doesn't make much sense, does it? But you see, Mrs. Halldorfson was only part-time and the Council seems to think that's what her replacement should be."

"That doesn't make sense, either."

"Especially when you consider that the new library is twice the size of the old one."

Rorie had to bite her tongue to keep from saying

more. But she was appalled at the waste, the missed opportunities.

"We've been advertising for months for a part-time librarian, but so far we haven't found anyone interested. Not that I blame them—one look at the size of the job and no one wants to tackle it alone."

"A library is more than a place to check books in and out," Rorie said, gesturing dramatically. Her voice rose despite herself. This was an issue close to her heart, and polite silence was practically impossible. "A library can be the heart of a community. It can be a place for classes, community services, all kinds of things. Don't non-profit organizations use it for meetings?"

"I'm afraid not," Kate answered. "Everyone gets together at Nellie's when there's any kind of meeting. Nellie serves great pies," she added, as though that explained everything.

Realizing that she'd climbed onto her soapbox, Rorie dropped her hands and shrugged. "It's a very nice building, Kate, and you have every reason to be proud. I didn't mean to sound so righteous."

"But you're absolutely correct," Kate said thoughtfully. "We're not using the library to its full potential, are we? Volunteers can only do so much. As it is, the library's only open three afternoons a week." She sighed expressively. "To be honest, I think Dad and the other members of the Town Council are expecting Mrs. Halldorfson to come back in the fall, but that's unfair to her. She's served the community for over twenty years. She deserves to retire in peace without being blackmailed into coming back because we can't find a replacement."

"Well, I hope you find someone soon."

"I hope so, too," Kate murmured.

They ate a leisurely lunch, and as she'd promised, Kate gave Rorie a tour of the town. After showing her several churches, the elementary school where she taught second grade and some of the nicer homes on the hill, Kate ended the tour on the outskirts of town near Garner's Feed and Supply.

"Luke's here," Kate said, easing into the parking place next to a dusty pickup truck.

"Luke?"

"Our foreman. I don't know what Dad would do without him. He runs the ranch and has for years—ever since I was in high school. Dad's retirement age now, and he's more than willing to let Luke take charge."

Kate got out of the car and leaned against the front fender, crossing her arms over her chest. Rorie joined her.

"He'll be out in a minute," Kate said.

True to her word, a tall, deeply tanned man appeared with a sack of grain slung over his shoulder. His eyes were so dark they gleamed like onyx, taking in everything around him, but revealing little of his own thoughts. His strong square chin was balanced by a high intelligent brow. He was lean and muscular and strikingly handsome.

"Need any help, stranger?" Kate asked with a laugh.

"You offering?"

"Nope."

Luke chuckled. "That's what I figured. You wouldn't want to ruin those pretty nails of yours now, would you?"

"I didn't stop by to be insulted by you," Kate chastised, clearly enjoying the exchange. "I wanted you to meet Rorie Campbell—she's the one Clay was telling us about the other night, whose car broke down."

"I remember." For the first time the foreman's gaze left Kate. He tossed the sack of grain into the back of the truck and used his teeth to tug his glove free from his right hand. Then he presented his long callused fingers to Rorie. "Pleased to meet you, ma'am."

"The pleasure's mine." Rorie remembered where she'd heard the name. Skip had mentioned Luke Rivers when he'd told her about the Grange square dance. He'd said something about all the girls being attracted to the foreman. Rorie could understand why.

They exchanged a brief handshake before Luke's attention slid back to Kate. His eyes softened perceptibly.

"Luke's like a brother to me," Kate said fondly.

He frowned at that, but didn't comment.

"We're going to let you escort us to the dance tonight," she informed him.

"What about Clay?"

"Oh, he'll meet us there. I thought the three of us could go over together."

Rorie wasn't fooled. Kate was setting her up with Luke, who didn't look any too pleased at having his evening arranged for him.

"Kate, listen," she began, "I'd really rather skip the dance tonight. I've never done any square dancing in my life—"

"That doesn't matter," Kate interrupted. "Luke will be glad to show you. Won't you, Luke?"

"Sure," he mumbled, with the enthusiasm of a man offered the choice between hanging and a firing squad.

"Honestly, Luke!" Kate gave an embarrassed laugh.

"Listen," Rorie said quickly. "It's obvious Luke has his own plans for tonight. I don't want to intrude—"

He surprised her by turning toward her, his eyes searching hers. "I'd be happy to escort you, Rorie."

"I'm likely to step all over your toes… I really think I should sit the whole thing out."

"Nonsense," Kate cried. "Luke won't let you do that and neither will I!"

"We'll enjoy ourselves," the foreman said. "Leave everything to me."

Rorie nodded reluctantly.

A moment of awkward silence fell over the trio. "Well, I suppose I should get Rorie back to Circle L and see about finding her a dress," Kate said, smiling. She playfully tossed her car keys in the air and caught them deftly.

Luke tipped his hat when they both returned to the car. Rorie didn't mention his name until they were back on the road.

"Luke really is attractive, isn't he?" she asked, closely watching Kate.

The other woman nodded eagerly. "It surprises me that he's not married. There are plenty of girls around Nightingale who'd be more than willing, believe me. At every Grange dance, the ladies flirt with him like crazy. I love to tease him about it—he really hates that. But I wish Luke *would* get married—I don't like the idea of him living his life alone. It's time he thought about settling down and starting a family. He was thirty last month, but when I said something about it, he nearly bit my head off."

Rorie nibbled on her lower lip. She inhaled a deep breath and released it slowly. Her guess was that Luke Rivers had his heart set on someone special, and that someone was engaged to another man. God help him, Rorie thought. She knew exactly how he felt.

The music was already playing by the time Luke, Kate and Rorie arrived at the Grange Hall in Luke's ten-year-old four-door sedan. Rorie tried to force some enthusiasm for this outing, but had little success. She hadn't exchanged more than a few words with the foreman during the entire drive. He, apparently, didn't like this arranged-date business any better than she did. But they were stuck with each other, and Rorie at least was determined to make the best of it.

They entered the hall and were greeted by the cheery voice of the male caller:

Rope the cow, brand the calf
Swing your sweetheart, once and a half...

Rorie hadn't known what to expect, but she was surprised by the smooth-stepping, smartly dressed dancers who twirled around the floor following the caller's directions. She felt more daunted than ever by the evening ahead of her. And to worsen matters, Kate had insisted Rorie borrow one of her outfits. Although Rorie liked the bright blue colors, she felt awkward and self-conscious in the billowing skirts.

The Grange itself was bigger than Rorie had anticipated. On the stage stood the caller and several fiddlers. Refreshment tables lined one wall and the polished dance floor was so crowded Rorie wondered how anyone could move without bumping into others. The entire meeting hall was alive with energy and music, and despite herself, she felt her mood lift. Her toes started tapping out rhythms almost of their own accord. Given time, she'd be out there, too, joining the vibrant, laughing dancers. It was unavoidable, anyway. She knew Kate wouldn't allow her to sit sedately in the background and watch. Neither would Clay and Skip, who'd just arrived.

"Oh, my feet are moving already." Kate was squirming with eagerness. Clay smiled indulgently, tucked his arm around her waist and the two of them stepped onto the dance floor. He glanced back once at Rorie, before a circle of eight opened up to admit them.

"Shall we?" Luke asked, eyeing the dance floor.

He didn't sound too enthusiastic and Rorie didn't blame him. "Would it be all right if we sat out the first couple of dances?" she asked. "I'd like to get more into the swing of things."

"No problem."

Luke looked almost grateful for the respite, which didn't lend Rorie much confidence. No doubt he assumed this city slicker was going to make a fool of herself and of him—and she probably would. When he escorted her to the row of chairs, Rorie made the mistake of sitting down. Instantly her skirts leaped up into her face. Embarrassed, she pushed them down, then tucked the material under her thighs in an effort to tame the layers of stiff petticoats.

"Hello, Luke." A pretty blonde with sparkling blue eyes sauntered over. "I didn't know if you'd show tonight or not. Glad you did."

"Beth Hammond, this is Rorie Campbell."

Rorie nodded. "It's nice to meet you, Beth."

"Oh, I heard about you at the drugstore yesterday.

You're the gal with the broken-down sports car, aren't you?"

"That's me." By now it shouldn't have surprised Rorie that everyone knew about her troubles.

"I hope everything turns out okay."

"Thanks." Although Beth was speaking to Rorie, her eyes didn't leave Luke. It was patently obvious that she expected an invitation to dance.

"Luke, why don't you dance with Beth?" Rorie suggested. "That way I'll gather a few pointers from watching the two of you."

"What a good idea," Beth chirped eagerly. "We'll stay on the outskirts of the crowd so you can see how it's done. Be sure and listen to Charlie—he's the caller. Then you'll see what each step is."

Rorie nodded agreeably.

Luke gave Rorie a long sober look. "You're sure?"

"Positive."

All join hands, circle right around
Stop in place at your hometown...

Studying the dancers, Rorie quickly picked up the terms *do se do, allemande left* and *allemande right* and a number of others, which she struggled to keep track of. By the end of the dance, her foot was tapping out the lively beat of the fiddlers' music and a smile formed as she listened to the perfectly rhyming words.

"Rorie," Skip said, suddenly standing in front of her. "May I have the pleasure of this dance?"

"I… I don't think I'm ready yet."

"Nonsense." Without listening to her protest, he grabbed her hand and hauled her to her feet.

"Skip, I'll embarrass you," she protested in a low whisper. "I've never done this before."

"You've got to start sometime." He tucked his arm around her waist and led her close to the stage.

"We got a newcomer, Charlie," Skip called out, "so make this one simple."

Charlie gave Skip a thumbs-up and reached for the microphone. "We'll go a bit slower this time," Charlie announced to his happy audience. "Miss Rorie Campbell from San Francisco has joined us and it's her first time on the floor."

Rorie wanted to curl up and die as a hundred faces turned to stare at her. But the dancers were shouting and cheering their welcome and Rorie shyly raised her hand, smiling into the crowd.

Getting through that first series of steps was the most difficult, but soon Rorie was in the middle of the floor, stepping and twirling—and laughing. Something she'd always assumed to be a silly, outdated activity turned out to be great fun.

By the time Skip led her back to her chair, she was breathless. "Want some punch?" he asked. Rorie nodded eagerly. Her throat felt parched.

When Skip left her, Luke Rivers appeared at her side. "You did just great," he said sincerely.

"For a city girl, you mean," she teased.

"As good as anyone."

"Thanks."

"I suspect I owe you an apology, Rorie."

"Because you didn't want to make a fool of yourself with me on the dance floor?" she asked with a light laugh. "That's understandable. Kate and Clay practically threw me in your lap. I'm sure you had other plans for tonight, and I'm sorry for your sake that we got stuck with each other."

Luke grinned. "Trust me, I've had plenty of envious looks from around the room. Any of a dozen different men would be more than happy to be 'stuck' with you."

That went a long way toward boosting her ego. She would have commented, but Skip came back just then carrying a paper cup filled with bright pink punch. A teenage girl was beside him, clutching his free arm and smiling dreamily up at him.

"I'm going to dance with Caroline now, okay?" he said to Rorie.

"That's fine," she answered, smiling, "and thank you for braving the dance floor with me." Skip blushed as he slipped an arm around Caroline's waist and hurried her off.

"You game?" Luke nodded toward the dancing couples.

Rorie didn't hesitate. She swallowed the punch in three giant gulps, and gave him her hand. Together they moved onto the crowded floor.

By the end of the third set of dances, Rorie had twirled around with so many different partners, she lost track of them. She'd caught sight of Clay only once, and when he saw her he waved. Returning the gesture, she promptly missed her footing and nearly fell into her partner's waiting arms. The tall sheriff's deputy was all too happy to have her throw herself at him and told her as much, to Rorie's embarrassment.

Although it was only ten o'clock, Rorie was exhausted and so warm the perspiration ran in rivulets down her face and neck. She had to escape. Several times, she'd tried to sit out a dance, but no one would listen to her excuses.

In an effort to catch her breath and cool down, Rorie took advantage of a break between sets to wander outside. The night air was refreshing. Quite a few other people had apparently had the same idea; the field that served as a car park was crowded with groups and strolling couples.

As she made her way through the dimly lit field, she saw a handful of men passing around a flask of whiskey and entertaining each other with off-color jokes. She steered a wide circle around them and headed toward Luke's parked car, deciding it was far enough away to discourage anyone from following her. In her eagerness to escape, she nearly stumbled over a couple locked in a passionate embrace against the side of a pickup.

Rorie mumbled an apology when the pair glanced up at her, irritation written all over their young faces. Good grief, she'd only wanted a few minutes alone in order to get a breath of fresh air—she hadn't expected to walk through an obstacle course!

When she finally arrived at Luke Rivers's car, she leaned on the fender and slowly inhaled the clean country air. All her assumptions about this evening had been wrong. She'd been so sure she'd feel lonely and bored and out of place. And she'd felt none of those things. If she were to tell Dan about the Grange dance, he'd laugh at the idea of having such a grand time with a bunch of what he'd refer to as "country bumpkins." The thought annoyed her. These were good, friendly, fun-loving people. They'd taken her under their wing, expressed their welcome without reserve, and now they were showing her an uncomplicated lifestyle that had more appeal than Rorie would have believed possible.

"I thought I'd find you out here."

Rorie's whole body tensed as she recognized the voice of the man who'd joined her.

"Hello, Clay."

Eight

Rorie injected a cheerful note into her voice. She turned around, half expecting Kate to be with him. The two had been inseparable from the minute Clay had arrived. It was just as well that Kate was around, since her presence prevented Clay and Rorie from giving in to any temptation.

Clay's hands settled on her shoulders and Rorie flinched involuntarily at his touch. With noticeable regret, Clay dropped his hands.

"Are you having a good time?" he asked.

She nodded. "I didn't think I would, which tells you how prejudiced I've been about country life, but I've been pleasantly surprised."

"I'm glad." His hands clenched briefly at his sides, then he flexed his fingers a couple of times. "I would've danced with you myself, but—"

She stopped him abruptly. "Clay, no. Don't explain… it isn't necessary. I understand."

His eyes held hers with such tenderness that she had to look away. The magical quality was in the air again—Rorie could feel it as forcefully as if the stars had spelled it out across the heavens.

"I don't think you do understand, Rorie," Clay said, "but it doesn't matter. You'll be gone in a couple of days and both our lives will go back to the way they were meant to be."

Rorie agreed with a quick nod. It was too tempting, standing in the moonlight with Clay. Much too tempting. The memory of another night in which they'd stood and gazed at the stars returned with powerful intensity. Rorie realized that even talking to each other, alone like this, was dangerous.

"Won't Kate be looking for you?" she asked carefully.

"No. Luke Rivers is dancing with her."

For a moment she closed her eyes, not daring to look up at Clay. "I guess I'll be going inside now. I just came out to catch my breath and cool down a little."

"Dance with me first—here in the moonlight."

A protest rose within her, but the instant Clay slid his arms around her waist, Rorie felt herself give in. Kate would have him the rest of her life, but Rorie only had these few hours. Almost against her will, her hands found his shoulders, slipping around his neck with an ease that brought a sigh of pleasure to her lips. Being held by Clay shouldn't feel this good.

"Oh, Rorie," he moaned as she settled into his embrace.

They fitted together as if they'd been created for each other. His chin touched the top of her head and he caressed her hair with his jaw.

"This is a mistake," Rorie murmured, closing her eyes, savoring the warm, secure feel of his arms.

"I know…"

But neither seemed willing to release the other.

His mouth grazed her temple and he kissed her there. "God help me, Rorie, what am I going to do? I haven't been able to stop thinking about you. I can't sleep, I hardly eat..." His voice was raw, almost savage.

"Oh, please," she said with a soft cry. "We can't...we mustn't even talk like this." His gray eyes smoldered above hers, and their breaths merged as his mouth hovered so close to her own.

"I vowed I wouldn't touch you again."

Rorie looked away. She'd made the same promise to herself. But it wasn't in her to deny him now, although her mind searched frantically for the words to convince him how wrong they were to risk hurting Kate—and each other.

His hands drifted up from her shoulders, his fingertips skimming the sides of her neck, trailing over her cheeks and through the softness of her hair. He placed his index finger over her lips, gently stroking them apart.

Rorie moaned. She moistened her lips with the tip of her tongue. Clay's left hand dug into her shoulders as her tongue caressed the length of his finger, drawing it into her mouth and sucking it gently. She needed him so much in that moment, she could have wept.

"Just this once...for these few minutes," he pleaded, "let me pretend you're mine." His hands cupped her face and slowly brought her mouth to his, smothering her whimper of part welcome, part protest.

A long series of kisses followed. Deep, relentless, searching kisses that sent her heart soaring. Kisses that only made the coming loneliness more painful. A sob swelled within her and tears burned her eyes as she twisted away and tore her mouth from his.

"No," she cried, covering her face with her hands and turning her back to him. "Please, Clay. We shouldn't be doing this."

He was silent for so long that Rorie suspected he'd left her. She inhaled a deep, calming breath and dropped her hands limply to her sides.

"It would be so easy to love you, Rorie."

"No," she whispered, shaking her head vigorously as she faced him again. "I'm not the right person for you—it's too late for that. You've got Kate." She couldn't keep the pain out of her voice. Anything between them was hopeless, futile. Within a day or two her car would be repaired and she'd vanish from his life as suddenly as she'd appeared.

Clay fell silent, his shoulders stiff and resolute as he stood silhouetted against the light of the Grange Hall. His face was masked by shadows and Rorie couldn't read his thoughts. He drew in a harsh breath.

"You're right, Rorie. We can't allow this…attraction between us to get out of hand. I promise you, by all I hold dear, that I won't kiss you again."

"I'll…do my part, too," she assured him, feeling better now that they'd made this agreement.

His hand reached for hers and clasped it warmly. "Come on, I'll walk you back to the hall. We're going to be all right. We'll do what we have to do."

Clay's tone told her he meant it. Relieved, Rorie silently made the same promise to herself.

Rorie slept late the next morning, later than she would have thought possible. Mary was busy with lunch preparations by the time she made her way downstairs.

"Did you enjoy yourself last night?" Mary immediately asked.

In response, Rorie curtsied and danced a few steps with an imaginary partner, clapping her hands.

Mary tried to hide a smile at Rorie's antics. "Oh, get away with you now. All I was looking for was a yes or a no."

"I had a great time."

"It was nothing like those city hotspots, I'll wager."

"You're right about that," Rorie told her, pouring herself a cup of coffee.

"You seeing Kate today?"

Rorie shook her head and popped a piece of bread in the toaster. "She's got a doctor's appointment this morning and a teachers' meeting this afternoon. She's going to stop by later if she has a chance, but if not I'll be seeing her for sure tomorrow." Rorie intended to spend as much time as she could with Clay's fiancée. She genuinely enjoyed her company, and being with her served two useful purposes. It helped keep Rorie occupied, and it prevented her from being alone with Clay.

"What are you going to do today, then?" Mary asked, frowning.

Rorie laughed. "Don't worry. Whatever it is, I promise to stay out of your way."

The housekeeper gave a snort of amusement—or was it relief?

"Actually, I thought I'd finish putting the data Clay needs for his pedigree-research program into the computer. There isn't much left and I should be done by this afternoon."

"So if someone comes looking for you, that's where you'll be?"

“That’s where I’ll be,” Rorie echoed. She didn’t know who would “come looking for her,” as Mary put it. The housekeeper made it sound as though a posse was due to arrive any minute demanding to know where the Franklin men were hiding Rorie Campbell.

Taking her coffee cup with her, Rorie walked across the yard and into the barn. Once more, she was impressed with all the activity that went on there. She’d come to know several of the men by their first names and returned their greetings with a smile and a wave.

As before, she found the office empty. She set down her cup while she turned on the computer and collected Clay’s data. She’d just started to type it in when she heard someone enter the room. Pausing, she twisted around.

“Rorie.”

“Clay.”

They were awkward with each other now. Almost afraid.

“I didn’t realize you were here.”

She stood abruptly. “I’ll leave…”

“No. I came up to get something. I’ll be gone in a minute.”

She nodded and sat back down. “Okay.”

He walked briskly to his desk and sifted through the untidy stacks of paper. His gaze didn’t waver from the task, but his jaw was tight, his teeth clenched. Impatience marked his every move. “Kate told me you’re involved with a man in San Francisco. I…didn’t know.”

“I’m not exactly involved with him—at least not in the way you’re implying. His name is Dan Rogers, and we’ve been seeing each other for about six months. He’s divorced. The MG is his.”

Clay's mouth thinned, but he still didn't look at her. "Are you in love with him?"

"No."

Lowering his head, Clay rubbed his hand over his eyes. "I had no right to ask you that. None. Forgive me, Rorie." Then, clutching his papers, he stalked out of the office without a backward glance.

Rorie was so shaken by the encounter that when she went back to her typing, she made three mistakes in a row and had to stop to regain her composure.

When the phone rang, she ignored it, knowing Mary or one of the men would answer it. Soon afterward, she heard running footsteps behind her and swivelled around in the chair.

A breathless Skip bolted into the room. Shoulders heaving, he pointed in the direction of the telephone. "It's for you," he panted.

"Me?" It could only be Dan.

He nodded several times, his hand braced theatrically against his heart.

She picked up the extension. "Hello," she said, her fingers closing tightly around the receiver. "This is Rorie Campbell."

"Miss Campbell," came the unmistakable voice of George, the mechanic in Riversdale, "let me put it to you like this. I've got good news and bad news."

"Now what?" she cried, pushing her hair off her forehead with an impatient hand. She had to get out of Elk Run.

"My man picked up the water pump for your car in Portland just like we planned."

"Good."

George sighed heavily. "There's a minor problem, though."

"Minor?" she repeated hopefully.

"Well, not that minor actually."

"Oh, great… Listen, George, I'd prefer not to play guessing games with you. Just tell me what happened and how long it's going to be before I can get out of here."

"I'm sorry, Miss Campbell, but they shipped the wrong part. It'll be two, possibly three more days."

Nine

"What's the matter?" Skip asked when Rorie indignantly replaced the receiver.

She crossed her arms over her chest and breathed deeply, battling down the angry frustration that boiled inside her. The problem wasn't George's fault, or Skip's, or Kate's, or anyone else's.

"Rorie?" Skip asked again.

"They shipped the wrong part for the car," she said flatly. "I'm going to be stuck here for another two or possibly three days."

Skip didn't look the least bit perturbed at this information. "Gee, Rorie, that's not so terrible. We like having you around—and you like it here, don't you?"

"Yes, but..." How could she explain that her reservations had nothing to do with their company, the farm or even with country life? She couldn't very well blurt out that she was falling in love with his brother, that she had to escape before she ruined their lives.

"But what?" Skip asked.

"My vacation."

"I know you had other plans, but you can relax and enjoy yourself here just as well, can't you?"

She didn't attempt to answer him, but closed her eyes and nodded, faintly.

"Well, listen, I've got to get back to work. Do you need me for anything?"

She shook her head. When the office door closed, Rorie sat down in front of the computer again and poised her fingers over the keyboard. She sat like that, unmoving, for several minutes as her thoughts churned. What was she going to do? Every time she came near Clay the attraction was so strong that trying to ignore it was like swimming upstream. Rorie had planned on leaving Elk Run the following day. Now she was trapped here for God only knew how much longer.

She got up suddenly and started pacing the office floor. Dan hadn't called her, either. She might have vanished from the face of the earth as far as he was concerned. The stupid car was his, after all, and the least he could do was make some effort to find out what had happened. Rorie knew she wasn't being entirely reasonable, but she was caught up in the momentum of her anger and frustration.

Impulsively she snatched up the telephone receiver, had the operator charge the call to her San Francisco number and dialed Dan's office.

"Rorie, thank God you phoned," Dan said.

The worry in his voice appeased her a little. "The least you could've done was call me back," she fumed.

"I tried. My secretary apparently wrote down the wrong number. I've been waiting all this time for you to call me again. Why didn't you? What on earth is going on?"

She told him in detail, from the stalled car to her recent conversation with the mechanic. She didn't tell him about Clay Franklin and the way he made her feel.

"Rorie, baby, I'm so sorry."

She nodded mutely, close to tears. If she wasn't so dangerously close to falling in love with Clay, none of this would seem such a disaster.

The silence lengthened while Dan apparently mulled things over. "Shall I come and get you?" he finally asked.

"With what?" she asked with surprising calm. "My car? You were the one who convinced me it would never make this trip. Besides, how would you get the MG back?"

"I'd figured something out. Listen, I can't let you sit around in some backwoods farm town. I'll borrow a car or rent one." He hesitated, then expelled his breath in a short burst of impatience. "Damn, forget that. I can't come."

"You can't?"

"I've got a meeting tomorrow afternoon. It's important—I can't miss it. I'm sorry, Rorie, I really am, but there's nothing I can do."

"Don't worry about it," she said, defeat causing her voice to dip slightly. "I understand." In a crazy kind of way she did. Dan was a rising stockbroker, so career moves were critical to him, more important than rescuing Rorie, the woman he claimed to love… Somehow Rorie couldn't picture Clay making the same decision. In her heart she knew Clay would come for her the second she asked.

They spoke for a few more minutes before Rorie ended the conversation. She felt trapped, as though the walls were closing in around her. So far she and Clay had managed to disguise their feelings, but they wouldn't be able to keep it up much longer before someone guessed. Kate wasn't blind, and neither was Mary.

"Rorie?" Clay called her name as he burst into the office. "What happened? Skip told me you were all upset—something about the car? What is it?"

"George called." She whirled around and pointed toward the phone. "The water pump arrived just like it was supposed to—but it's the wrong one."

Clay dropped his gaze, then removed his hat and wiped his forehead. "I'm sorry."

"I am, too, but that doesn't help, does it?" The conversation with Dan hadn't improved matters, and taking her frustration out on Clay wasn't going to change anything, either. "I'm stuck here, and this is the last place on earth I want to be."

"Do you think I like it any better?" he challenged.

Rorie blinked wildly at the tears that burned for release.

"I wish to God your car had broken down a hundred miles from Elk Run," he said. "Before you bombarded your way into my home, my life was set. I knew what I wanted, where I was headed. In the course of a few days you've upended my whole world."

Emotion clogged Rorie's throat at the unfairness of his accusations. She hadn't asked for the MGB to break down where it had. The minute she could, she planned to get out of his life and back to her own.

No, she decided, they couldn't wait that long—it was much too painful for them both. She had to leave now. "I'll pack my things and be gone before evening."

"Just where do you plan to go?"

Rorie didn't know. "Somewhere…anywhere." She had to leave for his sake, as well as hers.

"Go back inside the house, Rorie, before I say or do something else I'll regret. You're right—we can't be in the same room together. At least not alone."

She started to walk past him, eyes downcast, her heart heavy with misery. Unexpectedly his hand shot out and caught her fingers, stopping her.

"I didn't mean what I said." His voice rasped, warm and hoarse. "None of it. Forgive me, Rorie."

Her heart raced when his hand touched hers. It took all the restraint Rorie could muster, which at the moment wasn't much, to resist throwing herself into his arms and holding on for the rest of her life.

"Forgive me, too," she whispered.

"Forgive you?" he asked, incredulous. "No, Rorie. I'll thank God every day of my life for having met you." With that, he released her fingers, slowly, reluctantly. "Go now, before I make an even bigger fool of myself."

Rorie ran from the office as though a raging fire were licking at her heels, threatening to consume her.

And in a way, it was.

For two days, Rorie managed to stay completely out of his way. They saw each other only briefly and always in the company of others. Rorie was sure they gave Academy Award performances every time they were together. They laughed and teased and joked and the only one who seemed to suspect things weren't quite right was Mary.

Rorie was grateful the housekeeper didn't question her, but the looks she gave Rorie were frowningly thoughtful.

Three days after the Grange dance, Mary's sister arrived in Riversdale. Revealing more excitement than Rorie had seen in their acquaintance, Mary fussed with her hair and dress, and as soon as she'd finished the lunch dishes she was off.

Putting on Mary's well-worn apron, Rorie looped the long strands around her waist twice and set to work. Kate joined her mid-afternoon, carrying a large bag of ingredients for the dessert she was going to prepare.

"I've been cooking from the moment Mary left," Rorie told Kate, pushing the damp hair from her forehead as she stirred wine into a simmering sauce. Rorie intended to dazzle Clay and Skip with her one specialty—seafood fettuccine. She hadn't admitted to Mary how limited her repertoire of dishes was, although the housekeeper had repeatedly quizzed her about what she planned to make for dinner. Rorie had insisted it was a surprise. She'd decided that this rich and tasty dish stood a good chance of impressing the Franklin men.

"And I'm making Clay his favorite dessert—homemade lemon meringue pie." Kate reached for the grocery bag on the kitchen counter and six bright yellow lemons rolled out.

Rorie was impressed. The one and only time she'd tried to bake a lemon pie, she'd used a pudding mix. Apparently, Kate took the homemade part seriously.

"Whatever you're cooking smells wonderful," Kate said, stepping over to the stove. Crab, large succulent shrimp and small bite-sized pieces of sole were waiting in the refrigerator, to be added to the sauce just before the dish was served.

Kate was busy whipping up a pie crust when the

phone rang several minutes later. She glanced anxiously at the wall, her fingers sticky with flour and lard.

Rorie looked over at her. "Do you suppose I should answer that?"

"You'd better. Clay usually relies on Mary to catch the phone for him."

Rorie lifted the receiver before the next peal. "Elk Run."

"That Miss Campbell?"

Rorie immediately recognized the voice of the mechanic from Riversdale. "Yes, this is Rorie Campbell."

"Remember I promised I'd call you when the part arrived? Well, it's here, all safe and sound, so you can stop fretting. Just came in a few minutes ago—haven't even had a chance to take it out of the box. Thought you'd want to know."

"It's the right one this time?"

"Here, I'll check it now… Yup, this is it."

Rorie wasn't sure what she felt. Relief, yes, but regret, too. "Thank you. Thank you very much."

"It's a little late for me to be starting the job this afternoon. My son's playing a Little League game and I promised him I'd be there. I'll get to this first thing in the morning and should be finished before noon. Give me a call before you head over here and I'll make sure everything's running the way it should."

"Yes, I'll do that. Thanks again." Slowly Rorie replaced the receiver. She leaned against the wall sighing deeply. At Kate's questioning gaze, she smiled weakly and explained, "That was the mechanic. The water pump for my car arrived and he's going to be working on it first thing in the morning."

"Rorie, that's great."

"I think so, too." She did—and she didn't. Part of her longed to flee Elk Run, and another part of her realized that no matter how far she traveled, no matter how many years passed, she'd never forget these days with Clay Franklin.

"Then tonight's going to be your last evening here," Kate murmured. "Selfish as it sounds, I really hate the thought of you leaving."

"We can keep in touch."

"Oh, yes, I'd like that. I'll send you a wedding invitation."

That reminder was the last thing Rorie needed. But once she was on the road again, she could start forgetting, she told herself grimly.

"Since this is going to be your last night, we should make it special," Kate announced brightly. "We're going to use the best china and set out the crystal wineglasses."

Rorie laughed, imagining Mary's face when she heard about it.

Even as she spoke, Kate was walking toward the dining-room china cabinet. In a few minutes, she'd set the table, cooked the sauce for the pie and poured it into the cooling pie shell that sat on the counter. The woman was a marvel!

Rorie was busy adding the final touches to the fettuccine when Clay and Skip came in through the back door.

"When's dinner?" Skip wanted to know. "I'm starved."

"Soon." Rorie tested the boiling noodles to be sure they'd cooked all the way through but weren't overdone.

"Upstairs with the both of you," Kate said, shooing them out of the kitchen. "I want you to change into something nice."

"We're supposed to dress up for dinner?" Skip complained. He'd obviously recovered from any need to impress her with his sartorial elegance, Rorie noted, remembering that he'd worn his Sunday best that first night. "We already washed—what more do you want?"

"For you to change your clothes. We're having a celebration tonight."

"We are?" The boy looked from Kate to Rorie and then back again.

"That's right," Kate continued, undaunted by his lack of enthusiasm. "And when we're through with dinner, there's going to be a farewell party for Rorie. We're going to send her off country-style."

"Rorie's leaving?" Skip sounded shocked. "But she just got here."

"The repair shop from Riversdale called. Her car will be finished tomorrow and she'll be on her way."

Clay's eyes burned into Rorie's. She tried to avoid looking at him, but when she did chance to meet his gaze, she could feel his distress. His jaw went rigid, and his mouth tightened as though he was bracing himself against Kate's words.

"Now hurry up, you two. Dinner's nearly ready," Kate said with a laugh. "Rorie's been cooking her heart out all afternoon."

Both men disappeared and Rorie set out the fresh green salad she'd made earlier, along with the seven-grain dinner rolls she'd warmed in the oven.

Once everyone was seated at the table and waiting, Rorie ceremonially carried in the platter of fettuccine, thick with seafood. She'd spent at least ten minutes arranging it to look as attractive as possible.

"Whatever it is smells good," Skip called out as she

entered the dining room. “I’m so hungry I could eat a horse.”

“Funny, Skip, very funny,” Kate said.

Rorie set the serving dish in the middle of the table and stepped back, anticipating their praise.

Skip raised himself halfway out of his seat as he glared at her masterpiece. “That’s it?” His voice was filled with disappointment.

Rorie blinked, uncertain how she should respond.

“You’ve been cooking all afternoon and you mean to tell me that’s everything?”

“It’s seafood fettuccine,” she explained.

“It just looks like a bunch of noodles to me.”

Ten

"I'll have another piece of lemon pie," Skip said, eagerly extending his plate.

"If you're still hungry, Skip," Clay remarked casually, "there are a few dinner rolls left."

Skip's gaze darted to the small wicker basket and he wrinkled his nose. "No, thanks. Too many seeds in those things. I got one caught in my tooth earlier and spent five minutes trying to suck it out."

Rorie did her best to smile.

Skip must have noticed how miserable she was because he added, "The salad was real good though. What kind of dressing was that?"

"Vinaigrette."

"Really? It tasted fruity."

"It was raspberry flavored."

Skip's eyes widened. "I've never heard of that kind of vinegar. Did you buy it here in Nightingale?"

"Not exactly. I got the ingredients while Kate and I were out the other day and mixed it up last night."

"*That* tasted real good." Which was Skip's less-than-subtle method of telling her nothing else had. He'd barely touched the main course. Clay had made a show of asking for seconds, but Rorie was all too aware that his display of enthusiasm had been an effort to salve her injured ego.

Rorie wasn't fooled—no one had enjoyed her special dinner. Even old Blue had turned his nose up at it when she'd offered him a taste of the leftovers.

Clay and Skip did hard physical work; they didn't sit in an office all day like Dan and the other men she knew. She should have realized that Clay and his brother required a more substantial meal than noodles swimming in a creamy sauce. Rorie wished she'd discussed her menu with either Mary or Kate. A tiny voice inside her suggested that Kate might have said something to warn her…

"Anyone else for more pie?" Kate was asking.

Clay nodded and cast a guilty glance in Rorie's direction. "I could go for a second piece myself."

"The pie was delicious," Rorie told Kate, meaning it. She was willing to admit Kate's dessert had been the highlight of the meal.

"Kate's one of the best cooks in the entire country," Skip announced, licking the back of his fork. "Her lemon pie won a blue ribbon at the county fair last year." He leaned forward, planting his elbows on the table. "She's got a barbecue sauce so tangy and good that when she cooks up spareribs I just can't stop eating 'em." His face fell as though he was thinking about those ribs now and would have gladly traded all of Rorie's fancy city food for a plateful.

"I'd like the fettuccine recipe if you'd give it to me," Kate told Rorie, obviously attempting to change the subject and spare Rorie's feelings. Perhaps she felt a little guilty, too, for not giving her any helpful suggestions.

Skip stared at Kate as if she'd volunteered to muck out the stalls.

"I'll write it down before I leave."

"Since Rorie and Kate put so much time and effort into the meal, I think Skip and I could be convinced to do our part and wash the dishes."

"We could?" Skip protested.

"It's the least we can do," Clay returned flatly, frowning at his younger brother.

Rorie was all too aware of Clay's ploy. He wanted to get into the kitchen so they could find something else to eat without being conspicuous about it. Something plain and basic, no doubt, like roast-beef sandwiches.

"Listen, you guys," Rorie said brightly. "I'm sorry about dinner. I can see everyone's still hungry. You're all going out of your way to reassure me, but it isn't necessary."

"I don't know what you're talking about, Rorie. Dinner was excellent," Clay said, patting his stomach.

Rorie nearly laughed out loud. "Why don't we call for a pizza?" she said, pleased with her solution. "I bungled dinner, so that's the least I can do to make it up to you."

Three faces stared at her blankly.

"Rorie," Clay said gently. "The closest pizza parlour is thirty miles from here."

"Oh."

Undeterred, Skip leaped to his feet. "No problem… You phone in the order and I'll go get it."

Empty pizza boxes littered the living-room floor, along with several abandoned soft-drink cans.

Skip lay on his back staring up at the ceiling. "Anyone for a little music?" he asked lazily.

"Sure." Kate got to her feet and sat down at the piano. As her nimble fingers ran over the keyboard, the rich sounds echoed against the walls. "Some Lee Greenwood?"

"All *right,*" Skip called out with a yell, punching his fist into the air. He thrust two fingers in his mouth and gave a shrill whistle.

"Who?" Rorie asked once the commotion had died down.

"He's a country singer," Clay explained. Blue ambled to his side, settling down at his feet. Clay gently stroked his back.

"I guess I haven't heard of him," Rorie murmured.

Once more she discovered three pairs of eyes studying her curiously.

"What about Johnny Cash?" Kate suggested next. "You probably know who he is."

"Oh, sure." Rorie looped her arms over her bent knees and lowered her voice to a gravelly pitch. "I hear that train a comin'."

Skip let loose with another whistle and Rorie laughed at his boisterous antics. Clay left the room; he returned a moment later with a guitar, then seated himself on the floor again, beside Blue. Skip crawled across the braided rug in the center of the room and retrieved a harmonica from the mantel. Soon Kate and the two men were making their own brand of music—country songs, from the traditional to the more recent. Rorie didn't know a single one, but she clapped her hands and tapped her foot to the lively beat.

"Sing for Rorie," Skip shouted to Clay and Kate. "Let's show her what she's been missing."

Clay's rich baritone joined Kate's lilting soprano, and Rorie's hands and feet stopped moving. Her eyes darted from one to the other in openmouthed wonder at the beautiful harmony of their two voices, male and female. It was as though they'd been singing together all their lives. She realized they probably had.

When they finished, Rorie blinked back tears, too dumbfounded for a moment to speak. "That was wonderful," she told them and her voice caught with emotion.

"Kate and Clay sing duets at church all the time," Skip explained. "They're good, aren't they?"

Rorie nodded, gazing at the two of them. Clay and Kate were right for each other—they belonged together, and once she was gone they would blend their lives as beautifully as they had their voices. Rorie happened to catch Kate's eye. The other woman slipped her arms around Clay's waist and rested her head against his shoulder, laying claim to this man and silently letting Rorie know it. Rorie couldn't blame Kate. In like circumstances she would have done the same.

"Do you sing, Rorie?" Kate asked, leaving Clay and sliding onto the piano bench.

"A little, and I play some piano." Actually her own singing voice wasn't half bad. She'd participated in several singing groups while she was in high school and had taken five years of piano lessons.

"Please sing something for us." Rorie recognized a hint of challenge in the words.

"Okay." She replaced Kate at the piano seat and started out with a little satirical ditty she remembered from her college days. Skip hooted as she knew he would at the clever words, and all three rewarded her with a round of applause.

"Play some more," Kate encouraged. "It's nice to have someone else do the playing for a change." She sat next to Clay on the floor, once again resting her head against his shoulder. If it hadn't been for the guitar in his hands, Rorie knew he would've placed his arm around her and drawn her even closer. It would have been the natural thing to do.

"I don't know the songs you usually sing, though." Rorie was more than a little reluctant now. She'd never heard of this Greenwood person they seemed to like so well.

"Play what you know," Kate said, "and we'll join in."

After a few seconds' thought, Rorie nodded. "This is a song by Billy Joel. I'm sure you've heard of him—his songs are more rock than country, but I think you'll recognize the music." Rorie was only a few measures into the ballad before she realized that Kate, Clay and Skip had never heard this song.

She stopped playing. "What about Whitney Houston?"

Skip repeated the name a couple of times before his eyes lit up with recognition. "Hasn't she done Coke commercials?"

"Right," Rorie said, laughing. "She's had several big hits."

Kate slowly shook her head. "Sorry, I don't think I can remember the words to her songs."

"Barbra Streisand?"

"I thought she was an actress," Skip said with a puzzled frown. "You mean she sings, too?"

Reluctantly Rorie rose from the piano seat. "Kate, you'll have to take over. It seems you three are a whole lot country and I'm a little bit rock and roll."

"We'll make you into a country girl yet!" Skip insisted, sliding the harmonica across his mouth with an ease Rorie envied.

Clay glanced at his watch. "We aren't going to be able to convert Rorie within the next twelve hours."

A gloom settled over them as Kate took Rorie's place at the piano.

"Are you sure we can't talk you into staying a few extra days?" Skip asked. "We're just getting to know each other."

Rorie shook her head, more determined than ever to leave as soon as she could.

"It would be a shame for you to miss the county fair next weekend. Maybe you could stop here on your way back through Oregon, after your trip to Canada," Kate added. "Clay and I are singing, and we're scheduled for the square dance competition, too."

"Yeah," Skip cried. "And we've got pig races planned again this year."

"Pig races?" Rorie echoed faintly.

"I know it sounds silly, but it's really fun. We take the ten fastest pigs in the area and let them race toward a bowl of Oreos. No joke—cookies! Everyone bets on who'll win and we all have a lot of fun." Skip's eyes shone with eagerness. "Please think about it, anyway, Rorie."

"Mary's entering her apple pie again," Clay put in. "She's been after that blue ribbon for six years."

A hundred reasons to fade out of their lives flew across Rorie's mind like particles of dust in the wind.

And yet the offer was tempting. She tried, unsuccessfully, to read Clay's eyes, her own filled with a silent appeal. This was a decision she needed help making. But Clay wasn't helping. The thought of never seeing him again was like pouring salt onto an open wound; still, it was a reality she'd have to face sooner or later.

So Rorie volunteered the only excuse she could come up with at the moment. "I don't have the time. I'm sorry, but I'd be cutting it too close to get back to San Francisco for work Monday morning."

"Not if you canceled part of your trip to Canada and came back on Friday," Skip pointed out. "You didn't think you'd have a good time at the square dance, either, but you did, remember?"

It wasn't a matter of having a good time. So much more was involved…though the pig races actually sounded like fun. The very idea of such an activity would have astounded her only a week before, Rorie reflected. She could just imagine what Dan would say.

"Rorie?" Skip pressed. "What do you think?"

"I… I don't know."

"The county fair is about as good as it gets around Nightingale."

"I don't want to impose on your hospitality again." Clay still wasn't giving her any help with this decision.

"But having you stay with us isn't a problem," Skip insisted. "As long as you promise to stay out of the kitchen, you're welcome to stick around all summer. Isn't that right, Clay?"

His hesitation was so slight that Rorie doubted anyone else had noticed it. "Naturally Rorie's welcome to visit us any time she wants."

"If staying with these two drives you crazy," Kate

inserted, "you could stay at my house. In fact, I'd love it if you did."

Rorie dropped her gaze, fearing what she might see in Clay's eyes. She sensed his indecision as she struggled with her own. She had to leave. Yet she wanted to stay....

"I think I should take the rest of my vacation in Victoria," she finally told them.

"I know you're worried about getting back in time for work, but Skip's right. If you left Victoria one day early, then you could be here for the fair," Kate suggested again, but her offer didn't sound as sincere as it had earlier.

"Rorie said she doesn't have the time," Clay said after an awkward silence. "I think we should respect her decision."

"You sound as if you don't want her to come back," Skip accused.

"No," Clay murmured, his eyes meeting hers. "I want her here, but Rorie should try to salvage some of the vacation she planned. She has to do what she think's best."

Rorie could feel his eyes moving over her hair and her face in loving appraisal. She tensed and prayed that Kate and Skip weren't aware of it.

During the next hour, Skip tried repeatedly to convince Rorie to visit on her way back or even to stay until the fair. As far as Skip could see, there wasn't much reason to go to Canada now, anyway. But Rorie resisted. Walking away from Clay once was going to be painful enough. Rorie didn't know if she could do it twice.

Skip was yawning by the time they decided to call an end to the evening. With little more than a mumbled good-night, he hurried up the stairs, abandoning the others.

Rorie and Kate took a few extra minutes to straighten the living room, while Clay drove his pickup around to the front of the house. "I'd better burn the evidence before Mary sees these pizza boxes," Rorie joked. "She'll have my hide once she hears about dinner."

Kate laughed good-naturedly as she collected her belongings. When they heard Clay's truck, she put down her bags and ran to Rorie. "You'll call me before you leave tomorrow?"

Rorie nodded and hugged her back.

"If something happens and you change your mind about the fair, please know that you're welcome to stay with me and Dad—we'd enjoy the company."

"Thank you, Kate."

The house felt empty and silent once Kate had left with Clay. Rorie knew it would be useless to go upstairs and try to sleep. Instead she went out to the front porch, where she'd sat in the swing with Clay that first night. She sank down on the steps, one arm wrapped around a post, and gazed upward. The skies were glittered with the light of countless stars—stars that shone with a clarity and brightness one couldn't see in the city.

Clay belonged to this land, this farm, this small town. Rorie was a city girl to the marrow of her bones. This evening had proved the hopelessness of any dream that she and Clay might have of finding happiness together. There was his commitment to Kate. And there was the fact that he and Rorie were too different, their tastes too dissimilar. She certainly couldn't picture him making a life away from Elk Run.

Clay had accepted the hopelessness of it, too. That was the reason he agreed she should travel to Canada.

This evening Rorie had sensed a desperation in him that rivaled her own.

It was a night filled with insights. Sitting under the heavens, she was beginning to understand some important things about life. For perhaps the first time, she'd fallen in love. During the past six days she'd tried to deny what she was feeling, but on the eve of her departure it seemed silly to lie to herself any longer. Rorie couldn't believe something like this had actually happened to her. Meeting someone and falling in love with him in the space of a few days was an experience reserved for novels and movies. This wasn't like her normal sane, sensible self at all. Rorie had always thought she was too levelheaded to fall so easily in love.

Until she met Clay Franklin.

On the wings of one soul-searching realization came another. Love wasn't what she'd expected. She'd assumed it meant a strong sensual passion that overwhelmed the lovers and left them powerless before it. But in the past few days, she'd learned that love marked the soul as well as the body.

Clay would forever be a part of her. Since that first night when Nightsong was born, her heart had never felt more alive. Yet within a few hours she would walk away from the man she loved and consider herself blessed to have shared these days with him.

A tear rolled down the side of her face, surprising her. This wasn't a time for sadness, but joy. She'd discovered a deep inner strength she hadn't known she possessed. She wiped the moisture away and rested her head against the post, her eyes fixed on the heavens.

The footsteps behind Rorie didn't startle her. She'd known Clay would come to her this one last time.

Eleven

Clay draped his arm over Rorie's shoulders and joined her in gazing up at the sky. Neither spoke for several minutes, as though they feared words would destroy the tranquil mood. Rorie stared, transfixed by the glittering display. Like her love for this man, the stars would remain forever distant, unattainable, but certain and unchanging.

A ragged sigh escaped her lips. "All my life I've believed that everything that befalls us has a purpose."

"I've always thought that, too," Clay whispered.

"Everything in life is deliberate."

"Our final hours together you're going to become philosophical?" He rested his chin on her head, gently ruffling her hair. "Are you sad, Rorie?"

"Oh, no," she denied quickly. "I can't be… I feel strange, but I don't know if I can find the words to explain it. I'm leaving tomorrow and I realize we'll probably never see each other again. I have no regrets—not a single one—and yet I think my heart is breaking."

His hand tightened on her shoulder in silent protest

as if he found the idea of relinquishing her more than he could bear.

"We can't defy reality," she told him. "Nothing's going to change in the next few hours. The water pump on the car will be replaced, and I'll go back to my life. The way you'll go back to yours."

"I have this gut feeling there's going to be a hole the size of the Grand Canyon in mine the minute you drive away." He dropped his arm and moved away from her. His eyes held a weary sadness, but Rorie found an acceptance there, too.

"I'm an uncomplicated man," he said evenly. "I'm probably nothing like the sophisticated man you're dating in San Francisco."

Her thoughts flew to Dan, so cosmopolitan and… superficial, and she recognized the truth in Clay's words. The two men were poles apart. Dan's interests revolved around his career and his car, but he was genuinely kind, and it was that quality that had attracted Rorie.

"Elk Run's given me a good deal of satisfaction over the years. My life's work is here and, God willing, some day my son will carry on the breeding programs I've started. Everything I've ever dreamed of has always been within my grasp." He paused, holding in a long sigh and releasing it slowly. "And then you came," he whispered, and a brief smile crossed his lips, "and, within a matter of days, I'm reeling from the effects. Suddenly I'm left doubting what's really important in my life."

Rorie lowered her eyes. "Who'd have believed a silly water pump would be responsible for all this wretched soul-searching?"

"I've always been the type of man who's known what

he wants, but you make me feel like a schoolboy no older than Skip. I don't know what to do anymore, Rorie. In a few hours, you'll be leaving and part of me says if you do, I'll regret it the rest of my life."

"I can't stay." Their little dinner party had shown her how different their worlds actually were. She wouldn't fit into his life and he'd be an alien in hers. But Kate... Kate belonged to his world.

Clay rubbed his hands across his eyes and harshly drew in a breath. "I know you feel you should leave, but that doesn't mean I have to like it."

"The pull to stay is there for me, too," she whispered. "And it's tearing both of us apart."

Rorie shook her head. "Don't you see? So much good has come out of meeting you, Clay." Her voice was strong. She had to make him understand that she'd always be grateful for the things he'd taught her. "In some ways I grew up tonight. I feel I'm doing what's right for both of us, although it's more painful than anything I've ever known."

He looked at her with such undisguised love that she ached.

"Let me hold you once more," he said softly. "Give me that, at least."

Rorie shook her head. "I can't... I'm sorry, Clay, but this is how it has to be with us. I'm so weak where you're concerned. I couldn't bear to let you touch me now and then leave tomorrow."

His eyes drifted shut as he yielded to her wisdom. "I don't know that I could, either."

They were only a few feet apart, but it seemed vast worlds stood between them.

"More than anything I want you to remember me

fondly, without any bitterness," Rorie told him, discovering as she spoke the words how much she meant them.

Clay nodded. "Be happy, Rorie, for my sake."

Rorie realized that contentment would be a long time coming without this man in her life, but she would find it eventually. She prayed that he'd marry Kate the way he'd planned. The other woman was the perfect wife for him—unlike herself. A thread of agony twisted around Rorie's heart.

She turned to leave him, afraid she'd dissolve into tears if she remained much longer. "Goodbye, Clay."

"Goodbye, Rorie."

She rushed past him and hurried up the stairs.

The following morning, both Clay and Skip had left the house by the time Rorie entered the kitchen.

"Good morning, Mary," she said with a note of false cheer in her voice. "How did the visit with your sister go?"

"Fine."

Rorie stepped around the housekeeper to reach the coffeepot and poured herself a cup. A plume of steam rose enticingly to her nostrils and she took a tentative sip.

"I found those pizza boxes you were trying so hard to hide from me," Mary grumbled as she wiped her hands on her apron. "You fed these good men restaurant pizza?"

Unable to stop herself, Rorie chuckled at the housekeeper's indignation. "Guilty as charged. Mary, you should've known better than to leave their fate in my evil hands."

"Near as I can figure, the closest pizza parlour is a

half hour away. Did you drive over and get it yourself or did you send Skip?"

"Actually he volunteered," she admitted reluctantly. "Dinner didn't exactly turn out the way I'd hoped."

The housekeeper snickered. "I should've guessed. You city slickers don't know nothing about serving up a decent meal to your menfolk."

Rorie gave a hefty sigh of agreement. "The only thing for me to do is stay on another couple of months and have you teach me." As she expected, the housekeeper opened her mouth to protest. "Unfortunately," Rorie continued, cutting Mary off before she could launch into her arguments, "I'm hoping to be gone by this afternoon."

Mary's response was a surprise. The older woman's expression grew troubled and intense.

"I suspected you'd be going soon enough," she said in a tight voice, pulling out a chair. She sat down heavily and brushed wisps of gray hair from her forehead. Her weathered face was thoughtful. "It's for the best, you know."

"I knew you'd be glad to get rid of me."

Mary shrugged. "It's other reasons that make it right for you to leave. You know what I'm talking about, even if you don't want to admit it to me. As a person you tend to grow on folks. Like I said before, for a city girl, you ain't half bad."

Rorie took a banana from the fruit bowl in the center of the table. "For a stud farm, stuck out here in the middle of nowhere, this place isn't half bad, either," she said, trying to lighten the mood, which had taken an unexpected turn toward the serious. "The people are friendly and the apple pie's been exceptional."

Mary ignored the compliment on her pie. "By people, I suppose you're referring to Clay. You're going to miss him, aren't you, girl?"

The banana found its way back into the bowl and with it went her cheerful facade. "Yes. I'll miss Clay."

The older woman's frown deepened. "From the things I've been noticing, he's going to be yearning for you, as well. But it's for the best," she said again. "For the best."

Rorie nodded and her voice wavered. "Yes…but it isn't easy."

The housekeeper gave her a lopsided smile as she gently patted Rorie's hand. "I know that, too, but you're doing the right thing. You'll forget him soon enough."

A strong protest rose in her breast, closing off her throat. She wouldn't forget Clay. Ever. How could she forget the man who had so unselfishly taught her such valuable lessons about life and love? Lessons about herself.

"Kate Logan's the right woman for Clay," Mary said abruptly.

Those few words cut Rorie to the quick. Hearing another person voice the truth made it almost unbearably painful.

"I…hope they're very happy."

"Kate loves him. She has from the time she was knee-high to a June bug. And there's something you don't know. Years back, when Clay was in college, he fell in love with a girl from Seattle. She'd been born and raised in the city. Clay loved her, wanted to marry her, even brought her to Elk Run to meet the family. She stayed a couple of days, and the whole time, she was as restless as water on a hot skillet. Apparently she had words with Clay because the next thing I knew, she'd packed her bags and headed home. Clay never said much about her after that, but she hurt him bad. It wasn't until Kate got home from college that Clay thought seriously about marriage again."

Mary's story explained a lot about Clay.

"Now, I know I'm just an old woman who likes her soaps and Saturday-night bingo. Most folks don't think I've got a lick of sense, and that's all right. What others choose to assume don't bother me much." She paused, and shook her head. "But Kate Logan's about the kindest, dearest person this town has ever seen. People like her—they can't help themselves. She's always got a kind word and there's no one in this world she's too good for. She cares about the people in this community. Those kids she teaches over at the grade school love her like nothing you've ever seen. And she loves them. When it came to building that fancy library, it was Kate who worked so hard convincing folks they'd be doing what was best for Nightingale by voting for that bond issue."

Rorie kept her face averted. She didn't need Mary to tell her Kate was a good person; she'd seen the evidence of it herself.

"What most folks don't know is that Kate's seen plenty of pain in her own life. She watched her mother die a slow death from cancer. Took care of her most of the time herself, nursing Nora when she should've been off at college having fun like other nineteen-year-olds. Her family needed her and she was there. Kate gave old man Logan a reason to go on living when Nora passed away. She still lives with him, and it's long past time for her to be a carefree adult on her own. Kate's a good person clean through." Mary hesitated, then drew in a solemn breath. "Now, you may think I'm nothing but a meddling old fool. But I'm saying it's a good thing you're leaving Elk Run before you break that girl's heart. She's got a chance now for some happiness, and God knows she deserves it. If she loses Clay, I can tell you it'd break her heart. She's too good to have that happen to her over some fancy city girl who's only passing through."

Rorie winced at the way Mary described her.

"I'm a plain talker," Mary said on the end of an abrupt laugh. "Always have been, always will be. Knowing Clay—and I do, as well as his mother did, God rest her soul—he'll pine for you awhile, but eventually everything will fall back into place. The way it was before you arrived."

Tears stung Rorie's eyes. She felt miserable as it was, and Mary wasn't helping. She'd already assured the housekeeper she was leaving, but Mary apparently wanted to be damn sure she didn't change her mind. The woman didn't understand…but then again, maybe she did.

"Have you ever been in love, Mary?"

"Once," came the curt reply. "Hurt so much the first time I never chanced it again."

"Are you sorry you lived your life alone now?" That was what Rorie saw for herself. Oh, she knew she was being melodramatic and over-emotional, but she couldn't imagine loving any man as much as she did Clay.

Mary lifted one shoulder in a shrug. "Some days I have plenty of regrets, but then on others it ain't so bad. I'd like to have had a child, but God saw to it that I was around when Clay and Skip needed someone.… That made up for what I missed."

"They consider you family."

"Yeah, I suppose they do." Mary pushed out her chair and stood up. "Well, I better get back to work. Those men expect a decent lunch. I imagine they're near starved after the dinner you fed them last night."

Despite her heartache, Rorie smiled and finished her coffee. "And I'd better get upstairs and pack the rest of my things. The mechanic said my car would be ready around noon."

On her way to the bedroom, Rorie paused at the framed photograph of Clay's parents that sat on the piano. She'd passed it a number of times and had given it little more than a fleeting glance. Now it suddenly demanded her attention, and she stopped in front of it.

A tremor went through her hand as she lightly ran her finger along the brass frame. Clay's mother smiled serenely into the camera, her gray eyes so like her son's that Rorie felt a knot in her stomach. Those same eyes seemed to reach across eternity and call out to Rorie, plead with her. Rorie's own eyes narrowed, certain her imagination was playing havoc with her troubled mind. She focused her attention on the woman's hair. That, too, was the same dark shade as Clay's, brushed away from her face in a carefully styled chignon. Clay had never mentioned his parents to her, not once, but studying the photograph Rorie knew intuitively that he'd shared a close relationship with his mother. Blue wandered out from the kitchen and stood at Rorie's side as though offering consolation. Grateful, she bent down to pet him.

Looking back at the photograph, Rorie noted that Skip resembled his father, with the same dancing blue eyes that revealed more than a hint of devilry.

Rorie continued to study both parents, but it was

Clay's mother who captured her attention over and over again.

The phone ringing in the distance startled her, and her wrist was shaking when she set the picture back on the piano.

"Phone's for you," Mary shouted from the kitchen.

Rorie assumed it was George at the repair shop in Riversdale; she'd been waiting all morning to hear from him.

"Hello," she said, her fingers closing tightly around the receiver. Her biggest fear was that something had happened to delay her departure a second time.

"Miss Campbell," said the mechanic, "everything's fine. I got that part in and working for you without a hitch."

"Thank God," she murmured. Her hold on the telephone receiver relaxed, a little.

"I've got a man I could spare if you'd like to have your car delivered to Elk Run. But you've got to understand fifty miles is a fair distance and I'm afraid I'll have to charge you extra for it."

"That's fine," Rorie said eagerly, not even bothering to ask the amount. "How soon can he be here?"

Twelve

"So you're really going," Skip said as he picked up Rorie's bags. "Somehow I figured I might've talked you into staying on for the county fair."

"You seem intent on bringing me to ruin, Skip Franklin. I'm afraid I'd bet all my hard-earned cash on those pig races you were telling me about," Rorie teased. Standing in the middle of the master bedroom, she surveyed it to be sure she hadn't forgotten anything.

A pang of wistfulness settled over her as she slowly looked around. Not for the first time, Rorie felt the love and warmth emanating from these brightly papered walls. Lazily, almost lovingly, she ran her fingertips along the top of the dresser, letting her hand linger there a moment, unwilling to pull herself away. This bedroom represented so much of what she was leaving behind. It was difficult to walk away.

Skip stood in the doorway impatiently waiting for her. "Kate phoned and said she's coming over. She wants to say goodbye."

"I'll be happy to see her one last time." Rorie wished Skip would leave so she could delay her parting with this room a little longer. Until now, Rorie hadn't realized how much sleeping in Clay's parents' room had meant to her. Her appreciation had come too late.

"Mary's packing a lunch for you," Skip announced with a wry chuckle, "and knowing Mary, it'll be enough to last you a week."

Rorie smiled and reluctantly followed him down the stairs. As Skip had claimed, the housekeeper had prepared two large bags, which sat waiting on the kitchen table.

"Might as well take those with you, too," Mary muttered gruffly. "I hate the thought of you eating restaurant food. This, at least, will stick to your ribs."

"Goodbye, Mary," Rorie said softly, touched by the housekeeper's thoughtfulness. On impulse she hugged the older woman. "Thank you for everything—including our talk this morning." The impromptu embrace surprised Rorie as much as it obviously did Mary.

"You drive careful now, you hear?" the housekeeper responded, squeezing Rorie tightly and patting her back several times.

"I will, I promise."

"A letter now and again wouldn't be amiss."

"All right," Rorie agreed, and used her sleeve to blot tears from the corners of her eyes. These people had touched her in so many ways. Leaving them was even more difficult than she'd imagined.

The housekeeper rubbed the heel of her hand over her right eye. "Time for you to get on the road. What are you doing standing in the kitchen chitchatting with me?" she asked brusquely.

"I'm going, I'm going." Mary's gruff voice didn't fool Rorie. The housekeeper's exterior might be a little crusty, and her tongue a bit surly, but she didn't succeed in disguising a generous, loving heart.

"I don't know where Clay is," Skip complained after he'd loaded the luggage into the MG's trunk. "I thought he'd want to see you before you left. I wonder where he got off to."

"I'm…sure he's got better things to do than say goodbye to me."

"No way," Skip said, frowning. "I'm going to see if I can find him."

Rorie's first reaction was to stop Skip, then she quickly decided against it. If she made too much of a fuss, Skip might suspect something. She understood what had prompted Clay to stay away from the house all morning, and in truth she was grateful. Leaving Elk Run was hard enough without prolonging the agony in lengthy farewells.

Skip hesitated, kicking at the dirt with the pointed toe of his cowboy boot. "You two didn't have a fight or anything, did you?"

"No. What makes you ask?"

Skip shrugged. "Well… It's just that every time I walked into a room with the two of you, I could feel something. If it wasn't for Kate, I'd think my big brother was interested in you."

"I'm sure you're imagining things."

"I suppose so," Skip said with a nod, dismissing the notion. "Ever since you got here, though, Clay's been acting weird."

"How do you mean?"

"Sort of cranky."

"My unexpected arrival added to his problems, don't you think?" In so many ways it was the truth, and she felt guilty about that. The responsibilities for the farm and for raising Skip were sobering enough; he didn't need her there to wreak havoc with his personal life.

"You weren't any problem," Skip answered sharply. "In fact, having you around was fun. The only trouble is you didn't stay long enough."

"Thank you, Skip." Once again she felt her throat clog with tears. She was touched by his sweet, simple hospitality and reminded of how much she'd miss him.

"I still kinda wish you were going to stay for the fair," he mumbled. "You'd have a good time, I guarantee it. We may not have all the fancy entertainment you do in San Francisco, but when we do a county fair, we do it big."

"I'm sure it'll be great fun."

Skip braced his foot against the bumper of the faded blue pickup, apparently forgetting his earlier decision to seek out Clay, which was just as well.

"You don't like the country much, do you, Rorie?"

"Oh, but I do," she said. "It's a different way of life, though. Here on Elk Run, I feel like a duck in a pond full of swans."

Skip laughed. "I suppose folks there in the big city don't think much of the country."

"No one has time to think," Rorie said with a small laugh.

"That doesn't make any sense. Everyone's got thoughts."

Rorie nodded, not knowing how to explain something so complex. When Skip had spent some time in the city, he'd figure out what she meant.

"The one thing I've noticed more than anything is how quiet it is here," she said pensively, looking around, burning into her memory each detail of the farmhouse and the yard.

"I like the quiet. Some places, the noise is so bad I worry about ear damage," Skip said.

"I imagine if I lived here, I'd grow accustomed to the silence, too. But to be honest, I hadn't realized how much I enjoy the sounds of the city. There's something invigorating about the clang of the trolley cars or the foghorn on the Bay early in the morning."

Skip frowned and shook his head. "You honestly like all that racket?"

Rorie nodded. "It's more than that. The city's exciting. I hadn't really known how much living there meant to me before coming to Elk Run." Rorie wasn't sure how to describe the aroma of freshly baked sourdough bread, or the perfumed scent of budding rosebushes in Golden Gate Park, to someone who'd never experienced them. Country life had its appeal, she couldn't deny that, but she belonged to the city. At least, that was what she told herself over and over again.

"Ah," Skip said, and his foot dropped from the bumper with a thud, "here's Clay now."

Rorie tensed, clasping her hands in front of her. Clay's lengthy strides quickly diminished the distance between the barn and the yard. Each stride was filled with purpose, as though he longed to get this polite farewell over with.

Rorie straightened and walked toward him. "I'll be leaving in a couple of minutes," she said softly.

"Kate's coming to say goodbye," Skip added.

Rorie noted how Clay's eyes didn't quite meet her own. He seemed to focus instead on the car behind her.

They'd already said everything there was to say and this final parting only compounded the pain.

"Saying thank you seems so inadequate," Rorie told him in a voice that wasn't entirely steady. "I've appreciated your hospitality more than you'll ever know." Hesitantly she held out her hand to him.

Clay's hard fingers curled around her own, his touch light and impersonal. Rorie swallowed hard, unable to hold back the emotion churning so violently inside her.

His expression was completely impassive, but she sensed that he held on to his self-control with the thinnest of threads. In that moment, Rorie felt the longing in him and knew that he recognized it in her, too.

"Oh, Clay..." she whispered, her eyes brimming with tears. The impulse to move into his arms was like a huge wave, threatening to sweep over her, and she didn't know how much longer she'd have the strength to resist.

"Don't look at me like that," Clay muttered grimly.

"I...can't help it." But he belonged to Kate and nothing was likely to change that.

He took a step toward her and stopped himself, suddenly remembering they weren't alone.

"Skip, go hold Thunder for Don. Don's trying to paste-worm him, and he's getting dragged all over the stall." Clay's words were low-pitched, sharp, full of demand.

"But, Clay, Rorie's about to—"

"Do it."

Mumbling something unintelligible, Skip trudged off to the barn.

The minute his brother was out of sight, Clay caught Rorie's shoulders, his fingers rough and urgent through the thin cotton of her blouse. The next instant, she was locked against him. The kiss was inevitable, Rorie knew, but when his mouth settled over hers she wanted to weep for the joy she found in his arms. He kissed her temple, her cheek, her mouth, until she clung to him with hungry abandon. They were standing in the middle of the yard in full view of farmhands, but Clay didn't seem to care and Rorie wasn't about to object.

"I told myself I wouldn't do this," he whispered huskily.

Rorie's heart constricted.

At the sound of a car in the distance, Clay abruptly dropped his arms, freeing her. His fingers tangled in her hair as if he had to touch her one last time.

"I was a fool to think I could politely shake your hand and let you leave. We're more than casual friends and I can't pretend otherwise—to hell with the consequences."

Tears flooded Rorie's eyes as she stared up at Clay. Then, from behind him, she saw the cloud of dust that announced Kate's arrival. She inhaled a deep breath in an effort to compose herself and, wiping her damp cheeks with the back of one hand, forced a smile.

Clay released a ragged sigh as he trailed a callused hand down the side of her face. "Goodbye, Rorie," he whispered. With that, he turned and walked away.

Thick fog swirled around Rorie as she paused to catch her breath on the path in Golden Gate Park. She bent forward and planted her hands on her knees, driving the oxygen into her heaving lungs. Not once in the two weeks she'd been on vacation had she followed her jogging routine, and now she was paying the penalty. The muscles in her calves and thighs protested the strenuous exercise and her heart seemed about to explode. Her biggest problem was trying to keep up with Dan, who'd run ahead, unwilling to slow his pace to match hers.

"Rorie?"

"Over here." Her voice was barely more than a choked whisper. She meant to raise her hand and signal to him, but even that required more effort than she could manage. Seeing a bench in the distance, she stumbled over and collapsed into it. Leaning back, she stretched out her legs.

"You *are* out of shape," Dan teased, handing her a small towel.

Rorie wiped the perspiration from her face and smiled her appreciation. "I can't believe two weeks would make such a difference." She'd been back in San Francisco only a couple of days. Other than dropping off the MG at Dan's place, this was the first time they'd had a chance to get together.

Dan stood next to her, hardly out of breath—even after a three-mile workout.

"Two weeks *is* a long time," he said with the hint of a smile. "I suppose you didn't keep up with your vitamin program, either," he chastised gently. "Well, Rorie, it's obvious how much you need me."

She chose to ignore that comment. "I used to consider myself in top physical condition. Not anymore. Good grief, I thought my heart was going to give out two miles back."

Dan, blond and debonair, was appealingly handsome in a clean-cut boyish way. He draped the towel around his neck and grasped the ends. Rorie's eyes were drawn to his hands, with their finely manicured nails and long tapered fingers. Stockbroker fingers. Nice hands. Friendly hands.

Still, Rorie couldn't help comparing them with another pair of male hands, darkly tanned from hours in the sun and roughly callused. Gentle hands. Working hands.

"I meant what I said about you needing me," Dan murmured, watching her closely. "It's time we got serious, Rorie. Time we made some important decisions about our future."

When she least expected it, he slid closer on the bench beside her. With his so smooth fingers, he cupped her face, his thumbs stroking her flushed cheeks. "I did a lot of thinking while you were away."

She covered his fingers with her own, praying for an easier way to say what she must. They'd been seeing each other for months and shc hated to hurt him, but it would be even crueler to lead him on. When they'd started dating, Dan had been looking for a casual relationship. He'd recently been divorced and wasn't ready for a new emotional commitment.

"Oh, Dan, I think I know what you're going to say. Please don't."

He paused, searching her face intently. "What do you mean?"

"I did some thinking while I was away, too, and I realized that although I'll always treasure your friendship, we can't ever be more than friends."

His dark eyes ignited with resistance. "What happened to you on this vacation, Rorie? You left, and two weeks later you returned a completely different woman."

"You're exaggerating," Rorie objected weakly. She knew she *was* different, from the inside out.

"You've hardly said a word to me about your trip," Dan complained, in a tone that suggested he felt hurt by her reticence. "All you've said is that the car broke down in the Oregon outback and you were stuck on some farm for days until a part could be delivered. You don't blame me for that, do you? I had no idea there was anything wrong with the water pump."

She laughed at his description of Nightingale as the outback.

"You completely missed the writers' conference, didn't you?"

"That couldn't be helped, but I enjoyed the rest of my vacation. Victoria was like stepping into a small piece of England," she said, in an effort to divert his attention from the time she'd spent on the Franklin farm. Victoria had been lovely, but unfortunately she hadn't been in the proper mood to appreciate its special beauty.

"You didn't so much as mail me a postcard."

"I know," she said with a twinge of guilt.

"I was lonesome without you," Dan said slowly, running his hand over her hair. "Nothing felt right with you gone."

Rorie knew it had taken a lot for him to admit that, and it made what she had to tell him all the more difficult.

"Dan, please," she said, breaking away from him and standing. "I... I don't love you."

"But we're friends."

"Of course."

He seemed both pleased and relieved by that. "Good friends?" he coaxed.

Rorie nodded, wondering where this was leading.

"Then there's really no problem, is there?" he asked,

his voice gaining enthusiasm. "You went away, and I realized how much I love you, and you came back deciding you value my friendship. That, at least, is a beginning."

"Dan, honestly!"

"Well, isn't it?"

"Our relationship isn't going anywhere," she told him, desperate to clarify the issue. Dan was a good person and he deserved someone who was crazy in love with him. The way she was with Clay.

To Rorie's surprise, Dan drew her forward and kissed her. Startled, she stood placidly in his arms, feeling his warm mouth move over hers. She experienced no feeling, no excitement, nothing. Kissing Dan held all the appeal of drinking flat soda.

Frustrated, he tried to deepen the kiss.

Rorie braced her hands against his chest and tried to pull herself free. He released her immediately, then stepped back, frowning. "Okay, okay, we've got our work cut out for us. But the electricity will come, in time."

Somehow Rorie doubted that.

Dan dropped her off in front of her apartment. "Can I see you soon?" he asked, his hands clenching the steering wheel. He didn't look at her but stared straight ahead as though he feared her answer.

Rorie hesitated. "I'm not going to fall in love with you, Dan, and I don't want to take advantage of your feelings. I think it'd be best if you started seeing someone else."

He appeared to consider that for an awkward moment. "But the decision should be mine, shouldn't it?"

"Yes, but—"

"Then leave everything to me, and stop worrying. If I choose to waste my time on you, that's my problem, not yours. I think you're going to change your mind, Rorie. Because I love you enough for both of us."

"Oh, Dan." Her shoulders sagged with defeat. He hadn't believed a single word she'd said.

"Now don't look so depressed. How about a movie on Sunday? It's been a while since we've done that."

Exhausted, she shook her head. "Dan, no."

"I insist, so stop arguing."

She didn't have the energy to argue. "All right," she murmured. He'd soon learn she meant what she'd said. "All right."

"Good. I'll pick you up at six."

Rorie climbed out of the MG and closed the door, turning to give Dan a limp wave. She paused in the foyer of her apartment building to unlock her mailbox.

There was a handful of envelopes. Absently, she shuffled through a leaflet from a prominent department store, an envelope with a Kentucky postmark and an electric bill. It wasn't until she was inside her apartment that Rorie noticed the letter postmarked Nightingale, Oregon.

Thirteen

Rorie set the letter on her kitchen counter and stared at it for a moment. Her chest felt as if a dead weight were pressing against it. Her heart was pounding and her stomach churned. The post-office box number for the return address didn't tell her much. The letter could as easily be from Kate as Clay. It could even be from Mary.

Taking a deep, calming breath, Rorie reached for the envelope from Kentucky first. The return address told her nothing—she didn't know anyone who lived in that state.

The slip of paper inside confused her, too. She read it several times, not understanding. It appeared to be registration papers for Nightsong, from the National Show Horse Association. Rorie Campbell was listed as owner, with Clay's name as breeder. The date of Nightsong's birth was also recorded. Rorie slumped into a kitchen chair and battled an attack of memories and tears.

Clay was giving her Nightsong.

It was Nightsong who'd brought them together and it was through Nightsong that they'd remain linked. Life would go on; the loss of one couple's love wouldn't alter the course of history. But now there was something—a single piece of paper—that would connect her to Clay, something that gave testimony to their sacrifice.

Rorie had needed that and Clay had apparently known it.

They'd made the right decision, Rorie told herself for the hundredth time. Clay's action confirmed it.

Clay was wide-open spaces and sleek, well-trained horses, while she thrived in the crowded city.

His strength came from his devotion to the land; hers came from the love of children and literature and the desire to create her own stories.

They were dissimilar in every way—and alike. In the most important matters, the most telling, they were actually very much alike. Neither of them was willing to claim happiness at the expense of someone else.

Tears spilled down her cheeks, and sniffling, Rorie wiped them aside. The drops dampened her fingertips as she picked up the second envelope, blurring the return address. But even before she opened it, Rorie realized the letter was from Kate. Clay wouldn't write her, and everything Mary had wanted to say she'd already said the morning Rorie left Elk Run.

Three handwritten sheets slipped easily from the envelope, with Kate's evenly slanted signature at the bottom of the last.

The letter was filled with chatty news about Nightingale and some of the people Rorie had met. There were so many, and connecting names with faces taxed her memory. Kate wrote about the county fair, telling Rorie that she'd missed a very exciting pig race. The biggest news of all was that after years of trying, Mary had finally won a blue ribbon for her apple pie—an honor long overdue in Kate's opinion.

Toward the end of the letter, Clay's fiancée casually mentioned that Clay would be in San Francisco the first week of September for a horse show. The American Saddlebreds from Elk Run were well-known throughout the Pacific coast for their fire and elegance. Clay had high hopes of repeating last year's wins in the Five Gaited and Fine Harness Championships.

Rorie's pulse shifted into overdrive and her fingers tightened on the letter. Clay was coming to San Francisco. He hadn't said anything about the show to Rorie—although he must've known about it long before she'd left Nightingale.

Kate went on to say that she'd asked Clay if he planned to look up Rorie while he was in town, but he'd claimed there wouldn't be time. Kate was sure Rorie would understand and not take offense. She closed by saying that her father might also be attending the horse show and, if he did, Kate would try to talk him into letting her tag along. Kate promised she'd phone Rorie the minute she arrived in town, if she could swing it with her father.

Not until Rorie folded the letter to return it to the envelope did she notice the postscript on the back of the last page. She turned over the sheet of pink stationery. The words seemed to jump off the page: Kate was planning an October wedding and would send Rorie an invitation. She ended with, "Write soon."

Rorie's breath caught in her lungs. An October wedding… In only a few weeks, Kate would belong to Clay. Rorie closed her eyes as her heart squeezed into a knot of pain. It wasn't that she hadn't known this was coming. Kate and Clay's wedding was inevitable, but Rorie hadn't thought Clay would go through with it quite so soon. With trembling hands, she set the letter aside.

"Rorie, love, I can't honestly believe you want to go to a horse show," Dan complained, scanning the entertainment section of the Friday-evening paper. They sat in the minuscule living room in her apartment and sipped their coffee while they tossed around ideas for something to do.

Rorie smiled blandly, praying Dan couldn't read her thoughts. He'd offered several suggestions for the night's amusement, but Rorie had rejected each one. Until she pretended to hit upon the idea of attending the horse show…

"A horse show?" he repeated. "You never told me you were interested in horses."

"It would be fun, don't you think?"

"Not particularly."

"But, Dan, it's time to broaden our horizons—we might learn something."

"Does this mean you're going to insist we attend a demolition derby next weekend?"

"Of course not. I read an article about this horse show and I just thought we'd enjoy the gaited classes and harness competitions. Apparently, lots of Saddlebreds and National Show Horses are going to be performing. Doesn't that interest you?"

"No."

Rorie shrugged, slowly releasing a sigh. "Then a movie's fine," she said, not even trying to hide her disappointment. They'd seen each other only a handful of times since Rorie's return. Rorie wouldn't be going out with him tonight if he hadn't persisted. She hoped he'd get the message and start dating other women, but that didn't seem to be happening.

"I have no idea why you'd want to see a horse show," Dan said once more.

For the past few days the newspapers had been filled with information regarding the country-wide show in which Kate had said several of Elk Run's horses would be participating. In all the years she'd lived in San Francisco, Rorie couldn't remember reading about a single equine exhibition, but then she hadn't exactly been looking for one, either.

If Dan refused to go with her, Rorie was determined to attend the event on her own. She didn't have any intention of seeking out Clay, but the opportunity to see him, even from a distance, was too tempting to let pass. It would probably be the last time she'd ever see him.

"I don't know what's got into you lately, Rorie," Dan muttered. "Just when I think our lives are on track, you throw me for a loop."

"I said a movie was fine." Her tone was testier than she meant it to be, but Dan had been harping on the same subject for weeks and she was tired of it.

If he didn't want her company, he should start dating someone else. She wasn't going to suddenly decide she was madly in love with him, as he seemed to expect. Again and again, Dan phoned to tell her he loved her, that his love was enough for both of them. She always stopped him there, unable to imagine spending the rest of her life with him. If she couldn't have Clay—and she couldn't—then she wasn't willing to settle for anyone else.

"I'm talking about a lot more than seeing a movie."

He laid the newspaper aside and seemed to carefully consider his next words.

"Really, Dan, you're making a mountain out of a molehill," Rorie said. "Just because I wanted to do something a little out of the ordinary…"

"Eating at an Armenian restaurant is a little out of the ordinary," he said, frowning, "but horse shows… I can't even begin to understand why you'd want to watch a bunch of animals running around in circles."

"Well, you keep insisting I've changed," she said flippantly. If she'd known Dan was going to react so strongly to her suggestion, she'd never have made it. "I guess this only goes to prove you're right."

"How much writing have you done in the past month?"

The question was completely unexpected. She answered him with a shrug, hoping he'd drop the subject, knowing he wouldn't.

"None, right? I've seen you sitting at your computer, staring into space with that sad look on your face. I remember how you used to talk about your stories. Your eyes would light up. Enthusiasm would just spill out of you." His hand reached for hers, tightly squeezing her fingers. "What happened to you, Rorie? Where's the joy? Where's the energy?"

"You're imagining things," she said, nearly leaping to her feet in an effort to sidestep the issues he was raising. She grabbed her purse and a light sweater, eager to escape the apartment, which suddenly felt too small. "Are you going to take me to that movie, or are you going to sit here and ask questions I have no intention of answering?"

Dan stood, smiling faintly. "I don't know what happened while you were on vacation, and it's not important that I know, but whatever it was hurt you badly."

Rorie tried to deny it, but couldn't force the lie past her tongue. She swallowed and turned her head away, eyes burning.

"You won't be able to keep pretending forever. Put whatever it is behind you. If you want to talk about it, I've got a sympathetic ear and a sturdy shoulder. I'm your friend, Rorie."

"Dan, please..."

"I know you're not in love with me," he said quietly. "I suspect you met someone else while you were away, but that doesn't matter to me. Whatever happened during those two weeks is over."

"Dan..."

He took her hand, pulling her back onto the sofa, then sitting down beside her. She couldn't look at him.

"Given time, you'll learn to love me," he cajoled, holding her hand, his voice filled with kindness. "We're already good friends, and that's a lot more than some people have when they marry." He raised her fingers to his mouth and kissed them lightly. "I'm not looking for passion. I had that with my first wife. I learned the hard way that desire is a poor foundation for a solid marriage."

"We've talked about this before," Rorie protested. "I can't marry you, Dan, not when I feel the way I do about...someone else." Her mouth trembled with the effort to suppress tears. Dan was right. As much as she hadn't wanted to face the truth, she'd been heartbroken from the moment she'd left Nightingale.

She'd tried to forget Clay, believing that was the best thing for them both, yet she cherished the memories, knowing those few brief days were all she'd ever have of this man she loved.

"You don't have to decide right now," Dan assured her.

"There isn't anything to decide," she persisted.

His fingers continued to caress hers, and when he spoke his voice was thick. "At least you've admitted there is someone else."

"Was," she corrected.

"I take it there isn't any chance the two of you—"

"None," she blurted, unwilling to discuss anything that had to do with Clay.

"I know it's painful for you right now, but all I ask is that you seriously consider my proposal. My only wish is to take care of you and make you smile again. Help you forget."

His mouth sought hers, and though his kiss wasn't unpleasant, it generated no more excitement than before, no rush of adrenaline, no urgency. She hadn't minded Dan's kisses in the past, but until she met Clay she hadn't known the warmth and magic a man's touch could create.

Dan must have read her thoughts, because he said in a soothing voice, "The passion will come in time—you shouldn't even look for it now, but it'll be there. Maybe not this month or the next, but you'll feel it eventually, I promise."

Rorie brushed the hair from her face, confused and uncertain. Clay was marrying Kate in just a few weeks. Her own life stretched before her, lonely and barren—surely she deserved some happiness, too. Beyond a doubt, Rorie knew Clay would want her to build a good life for herself. But if she married Dan, it would be an act of selfishness, and she feared she'd end up hurting him.

"Think about it," Dan urged. "That's all I ask."

"Dan…"

"Just consider it. I know the score and I'm willing to take the risk, so you don't have to worry about me. I'm a big boy." He rubbed his thumb against the inside of her wrist. "Now, promise me you'll think honestly about us getting married."

Rorie nodded, although she already knew what her answer would have to be.

Dan heaved a sigh. "Now, are you really interested in that horse show, or are we going to a movie?"

"The movie." There was no use tormenting herself with thoughts of Clay. He belonged to Kate in the same way that he belonged to the country. Rorie had no claim to either.

The film Dan chose was surprisingly good, a comedy, which was just what Rorie needed to lift her spirits. Afterward, they dined at an Italian restaurant and drank wine and discussed politics. Dan went out of his way to be the perfect companion, making no demands on her, and Rorie was grateful.

It was still relatively early when he drove her back to her apartment, and he eagerly accepted her invitation for coffee. As he eased the MG into a narrow space in front of her building, he suddenly paused, frowning.

"Do you have new neighbors?"

"Not that I know of. Why?"

Dan nodded toward the battered blue pickup across the street. "Whoever drives that piece of junk is about to bring down the neighborhood property values."

Fourteen

"Clay." His name escaped Rorie's lips on a rush of excitement. She jerked open the car door and stepped onto the sidewalk, her legs trembling, her pulse thundering.

"Rorie?" Dan called, agitated. "Who is this man?"

She hardly heard him. A door slammed in the distance and Rorie whirled around and saw that Clay had been sitting inside his truck, apparently waiting for her to return. He'd been parked in the shadows, and she hadn't noticed him.

Dan joined her on the pavement and placed his hand possessively on her shoulder. His grip was the only thing that rooted her in reality, his hand the restraining force that prevented her from flying into Clay's arms.

"Who is this guy?" Dan asked a second time.

Rorie opened her mouth to explain and realized she couldn't, not in a few words. "A...friend," she whispered, but that seemed so inadequate.

"He's a cowboy!" Dan hissed, making it sound as though Clay's close-fitting jeans and jacket were the garb of a man just released from jail.

Clay crossed the street and his long strides made short work of the distance separating him from Rorie.

"Hello, Rorie."

She heard the faint catch in his voice. "Clay."

A muscle moved in his cheek as he looked past her to Dan, who squared the shoulders of his Brooks Brothers suit. No one spoke, until Rorie saw that Clay was waiting for an introduction.

"Clay Franklin, this is Dan Rogers. Dan is the stockbroker I… I mentioned before. It was his sports car I was driving."

Clay nodded. "I remember now." His gaze slid away from Rorie to the man at her side.

Dan stepped around Rorie and accepted Clay's hand. She noticed that when Dan dropped his arm to his side, he flexed his fingers a couple of times, as though to restore the circulation. Rorie smiled to herself. Clay's handshake was the solid one of a man accustomed to working with his hands. When Dan shook hands, it was little more than a polite business greeting, an archaic but necessary exchange.

"Clay and his brother, Skip, were the family who helped me when the MG broke down," Rorie explained to Dan.

"Ah, yes, I remember your saying something about that now."

"I was about to make a pot of coffee," Rorie went on, unable to take her eyes off Clay. She drank in the sight of him, painfully noting the crow's-feet that fanned out from the corners of his eyes. She couldn't remember their being quite so pronounced before.

"Yes, by all means join us." Dan's invitation lacked any real welcome.

Clay said nothing. He just stood there looking at her. Almost no emotion showed in his face, but she could feel the battle that raged inside him. He loved her still, and everything about him told her that.

"Please join us," she whispered.

Any lingering hope that Dan would take the hint and make his excuses faded as he slipped his arm protectively around Rorie's shoulders. "I picked up some Swiss mocha coffee beans earlier," he said, "and Rorie was going to make a pot of that."

"Swiss mocha coffee?" Clay repeated, blinking quizzically.

"Decaffeinated, naturally," Dan hurried to add.

Clay arched his brows expressively, as if to say that made all the difference in the world.

With Dan glued to her side, Rorie reluctantly led the way into her building. "Have you been here long?" she asked Clay while they stood waiting for the elevator.

"About an hour."

"Oh, Clay..." Rorie felt terrible, although it wasn't her fault; she hadn't known he intended to stop by. Perhaps he hadn't known himself and had been lured to her apartment the same way she'd been contemplating the horse show.

"You should have phoned." Dan's comment was casual, but it contained a hint of accusation. "But then, I suppose, you folks tend to drop in on each other all the time. Things are more casual in the country, aren't they?"

Rorie sent Dan a furious glare. He returned her look blankly, as if to say he had no idea what could have angered her. Rorie was grateful that the elevator arrived just then.

Clay didn't comment on Dan's observation and the

three stepped inside, facing the doors as they slowly closed.

"When you weren't home, I asked the neighbors if they knew where you'd gone," Clay said.

"The neighbors?" Dan echoed, making no effort to disguise his astonishment.

"What did they tell you?" Rorie asked.

Clay smiled briefly, then sobered when he glanced at Dan. "They said they didn't know *who* lived next door, never mind where you'd gone."

"Frankly, I'm surprised they answered the door at all," Dan said conversationally. "There's a big difference between what goes on in small towns and big cities."

Dan spoke like a teacher to a grade-school pupil. Rorie wanted to kick him, but reacting in anger would only increase the embarrassment. She marveled at Clay's tolerance.

"Things are done differently here," Dan continued. "Few people have anything to do with their neighbors. People prefer to mind their own business. Getting involved leads to problems."

Clay rubbed the side of his face. "It seems to me *not* getting involved would lead to even bigger problems."

"I'm grateful Clay and Skip were there when *your* car broke down," Rorie said to Dan, hoping to put an end to this tiresome discussion. "Otherwise I don't know what would have happened. I could still be on that road waiting for someone to stop and help me," she said, forcing the joke.

"Yes," Dan admitted, clearing his throat. "I suppose I should thank you for assisting Rorie."

"And I suppose I should accept your thanks," Clay returned.

"How's Mary?" Rorie asked, quickly changing the subject as the elevator slid to a stop at her floor.

Humor sparked in Clay's gray eyes. "Mary's strutting around proud as a peacock ever since she won a blue ribbon at the county fair."

"She has reason to be proud." Rorie could just picture her. Knowing Mary, she was probably wearing the ribbon pinned to her apron. "What about Skip?" Rorie asked next, hungry for news about each one. She took the keys from her bag and systematically began unlocking the three bolts on her apartment door.

"Fine. He started school last week—he's a senior this year."

Rorie already knew that, but she nodded.

"Kate sends you her best," Clay said next, his voice carefully nonchalant.

"Tell her I said hello, too."

"She hasn't heard from you. No one has."

"I know. I'm sorry. She wrote after I got home from Canada, but I haven't had a chance to answer." On several occasions, Rorie had tried to make herself sit down and write Kate a letter. But she couldn't. At the end of her second week back home, she'd decided it was better for everyone involved if she didn't keep in touch with Kate. When the wedding invitation came, Rorie planned to mail an appropriate gift, and that would be the end of it.

Once they were inside the apartment, Rorie hung up her sweater and purse and motioned for both men to sit down. "It'll only take a minute to put on the coffee."

"Do you need me to grind the beans?" Dan asked, obviously eager to assist her.

"No, thanks. I don't need any help." His offer was an

excuse to question her about Clay, and Rorie wanted to avoid that if she could. At least for now.

Her apartment had never felt more cramped than it did when she rejoined the two men in her tiny living room. Clay rose to his feet as she entered, and the simple courtly gesture made her want to weep. He was telling her that he respected her and that…he cared for her…would always care for her.

The area was just large enough for one sofa and a coffee table. Her desk and computer stood against the other wall. Rorie pulled the chair away from the desk, turned it to face her guests and perched on the edge. Only then did Clay sit back down.

"So," Dan said with a heavy sigh. "Rorie never did tell me what it is you do in…in…"

"Nightingale," Rorie and Clay said together.

"Oh, yes, Nightingale," Dan murmured, clearing his throat. "I take it you're some kind of farmer? Do you grow soybeans or wheat?"

"Clay owns a stud farm, where he raises American Saddlebreds," Rorie said.

Dan looked as if she'd punched him in the stomach. He'd obviously made the connection between Clay and her earlier interest in attending the horse show.

"I see," he breathed, and his voice shook a little. "Horses. So you're involved with horses."

Clay glanced at him curiously.

"How's Nightsong?" Rorie asked, before Dan could say anything else. Just thinking about the foal with her wide curious eyes and long wobbly legs produced a feeling of tenderness in Rorie.

"She's a rare beauty," Clay told her softly, "showing more promise every day."

Rorie longed to tell Clay how much it had meant to her that he'd registered Nightsong in her name, how she cherished that gesture more than anything in her life. She also knew that Clay would never sell the foal, but would keep and love her all her life.

An awkward silence followed, and in an effort to smooth matters over she explained to Dan, "Clay was gone one night when Star Bright—one of the brood-mares—went into labor...if that's what they call it in horses?" she asked Clay.

He nodded.

"Anyway, I couldn't wake Skip, and I didn't know where Mary was sleeping and something had to be done—quick."

Dan leaned forward, his eyes revealing his shock. "You don't mean to tell me *you* delivered the foal?"

"Not exactly." Rorie wished now that she hadn't said anything to Dan about that night. No one could possibly understand what she and Clay had shared in those few hours. Trying to convey the experience to someone else only diminished its significance.

"I'll get the coffee," Rorie said, standing. "I'm sure it's ready."

From her kitchen, she could hear Dan and Clay talking, although she couldn't make out their words. She filled three cups and placed them on a tray, together with cream and sugar, then carried it into the living room.

Once more Clay stood. He took the tray out of her hands and set it on the coffee table. Rorie handed Dan the first cup and saucer and Clay the second. He looked uncomfortable as he accepted it.

"I'm sorry, Clay, you prefer a mug, don't you?" The

cup seemed frail and tiny, impractical, cradled in his strong hand.

"It doesn't matter. If I'm going to be drinking Swiss mocha coffee, I might as well do it from a china cup." He smiled into her eyes, and Rorie couldn't help reciprocating.

"Eaten any seafood fettuccine lately?" she teased.

"Can't say I have."

"It's my favorite dinner," Dan inserted, apparently feeling left out of the conversation. "We had linguini tonight, but Rorie's favorite is sushi."

Her eye caught Clay's and she saw that the corner of his mouth quirked with barely restrained humor. She could just imagine what the people of Nightingale would think of a sushi bar. Skip would probably turn up his nose, insisting that the small pieces of seaweed and raw fish looked like bait.

The coffee seemed to command everyone's attention for the next minute or so.

"I'm still reeling from the news of your adventures on this stud farm," Dan commented, laughing lightly. "You could have knocked me over with a feather when you said you'd helped deliver a foal. I would never have believed it of you, Rorie."

"I brought a picture of Nightsong," Clay said, cautiously putting down his coffee cup. He unsnapped the pocket of his wide-yoked shirt and withdrew two color photographs, which he handed to Rorie. "I meant to show these to you earlier...but I got sidetracked."

"Oh, Clay," she breathed, studying the filly with her gleaming chestnut coat. "She's grown so much in just the past month," she said, her voice full of wonder.

"I thought you'd be impressed."

Reluctantly Rorie shared the pictures with Dan, who barely glanced at them before giving them back to Clay.

"Most men carry around pictures of their wife and kids," Dan stated, his eyes darting to Clay and then Rorie.

Rorie supposed this comment was Dan's less-than-subtle attempt to find out if Clay was married. Taking a deep breath, she said, "Clay's engaged to a neighbor—Kate Logan."

"I see." Apparently he did, because he set aside his coffee cup, and got up to stand behind Rorie. Hands resting on her shoulders, he leaned forward and brushed his mouth over her cheek. "Rorie and I have been talking about getting married ourselves, haven't we, darling?"

Fifteen

No emotion revealed itself on Clay's face, but Rorie could sense the tight rein he kept on himself. Dan's words had dismayed him.

"Is that true, Rorie?" he said after a moment.

Dan's fingers tightened almost painfully on her shoulders. "Just tonight we were talking about getting married. Tell him, darling."

Her eyes refused to leave Clay's. She *had* been talking to Dan about marriage, although she had no intention of accepting his offer. Dan knew where he stood, knew she was in love with another man. But nothing would be accomplished by telling Clay that she'd always love him, especially since he was marrying Kate in a few weeks. "Yes, Dan has proposed."

"I'm crazy about Rorie and have been for months," Dan announced, squarely facing his competition. He spoke for a few more minutes, outlining his goals. Within another ten years, he planned to be financially secure and hoped to retire.

"Dan's got a bright future," Rorie echoed.

"I see." Clay replaced his coffee cup on the tray, then

glanced at his watch and rose to his feet. "I suppose I should head back to the Cow Palace."

"How…how are you doing in the show?" Rorie asked, distraught, not wanting him to leave. Kate would have him the rest of their lives; surely a few more minutes with him wouldn't matter. "Kate wrote that you were going after several championships."

"I'm doing exactly as I expected." The words were clipped, as though he was impatient to get away.

Rorie knew she couldn't keep him any longer. Clay's face was stern with purpose—and resignation. "I'll see you out," she told him.

"I'll come with you," Dan said.

She whirled around and glared at him. "No, you won't."

"Good to see you again, Rorie," Clay said, standing just inside her apartment, his hand on the door. His mouth was hard and flat and he held himself rigid, eyes avoiding hers. He stepped forward and shook Dan's hand.

"It was a pleasure," Dan said in a tone that conveyed exactly the opposite.

"Same here." Clay dropped his hand.

"I'm glad you came by," Rorie told him quietly. "It was…nice seeing you." The words sounded inane, meaningless.

He nodded brusquely, opened the door and walked into the hallway.

"Clay," she said, following him out, her heart hammering so loudly it seemed to echo off the walls.

He stopped and slowly turned around.

Now that she had his attention, Rorie didn't know what to say. "Listen, I'm sorry about the way Dan was acting."

He shook off her apology. "Don't worry about it."

Her fingers tightened on the doorknob, and she wondered if this was really the end. "Will I see you again?" she asked despite herself.

"I don't think so," he answered hoarsely. He looked past her as though he could see through the apartment door and into her living room where Dan was waiting. "Do you honestly love this guy?"

"He's…he's been a good friend."

Clay took two steps toward her, then stopped. As if it was against his better judgment, he raised his hand and lightly drew his finger down the side of her face. Rorie closed her eyes at the wealth of sensation the simple action provoked.

"Be happy, Rorie. That's all I want for you."

The rain hit during the last week of September, and the dreary dark afternoons suited Rorie's mood. Normally autumn was a productive time for her, but she remained tormented with what she felt sure was a terminal case of writer's block. She sat at her desk, her computer humming merrily as she read over the accumulation of an entire weekend's work.

One measly sentence.

There'd been a time when she could write four or five pages a night after coming home from the library. Perhaps the problem was the story she'd chosen. She wanted to write about a filly named Nightsong, but every time she started, her memories of the real Nightsong invaded her thoughts, crippling her imagination.

Here it was Monday night and she sat staring at the screen, convinced nothing she wrote had any merit. The only reason she kept trying was that Dan had pressured her into it. He seemed to believe her world would right itself once Rorie was back to creating her warm, lighthearted children's stories.

The phone rang and, grateful for a reprieve, Rorie hurried into the kitchen to answer it.

"Is this Miss Rorie Campbell of San Francisco, California?"

"Yes, it is." Her heart tripped with anxiety. In a matter of two seconds, every horrible scenario of what could have happened to her parents or her brother darted through Rorie's mind.

"This is Devin Logan calling."

He paused, as though expecting her to recognize the name. Rorie didn't. "Yes?"

"Devin Logan," he repeated, "from the Nightingale, Oregon, Town Council." He paused. "I believe you're acquainted with my daughter, Kate."

"Yes, I remember Kate." If her heart continued at this pace Rorie thought she'd keel over in a dead faint. Just as her pulse had started to slow, it shot up again. "Has anything happened?"

"The Council meeting adjourned about ten minutes ago. Are you referring to that?"

"No...no, I mean has anything happened to Kate?"

"Not that I'm aware of. Do you know something I don't?"

"I don't think so." This entire conversation was driving her crazy.

Devin Logan cleared his throat, and when he spoke his voice dropped to a deeper pitch. "I'm phoning in an official capacity," he said. "We voted at the Town Council meeting tonight to employ a full-time librarian."

He paused again, and, not knowing what else to say,

Rorie murmured, "Congratulations. Kate mentioned that the library was currently being run by part-time volunteers."

"It was decided to offer *you* the position."

Rorie nearly dropped the receiver. "I beg your pardon?"

"My daughter managed to convince the Council that we need a full-time librarian for our new building. She also persuaded us that you're the woman for the job."

"But..." Hardly able to take in what she was hearing, Rorie slumped against the kitchen wall, glad of its support. Logan's next remark was even more surprising.

"We'll match whatever the San Francisco library is paying you and throw in a house in town—rent-free."

"I..." Rorie's mind was buzzing. Kate obviously thought she was doing her a favor, when in fact being so close to Clay would be utter torment.

"Miss Campbell?"

"I'm honored," she said quickly, still reeling with astonishment, "truly honored, but I'm going to have to decline."

A moment of silence followed. "All right... I'm authorized to enhance the offer by ten percent over the amount you're currently earning, but that's our final bid. You'd be making as much money as the fire chief, and he's not about to let the Council pay a librarian more than he's bringing home."

"Mr. Logan, please, the salary isn't the reason I'm turning down your generous offer. I... I want you to know how much I appreciate your offering me the job. Thank you, and thank Kate on my behalf, but I can't accept."

Another, longer silence vibrated across the line, as though he couldn't believe what she was telling him.

"You're positive you want to refuse? Miss Campbell, we're being more than reasonable…more than generous."

"I realize that. In fact, I'm flattered by your proposal, but I can't possibly accept this position."

"Kate had the feeling you'd leap at the job."

"She was mistaken."

"I see. Well, then, it was good talking to you. I'm sorry we didn't get a chance to meet while you were in Nightingale. Perhaps next time."

"Perhaps." Only there wouldn't be a next time.

Rorie kept her hand on the receiver long after she'd hung up. Her back was pressed against the kitchen wall, her eyes closed.

She'd regained a little of her composure when the doorbell chimed. A glance at the wall clock told her it was Dan, who'd promised to drop by that evening. She straightened, forcing a smile, and slowly walked to the door.

Dan entered with a flourish, handing her a small white bag.

"What's this?" she asked.

"Frozen yogurt. Just the thing for a girl with a hot keyboard. How's the writing going?" He leaned forward to kiss her cheek.

Rorie walked into the kitchen and set the container in the freezer compartment of her refrigerator. "It's not. If you don't mind, I'll eat this later."

"Rorie." Dan caught her by her shoulders and studied her face. "You're as pale as chalk. What's wrong?"

"I… I just got off the phone. I was offered another job—as head librarian…"

"But, darling, that's wonderful!"

"…in Nightingale, Oregon."

The change in Dan's expression was almost comical. "And? What did you tell them?"

"I refused."

He gave a great sigh of relief. His eyes glowed and he hugged her impulsively. "Does this mean what I think it does? Are you finally over that cowpoke, Rorie? Will you finally consent to be my wife?"

Rorie lowered her gaze. "Oh, Dan, don't you understand? I'll never get over Clay. Not next week, not next month, not next year." Her voice was filled with pain, and with conviction. Everyone seemed to assume that, in time, she'd forget about Clay Franklin, but she wouldn't.

Dan's smile faded, and he dropped his arms to his sides. "I see." Leaning against the counter, he sighed pensively and said, "I'd do just about anything in this world for you, Rorie, but I think it's time we faced a few truths."

Rorie had wanted to confront them long before now.

"You're never going to love me the way you do that horseman. We can't go on like this. It isn't doing either of us any good to pretend your feelings are going to change."

He looked so grim and discouraged that she didn't point out that *he* was the one who'd been pretending.

"I'm so sorry to hurt you—it's the last thing I ever wanted to do," she told him sincerely.

"It isn't as if I didn't know," he admitted. "You've been honest with me from the start. I can't be less than honest with you. That country boy loves you. I knew it the minute he walked across the street without even noticing the traffic. The whole world would know," he said ruefully. "All he has to do is look at you and everything about him shouts his feelings. He may be engaged to another woman, but it's you he loves."

"I wouldn't fit into his world."

"But, Rorie, you're lost and confused in your own."

She bit her lower lip and nodded. Until Dan said it, she hadn't recognized how true that was. But it didn't change the fact that Clay belonged to Kate. And she was marrying him within the month.

"I'm sorry," Dan said, completely serious, "but the wedding's off."

She nearly laughed out loud at Dan's announcement. No wedding had ever been planned. He'd asked her to marry him at least ten times since she'd returned from her vacation, and each time she'd refused. Instead of wearing her down as he'd hoped, Dan had finally come to accept her decision. Rorie felt relieved, but she was sorry to lose her friend.

"I didn't mean to lead you on," she told him, genuinely contrite.

He shrugged. "The pain will only last for a while. I'm 'a keeper' as the girls in the office like to tell me. I guess it's time I put out the word that I'm available." He wiggled his eyebrows, striving for some humor.

"You've been such a good friend."

He cupped her face and gently kissed her. "Yes, I know. Now don't let that yogurt go to waste—you're too thin as it is."

She smiled and nodded. When she let him out of the apartment, Rorie bolted the door then leaned against it, feeling drained, but curiously calm.

Dan had been gone only a few minutes when Rorie's phone rang again. She hurried into the kitchen to answer it.

"Rorie? This is Kate Logan."

"Kate! How are you?"

"Rotten, but I didn't call to talk about me. I want to know exactly why you're refusing to be Nightingale's librarian—after everything I went through. I can't believe you, Rorie. How can you do this to Clay? Don't you love him?"

Sixteen

"Kate," Rorie demanded. "What are you talking about?"

"You and Clay," she said sharply, sounding quite unlike her usual self. "Now, do you love him or not? I've got to know."

This day had been sliding steadily downhill from the moment Rorie had climbed out of bed that morning. To admit her feelings for Clay would only hurt Kate, and Rorie had tried so hard to avoid upsetting the other woman.

"Well?" Kate said with a sob. "The least you can do is answer me!"

"Oh, Kate," Rorie said, her heart in her throat, "why are you asking me if I love Clay? He's engaged to you. It shouldn't matter one little bit if I love him or not. I'm out of your lives and I intend to stay out."

"But he loves you."

The tears in Kate's voice tore at Rorie's already battered heart. She would've given anything to spare her friend this pain. "I know," she whispered.

"Doesn't that mean anything to you?"

Only the world and everything in it. "Yes," she murmured, her voice growing stronger.

"Then how could you do this to him?"

"Do what?" Rorie didn't understand.

"Hurt him this way!"

"Kate," Rorie pleaded. "I have no idea what you're talking about—I'd never intentionally hurt Clay. If you insist on knowing, I do love him, with all my heart, but he's your fiancé. You loved him long before I even knew him."

Kate's short laugh was riddled with sarcasm. "What is this? First come, first served?"

"Of course not—"

"For your information, Clay isn't my fiancé anymore," Kate blurted, her voice trembling. "He hasn't been in weeks…since before he went to San Francisco for the horse show."

Rorie's head came up so fast she wondered whether she'd dislocated her neck. "He isn't?"

"That's…that's what I just told you."

"But I thought… I assumed…"

"I know what you assumed—that much is obvious—but it isn't like that now and it hasn't been in a long time."

"But you love Clay," Rorie muttered, feeling lightheaded.

"I've loved him from the time I was in pigtails. I love him enough to want to see him happy. Why…why do you think I talked my fool head off to a bunch of hard-nosed Council members? Why do you think I ranted and raved about what a fantastic librarian you are? I as good as told them you're the only person who could possibly assume full responsibility for the new library. Do you honestly think I did all that for the fun of it?"

"No, but, Kate, surely you understand why I have to refuse. I just couldn't bear to come between you and—"

Kate wouldn't allow her to finish, and when she spoke, her voice was high and almost hysterical. "Well, if you believe that, Rorie Campbell, then you've got a lot to learn about me…and even more about Clay Franklin."

"Kate, I'm sorry. Please listen to me. There's so much I don't understand. We've got to talk, because I can't make head or tail out of what you're telling me and I've got to know—"

"If you have anything to say to me, Rorie Campbell, then you can do it to my face. Now, I'm telling Dad and everyone else on the Council that you've accepted the position we so generously offered you. The job starts in two weeks and you'd damn well better be here. Understand?"

Rorie's car left a dusty trail on the long, curving driveway that led to the Circle L Ranch. It'd been a week since the telephone call from Kate, and Rorie still had trouble assimilating what the other woman had told her. Their conversation repeated itself over and over in her mind, until nothing made sense. But one thing stood out: Kate was no longer engaged to Clay.

Rorie was going to him, running as fast as she could, but first she had to settle matters with his former fiancée.

The sun had begun to descend in an autumn sky when Rorie parked her car at the Logan ranch and climbed out. Rotating her neck and shoulders to relieve some of the tension there, Rorie looked around, wondering if anyone was home. She'd been on the road most of the day, so she was exhausted. And exhilarated.

Luke Rivers strolled out of the barn, and stopped when he saw Rorie. His smile deepened. It could've been Rorie's imagination, but she sensed that the hard edge was missing from his look, as though life had unexpectedly tossed him a good turn.

"So you're back," he said by way of greeting.

Rorie nodded, then reached inside the car for her purse. "Is Kate here?"

"She'll be back any minute. Usually gets home from the school around four. Come inside and I'll get you a cup of coffee."

"Thanks." At the moment, coffee sounded like nectar from the gods.

Luke opened the kitchen door for her. "I understand you're going to be Nightingale's new librarian," he said, following her into the house.

"Yes." But that wasn't the reason she'd come back, and they both knew it.

"Good." Luke took two mugs from the cupboard and filled them from a coffeepot that sat on the stove. He placed Rorie's cup on the table, then pulled out a chair for her.

"Thanks, Luke."

The sound of an approaching vehicle drew his attention. He parted the lace curtain at the kitchen window and looked out.

"That's Kate now," he said, his gaze lingering on the driveway. "Listen, if I don't get a chance to talk to you later, I want you to know I'm glad you're here. I've got a few things to thank you for. If it hadn't been for you, I might've turned into a crotchety old saddle bum."

Before Rorie could ask what he meant, he was gone.

Kate burst into the kitchen a minute later and hugged

Rorie as though they were long-lost sisters. "I don't know when I've been happier to see anyone!"

Rorie's face must have shown her surprise because Kate hurried to add, "I suppose you think I'm a crazy woman after the way I talked to you on the phone last week. I don't blame you, but…well, I was upset, to put it mildly, and my thinking was a little confused." She threw her purse on the counter and reached inside the cupboard for a mug. She poured the coffee very slowly, as if she needed time to gather her thoughts.

Rorie's mind was whirling with questions she couldn't wait for Kate to answer. "Did I understand you correctly the other night? Did you tell me you and Clay are no longer engaged?"

Kate wasn't able to disguise the flash of pain that leaped into her deep blue eyes. She dropped her gaze and nodded. "We haven't been in weeks."

"But…"

Kate sat down across the table from Rorie and folded her hands around the mug. "The thing is, Rorie, I knew how you two felt about each other since the night of the Grange dance. A blind man would've known you and Clay had fallen in love, but it was so much easier for me to pretend otherwise." Her finger traced the rim of the mug. "I thought that once you went home, everything would go back to the way it was before…."

"I was hoping for the same thing. Kate, you've got to believe me when I tell you I would've done anything in the world to spare you this. When I learned you and Clay were engaged I wanted to—"

"Die," Kate finished for her. "I know exactly how you must have felt, because that's the way I felt later. The night of the Grange dance, Clay kept looking at you. Every time you danced with a new partner, he scowled. He might have had me at his side, but his eyes followed you all over the hall."

"He loves you, too," Rorie told her. "That's what makes this all so difficult."

"No, he doesn't," Kate answered flatly, without a hint of doubt. "I accepted that a long time before you ever arrived. Oh, he respects and likes me, and to Clay's way of thinking that was enough." She hesitated, frowning. "To my way of thinking, it was, too. We probably would've married and been content. But everything changed when Clay met you. You hit him right between the eyes, Rorie—a direct hit."

"I'm sure he feels more for you than admiration…."

"No." Kate rummaged in her purse for a tissue. "He told me as much himself, but like I said, it wasn't something I didn't already know. You see, I was so crazy about Clay, I was willing to take whatever he offered me, even if it was only second-best." She swabbed at the tears that sprang so readily to her eyes and paused in an effort to gather her composure. "I'm sorry. It's still so painful. But you see, through all of this, I've learned a great deal about what it means to love someone."

Rorie's own eyes welled with involuntary tears, which she hurriedly brushed aside. Then Kate's fingers clasped hers and squeezed tight in a gesture of reassurance.

"I learned that loving people means placing their happiness before your own. That's the way you love Clay, and it's the way he loves you." Kate squared her shoulders and inhaled a quavery breath.

"Kate, please, this isn't necessary."

"Yes, it is, because what I've got to say next is the

hardest part. I need to ask your forgiveness for that terrible letter I wrote after you left Nightingale. I don't have any excuse except that I was insane with jealousy."

"Letter? You wrote me a terrible letter?" The only one Rorie had received was the chatty note that had told her about Mary's prize-winning ribbon and made mention of the upcoming wedding.

"I used a subtle form of viciousness," Kate replied, her voice filled with self-contempt.

Rorie discounted the possibility that Kate could ever be malicious. "The only letter I got from you wasn't the least bit terrible."

Kate lowered her eyes to her hands, neatly folded on the table. Her grip tightened until Rorie was sure her nails would cut her palms.

"I lied in that letter," Kate continued. "When I told you that Clay wouldn't have time for you while he was at the horse show, I was trying to imply that you didn't mean anything to him anymore. I wanted you to think you'd slipped from his mind when nothing could have been further from the truth."

"Don't feel bad about it. I'm not so sure I wouldn't have done the same thing."

"No, Rorie, you wouldn't have. That letter was an underhand attempt to hold on to Clay… I was losing him more and more each day and I thought… I hoped that if you believed we were going to be married in October, then… Oh, I don't know, my thinking was so warped and desperate."

"Your emotions were running high at the time." Rorie's had been, too; she understood Kate's pain because she'd been in so much pain herself.

"But I was pretending to be your friend when in

reality I almost hated you." Kate paused, her shoulders shaking with emotion. "That was the crazy part. I couldn't help liking you and wanting to be your friend, and at the same time I was eaten alive with jealousy and selfish resentment."

"It's not in you to hate anyone, Kate."

"I… I didn't think it was, either, but I was wrong. I can be a terrible person, Rorie. Facing up to that hasn't been easy." She took a deep, shuddering breath.

"Then…a few days after I mailed that letter to you, Clay came over to the house wanting to talk. Almost immediately I realized I'd lost him. Nothing I could say or do would change the way he felt about you. I said some awful things to Clay that night…. He's forgiven me, but I need your forgiveness, too."

"Oh, Kate, of course, but it isn't necessary. I understand. I truly do."

"Thank you," she murmured, dabbing her eyes with the crumpled tissue. "Now I've got that off my chest, I feel a whole lot better."

"But if Clay had broken your engagement when he came to San Francisco, why didn't he say anything to me?"

Kate shrugged. "I don't know what happened while he was gone, but he hasn't been himself since. He never has been a talkative person, but he seemed to draw even further into himself when he came back. He's working himself into an early grave, everyone says. Mary's concerned about him—we all are. Mary said if you didn't come soon, she was going after you herself."

"Mary said that?" The housekeeper had been the very person who'd convinced Rorie she was doing the right thing by getting out of Clay's life.

"Well, are you going to him? Or are you planning to stick around here and listen to me blubber all day? If you give me any more time," she said, forcing a laugh, "I'll manage to make an even bigger fool of myself than I already have." Kate stood abruptly, pushing back the kitchen chair. Her arms were folded around her waist, her eyes bright with tears.

"Kate," Rorie murmured, "you are a dear, dear friend. I owe you more than it's possible to repay."

"The only thing you owe me is one godchild—and about fifty years of happiness with Clay Franklin. Now get out of here before I start weeping in earnest."

Kate opened the kitchen door and Rorie gave her an impulsive hug before hurrying out.

Luke Rivers was standing in the yard, apparently waiting for her. When she came out of the house he sauntered over to her car and held open the driver's door. "Did everything go all right with Kate?"

Rorie nodded.

"Well," he said soberly, "there may be more rough waters ahead for her. She doesn't know it yet, but I'm buying out the Circle L." Then he smiled, his eyes crinkling. "She's going to be fine, though. I'll make sure of that." He extended his hand, gripping hers in a firm handshake. "Let me be the first to welcome you to our community."

"Thank you."

He touched the rim of his hat in farewell, then glanced toward the house. "I think I'll go inside and see how Kate's doing."

Rorie's gaze skipped from the foreman to the house and then back again. "You do that." If Luke Rivers had anything to say about it, Kate wouldn't be suffering from a broken heart for long. Rorie had suspected Luke was in love with Kate. But, like her, he was caught in a trap, unable to reveal his feelings. Perhaps now Kate's eyes would be opened—Rorie fervently hoped so.

The drive from the Logans' place to the Franklins' took no more than a few minutes. Rorie parked her car behind the house, her heart pounding. When she climbed out, the only one there to greet her was Mary.

"About time you got here," the housekeeper complained, marching down the porch steps with a vengeance.

"Could this be the apple-pie blue-ribbon holder of Nightingale, Oregon?"

Mary actually blushed, and Rorie laughed. "I thought you'd never want to see the likes of me again," she teased.

"Fiddlesticks." The weathered face broke into a smile.

"I'm still a city girl," Rorie warned.

"That's fine, 'cause you got the heart of a country girl." Wiping her hands dry on her apron, Mary reached for Rorie and hugged her.

After one brief, bone-crushing squeeze, she set her free. "I'm a meddling old woman, sure enough, and I suspect the good Lord intends to teach me more than one lesson in the next year or two. I'd best tell you that I never should've said those things I did about Kate being the right woman for Clay."

"Mary, you spoke out of concern. I know that."

"Clay doesn't love Kate," she continued undaunted, "but my heavens, he does love you. That boy's been pining his heart out for want of you. He hasn't been the same from the minute you drove out of here all those weeks ago."

Rorie had suffered, too, but she didn't mention that to Mary. Instead, she slipped her arm around the housekeeper's broad waist and together they strolled toward the house.

"Clay's gone for the day, but he'll be back within the hour."

"An hour," Rorie repeated. She'd waited all this time; another sixty minutes shouldn't matter.

"Dinner will be ready then, and it's not like Clay or Skip to miss a meal. Dinner's been at six every night since I've been cooking for this family, and that's a good many years now." Mary's mouth formed a lopsided grin. "Now what we'll do is this. You be in the dining room waiting for him and I'll tell him he's got company."

"But won't he notice my car?" Rorie twisted around, gesturing at her old white Toyota—her own car this time—parked within plain sight.

Mary shook her head. "I doubt it. He's never seen your car, so far as I know, only that fancy sports car. Anyway, the boy's been working himself so hard, he'll be too tired to notice much of anything."

Mary opened the back door and Rorie stepped inside the kitchen. As she did, the house seemed to fold its arms around her in welcome. She paused, breathing in the scent of roast beef and homemade biscuits. It might not be sourdough and Golden Gate Park roses, but it felt right. More than right.

"Do you need me to do anything?" Rorie asked.

Mary frowned, then nodded. "There's just one thing I want you to do—make Clay happy."

"Oh, Mary, I intend to start doing that the second he walks through that door."

An hour later, almost to the minute, Rorie heard Skip and Clay come into the kitchen.

"What's for dinner?" Skip asked immediately.

"It's on the table. Now wash your hands."

Rorie heard the teenager grumble as he headed down the hallway to the bathroom.

"How'd the trip go?" Mary asked Clay.

He mumbled something Rorie couldn't hear.

"The new librarian stopped by to say hello. Old man Logan and Kate sent her over—thought you might like to meet her."

"I don't. I hope you got rid of her. I'm in no mood for company."

"Nope," Mary said. "Fact is, I invited her to stay for dinner. The least you can do is wipe that frown off your face and go introduce yourself."

Rorie stood just inside the dining room, her heart ready to explode. By the time Clay stepped into the room, tears had blurred her vision and she could hardly make out the tall, familiar figure that blocked the doorway.

She heard his swift intake of breath, and the next thing she knew she was crushed in Clay's loving arms.

Seventeen

Rorie was locked so securely in Clay's arms that for a moment she couldn't draw a breath. But that didn't matter. What mattered was that she was being hugged by the man she loved and he was holding on to her as though he didn't plan to ever let her go.

Clay kissed her again and again, the way a starving man took his first bites of food, initially hesitant, then eager. The palms of Rorie's hands were pressed against his chest and she felt the quick surge of his heart. His own hand was gentle on her hair, caressing it, running his fingers through it.

"Rorie… Rorie, I can't believe you're here."

Rorie felt the power of his emotions, and they were strong enough to rock her, body and soul. This man loved her. He was honest and hardworking, she knew all that, but even more, Clay Franklin was *good,* with an unselfishness and a loyalty that had touched her profoundly. In an age of ambitious, hardhearted, vain men, she had inadvertently stumbled on this rare man of character. Her life would never be the same.

Clay exhaled a deep sigh, and his hands framed her

face as he pulled his head back to gaze into her eyes. The lines that marked his face seemed more deeply incised now, and she felt another pang of sorrow for the pain he'd endured.

"Mary wasn't teasing me, was she? You *are* the new librarian?"

Rorie nodded, smiling up at him, her happiness shining from her eyes. "There's no going back for me. I've moved out of my apartment, packed everything I own and quit my job with barely a week's notice."

Rorie had fallen in love with Clay, caught in the magic of one special night when a foal had been born. But her feelings stretched far beyond the events of a single evening and the few short days they'd spent together. Her love for Clay had become an essential part of her. Rorie adored him and would feel that way for as long as her heart continued to beat.

Clay's frown deepened and his features tightened briefly. "What about Dan? I thought you were going to marry him."

"I couldn't," she said, then smiled tenderly, tracing his face with her hands, loving the feel of him beneath her fingertips.

"But—"

"Clay," she interrupted, "why didn't you tell me when I saw you in San Francisco that you'd broken your engagement to Kate?" Her eyes clouded with anguish at the memory, at the anxiety they'd caused each other. It had been such senseless heartache, and they'd wasted precious time. "Couldn't you see how miserable I was?"

A grimace of pain moved across his features. "All I noticed was how right you and that stockbroker looked together. You both kept telling me what a bright future he had. I couldn't begin to offer you the things he could. And if that wasn't enough, it was all too apparent that Dan was in love with you." Gently Clay smoothed her hair away from her temple. "I could understand what it meant to love you, and, between the two of us, he seemed the better man."

Rorie lowered her face, pressing her forehead against the hollow of his shoulder. She groaned in frustration. "How could you even *think* such a thing, when I love you so much?"

Clay moved her face so he could meet her eyes. "But, Rorie..." He stopped and a muscle jerked in his jaw. "Dan can give you far more than I'll ever be able to. He's got connections, background, education. A few years down the road, he's going to be very wealthy—success is written all over him. He may have his faults, but basically he's a fine man."

"He *is* a good person and he's going to make some woman a good husband. But it won't be me."

"He could give you the kinds of things I may never be able to afford...."

"Clay Franklin, do you love me or not?"

Clay exhaled slowly, watching her. "You know the answer to that."

"Then stop arguing with me. I don't love Dan Rogers. I love you."

Still his frown persisted. "You belong in the city."

"I belong with you," she countered.

He said nothing for a long moment. "I can't argue with that," he whispered, his voice husky with emotion. "You do belong here, because God help me, I haven't got the strength to let you walk away a second time."

Clay kissed her again, his mouth sliding over hers

as though he still couldn't believe she was in his arms. She held on to him with all her strength, soaking up his love. She was at home in his arms. It was where she belonged and where she planned to stay.

The sound of someone entering the room filtered through to Rorie's consciousness, but she couldn't bring herself to move out of Clay's arms.

"Rorie!" Skip cried, his voice high and excited, "What are you doing here?"

Rorie finally released Clay and turned toward the teenager who had come to her rescue that August afternoon.

"Hello, Skip," she said softly. Clay slipped his arm around her waist and she smiled up at him, needing his touch to anchor her in the reality of their love.

"Are you back for good?" Skip wanted to know.

She nodded, but before she could answer Clay said, "Meet Nightingale's new librarian." His arm tightened around her.

The smile that lit the teenager's eyes was telling. "So you're going to stick around this time." He blew out a gusty sigh. "It's a damn good thing, because since you left, my brother's been as hard to live with as a rattlesnake."

"I'd say that was a bit of an exaggeration," Clay muttered, clearly not approving of his brother's choice of description.

"You shouldn't have gone," Skip said, sighing again. "Especially before the county fair."

Rorie laughed. "You're never going to forgive me for missing that, are you?"

"You should've been here, Rorie. It was great."

"I'll be here next summer," she promised.

"The fact is, Rorie's going to be around for a lifetime

of summers," Clay informed his brother. "We're going to be married as soon as we can arrange it." His eyes held hers but they were filled with questions, as if he half expected her, even now, to refuse him.

Rorie swallowed the emotion that bobbed so readily to the surface and nodded wildly, telling him with one look that she'd marry him anytime he wanted.

Skip crossed his arms over his chest and gave them a smug look. "I knew something was going on between the two of you. Every time I was around you guys it was like getting zapped with one of those stun guns."

"We were that obvious?" It still troubled Rorie that Kate had known, especially since both she and Clay had tried so hard to hide their feelings.

Skip's shrug was carefree. "I don't think so, but I don't care about love and all that."

"Give it time, little brother," Clay murmured, "because when it hits, it'll knock you for a loop."

Mary stepped into the room, carrying a platter of meat. "So the two of you are getting hitched?"

Their laughter signaled a welcome release from all the tensions of the past weeks. Clay pulled out Rorie's chair, then sat down beside her. His hand reached for hers, lacing their fingers together. "Yes," he said, still smiling, "we'll be married as soon as we can get the license and talk to the pastor."

Mary pushed the basket of biscuits closer to Skip. "Well, you don't need to fret—I'll stay for a couple more years until I can teach this child the proper way to feed a man. She may be pretty to look at, but she don't know beans about whipping up a decent meal."

"I'd appreciate that, Mary," Rorie said. "I could do with a few cooking lessons."

The housekeeper's smile broadened. "Now, go ahead and eat before the potatoes get cold and the gravy gets lumpy."

Skip didn't need any further inducement. He helped himself to the biscuits, piling three on the edge of his plate.

Mary playfully slapped his hand. "I've got apple pie for dessert, so don't go filling yourselves up on my buttermilk biscuits." Her good humor was evident as she surveyed the table, glancing at everyone's plate, then bustled back to the kitchen.

Rorie did her best to sample a little of everything. Although the meal was delicious, she was too excited to do anything as mundane as eat.

After dinner, Skip made himself scarce. Mary delivered a tray with two coffee cups to the living room, where Clay and Rorie sat close together on the couch. "You two have lots to talk about, so you might as well drink this while you're doing it."

"Thank you, Mary," Clay said, exchanging a smile with Rorie.

The older woman set the tray down, then patted the fine gray hair at the sides of her head. "I want you to know how pleased I am for you both. Have you set the date yet?"

"We're talking about that now," Clay answered. "We're going to call Rorie's family in Arizona this evening and discuss it with them."

Mary nodded. "She's not the woman I would've chosen for you, her being a city girl and all, but she'll make you happy."

Clay's hand clasped Rorie's. "I know."

"She's got a generous soul." The housekeeper looked at Rorie and her gaze softened. "Fill this house with children—and with love. It's been quiet far too long."

The phone rang in the kitchen and, with a regretful glance over her shoulder, Mary hurried to answer it. A moment later, she stuck her head around the kitchen door.

"It's for you, Clay. Long distance."

Clay's grimace was apologetic. "I'd better get it."

"You don't need to worry that I'll leave," Rorie said with a laugh. "You're stuck with me for a lot of years, Clay Franklin."

He kissed her before he stood up, then headed toward the kitchen. Rorie sighed and leaned back, cradling her mug. By chance, her gaze fell on the photograph of Clay's parents, which rested on top of the piano. Once more, Rorie felt the pull of his mother's eyes. She smiled now, understanding so many things. The day she'd planned to leave Elk Run, this same photograph had captured her attention. The moment she'd walked into this house, Rorie had belonged to Clay and he to her. Somehow, looking at his mother's picture, she'd sensed that. She belonged to this home and this family.

Clay returned a few minutes later, with Blue trailing him. "Just a call from the owner of one of the horses I board," he said, as he sat down beside Rorie and placed his arm around her shoulders. His eyes followed hers to the photo. "Mom would have liked you."

Rorie sipped her coffee and smiled. "I know I would have loved her." Setting her cup aside, she reached up and threw both arms around Clay's neck. Gazing into his eyes, she brought his mouth down to hers.

Perhaps it was her imagination or an optical illusion—in fact, Rorie was sure of it. But she could have sworn the elegant woman in the photograph smiled.

* * * * *

Also by Lee Tobin McClain

Love Inspired

Rescue Haven

The Secret Christmas Child
Child on His Doorstep
Finding a Christmas Home

Rescue River

Engaged to the Single Mom
His Secret Child
Small-Town Nanny
The Soldier and the Single Mom
The Soldier's Secret Child
A Family for Easter

HQN

The Off Season

Cottage at the Beach
Reunion at the Shore
Christmas on the Coast
Home to the Harbor
First Kiss at Christmas
Forever on the Bay

Safe Haven

Low Country Hero
Low Country Dreams
Low Country Christmas

Visit her Author Profile page at Harlequin.com, or leetobinmcclain.com, for more titles!

HER EASTER PRAYER

Lee Tobin McClain

Dedicated to my sister,
who teaches adult GED students with sensible good humor and no expectation of applause.
Thank you for all you do, Sue Spore!

Weeping may endure for a night,
but joy cometh in the morning.
—*Psalm* 30:5

One

He was watching her and the students again.

Emily Carver deliberately looked away from the dark-eyed handyman who kept finding things to repair in her library's teaching space. There had been a time, in her carefree twenties, when she'd have smiled at a handsome man who seemed to take an interest in her, but not anymore.

Anyway, his expression wasn't flirtatious so much as curious, watchful, assessing. Well. If he had a problem with the way she conducted her reading class—or the scars on her arms—so be it. She had to shepherd nine students on to their lunch hour, a task sometimes easier said than done with this particular group.

The Bright Tomorrows Residential Academy wasn't fancy, but most classrooms featured views of the Colorado Rocky Mountains. In early April, they were a marvel of snowfields and evergreen forests and giant boulder peaks, reaching toward a sky as blue as a baby's eyes. Emily had only to glance out a window to remind herself that God's creation was far bigger than her human-size problems.

She put on a smile—easy enough when she looked at her beloved students. "Angus, remember to keep your hands to yourself," she said to a fifth grader who was pestering the boy in front of him. "Shane, you forgot your book. It's fine, here you go," she added, handing the child his copy of *The Secret Garden*. Shane tended to burst into tears at the smallest provocation.

Something Emily understood quite well. She'd been there.

Automatically she reached for Lady, but her service dog wasn't by her side. She looked back and saw her new student, Landon McCarthy, kneeling beside Lady, rubbing the shaggy poodle mix's cream-colored head.

She double-checked that the rest of her students were under the care of the lunch aide and noticed that the hyper-observant handyman had left the library, not that she was all that interested, no way. And then she walked back to Landon. The boy hadn't spoken during their reading class, but that was normal for new kids at Bright Tomorrows Academy. And if petting a service dog was his worst problem…

She reached the pair. "Landon, I didn't get the chance to tell you before class, but service dogs shouldn't be petted or touched while they're…" She trailed off and stared at the bright blue circles around Lady's eyes. "What are you *doing*? Give me that marker right now!"

He didn't, so she reached out and pulled it from his fingers. "Lady. Down." She pointed at a spot on the floor well away from the boy. "Landon, wait right here while I make sure she's okay."

"I didn't hurt her." The boy's tone was gruff.

A quick check of the dog assured her that he was

telling the truth, although… She looked down at the marker. Sure enough, it was permanent.

Even if Emily was able to remove the worst of the ink, Lady would be sporting blue eye shadow for the foreseeable future.

Visions of a leisurely lunchtime—the ham-and-cheese sandwich stowed in the teachers' lounge's refrigerator, a walk with her coworkers—faded away. It was more important to handle this behavior issue. She turned back to the child. "Landon, sit down and tell me what you were doing."

"She needed decorating." He looked at his hands, also stained with blue. "Can I go to lunch?"

"Why on earth did you think she needed decorating? We don't do things like that to animals. The ink could hurt her."

He shrugged and stared at the floor.

So he wasn't going to explain. Probably, he couldn't. Being a new kid in a boarding school for boys with issues was reason enough to act out.

She looked around the library, trying to figure out an appropriate consequence that wasn't too harsh. She wasn't going to have him scrub Lady's face, but maybe he could clean up something else instead, she decided. And working together might give her a chance to know the new boy a little better, even help him feel he had a place here.

"I'm going to have to spend extra time cleaning the marker off Lady," she said, "so I'd like for you to help me straighten up the library before you go to lunch. You can start with picking up the paper on the floor." She pointed to the corner of the room, where several crumpled balls of paper had missed the trash can. "After that, you can help me put our chairs back at the tables."

"Fine." Landon blew out a heavy, dramatic sigh and headed toward the messy corner.

Relieved that he hadn't gotten belligerent, Emily reshelved the books she'd been showing the kids. The library was small, but the shelves lined with books gave her a peaceful, expansive feeling. You were never trapped when there was a book to read. She'd have to try to find out Landon's reading tastes.

Lady had been watching Emily, but now she rested her blue-tinted head on her paws. Obviously, the service dog hadn't detected any unusual nervousness or tension. And she was right. Kids misbehaving was just part of the job at Bright Tomorrows Academy.

The new handyman strode into the library and looked from Landon, crushing down paper into the overfull wastebasket, to Emily, and back again. Then he knelt in front of the boy. "Why are you cleaning? You're a student here."

Seeing the two dark heads together made it click for Emily: they had to be father and son. New handyman, new student. No wonder the handyman had paid extra attention to the class. His son was in it.

Landon ducked away from his dad and hustled over to the chairs, moving them back to their original locations at tables. He didn't volunteer why he was in trouble, of course.

Emily opened her mouth to explain and then snapped it closed again as the handyman advanced on her, brows drawn together, mouth pressed into a flat line. He gestured at Landon. "He's the custodian's kid, not the custodian," he growled in a low voice, obviously not wanting Landon to hear. "I won't have him doing cleaning work."

He was big and angry, and Emily sucked in a breath and took a step backward. Lady got to her feet, trotted toward them and pushed her nose into Emily's hand.

The movement caught the handyman's attention, and his eyes widened. "What happened to your dog?"

Emily was tempted to take another step back, away from his looming intensity, but she forced herself to stay put. "Landon happened," she explained. "He decided the dog needed to be more colorful. Since he made a mess, I asked him to clean up a mess as a consequence. I'm Emily Carver," she added, sticking out her hand.

"Dev McCarthy," he said, automatically shaking hers, still frowning.

His hands were callused, as you'd expect from his line of work. Muscular arms strained the sleeves of his polo shirt, and his hair was graying at the temples, though he didn't look much older than Emily was. Forty at most.

The lines in his forehead smoothed out, though a slight frown remained.

Having defused the situation and calmed everyone down, as usual, Lady nudged Emily one last time, glanced up at her and then settled on the floor a few feet away.

Landon finished straightening the chairs but didn't approach his father and Emily. He stood beside one of the tables, fidgeting from foot to foot.

Emily glanced from the child to Dev. "As far as I'm concerned, he's made up for what he did and can go to lunch," she said quietly. "I'll walk him down, unless you'd like to talk with him first?"

"I can walk my own kid to lunch." He beckoned to Landon, and the two of them left the library.

"Thanks for helping," Emily called after the boy.

He glanced back and then hurried after his father.

That went well. Not.

In her tiny office in the back of the library, Emily checked her phone. Three messages from the same number, and…uh-oh.

She sank into her desk chair and returned the call, identifying herself. "Is my mom okay?"

"She's fine." The business office manager's voice sounded impatient. "It's about your account."

Emily blew out a breath and leaned back, staring up at the industrial-tile ceiling. "I know my payment is late. I had an unexpected car repair, but my tax refund check will arrive any day, and as soon as it does, I'll send the money."

"With the late fee," the woman reminded her.

"Right. Of course." She ended the call, adding up numbers in her mind. She knew the amount of the late fee because she'd paid it before.

Which just spoke to the fact that her situation wasn't sustainable.

But Mom was getting great care—care that Emily couldn't provide at home. Her stomach churned.

"What's wrong?" Her friend Hayley, who managed food services at the school, stuck her head in the door. "You didn't come walk. We missed you."

"Little problem with the new student. And then a call from Mom's care center. I'm late paying."

"Ugh." Hayley came in and perched on the edge of Emily's desk. "Hey, did you meet the new handyman? He's good to look at."

"Nope. Not interested." No one who looked like the new handyman would give her a second glance.

Which was fine. She had plenty of problems without adding a handsome, surly man into the mix. Plus, she'd had her chance and she'd blown it, lost everything. She didn't deserve another try at relationships.

"You're not doing the whole 'I don't deserve happiness' thing, are you? Because you *do* deserve it. No matter what happened in the past, we're forgiven and can make a fresh start."

"Right." At least in theory, but the practical truth was that Emily would never let herself get involved with a man, given what had happened in the past, even though her biological clock seemed to tick louder every year. "I need to focus on making some extra money. Do you need any part-time help in the kitchen? I could work the dinner shift."

"You shouldn't work two jobs, should you? Think of the stress."

As if to prove Hayley right, Lady shoved her nose into Emily's hand, then leaned against her.

Emily stroked the big dog, and her nerves settled. "I'm pretty sure I'll have to find a second job," she said. "And if I do, I'd rather work with you, here at Bright Tomorrows, than flip burgers in town."

"And I'd love to have you work with me, but we're fully staffed. No budget for a new hire." Hayley's dark eyes were warm with sympathy. "God will help you find a way."

Emily sure hoped so. And the sooner, the better.

At the end of the school day, Dev waited for the students to be dismissed to their dorm parents. The few day students boarded their vans or climbed into cars. When it was Landon's turn for dismissal, the boy looked around for Dev, and there was relief in his eyes when he saw his father.

Which just about gutted Dev. Landon had lived mostly with his mom, back in Denver, and she hadn't always been reliable about things like picking up her son at the scheduled time. Especially as she'd gotten more into dating. When the marriage had ended three years ago, she hadn't wanted Dev to have but every other weekend with Landon. As time went on, she'd allowed more and more visitation until Dev had Landon most weekends. Just last month, he'd found the opening at Bright Tomorrows and proposed taking Landon full-time. Frustrated with Landon's school and behavior problems, she'd agreed with the plan, and here they were.

Dev had plenty of inadequacies, but he'd do everything within his power to show up for his son, because he knew from personal experience what it was like to be the last kid left waiting in front of the school.

And he'd also do his best to be a good parent, which meant teaching interpersonal skills. He beckoned to Landon. "We need to apologize to Ms. Carver before we go home."

"Aw, I already did her chores," Landon protested. "And Lady—that's her dog—is okay. She said so."

"We didn't tell her we were sorry. Come on."

Landon fell into step beside him, dragging his feet. "You mean me."

"What?"

"Me. *I* need to tell her, not we."

At eight, Landon was starting to analyze the details

of what Dev said, often with an eye toward rebelling against whatever Dev told him. "Truth is," Dev said, "I need to apologize as well. I was short with her when I saw you doing the cleaning."

"You're gonna apologize for that?"

"Uh-huh." Even though it might not be well received. Emily Carver, a reading teacher, of all things, had reason to be already set against Landon, although Dev hoped she wasn't that quick to judge a kid. And she might not think well of a lowly handyman like Dev.

But for his son's sake, to set a good example, he'd put in an effort.

There was another reason as well. Dev had gotten the impression, from report cards and from a few things his ex had said, that Landon was struggling in school. It didn't seem all that serious a problem, and Dev wasn't too worried about it, but he also didn't want Landon to face the challenges Dev faced himself. That was why he'd been watching Ms. Carver's class so closely. If Landon needed a tutor, Dev wanted to find him a good one. Ms. Carver seemed like she just might fit the bill, though after his annoyance with her earlier today, he felt less sure.

As they approached the library, Landon hung back and spoke to a kid passing by. That was good—Dev wanted his son to make friends in the new school, so he continued on to the library door and stood waiting.

He could see Ms. Carver in her glassed-in cube of an office, her dog beside her. Reddish-brown hair to her shoulders, in a simple style that suited her matter-of-fact attitude and friendly smile. She seemed to be on the phone—that or she was talking to herself. She looked young and fresh-faced, but he'd seen the tiny wrinkles fanning out from her eyes and figured she wasn't that much younger than he was. She just wore it better.

Beyond the office were the library's shelves and shelves of books. They held worlds that were closed to Dev, but with the help of this school, they'd be open to Landon. It was worth the pay cut to get the free tuition and pull Landon away from bad influences, including his mother's flavor-of-the-week boyfriends. Her unsteady lifestyle had meant lots of school moves for Landon, and the academic struggles that went along with that. Dev hoped a consistent stretch at a private school would solve those problems quickly. If not, he'd get serious about hiring a tutor, maybe even pretty-but-uptight Ms. Carver. So it was time to make nice.

He looked back to see his son wandering toward him, kicking the wall every few steps.

"Come on, Landon," he said. "Now."

Landon walked marginally faster, and they entered the library together.

He cleared his throat. "Ms. Carver?"

She looked up, but her phone buzzed. She raised a finger, her face apologetic. "Be right with you," she said and then took the call.

"Thank you for calling me back. I need something part-time. Right." She listened for a moment. "Right, I understand. Is it okay if I call you back in a couple of weeks and see if anything has opened up?" She listened another few seconds. "Sure. Thanks."

She came out the half-opened door and flipped back her hair, which he was already starting to recognize as a nervous gesture. "Hi, Landon. Mr. McCarthy."

"You can call me Dev."

"And I'm Emily," she said with an impersonal smile.

"Reading teacher and librarian for Bright Tomorrows. It's a small school, so we tend to play more than one role here."

He'd already realized that, when he'd walked around with the school principal and seen that he was expected to fix the furnace and repair the malfunctioning bell system as well as cleaning classrooms and trimming hedges. Which was fine with him. He had a knack for fixing things, and he liked to work hard.

He refocused on Emily, who was looking at him expectantly. "We wanted to apologize," he said.

"No need. We're fine."

"No." His mouth was dry and he swallowed, conscious of the need to set an example, not just of the importance of apologies, but of how to do them. "I spoke sharply to you earlier, and I had no call to do that. I'm sorry."

Her face broke into a genuine, open smile that looked like sunshine. "Thank you. Really, it's fine."

It was hard to look away from her, but he made himself turn toward his son, put a hand on the boy's shoulder. "Landon?"

Landon squared his shoulders. "I'm sorry I put marker on your dog. Is she okay?"

There was that sunshiny smile again. "Thank you for apologizing. Lady's fine." She turned and spoke to the dog, and the white poodle mix stood, stretched with her front legs out and back end high, and then trotted over.

The dog's eyes were now surrounded by pale blue circles. Apparently, Emily had gotten some of the marker out of the dog's fur, but not all. Definitely not a good start for Landon.

But Emily seemed to take it in stride. She slipped

off the dog's red vest. "Would you like to pet her?" she asked Landon. "You can, as long as she's out of harness."

"Yeah!" Landon knelt in front of the dog and stuck out a tentative hand. As far as Dev knew, the boy hadn't had much experience with animals, but he seemed to love them.

Emily pulled a toy out of a basket just inside her office door. She knelt beside Landon. "You'd be doing me a favor if you'd play with her for a few minutes. She's been sitting still most of the day. It's not easy being a service dog."

Landon took the tug toy with a shy smile at Emily, and Dev was pretty sure the boy had just become a fan of the pretty librarian.

Dev was starting to like her better himself, because she wasn't holding Landon's earlier misbehavior against him. Instead, she seemed to be trying to build a bridge and help Landon feel comfortable at his new school. Dev appreciated that.

He wondered what kind of service dog Lady was, since Emily had no visible disability. But it would be rude to ask her outright.

Landon had no such scruples. As he played a game of tug-of-war with the dog, he looked up at Emily. "How come you have a service dog?"

Dev winced. "Landon. That's Ms. Carver's private business."

"It's okay. All the kids know." She glanced up at Dev and then knelt down to the level of Landon and the dog. "I had something bad happen to me, and I still get nervous and upset sometimes. Lady helps me stay calm."

"What was the—" Landon cut off his question and looked up at Dev. "Sorry. It's your private business."

Good. Dev gave Landon an approving smile and a slight head nod.

Dev was curious, too. Sounded like a PTSD dog, making him wonder if Emily was a veteran. It was hard to imagine the petite, almost delicate woman in a uniform, but that was just his own sexism talking. All kinds of women did all kinds of things in the military these days.

She straightened and brushed her hands together. "How are you both liking the school? Where'd you move from?"

"It's a good change for both of us, I think," Dev said, because Landon wasn't answering. "We moved from Denver."

"Great city. You'll find it a lot quieter here." She flipped her hair again, and a whiff of strawberry tickled his nose.

Longing flashed through him, hard and sharp. He missed being close with a woman, but that wasn't on his playlist, not now. He needed to focus on Landon.

"Quiet's good," he said, stepping back. "We don't want to keep you. I'm sure you're eager to get home at the end of a school day."

"I definitely get tired, but it's a good tired." She stepped back into her office and started loading books into an old-fashioned brown satchel. "We just got a pile of new books in, and I'm eager to dig in. Book nerd," she added.

A skittery feeling turned his stomach over. "Uh-huh. Landon, we need to go," he said.

Since his divorce, he'd stayed well away from women who might discover his reading problems. No way was he inviting the kind of disrespect and ridicule he'd gotten from his ex because he couldn't read well.

He needed to keep his distance from pretty, complicated Emily Carver. Even if he did ask her to tutor Landon, he'd make sure everything was strictly professional.

"Come on," he repeated to Landon, who was dawdling, playing with the dog.

Landon stood immediately, and Dev realized he'd spoken more sharply than he'd intended.

"I'll walk out with you," Emily said easily. She slipped Lady's service vest and harness back onto her, then picked up her loaded satchel, struggling a little.

Dev held out a hand. "I can carry that out for you."

She looked surprised. "Oh! Well, sure. Thanks."

It was as if she wasn't used to a man helping her out, making Dev wonder even more about her background. He picked up her satchel, and the three of them headed out of the school.

The silence between them felt awkward, at least to Dev, and he was relieved when they got to the parking area. He handed her the heavy satchel. "We'll be seeing you," he said, turning toward the road that led to the staff cabins.

"Actually, I live over in the cabins." She and her dog turned in the same direction.

"We live there, too." Landon sounded amazed. "We just moved in."

Her eyebrows lifted a fraction at the same moment that Dev got a sinking feeling. "Which one?" he asked.

"Cabin six," she said.

"We're in five." And a pretty reading teacher wasn't exactly whom he'd have chosen as a next-door neighbor.

Seeing her on a day-to-day basis, at home as well as at work, was just going to rub in the fact that he couldn't dream of connecting with a woman whose life was all about books and reading.

He had to keep his distance to conceal the embarrassing fact that he could barely read.

Two

The week flew by quickly, as most of them did at the busy school, and the weekend passed even faster. Emily spent most of Saturday with friends in town, not *necessarily* to avoid her new neighbors, but partly so. She felt a little too intrigued by Dev, and she wanted to avoid letting that interest build at all, since she'd never pursue it. And Landon…well. He was a cute kid, and he tugged at her heartstrings. That happened to all teachers, and wasn't necessarily a bad thing. But for Emily, with her anxiety issues, it felt wrong and dangerous to develop an affection for Landon.

Since the school started with grade three, this was the first year she'd taught kids the same age her son, James, would have been, if he'd lived. Landon had the same coloring, too, right down to the unusual hazel eyes, and for some reason, that combination was kicking her hard. Better to avoid the pair entirely.

Sunday, she drove an hour south to visit her mother, and Sunday evening, as the sun set over the Rockies, she pulled into her little driveway and shot up a prayer of thanks. Her loud, smoking beater of a car had made the weekly trip once more.

Across the road from the cabins, a lively picnic was in progress, with several people already sitting around a wooden table. At the sight, the tension left her shoulders.

She carried in her things, Lady trotting beside her. She really should go straight to bed. The drive and the visit had taken it out of her, and she had a busy week coming up. But after spending time with her mother and having an unpleasant conversation with the accounts manager of the Alpine Care Center, she needed cheering up.

"We'll go see our friends for just a little while but make it an early night," she said to Lady. *Do not pass go, do not look to the right or left, especially the left.*

Of course, she *did* look to the left, just in time to see Dev and Landon coming out the door of their cabin.

She considered turning around and going right back in. Although she and Dev had waved to each other last week, and although Landon had come to reading class all week, she hadn't had individual interactions with them.

Despite that, the handyman and his endearing son had been on her mind throughout the trip.

She'd be concerned about any new colleague or student. Wouldn't she?

"Hey, Emily."

Dev's low voice danced along her nerve endings, heating her face as she turned.

"Hi, Landon," she said, deliberately greeting the boy first. "Hi, Dev. Are you going to the picnic?"

"Didn't know about it, so probably not," Dev said. "It's a school night."

"That's the whole point of it." She leaned against the split-rail fence that stood between their yards. "Sunday nights can be gloomy. So the staff usually has a get-together to cheer up and stretch out the weekend as long as possible. You're welcome to come." She smiled at Landon. "It probably doesn't sound fun to hang around a bunch of teachers, but the boys usually have some kind of activity in the residence houses on Sunday nights. I'm sure you could join in."

"Actually," Dev said, "we came out because I heard your car."

Emily sighed. "I'm sorry. I know it's loud. You probably smelled it, too."

"Want me to take a look at it?"

She tipped her head to one side. "Really?"

"Dad's good at fixing cars," Landon said.

"I couldn't pay you—"

Something flashed in his eyes. "I'm just being neighborly. If you don't want me to look at it, it's okay."

"You can't afford to turn down an offer like that," Stan, the tall, white-haired math teacher, said as he approached from the cabin on the other side of Dev's. He stuck out a hand to Dev. "Stan Davidson. Seen you around the past week but didn't get the chance to say hello."

Dev greeted him and introduced Landon. It turned out Landon already knew the math teacher, and from the boy's frown, Emily guessed the connection wasn't a positive one.

"Wouldn't mind seeing what's going on under the hood of that vehicle myself," Stan said. "It'd probably be better if the whole thing just caught fire, so you could get the insurance money."

Emily flinched. *He means well, and he doesn't know what happened to you.* She thanked them both and left the two men, and Landon, studying her car.

As she approached the picnic, Hayley detached from the group. "You made it back! How was your visit?"

"It was good. Better than usual."

"Meaning..."

"Meaning Mom knew me." She wrinkled her nose. "But she didn't remember any of the bad stuff, which is a blessing. She was in a good mood."

"That's great. I'm so glad." Hayley put an arm around her. She was Emily's best friend, and one of the few people who knew about the family tragedy that had darkened Emily's past.

"They take such good care of her. And they're willing to work with me on payments, but the fact is, I need to pull together more money."

Beside her, Lady poked her nose into Emily's hand, reminding her to take deep breaths and relax her muscles.

Stan walked toward the picnic, Landon beside him. It looked like Stan was lecturing, and Landon grimaced and then took off running back toward his cabin.

"I hear he's not doing so well," Hayley said.

"Who, Landon? What do you mean?"

"Academics."

They both watched as Dev straightened from where he'd been looking under the hood of Emily's car and spoke sharply to Landon. Emily couldn't hear the words, but she could recognize a scolding, even from this distance.

"Poor kid," she murmured. "It can't be easy living

next door to two of your teachers when you're eight years old."

Hayley frowned. "Eight. That's about how old your son would have been. Are you thinking about that?"

Emily bit her lip and nodded, glancing around to make sure nobody had heard Hayley's blunt words. Fortunately, the five or six other people in the gathering were clustered together, roasting hot dogs over a small fire someone had built, talking and laughing.

She looked at the fire and got stuck there, spiraling into the horror that had happened six years ago. Hearing her mother's screams, but not her husband's, nor her baby's, because it was too late. The sirens, the sooty firefighters, the mess of water.

They'd done their best, but it hadn't been enough.

Leaving her baby with her difficult husband so she could go out with friends had been stupid enough, but when Mom was in the mix… It had been a huge mistake, one she'd paid for all too dearly. Mom had paid, too, since she'd left a pan burning on the stove and caused the fire. She was devastated when she remembered what she'd done, which thankfully was less and less often.

But James, her sweet two-year-old baby boy, and her husband as well, had paid with their lives.

"Hey, c'mon, let's get a hot dog," Hayley said. "You probably didn't have much to eat today."

Emily stroked Lady beside her and fought her way back to the present moment. "No, I didn't. A hot dog sounds good." She forced the words through a tight throat, but she got them out. "But I don't think I can…" She gestured toward the fire, her throat closing again.

She was getting better, but she knew her limits. She couldn't roast a hot dog over a fire without losing it.

"I'll make you one in a minute," Hayley said. "We've got company." She glanced past Emily.

Emily looked over her shoulder and saw Dev heading toward them, a concerned frown on his face, wiping oily hands on a rag. "I fixed the split hose that's causing your car to smoke like that," he said, "but it's temporary. The car needs a major overhaul."

It wasn't news to her, but hearing it said aloud pushed a heavy weight onto her shoulders. "Thank you for fixing what you could," she said, her throat still feeling tight. "You didn't have to do that. I appreciate it."

Hayley stood close beside her, and Lady leaned against her other side. Emily was enveloped by love, and she was truly grateful.

She just didn't know how to solve her money problems, which seemed to loom bigger all the time.

"Look," Hayley said, "you can do the car fix with a credit card, if need be."

"I don't like doing that." Her husband had gotten them into debt, and she'd had a terrible time paying it off. "Will the car run for a while?" she asked Dev. "I have to make weekly trips to Fort Collins, about an hour away. Aside from that and a stop at the grocery, that's all I need to drive."

He frowned. "Baby it along, and make sure you're not driving at night or on lonely stretches of highway."

"Hard to avoid in Colorado." She straightened. "But it's not your problem. I appreciate what you did, so much."

She'd just redouble her search for a second job.

The stress of working two jobs might affect her, but it couldn't be worse than this money stress.

And besides, working a second job would keep her from being around her new neighbors. The dad, with the piercing, soulful eyes and the talent for car repair.

And the son, who made her think of all she'd lost.

After cleaning up from the car repair, Dev reluctantly agreed to go out to the picnic with Landon.

As they approached, his eyes went immediately to Emily. Probably because she was at the center of the group. She'd seemed blue before, but now she was laughing at something the white-haired math teacher had said. The math teacher who'd apparently been scolding Landon for not turning in his math homework last week.

The sense that they were a community and he was on the outside was familiar. And a bunch of teachers was just the group to heighten his feelings of inadequacy. But for Landon's sake, he'd go make nice. Set the example of being friendly, not having a chip on his shoulder, not taking things personally.

And if Stan the math teacher gave Landon a hard time again, Dev would take the man aside and have a word with him.

"Hey, it's our new superhero!" That was Annabel Andrews, the art teacher. "This guy made the furnace stop blowing nonstop heat into the art studio. I can finally teach without the windows open."

"And he *got* the cafeteria windows open, so we're not eating surrounded by the smell of kid sweat," Hayley said, then glanced at Landon. "Sorry, kiddo. I'm not talking about you, but when you get a group of teen and preteen boys in a small room and turn up the heat, things get smelly."

"I know, I've smelled a locker room," Landon said wryly, and everyone laughed. It made Dev proud of his son, that he could speak to a group of adults without acting all shy and embarrassed.

"He's not going to live with the boys?" Stan asked, his voice hearty.

"No. He needs to stay with me." No way was he gaining custody of his son and then shipping him off to boarding school, even if Landon's quarters would be just on the other side of the school grounds.

"The kids are seeing a movie tonight," Annabel said. "Something horrible, with monsters. I'm sure you could join them just for the movie, Landon, if you want to."

"Can I, Dad?"

It was a good plan. Landon would get to know some of the other boys better, and this group of teachers wouldn't have a student in their midst, inhibiting their conversation. "Sure, I'll walk you down. Where is it?" he asked the group.

"Big brick building behind the barn. Emily, could you show them?" That was Richard Cunningham, the vice principal of the school. Landon had already found out he was the man in charge of discipline.

"Um…sure. Of course." She forced a smile. "If we hurry, we'll get there in time for you to see the beginning of the movie, I think. They usually start at eight."

She led the way to the road and then stepped back to walk beside them. The sun's glow was fading behind the mountains, but it still cast enough light to see the rocks, tall pines and thin, lacy leaves of the wildflowers that would burst into bloom next month.

"It's cold out here," Landon said. He was walking close to Dev, Emily on the other side.

Dev found the air bracing, and the stars, beginning to grow visible, seemed thicker, denser than back in the city. It reminded him of living with his favorite foster family, the ones with the farm. He'd lived there for three years and had learned his basic handyman skills there.

The placement had been great, until it ended. Every placement had ended for Dev, some quicker than others. He hadn't been a bad kid—no worse than most, anyway—but his school struggles had made him act out.

Kind of like Landon. But that was going to change.

Landon and Emily were chatting about something, and Dev was glad. Emily was a good influence on his son, Dev could already tell. She didn't come on too strong, but she was truly interested in kids and seemed to respect what they had to say. Even now, she was listening closely as Landon went on and on about a movie he'd seen. She actually asked relevant questions about the plot and actors and said she wanted to see it, too.

More than Dev had done the last three times Landon had given him a blow-by-blow account of that same movie, he had to admit.

"Here we are," Emily said. She slid open a barn-style door and spoke to the woman inside. The smell of pizza filled the air.

"Movie's just starting," the woman said after introducing herself to Dev and greeting Landon. "Get yourself a drink and some pizza and find a seat."

Landon grabbed three slices, the hot dog he'd just eaten notwithstanding. He made his way to an empty seat, already stuffing pizza into his mouth.

"He's going to fit in fine," Emily said as they headed

back toward the bonfire. "He seems like a good kid, comfortable in his own skin."

"He is." That was the wonder of Landon: even with divorced parents, a dad with reading issues that had held him back professionally and a mom who was none too dependable, he was essentially secure. "I mean, I guess none of the kids here are what would really be considered good kids, since they're at a school for conduct issues."

She shrugged. "A lot of them made one mistake. Or they had school issues, undiagnosed learning disabilities and the like, and they acted out."

He liked that she saw it that way, realized that some things weren't a kid's fault. "You don't have kids?"

She didn't answer, didn't seem to hear. Instead, she knelt and focused on something on Lady's paw.

Dev breathed in the sharp, pine-scented air and lifted his face to study the emerging stars. So many, so far away.

"The stars are pretty, aren't they?" She stood and lifted her face to them, and they started to stroll again. He was conscious that she hadn't answered his question about kids, but maybe it had been a rude one. Women were always getting asked intrusive questions about their reproductive plans and issues—at least, that was what his ex had said.

"Do they make you feel small, the stars?" she asked him.

He'd never thought about it. "I guess…they make me feel like there are infinite possibilities." His cheeks heated. He wasn't normally the poetic type.

"I like that," she said. "Infinite possibilities. Hmm. What would you wish for?"

He knew the answer before she'd even gotten the

question out, but no way was he sharing it with her. So he said another wish, just as important if not more. "I want Landon to have everything he wants."

"So you're planning to spoil him?"

The question made his head whip around to glare at her, and then he realized she was joking. "Yeah, I'm buying him a pony and a sports car," he joked back.

"Get me a sports car, too, while you're at it."

He laughed. "What color?"

"Is there any color other than red?"

He could picture her in a sports car, her hair flying in the wind. "You'd look good in a red convertible."

She snorted. "Right. But back to Landon. Does he actually have a conduct issue, or did you just enroll him here because you got the job?" As soon as the words were out, she lifted her hands. "Sorry. That's personal and I have no right to know it, not unless it affects his work in my class."

"It's okay. He's like what you said before. He made one mistake." Then he wondered whether he was making excuses for Landon, like Roxy always did. He didn't want Landon to catch that habit, so he corrected himself. "It was a serious mistake, and the fact that there were serious consequences is good for him. He needs to learn to take responsibility for mistakes he makes."

"What did he do?" she asked, her voice curious, and then she clapped her hand over her mouth. "There I go again. Sorry."

"It's okay," he said. He figured she'd find out soon enough. He'd worked in a school before and knew that gossip spread faster than the flu. "He set a fire."

Three

The next day Emily was still reeling from the revelation that Landon had set a fire. So it just figured that she'd look at her individual consultation schedule and see Landon's name on it, in the last slot of the day. *Diagnostic Reading Test* was the notation beside his name.

She focused on reshelving books while she waited for him to arrive. It was no more than she deserved. If working with a child exactly the same age, coloring and gender her own son would have been—a kid who'd set a *fire* of all things—was part of the job, well, she'd suck it up and do it well. She owed Landon the help and support.

Her thoughts flickered to Landon's father. He'd noticed her gasp about the fire, of course, and had quickly explained that no one had been hurt. Landon had set the fire in a trash can in the school restroom after something upsetting had happened in class—Dev wasn't sure what—and he'd actually been trying to put it out when the fire alarm had gone off. But the school had a zero-tolerance policy for dangerous actions on the part of students, and now, he was barred from any regular schools in his own district. It had seemed like a good time for a change.

She'd been curious about Landon's mother, how she fit in, but Dev hadn't said anything about that. He'd only said that he'd gotten custody and permission to move Landon to Bright Tomorrows, two hours northwest of Denver.

She went back into her office and checked on Lady, who was napping on her rug. And then Lady lifted her head, and stood, and Landon was at the door.

"I hafta work with you," he said. He came into the library and dumped the contents of his backpack on the table, shoulders slumped. The cheerful kid from last night was gone.

She smiled at him. "You *get* to work with me, at least for today," she said. "But first, Lady wants to say hello. She perked right up when you came in." She slid the dog's harness off and let her go to Landon. Though she was Emily's service dog, she was good for the students, too. In practice, she was an unofficial therapy dog for the school. Not exactly best practice, according to the service dog training facility where Emily had gotten her and learned to work with her. But given Emily's life and her job, and Lady's personality, it all made sense.

Sure enough, Landon's tension eased.

"Okay, let's look at some books," she said, conscious that she only had half an hour with Landon.

He frowned. "Can Lady come?"

Normally, she wouldn't have done it, thinking the dog would be a distraction, but it was the last class of the day. Plus, she'd developed feelings for Landon. Which probably wasn't healthy, but there it was. "Sure, she can come. She might want us to look at the dog books first."

"She doesn't read books," Landon scoffed, but when she led him and Lady to the section where the animal books were shelved, he seemed marginally interested. They both knelt down to look at the low shelf.

"Go ahead and pull out three or four books that look good to you," she said. "Then we'll take a look and see which ones would be right for you to read." She always found that having students choose their own reading material worked best.

Landon pulled out a big encyclopedia of dogs and then a couple of books about specific breeds. Then he grabbed another featuring assistance animals, and one more about K-9 police dogs.

"Good choices," she said. "Now, let's do the finger test to see which is the best for you to read."

His mouth twisted to one side.

"You've probably done it before. Hold up one finger for each word you don't know on the first page."

He grabbed the encyclopedia of dogs, opened it up and looked at the first page. "I can read all the words," he said within seconds.

She was pretty sure he hadn't even glanced at the text but rather was drawn to the color photos of dogs. "You need to read it aloud," she said gently.

He looked at the text page for a minute and then thrust it aside. "I don't like this book."

"It's pretty hard," she said. "Want to try another?"

He picked up the one about K-9 police dogs. Good. It was at a second-grade reading level at most.

Landon opened to the first page, looked it over. Then, suddenly, he stood and hurled the book across the room. "I don't wanna read now! Reading is dumb!" He kicked at the other books.

"Landon! Stop it." She pulled the scattered volumes out of the way of his kicking feet. "We treat books with respect. Especially library books. They're for everyone."

"Not for me!" He rubbed a fist under his eye and ran toward the door.

His father was coming in, and Landon crashed into him. Dev caught the boy by the upper arms. "Hey, hey, no running in school. What's going on?"

Emily took a moment to shelve the books, all but the one he'd thrown. Dev had led Landon back into the library.

"She said books are for everybody, but they're not for me." Landon kicked at a table leg.

"What's this all about?" Dev asked Emily.

"I did say books are for everyone," she said, deliberately calming her voice. "We were talking about taking good care of books, after Landon threw one and kicked some others."

"Whoa. You can't do that." Dev's voice went deeper, and Landon looked just a little scared.

She picked up the police dog book and held it out to Dev. "This is the one he threw," she said. "I think he was frustrated because it looks so interesting, but it's a little too hard for him to read."

A pained look crossed Dev's face, so quickly she might have imagined it. "You need to apologize," he told Landon. "And if Ms. Carver wants to assign you another chore, you need to do it. You'll definitely have an extra chore at home."

"If you're giving him a consequence, that's plenty," Emily said. "And maybe you two would like to check out the book. Landon, after you've done your chore, your dad can read it with you."

Identical frowns crossed the two faces.

"He won't read it to me," Landon said.

So much for her brilliant idea.

"That's not my job, it's yours." Dev's voice was sharp as he handed the book back to her.

"Fine." Emily pressed her lips together to keep from snapping at them both. She carried the book back to the shelf to give herself time to cool down.

Why did men think they didn't need to model reading, or that the job of reading aloud fell to the mother? She took a couple of deep breaths. Lady, who'd been dozing in her office, came trotting out to her side.

She walked back toward Dev and Landon. Dev stood, arms crossed, while Landon loaded schoolbooks and papers back into his backpack. Clearly Landon had been scolded; he was blinking away tears.

"Tell her you're sorry."

"I'm sorry."

"Tell her what you're sorry for."

"I'm sorry I threw and kicked the books."

"Apology accepted." She felt the strongest urge to reach out and give Landon a hug. He was still just a little boy, really. "We can meet another day to talk about reading."

He nodded, looking down at the floor.

She looked up at Dev. "And maybe you and I should have a talk soon, too," she said.

He rubbed the back of his neck. "Sure," he said. "Sometime." And then he and Landon hurried out of the library.

Don't get involved. They're not your responsibility outside school hours.

Yet she had to admit, she was curious about the father-son pair. Drawn to them, even. Rudeness and all.

Friendliness and surliness alternated in both of them like a spinning coin—you never knew ahead of time which side would turn up. That wasn't unusual for new students here, and the reasons for it weren't her business. A better teacher would stay objective, focused on academics, and let the school counselors handle the emotions.

But there was something about the pair that kept plucking at her, drawing her in, making her care.

All the more reason to keep them at a distance, so she didn't start hoping for things she didn't deserve and couldn't have.

The day after Landon's disastrous reading experience, Dev walked into the school office and found a note in his little mailbox, one of a row in a wooden grid of open-front boxes. He studied the handwriting, then looked through the office's glass wall. Outside it, kids milled around in the lobby area, talking, laughing, play-punching each other.

He studied the note again, the letters swimming before his eyes, then glanced over at Mrs. Henry, the office secretary. "Forgot my glasses," he said, holding the note far away from him and squinting at it. "What's this about?"

"Let me see."

He handed her the note, relieved.

She looked at it and laughed. "Dr. Green has terrible handwriting. She wants to see you in her office sometime this morning, at your convenience."

"Thanks." He smiled at her. "No time like the present, I guess."

He tapped on the principal's half-opened door. "Dr. Green? You wanted to see me?"

"Come in," she said from behind her computer, and he walked into a book-lined office furnished with an old, scarred desk and gray metal filing cabinets.

Ashley Green had hired Dev and was well respected by students and staff alike, as far as Dev could see. Pretty, too, if you liked the buttoned-up type.

She peered out at him from behind thick glasses, then stood. "Ah, yes, Dev. And please, call me Ashley."

"Sure." Though she seemed like a formal-titles type. Every inch a principal and a boss.

"Thank you for stopping in. I need to talk to you about Landon. Close the door, would you? And then have a seat."

Dev's stomach turned over as he closed the door, then sat in one of the chairs in front of her desk. She picked up a paper file and then sat in the chair beside him.

"Is Landon in trouble?" he asked. He'd punished the boy for throwing the book, but he hadn't explored the incident in too much detail. It struck too close to home.

Had Emily ratted Landon out?

But he shouldn't think of it that way. It might be that she was obligated to report the incident.

"No, he's not in trouble," she said. "He's a nice boy and seems to be fitting in well."

"Okay, good." Then what was this about?

"But he's behind in academics." Ashley tapped the folder she held. "We always consult about new students after their first week, see whether their placement is correct and whether they need extra help. Landon's records indicate that he passed second grade last year, so he was placed in third grade. But he's not doing so well there, at least from the looks of things."

"He's still adjusting," Dev said. His head spun with worries. He'd never been in an academic conference about Landon before; Landon's mom had always handled that end of things, or at least she'd told him she was handling it. Only lately had he learned that Roxy had been a no-show at most of the conferences the teachers at Landon's old school had tried to schedule.

He didn't know whether he was even allowed to argue, if disagreeing with a principal was inappropriate, but what else could he do? "He's a very smart boy. It's just that everything's new to him."

"Of course," the principal said, her voice soothing. "It'll take him a while to get his feet on the ground, and maybe that's all this is. But all three of his teachers indicated that he didn't seem to pay attention to what they were writing on the board, though he did fine in class discussions. That's why we decided to have him visit Emily, but she said the preliminary reading test didn't go well. Didn't even happen, as a matter of fact."

"Right." He sighed. "I'm sorry Landon didn't behave. He was punished."

"Well, but more than that, we're wondering if he acted out because he's having problems with reading. It's at this grade level that those kinds of issues really catch up with kids, because they need to be able to read in various subjects, not just language arts."

"But he's so young," Dev said. "You can't expect him to read history or philosophy."

She smiled. "Of course not. But all children's textbooks require some reading skills. Science, social studies. Even math has word problems."

"Can't the teachers work with him?" He wondered whether Landon would get poorer treatment because he wasn't a tuition-paying student.

"Of course. Emily, in particular, can help him with reading skills."

"Good." His face heated as he remembered how he'd rudely told her that teaching Landon was her job. She'd only been making a normal suggestion, that he read to his son at home.

He thought of how she'd looked, shelving the books. Nimble, quick, athletic. She seemed to be in great shape, somehow not what he'd expect from a librarian and reading teacher.

She appealed to him like honey to a bear who'd just come out of hibernation. And he shouldn't feel that way, because a woman like her wouldn't have anything to do with a man like him, especially if she found out his secret inadequacy.

A better person would just breezily confess he had trouble reading, act confident, get help. But Dev wasn't that kind of person. Too many years of being told he was stupid and worthless. Words said when you were a kid really stuck with you, made you who you were. That was why he was always careful to boost Landon's self-image when he could.

But parents weren't the only influence. At Landon's age, peers and teachers played an increasingly big role in what he thought of himself.

He had to make sure Landon wasn't seen as stupid or treated as deficient.

"...I'd also like for you to think about the possibility of holding him back a grade," the principal was saying.

Dev tuned back in and stared at her. "What?"

"Having him repeat third grade might be the best thing to do. That way, he'd—"

"No." He barked out the word without thought, because he instantly knew holding Landon back would be the wrong thing to do.

She tilted her head to one side. "Of course it's early times, and we'll have to see how he does between now and the end of school. But if he can't catch up, if he fails in the final grading period, we really wouldn't have a choice."

"No way. I don't want him to repeat third grade." Dev gripped the arms of the chair, hard.

"We don't do social passes here at Bright Tomorrows." Her voice was firm. "And there's no shame in repeating a grade."

Yes, there is. Landon was already big for his age, and if he was held back a year, he'd be a giant. He'd be that big kid in the class who was behind the younger, smaller, smarter kids. Who was ridiculed and labeled.

Like Dev had been.

"You'll need to work with him, then," she said. "Sit with him while he's doing his homework. Help him understand his textbooks. Possibly, get him some extra tutoring, beyond what we do here at the school."

He nodded quickly, stood. "I'll do it. We'll get him caught up. Thanks, Ashley." He turned and hurried out of the office, even though he could tell from her face that she wasn't finished talking to him.

He walked down the hall, but the place seemed too stifling for him. Memories of his own childhood, going from new school to new school, having a week or so of grace until someone discovered his lack of academic skills—all of it pressed in on him.

He'd survived, but it had been miserable. He wanted so much more for Landon.

He strode out through the double doors and walked toward the river that wound its way beside the school. The water sparkled and rushed. It was a perfect stream for trout.

He wanted to take Landon fishing, teach him how to read the water, show him how to dig for bait. He wanted to fry up fish for dinner, fish they'd just caught that day. It was part of what he'd dreamed of when he'd gotten the chance to move to the mountains.

But it looked like Landon would have another use for his free time. Homework. Studying. Tutoring.

Landon needed help with homework. He needed someone to read him books that interested him. Someone to help him catch up and get on track to a better life.

But that person definitely wasn't Dev. Not when he could barely read himself.

He was going to have to suck it up and ask Emily to tutor Landon, even though the very notion made him a little sick, thinking how hard it would be to hide his own inadequacies from someone who was around all the time, tutoring his son.

He hated to admit to himself that the notion of spending more time around Emily revved him up, like an old, decrepit car engine finally turning over and starting to run. Which was ridiculous and wrong. He should advertise for another tutor, since Emily, off-limits Emily, awakened so much that had been safely dormant in him.

But he couldn't tame the excitement that stirred in

him at the thought of working with her to help Landon. She was sweet and caring, the opposite of Landon's mom in many ways. She'd be good for Landon, he knew it.

He listened to the sound of the rushing water, smelled the sage-scented breeze and let it cool him. If Dev took Landon fishing, and he liked it, no doubt Emily would find him a book on fishing to read. She seemed to pay close attention to kids' interests and build on them.

The trouble was, if Landon brought home books and wanted help reading them, Dev couldn't help. And that awareness opened a hollow wound in his chest that no excitement about a pretty reading teacher could fill.

Four

It was the Saturday before Easter, and Emily was still feeling troubled about Dev and Landon and all they'd stirred up inside her. She hoped helping with the church's annual Easter Egg hunt would heal that, would help her get it off her mind and move her toward a sense of Easter peace.

Hayley, though, apparently had other ideas.

"I'm so glad you came early to help hide the eggs," she said, tucking a pink plastic one behind a rock. "I wanted to ask you how your reading lesson with Landon went, but with being away visiting my family, I haven't seen you."

"It went okay. Do you think we should put some of these out in plain sight, for the little kids?"

"Definitely. And some well hidden, because they're letting kids up to age twelve participate. What do you mean, it went okay?"

Emily shrugged, placing a couple of eggs out in the open and then standing, pushing her hands on her lower back to stretch.

The white church nestled against the foothills that

surrounded the town of Little Mesa. A couple of backpackers walked by, talking and laughing, no doubt headed for the popular hiking trail that skirted the town.

They were accompanied by a golden retriever with a small pack of his own. Beside Emily, Lady watched the other dog but didn't bark or lunge. "Good girl," Emily murmured and gave her a small treat.

She breathed in the pine-scented air from the foothills. *Calm. Peace.*

Hayley nudged her. "Come on, let's hide some in back. Was the session with Landon really that bad?"

So much for peace, but maybe it would help to talk to Hayley about it. "Cone of silence," she said, and Hayley nodded. "He got very upset when I tried to get him to read aloud. Threw a book, in fact. When his dad came to get him and I suggested they check out a book and read together, Dev told me helping Landon was my job."

Hayley frowned. "That doesn't sound like Dev. From what I've seen, he seems like an involved dad."

"He does," Emily agreed, kneeling to tuck a couple of eggs in the stone wall that separated the church from the mountain. "Maybe he just doesn't think reading is important. Or maybe it doesn't seem manly to him. Lots of men are like that."

"Finished, ladies?" Nate Fisher came out the back door of the church and surveyed their work. "The kids are starting to arrive out front. I think Mrs. Poole has bunny ears for you."

Hayley raised an eyebrow. "Where are *your* bunny ears, Pastor?"

He grinned. "I have to put on the whole bunny suit. You got off easy with just the ears."

They went around front, and sure enough, Mrs. Poole,

who ran most things in the church, handed them ears and directed them to their stations. Kids of all ages and sizes were trickling toward the church, and the sight stirred something deep inside Emily.

She was thirty-five, and she wasn't going to have the chance to have another baby, but that didn't mean she didn't care. In fact, her biological clock seemed to be functioning particularly well these days.

Maybe helping out at kids' events wasn't the best way to gain a sense of peace and acceptance about her life.

"Senorita Emily!" A dark-haired little boy hurled himself into her arms. "I'm going to get all the eggs!"

She knelt to hug him. "There's a limit. Five eggs per kid, I think."

He pouted.

His grandmother appeared behind him and greeted Emily in Spanish, and they discussed the event and their Easter plans. "There's a short lesson for the children before the egg hunt starts," Emily explained. *"Muy corto,"* she added as Mateo's eyebrows drew together, holding her forefinger and thumb an inch apart. "And afterward, you'll get to run around and find all kinds of sweets, if it's okay with your *abuela*."

"I want the sweets first," he said, earning a short lecture from his grandmother.

Hayley came over and heard the tail end of the conversation. "Can you help? Unbeknownst to me, Pastor Nate scheduled me to teach the lesson, and I need someone to translate into Spanish." Some of the families in their church spoke Spanish as their primary language. One service each week was conducted in Spanish, but since church events brought all members together, Pastor Nate tried to make them bilingual. Emily was fluent in Spanish, while Hayley was a beginner.

Hayley taught a simple lesson about Christ's sacrifice and how sins could be forgiven because of it, and Emily translated, and the kids were adorable. "If I yelled at my brother, could I be forgiven?" one little girl asked, glancing at the toddler on her mother's lap.

"Yes, absolutely," Hayley said. "But we try to do better all the time, because we love Jesus."

"Will I be forgiven if I take some extra eggs?" Mateo asked with a grin, earning another frown from his *abuela*.

"Forgiven, yes, but there are likely to be consequences," Emily said.

She felt a longing for the simple faith the children had. A longing to ask if she, too, could be forgiven for her own sins, so much vaster than these children's.

Of course, she knew in her head that God was all powerful and could forgive all sins. But in her heart, she didn't quite believe it.

Once the egg hunt started, Emily and Hayley and the other helpers stayed busy. The little kids were allowed to go first, and when the bigger ones joined, they were warned to be careful of the smaller ones. Most of the kids were great about it, the older ones helping and sharing, and Emily was touched. Her skills at speaking Spanish came in handy a couple more times, and she reminded herself that life could be good as a single person, that she could do a lot of good.

She was starting to feel the peace she'd been looking for. To open to the reality of Easter, the reawakening of the spring world around her, the possibility of new life.

As she leaned against the stone wall, watching the

colorfully dressed children running around to try to find the last eggs, she noticed someone running toward the church. Two people, actually.

Dev and Landon.

Landon's brow was wrinkled, and he kept turning to gesture toward Dev, beckoning for him to hurry up. He must realize he'd missed most of the egg hunt. Dev was yelling at him to slow down and watch for cars.

Both of them spotted Emily and came toward her.

Even though they'd parted on a bad note, a rude note.

Great. What was Dev going to do now—tell her it was her job to fix the egg hunt for Landon?

Dev slowed to a walk as Landon sprinted toward Emily.

She stood beside a shorter, older woman as the activity of the egg hunt swirled around them. Wound down, unfortunately. It looked like things were over.

Emily looked fresh-faced and young in a pink sweater, jeans and bunny ears. He found himself wondering if she smelled like strawberries, the way she had last week.

As Landon approached and started talking to her, she held up a finger, indicating that he should wait until she'd finished her conversation with the older lady. Good. Dev caught up in time to catch the tail end of it; she was telling the woman, in Spanish, that it was fine that her grandson had snagged an extra egg, but maybe they could ask him to share it with someone who hadn't gotten their share.

"What's she saying, Dad?" Landon asked.

Dev explained. "It sounds like the hunt is over, but there may be a few kids with extra eggs who can share."

Emily glanced at him, looking surprised. *"Hablas español?"*

"Si, un poco." He normally didn't think much about the fact that he spoke and understood Spanish pretty well, but now he was glad. He smiled at the older lady. *"Buenas días, Señora,"* he added, and Emily introduced them. They chatted for a moment, and then the woman excused herself and hurried over to a little boy who was stuffing candy into his mouth.

Landon was near tears. "I made us late and now I missed the hunt," he said, his voice shaky. He started to pet Lady, but Emily pointed to the service dog's vest and shook her head.

Landon's tears overflowed.

Dev tensed and then reminded himself to take deep breaths. Of course, it was okay for boys to cry, but that didn't mean it was comfortable for Dev to see it happen. He'd had one foster father who'd beaten him for it, and others who'd made fun, and he'd quickly learned not to show the softer emotions himself.

But he wanted Landon to have a different sort of childhood, different values. "There'll be other candy for Easter," he said, putting a hand on his son's shoulder.

"But I wanted to *hunt*!"

Emily snapped her fingers. "You know what? We may need someone to help us as things wind down. We kept count of all the eggs so nothing gets left around for animals to get into." She called to Hayley, the cafeteria head from the school, who also sported bunny ears. "Any eggs still missing?"

"Three," Hayley called back.

"I have a helper who will find them, maybe." She raised an eyebrow at Dev, who nodded permission, and she put an arm around Landon and guided him around the side of the church.

"Nice girl," said a voice behind Dev, and he turned to see his cousin Nate, who'd helped him get the job at Bright Tomorrows. "How's it going?"

"Everything's good now," Dev said. "You know Emily?" He didn't want to ask, but he couldn't help it; the woman made him curious.

"Yes. She hasn't had an easy time of it. Well, neither have you and I, for that matter, but her situation was a lot worse than ours."

"Really? She seems to have it together." Although she did have her service dog at her side today, like usual.

"She's resilient. But I pray for her."

Devon looked sharply at his cousin. "Why? Are you interested in her?"

Nate laughed. "No. I pray for a lot of people. You included." He lifted an eyebrow. "Sounds like *you're* interested."

Dev's face heated. "No. No way. A teacher's not my type."

"Dad! Dad!" Landon came running from behind the church, three eggs in his hands. Emily followed, laughing, a lilting sound like bells. The wind blew her hair across her face, and she brushed it back.

"You sure she's not your type?" Nate said in a low voice.

"Can it." He bent to look at Landon's eggs, then straightened and met Emily's eyes. "Thank you for helping him. I appreciate the second chance."

"Everyone needs a second chance sometimes," she said evenly, meeting his gaze.

Their eyes held for a moment longer than they should have.

Landon sat down on the ground and opened the first egg. Several pieces of brightly wrapped candy were there, along with a slip of pink paper. Landon studied it, then handed it up to Dev. "What's this say, Dad?"

Dev's insides constricted. Emily was standing there, and so was his cousin. He studied the paper, the letters dancing in front of him.

He was forty years old and couldn't read a piece of paper meant for kids. What did that say about him?

Given time, he might be able to puzzle it out. But not when he was on the spot, with an audience.

His heart rate picked up, heating his face, his whole body. Wasn't that just like a teacher, a pastor, a church, putting something to read inside an Easter egg? Ridiculous.

But she and Nate had been nothing but kind to him and Landon. It was wrong of him to be angry. He shouldn't—couldn't—let them see how he felt.

Mostly, he was mad at himself for being such an idiot.

He looked at the families around him and saw mothers and fathers oohing and aahing over their children's treasures. No doubt they were all easily able to read the papers to their children.

"Can I see?" Nate asked, taking the paper from Dev's hand. "I didn't get a chance to look these over before Mrs. Poole organized everyone and got the eggs stuffed." He read aloud. "'He is risen! He is not here.' Oh, good, the verses are in Spanish and English." He knelt and held the paper out to Landon. "See? There's a picture of an empty tomb. We'll talk about it more in church tomorrow."

"Cool." Landon was more occupied with the candy.

As for Dev, the sweat dripped down his back as his heart rate settled back to normal. Relief. Emily hadn't noticed anything.

Nate, though, was looking at him thoughtfully. His cousin the pastor was pretty smart. If he put what had just happened together with the kind of support he'd had to give Dev to help him get the job…yeah.

If he hadn't already, he might very soon guess Dev's secret.

The next day was Easter. After the sunrise service, Emily helped put chairs away. So did Landon and Dev. She hadn't realized that they were related to the pastor until yesterday, but now she could see a slight family resemblance. Both tall, square jawed, muscular. Landon, at eight, was headed in the same direction, big and strong for his age.

They walked out together to the parking lot. Emily was relieved they'd gotten friendly again, although she was also still irritated that he didn't want to help his son with reading. She wished them a happy Easter and got in her car.

When she turned it on—or tried to—nothing happened.

"Come on, come on…" She didn't need this delay. She needed to get going if she was going to make it over the mountain and to her mother's care center in time for the big Easter dinner.

She tried again, and this time the car turned over, made a horrible sound and died.

She let her head rest on the steering wheel for just a minute.

It was Easter. She *had* to visit her mom.

Granted, Mom might not even recognize her, know she was there or remember it later, but what if she did? What if today was a rare good day, and Emily missed it…and worse, Mom felt alone and abandoned on this holiday?

There was a knock on her car window. She turned her head to the side and recognized Landon's concerned face. She read his lips as he asked, "What's wrong, Miz Carver?"

She sighed and got out of the car. "It won't start," she said. She shivered in the cool mountain air. She'd worn an Easter dress, but it really wasn't warm enough for it. She'd welcomed the outdoor heaters Pastor Nate had put around the courtyard where they'd held the service.

Landon nodded. "That's what Dad thought. You can get a ride home with us."

"I was supposed to visit my mother," she said, biting her lip. She looked across the parking lot and saw Dev climbing out of his truck.

"My dad doesn't have time to fix your car today," Landon said as Dev approached, "because *my* mom's coming to see me today." He sounded excited.

Surprised, she looked at Dev.

"He's right, we do have to get back to the cabin," Dev said. "But we can run you home. At least you won't be stuck here."

"Come on, Ms. Carver, hurry!"

What else could she do? It wasn't as if she was going to fix the car herself, here in the church parking lot in her Easter finery.

Besides, she admitted to herself, she was curious about Landon's mother. What kind of woman had Dev chosen for a wife?

What kind of woman would let Dev and Landon go?

The ride back to the cabins went quickly. Landon chattered away about what he and his mother were going to do and what she might bring him.

Emily was grateful for the distraction. She felt awful about not seeing her own mom.

When they arrived at the cabins, a white SUV was pulling into Dev's driveway. Landon barreled out the moment the truck stopped. He ran toward the car. "Mom!"

Emily was watching him, so she saw the moment when he slowed, stopped and stepped back.

A woman got out of the passenger side. A man got out of the driver's side.

Dev muttered something under his breath, got out of the car and strode over.

There was nothing for Emily to do but get out, too. So she heard the unhappy little family drama.

"She brought her boyfriend," Landon said to his father, sounding deflated.

"He has a name," the woman said with a forced-sounding laugh. "Landon, Dev, this is Adam."

The man, a very handsome, fine-featured man in hiking clothes, stuck out a hand. "Glad to meet you both," he said.

Landon ignored the offered handshake, but Dev shook the other man's hand, his expression as impassive as the high rocky cliffs that surrounded them.

The man named Adam, oblivious, looked over Dev's shoulder and gave Emily a wave, too. "Hey. Nice day."

"Look," Landon's mom said, strolling over and putting a casual arm around Landon, "I didn't realize you were this far out in the middle of nowhere. Our ski group is meeting up in Vail. So do you mind if we just hang out here instead of going out and doing something?"

She was acting so casual and blasé about the chance to spend time with her son, as if she were a distant relative or a friend, not Landon's mom. Emily shouldn't judge—she didn't know the woman. But she'd lost her chance to hold her own child six years ago. Seeing Landon's mother reach out a hand for her boyfriend, even as she was supposed to be focused on her son, made Emily furious.

"Come on," the woman said, looking from the boyfriend to Landon and back again. "Let's hang out on the porch. Landon will get us something to drink."

To his credit, the outdoorsy boyfriend backed off, hands out. "I'll give you two some mother-son time. Do a little hiking around."

Relief was evident on Landon's face. Obviously, he wanted his mom to himself. "I'll show you my room and my school, Mom," he said, hugging her and holding on, his arms wrapped tightly around her.

She looked sad and happy at the same time, and some of Emily's anger drained away. It had to be hard to live two hours away from your child. Maybe the mother's distant attitude and focus on her boyfriend was an effort to protect her heart.

"How long can you stay, Mom?" Landon let go of her waist and grabbed her hand, clinging onto it with both hands, bouncing up and down.

"Oh, most of the day," she said. "If that's okay with your dad."

From behind him, Emily saw Dev square his shoulders. “That’s fine,” he said. “I’ll just…give you a little space, too.”

“Good idea,” Landon’s mom said promptly.

Adam opened the door of the SUV. “I’ll drive over to the trailhead we passed on the way up,” he said to Landon’s mother. “Call me when you’re ready to go.”

He climbed in and roared off.

“Come on!” Landon tugged at his mother’s hand, and they disappeared into Dev’s cabin.

Dev stood watching them and then turned back toward his truck. His shoulders sagged a little. He seemed surprised to see Emily still standing there.

She couldn’t help it; she was concerned. “Are you okay?” she asked him bluntly.

“Ah, sure. Whatever works for them.” Then he tilted his head to one side. “How about I drive you for a quick visit with your mom?”

The thought of spending two hours in the truck with Dev brought mingled horror and joy into Emily’s heart. “Oh, Dev, you don’t have to do that.”

He lifted his hands, palms up. “I’ve got nowhere else to go, and your car’s not working. I’m in the way here.”

“Don’t you want to stick around in case Landon needs you?”

He shrugged. “Kind of, but he’s with his mom. He’s probably safer here with her than driving around somewhere.”

“Oh, well…” The chance to see her own mother trumped her worries. “If you’re sure.”

“I’d be glad to,” he said. “Let’s go.”

She followed him to his truck and wondered, would a long drive with the handsome, mysterious handyman be an Easter blessing…or a big mistake?

Five

As they headed down the road toward Emily's mother's care home, Emily leaned back, enjoying the chance to take in the scenery rather than worrying about her temperamental car. To the right, the mountains stood like giants pushing up the sky. Here in the broad valley, morning sunshine cast a glow over the fields. Herds of cattle clustered along the foothills, seeming to need togetherness in the vastness of the land.

There was almost no traffic, and Emily felt like she and Dev were alone in the world. She'd even left Lady at home when she'd noticed the dog wasn't feeling well; Lady had a finicky stomach, and she didn't want to put her through the long day of driving and sitting quietly at the care home.

Dev had turned up the heat when they'd gotten in, and now she was warm enough that she started to slip off her sweater. And then a wave of self-consciousness hit her; he'd see her scars, up close and personal. A messy-looking red-and-white patchwork up and down both arms, a reminder of the night she'd dragged her mother from the fire that had ruined both of their lives.

There was plastic surgery that could help, but it was considered cosmetic, and she wouldn't spend that kind of money on such a vain thing, even if she had it to spend. She'd pay for her mother to have surgery sooner than she'd have it herself, and that wasn't happening. But what did it matter if Dev saw? Let him recoil in horror. She slid off her sweater and held it in her lap, her face warming.

But he didn't seem to notice. "Sorry if the scene back there made you uncomfortable. Landon really misses his mom, so the idea that she was coming to see him got him excited. It just didn't play out quite the way we'd discussed."

"It's nice she came to see him."

Dev let out a snort. "She *came* up into the mountains to ski. Landon's just a side trip."

He sounded bitter, and she couldn't blame him if what he'd said was true. "It did seem that way, a little. Are you... Do you get along? Was it a hostile breakup?"

He took a hand off the steering wheel, flattened it and tilted it from side to side. "Somewhat. She cheated, I took her back, she did it again. Lots of door slamming and yelling." He glanced over at her. "Not that unusual of a story, but it was hard on Landon. He was three when the worst of it started, five when we split for good."

"And she got custody?"

He hesitated. "She did, at first. I'm not..." He blew out a breath. "I'm not the smartest when it comes to legal stuff, and she was seeing a lawyer for a while, so...yeah."

"But she let you have custody now, right?"

He nodded. "She wanted custody, initially, to win out over me. And because of how it would look if she *didn't* have custody. But the truth is, she wants a fun lifestyle more than a family one."

Emily's heart ached for Landon and, just a little bit, for the rugged man beside her. His jaw was square, his expression revealing no emotion, but Emily had the feeling there was a world of pain behind his simple words.

The lines that fanned out from the corners of his eyes bespoke a level of experience that she shared. This man hadn't had it easy. He was a book that grabbed her attention, one she'd like to read.

But she ought to know better. Aside from the fact that he was out-of-her-league handsome, she'd already had her chance at a family, and she'd blown it. No way did she deserve another try.

She'd leave it at friendship, because it seemed like Dev needed a friend. No matter that she felt tempted to break her own rules and explore further.

How could any woman have chosen someone else over Dev? Not only was Dev handsome, but he had a thoughtful nature and a big heart full of love for his son.

"My life's not very interesting," he said. "What about you? Any sad love stories in your past?"

His words pulled her back from thinking about Dev as a romantic partner. What business did she have doing that? She bit her lip and stared out at the distant mountain peaks.

He'd told her about his past, and she ought to reciprocate by telling him something about hers. She'd gone through a fair amount of therapy after the fire, and one of the key takeaways was that keeping secrets kept you from healing.

"I'm a widow," she said, and held up a hand to halt his automatic expression of sympathy. "But before you feel all sorry for me, when I lost my husband, we were on the rocks." Then she felt bad for saying it. "Which doesn't mean it wasn't horrible to lose him. He had a family, parents who loved him and are still devastated by the fact that he died." And they blamed Emily for his death, still. "His life was cut short, and no matter the issues in our marriage, it was a terribly, terribly sad thing."

He nodded. "It can be tough to lose someone when you have unresolved issues," he said. "Me and Roxy, at least we can fight it out and get over it. When someone dies, you lose that chance."

"That's true." She'd wanted to rage at Mitch for being too drunk to stay awake and protect their son, but he'd paid the ultimate price. She couldn't find a focus for her anger, couldn't easily purge it.

She also couldn't bring herself to mention the loss of her son to Dev, but that was okay. A little at a time.

They rode along in silence that felt companionable, listened to music, pointed out features of the scenery. Finally, they got close to Mom's care home. "That's the turn, just up ahead." She pointed at the wooden sign that marked the home's long driveway.

Their conversation and Dev's company had distracted her, but now her stomach twisted into the usual knot that came from seeing her mother. It was compounded by the idea of Dev meeting her as well. Mom wasn't easy to be with now, even for Emily, who loved her.

"You don't have to come in," she said as they pulled into the parking lot. "I mean, you're welcome to, if you want. You could at least have Easter dinner with the group. They always have plenty of food. Although… don't get your expectations up too high. It's not exactly gourmet food."

"A little bland? Most places like this don't exactly pile on the spices."

"Exactly. Bland and easy to chew." She wrinkled her nose. "Still, the price of the meal is right, and we don't have to wash the dishes."

"Sounds good to me."

He pulled into a parking space by the side of the low-slung stone building. When he started to climb out, she put a hand on his arm to get his attention. "Mom has good and bad days," she said. "On bad days, she can be tough to be around."

His eyes crinkled, and he put his hand over hers and rubbed. "That's got to be hard," he said. "It's up to you. I don't have to come in, but I can. Either way."

She couldn't let the man sit in his truck for two hours after he'd been kind enough to drive her here. And she had to admit, it would be nice to have some companionship, not to face Mom and her issues alone. "Come on in," she said. "Welcome to my world."

Dev followed Emily into the care home. The woman was a puzzle, and though he shouldn't let himself get too interested in solving it—solving *her*—he found her hard to resist.

Her mom couldn't be very old, so she must have some condition or illness. Put that together with the fact that Emily was a widow who'd had a bad marriage, and his view of the smart, educated reading teacher with the perfect life was undergoing a change.

As soon as they reached the lobby, a woman in scrubs hurried over. "Hey, Emily. Your mom got upset this morning, and we felt like bringing her down to the group meal might upset her more. We can try it, now that you're here, or serve her lunch in her room."

Emily's forehead wrinkled. "Better serve her in her room. We'll keep her company while she eats."

"Want me to bring down a tray for you and your… friend?" She looked at Dev with frank interest, the type that told him Emily didn't often bring men to visit her mom.

That satisfied him way more than it should.

"That would be great, Abby. Thanks." She turned toward one of the hallways and then looked back at Dev. "You may not want to stay. She can get pretty agitated when she's confused or has some memories. It's one of the features of her condition." She must have seen his curious expression, because she added, "She has dementia. Probably early-onset Alzheimer's, although that's hard to diagnose."

"Whoa." Her matter-of-fact tone told him she'd been dealing with this for a while. "She's young, and you're young, to be dealing with that."

"Yeah. She's fifty-eight."

"Do you have other family?"

She shook her head. "Nope, Mom and I are it."

He got that, since his own family was untraditional, but he did have a pretty big network of cousins and former foster siblings. For her to be bearing this alone—not only the emotional pain of it, but the financial burden of care—that had to be tough.

But Emily's face told him that pity, or even an expression of sympathy, wouldn't be welcome right now. "I'll be interested to meet her."

She looked skeptical. "If you're sure."

"I'm sticking with you. At least I'll walk in there and

make sure you're both okay. If it upsets her for me to stay, then I'll go wait in the truck."

"Thanks." She led the way down a hallway and pushed open a door with a flowered wreath on it.

They walked into a simple but pretty room, decorated with a homey comforter and curtains, nature pictures on the walls. The hospital bed was moved to a sitting-up position, and an attendant sat talking to the woman in the bed.

A woman who looked just enough like Emily to be haunting. She had the same auburn hair, though streaked through with gray, the same wide, expressive eyes.

But while Emily had scars only on her arms, this woman had scars over every visible part of her body.

The woman looked up and saw Emily and immediately pushed away the attendant. "I know her. That's my sister Andrea."

"Mom, it's Emily," she said. "Your daughter." She walked over, kissed the woman's cheek and sat down beside her. "Happy Easter."

"Easter!" The woman looked around, eyes wide and eyebrows raised high. "It's not Easter."

"It is, Mom. Are you ready for lunch? They're going to bring us in a couple of trays."

"I'm not hungry." She studied Emily. "I know you from a fire."

Emily's smile seemed to wobble. "You know me because I'm your daughter."

"I'm sorry about the fire. I fell asleep." She looked around wildly. "Where's James?"

Emily's face cramped with pain. "It's okay, Mom. I know you didn't mean to cause the fire."

"Where is he?" She tried to climb out of the bed.

The attendant, who'd moved to stand against the wall, came back over. "Miss Annette, you need to ask for help if you want to get out of bed."

Curiosity flared in Dev. Who was James?

Emily's mother sank back against the headboard and looked around again, and this time, she seemed to see Dev and focus on him. "Who is that man?"

"Mom, this is Dev. He's my friend, and he was kind enough to drive me here to see you."

Dev walked forward, slowly so as not to distress the woman. He also didn't hold out his hand to shake, figuring the sight of a big male hand might make her uncomfortable. "It's nice to meet you. Happy Easter."

She shook her head, staring at him. "I know why you're here. You're here to investigate."

"Nope, I'm not," he said. "I'm just a friend."

"You're here to see if I set the fire or if Mitch did. But we didn't. Not on purpose." She picked at the covers on the bed. "You have to be careful when you're cooking. I know that, Officer."

Dev blew out a breath, sympathy for Emily filling his heart. He wished he could help but just didn't know how.

Emily caught his eyes and shook her head a little. "Mom, Dev is going to wait outside. He's just a friend who gave me a ride."

"It was nice to meet you," he said and walked out to the sound of her mother's voice rising in what sounded like questions.

It put a different perspective on Emily's life, that was for sure.

As he passed the office, he overheard two women arguing. "Leave her alone," one was saying. "It's Easter."

"She needs to get going on this payment plan. We're

working today—she can work, too." They saw him and lowered their voices, leading Dev to think they were talking about Emily.

Dev was starting to see that Emily's life was complicated. Bad enough to have a mother—your only family—in that condition. Having money problems piled on top of that seemed like too much.

He walked out of the building and crossed the parking lot slowly, thinking. This place was expensive; you could tell from how clean it was and how much personal attention the residents seemed to get.

But Emily no doubt was struggling to pay for it on a teacher's salary. Even if her mother received some kind of benefits or had insurance, it wasn't likely to be enough to cover a place like this.

Was there any way he could help?

And then it came to him, as suddenly as the storms rose over the mountains.

He'd been stalling on the request for tutoring, but it was time to take action. Having her tutor Landon would help solve her problems and his, both.

The fact that it might require them to spend more time together was a concern, yes. The more time he spent with Emily, the more interesting she became to him.

But her situation seemed pretty dire, and that trumped any discomfort he might feel.

When Emily emerged from the care center an hour later, dark semicircles of fatigue showed under her eyes, and strands of hair escaped her ponytail. It almost looked like she'd been in a fight, and maybe, in some sense, she had.

"Did the nursing administrator find you?" He hated to ask.

She nodded. "Nothing I didn't know about, but it's become a little more urgent. The money situation, I mean."

"Come on, let's go," he said. "We can pick up a pizza when we get close to home. I have the feeling you didn't eat much Easter dinner, and I also have a guess that Landon's mom isn't cooking him one. I doubt she even made him a peanut butter sandwich."

They climbed into the truck and drove a good ten minutes before she spoke. "Thank you for bringing me. I'm sorry you had to witness all that in there."

"I'm sorry you have to deal with that. It must be hard, seeing your mom that way."

She nodded. "It is. Mom never was perfect, but she loved to read and was a very smart woman. I got my interest in books and libraries from her. And now she can't read or understand anything."

"That's rough," Dev said, even as he was thinking, *It's all about the books with Emily, all about reading.*

As they drove along, he decided it was time to bring up his idea. "Listen, Emily, I've been thinking. Would you consider tutoring Landon after school?"

"Would I consider… Why, Dev?"

"He's not doing well in his academic subjects. They're suggesting that he repeat the third grade, and I really don't want that to happen. He'll be too big and old."

"Do they think tutoring is the answer?"

"Part of it, anyway." He didn't add that tutoring was the only part likely to work, since he himself wasn't able to work with Landon, who'd surpassed Dev's own reading ability last year.

"Hmm, I'll have to think about that," she said. "I need to get a second job to pay for Mom's care, so I won't have a lot of time."

"You don't understand. I'm not asking you to do it for free, I'm offering to pay you. For this to *be* your second job."

Her mouth twisted to one side, and she shook her head. "I need to make some real money, I'm afraid."

"How much do you need?" What she didn't know was that he had a significant nest egg. He'd been saving even before the divorce and more since then, scrimping on clothing for himself, cooking at home, taking advantage of free entertainment. He had earmarked the money for Landon's college education, but the first step was to get him through school and into college—which was less likely to happen if he failed third grade.

"Most private tutors make..." She googled on her phone. "Anywhere from twenty-five to eighty dollars per hour."

"I'll pay you the top end of the range," he said immediately. "And I'd like to start with five hours per week."

She stared at him. "That would basically solve all my money problems, but how..."

"How can I afford it?" He looked over at her. "I'm better off than I appear. Not exactly the millionaire next door, but I've done okay."

"I didn't mean to imply... It's just, I'd like to work for you for less. You've been so kind to me."

"There's no need to work for less. What do you think about taking the job?" He wanted her to do it, wanted to win her time in the same way he wanted to win every softball game he played. He should act neutral, leave it up to her, give her time to consider her situation and interests.

But Landon needed help now, and while she was trapped in the truck with him was probably the best time to make his case. “Landon’s touchy, but he knows and likes you. And I’ve watched you teach. I can tell you’re good at it and you care about the kids. You even live next door to us, so you could work with him after school without either of us having to drive anywhere. To me, it seems ideal. Will you do it?”

“I… Well, I’d love to work with Landon. He’s a good kid. And the salary would be a huge help.”

“Is that a yes?”

She chewed her lower lip, and he had to grip the steering wheel to keep himself from reaching out to her. To what end, he wasn’t quite sure.

“I… Maybe? Let me think about it a little bit.”

“Of course.” Again, there was the totally inappropriate urge to reach out to her.

He pulled into the pizza joint a few miles from the school, went in and ordered a pizza, then he came back out. He’d parked in the shade on the edge of the nearly empty parking lot.

“Twenty to thirty minutes,” he said, climbing back into the truck. “Should have called ahead.”

“I don’t mind waiting. Dev, I’ve decided for sure. I’d love to work with Landon.”

He did a fist pump. “Yes!”

She smiled at him. “And I’m so happy to have my money problems solved. You’ve made a huge difference in my life today. Thank you.”

She reached for him and squeezed his shoulder.

Could he be blamed for reaching up and touching her hand? And once he'd touched it, holding on?

He was just so grateful to her, as if he were the parent of a seriously ill child who'd just been given the medicine that could heal him. He was paying for her services, paying a lot, so he shouldn't feel beholden. A better man would look at this as a simple business transaction, beneficial to all parties, impersonal.

But few enough things in Dev's life had worked out so easily and well. He looked out at the mountains, rising up behind the little pizza place, and this time, they made him feel more than hopeful. They made him feel that God knew what He was doing.

He looked over to say something to that effect and saw that she was watching him. Watching him closely.

He still had his hand on top of hers. All of a sudden, the air in the truck seemed thicker. "Your hair's a mess," he said, reaching over with his other hand to straighten out a strand that had fallen in front of her eyes.

"I… I've had a rough day." She was looking at him, her lips full and maybe trembling a little. She wasn't pulling away.

He was ready to lean forward to kiss her, and from the looks of things, she was going to let him. And then reality slapped him in the face.

He'd possibly ruin Landon's tutoring if he started up something with Emily. Because whatever he started, he couldn't finish it. No way could there be a relationship between someone as smart as Emily and someone like him.

He pulled his hand back, cleared his throat. "Better check on that pizza," he said, making his voice hearty and friendly and unromantic. And then he nearly flung himself out of the truck.

How involved did a parent have to be in his child's tutoring? Because he was getting the feeling he'd better keep a safe distance from the reading teacher with the pretty brown eyes.

When they got back, Landon was sitting outside the cabin on the porch, alone.

Dev slammed on the brakes, jumped out of the truck and strode over. "Hey. Where's Mom?"

"S-s-she left." Landon was trying hard not to cry, Dev could tell, but there were tear tracks on his face.

Dev sat down next to Landon and put an arm around him, consciously unclenching his fists. She'd had less than a day with her son; did she have to leave early? Leave an eight-year-old alone? "How long ago?" he asked when he was sure he could govern his voice.

"A long time ago," he said. "She said she told you she had to leave after lunch."

Dev felt like the veins in his head were going to explode. She *hadn't* told him any such thing. But that was Roxy. She never took responsibility for her own omissions and mistakes.

And Dev was left in the position of either looking like a jerk himself, for not remembering what Roxy had told him, or making Roxy look like a liar. "We must have mixed up our signals," he managed to grit out, compromising.

Making them both look bad.

Emily had looked over at them, but she'd seemed to discern that Landon was okay and her presence wasn't needed. She'd gone into her cabin, and now she reemerged, letting Lady out to do her business.

"Lady!" Landon stood, then looked back at Dev. "Can I pet her?"

"If Ms. Carver says it's okay."

"Mom left a note," Landon called over his shoulder.

Dev did clench his fists at that. Roxy knew he wouldn't be able to read it. Oh, he'd try, sit down with a smartphone and puzzle out the letters in her messy handwriting, put them together and get the computer to speak the message. It would take all evening, but he'd do it.

Being with Emily all day, though, made Roxy's meanness stand out in stark contrast. Leaving him a written note, rather than a text he'd get right away and that he could have his phone read to him...it was just a way to torture him, to make excuses for her own behavior and then escape before he could call her on it.

She just plain stunk as a mother and as a coparent. It was on him to make it up to Landon.

Starting with hiring him an excellent tutor, and then making sure he didn't do anything to spoil the friendly, professional connection between them.

Six

They got started on tutoring right away, and Emily was mostly glad. Landon needed the help, and she needed the money.

But the first session had mixed results.

For one thing, it took place at the kitchen table in Landon and Dev's cabin, and Dev was there, moving in and out of the kitchen, putting on a pot of pasta for dinner, chopping onions, browning beef.

For another, Landon didn't want to be tutored. "I just sat around in school all day," he grumbled, even though she and Dev had arranged that he'd have an hour to be active and play before sitting down to his schoolwork. "I don't need tutoring."

"Yes, you do," Dev said without turning around. "I heard about your social studies test score. Even lower than the last one."

Landon's face, turned away from his father's, screwed up into a scowl.

"Tell you what," Emily said. "Let's talk about what's hardest in school, and what you like the best. That'll help me to plan lessons for you."

"It's all hard." Landon stared out the window, his shoe scuffing against the floor, his shoulders slumped. "I like outdoor time best."

Her heart went out to the child. Being behind in school was tough on a kid—tough on his ego, tough socially. The good news was that at Bright Tomorrows, lots of the kids struggled with academic problems. Landon wouldn't stand out as much as at a regular school. "Okay," she said. "What subject are you most worried about? What makes you feel most upset or unhappy, in the school day?"

Landon shrugged. "All of them."

Emily studied him, sending up a prayer that her creative teacher brain could come up with a way to reach this child. Even though he was acting indifferent, if not defiant, she could see through the facade to a discouraged child who didn't know how to break out of the cycle of failure.

At their feet, Lady shifted and sighed. Landon looked down, and for the first time, his expression lifted. "Can I pet her?"

There it was, the breakthrough idea she'd hoped for. "Yes, in a minute. First, I'm going to write down four words, and you tell me if you can read any of them. Only one is easy." On her big notepad, with a marker, she wrote *dog, poodle mix, lady*. She held the tablet out to Landon.

He glanced over at them. His finger gravitated to the shortest word, one he probably recognized by shape. "D-o-g. Dog."

"Yes, very good. Want to try one of the others?" She was really just trying to assess his reading level, and she had her own idiosyncratic way of doing it, focused on a child's interests. Since Landon didn't want to talk about school subjects, it looked like her one for-certain winner was dogs.

He looked at the next-shortest word. "L-ah-dee," he tried. "Lad?" And then his face fell. "But there's a *y* at the end. Lad-why. That's not a word."

"You're close. Did you ever learn about the *y* at the end of some words, how it can sound like 'eee'?"

He shrugged.

"Try it. Sound it out, with the '*y* that's an eee' sound."

"Lad-eee. Lad-eee." He frowned, and then his eyes widened as he got it. "Lady!" he shouted.

At the sound of her name, Lady looked up, panting, and nuzzled Landon. It was the perfect reinforcement. "Look, I can read your name," he told the dog, and he pointed to the word *Lady* as if the dog could learn to read it, as well.

"She's smart, but she's not that smart," Emily said. "Can you find her name on her tag?"

He knelt immediately, and Lady patiently allowed him to fumble with her collar. Landon did indeed find the word. They went on from there, figuring out "poodle mix," and then looking at other words that had the *y* or the *le* ending, until Landon started to get frustrated.

"English is hard," she said to him. "You're doing well."

"Español es mas fácil?" Dev said, making it sound like a question.

She'd almost forgotten Dev was there, and now she realized he'd been staying quiet and out of the way. "*Si*, it's easier to read. Do you read Spanish?"

He got a funny look on his face and then shook his head. "No, I never learned."

She shrugged. "You must have learned to speak it in the home, then," she said. "Rather than in a class, like I did."

"Yeah. A couple of the places I lived, Spanish was the main language. I had to learn enough to get by."

She studied him. "Places you lived?"

He nodded, added salt to the pasta sauce and tasted it.

"Military family?"

He shook his head. "I grew up in foster care. Lived in a few different homes."

"Eleven!" Landon said from where he lay on the floor, waving a toy in front of Lady's long nose. "Dad lived with eleven different families when he was a kid." He said it like it was some kind of achievement.

Emily looked quickly at Dev and caught the slightest pinch in his expression before he smiled. "Everybody's a record setter in some way or other."

"Sounds rough."

"It was at times, but hey. I learned Spanish and I learned to cook." He used a garlic press to squeeze garlic into a bowl of soft butter, stirred it and then spread it on a split-open loaf of Italian bread.

She leaned back, watching him.

Curiosity about this man who could make the best of a difficult childhood—and who actually owned a garlic press—flashed through her, warm and intense. She didn't want to be nosy, shouldn't be. His childhood wasn't her business, and she ought to be polite and drop the subject.

But this man and his son tugged at her. The more she learned about them, the more she felt for them. And maybe part of it was to do with Landon, with his being the same age her son would have been, but that wasn't all of it. They were a fascinating pair. They'd come through some challenges, Dev with his childhood and both of them with a divorce, and yet they were still positive. She really wanted to know how, what their secret was. "Did you grow up in the Denver area, or all over?"

"Denver and the farm country around it." He slid the bread into the oven. "How about you?"

"Just a few towns over on the other side of the mountain." Indeed, she'd spent most of her life, including her married life, in this part of the state.

He didn't volunteer any more information about himself and Landon, so she didn't press. Instead, she leaned down and showed Landon Lady's favorite spot to be scratched, right behind the ears. Now that they weren't working anymore, he was talkative and happy, asking her a million questions about the dog.

It was hard to leave the kitchen, cozy and warm, infused with the fragrances of garlic and tomato and bread. Her quiet home and the can of soup she'd likely heat up for dinner both seemed lonely after being here. But she had her own life and couldn't mooch off theirs. "I'd better let you men get on with your dinner," she said and started gathering up her books.

"You want to stay?" Dev asked.

The question, hanging in the air, ignited danger flares in her mind.

The answer was obvious: yes, she did want to stay. But an *Unwise! Unwise!* warning message seemed to flash in her head.

Spending even more time with Dev and Landon was no way to keep the distance she knew she had to keep. As appealing as this pair was, she couldn't risk getting closer. Her heart might not survive the wrenching away that would have to happen, sooner rather than later.

She fumbled with her book bag, reluctant to give the answer she knew she had to give.

Now, why had he gone and invited Emily to dinner?

It was bad enough to have the pretty reading teacher in his kitchen for the after-school hour, talking with and teasing and *teaching* Landon, getting more thinking and work out of him than Dev ever could've.

If she joined them for dinner, he and Landon would both start to get attached. And that was exactly what they couldn't do. They were her clients. Landon was her student. It was important that things stay at that same simple, professional level.

"It's a really nice offer, but I shouldn't stay." She stuffed the rest of her books and papers into a huge tote bag.

Relief and disappointment wrestled inside him. "That's fine. It was just a thought."

"Stay, Ms. Carver. I want to keep playing with Lady." Landon looked up at her. "I'll walk her for you after dinner."

"Ms. Carver needs to get home," Dev said, wishing it weren't so.

"Please? I worked really hard today." His eager face looked pleadingly from one adult to the other, his arm wrapped around Lady.

Emily glanced over at Dev, her expression amused, reflecting the way he felt. Manipulation. Kids were such pros at it. But who could say no to that face, those eyes?

She must have seen that he was caving. "Well," she said, "that garlic bread *does* smell really good."

"Yes!" Landon pumped his arm. "You'll love it. Dad's garlic bread is the best."

She smiled. "How could I turn that down?"

Dev's heart was light as he spooned spaghetti and sauce onto plates. Emily filled water glasses at his direction, and Landon got out the silverware and napkins. At the table, they held hands and prayed before digging in.

It could have been awkward—they didn't know each other well, and there *had* been that weird moment in the truck, when he'd gotten so tempted to pull her close—but Landon and Lady kept things light. Lady scarfed down a crust of bread that got knocked to the floor, so quickly that they all laughed. Landon talked about some of the boys in his classes in a way that suggested he was starting to make some decent friends. Which Dev was glad about but still wanted to keep an eye on, given that it was a school for troubled boys.

When they were clearing the dishes and Landon had gone into the front room to watch TV, Dev asked Emily about it. "Do you think there are kids here Landon should stay away from?"

She shook her head. "Not really. I don't know every boy's story, but I know if they've engaged in criminal behavior that's considered dangerous to others, they're not admitted. We're sort of midrange in terms of behavior issues."

He nodded, filling the sink with hot water, squirting in dish soap. "I guess from the outside, any kid's issues can look bad, including Landon's. I know he's not going to set another fire, but that's not obvious to everyone."

"He seems like a gentle kid." She brought over the rest of the dishes. "That's true of most of the kids here. Half of the trouble is that they didn't get the help they needed in school, and they fell behind and got frustrated."

"I hear that," he said, letting too much feeling leak into his voice.

And then he wished he hadn't, because her eyes darkened with sympathy. "It must have been tough living with all those different families, especially if it involved changing schools a lot, too."

He nodded and busied himself scrubbing the pan he'd used to brown the beef.

"Did you struggle in school?"

A flash of remembered frustration brought sweat to the back of his neck. Every school he'd attended had been at a different spot in the textbook. Every one had given different sorts of tests. And had different expectations of behavior.

He'd gotten assigned to low-level reading classes, and once he'd been pulled out of class for special help with reading. But just as he'd started to connect with the teacher and learn, he'd gotten moved to another foster home, another district. And the process of failing had started all over again.

He'd envied the kids comfortable enough in the classroom to joke around, the ones who could sneak a handheld game under their desk or pass notes and still manage to find their place in the book or come up with the right answer when the teacher called on them. Emily had probably been that kind of kid, though he already knew her well enough to speculate that she was more likely to have sneaked an unauthorized book to read than played video games or passed notes.

And that was just a reminder of why she wasn't for him. "Listen," he said without answering her question,

"I know you have things to do back at your place. I'll finish up here." He hated his own tone, abrupt, ungracious.

She'd been smiling, looking sympathetic, but at his rude dismissal, the smile slid off her face. "Oh, sure, okay," she said. She dried her hands without looking at him again, grabbed her bag, snapped her fingers to get Lady to her side. "See you in school tomorrow, Landon," she said, and she disappeared out the door before he could feel more than a pang of regret that he'd hurt her feelings by pushing her away.

Keeping his reading inadequacy a secret was going to be harder and harder the more Emily Carver infiltrated their lives.

Seven

On the Friday after she started tutoring Landon, Emily headed toward the group of students and staff clustered outside the school building with a firm goal: *not* to be assigned to the same hiking group as Dev and Landon.

It was Earth Day, and the school had taken advantage of the good weather with an outdoor activity—an all-day, all-school hike.

"Everyone listen up," Ashley Green called over the talking and laughing of students excited to be let out of class. She wore casual shorts and a Bright Tomorrows T-shirt, her hair in a simple ponytail instead of its usual neat bun, and Emily realized, with surprise, that she was pretty. She seemed less intimidating than usual, as well. Ashley was relatively new at Bright Tomorrows and didn't seem to have many friends yet. For the first time, Emily realized she ought to reach out to the woman, despite the fact that Ashley was her boss.

"Two rules," Ashley continued when everyone had quieted down. "No one hikes alone, which means you have to keep a lookout for slower members of your group. Don't keep going if they're falling behind. And rule number two, every student has to have an adult in sight at all times."

"Aw, they aren't much to look at," one of the older students yelled, earning glares from the adults and laughter from the students.

Ashley laughed, too, but then her face got serious. "It's no joke, Byron. Hiking in the Colorado mountains always has an element of risk. We've assigned someone trained in first aid and someone experienced with maps and compasses to each group, but everyone needs to have their wits about them."

So the groups were already assigned. It made sense. Emily looked across the crowd and spotted Landon and Dev. Of course they were already here; she'd waited until they were out of sight before leaving her cabin.

It was what she'd done the whole week since their first tutoring session, when Dev had invited her to share their cozy meal and then kicked her out.

The man was good to look at, as Hayley kept saying. Interesting, too, with a kindhearted side. A good dad. She couldn't deny that she felt a spark when she spent time around him.

Maybe he sensed it, and that was why he'd pushed her away. He was way out of her league lookswise, that was for sure.

But even if he'd looked more ordinary, like she did, nothing was going to happen between them. No-thing. Nothing. Emily didn't do relationships, not anymore.

Funny how often she was having to remind herself of that these days.

It was just that this was the first time she'd found a man appealing since she'd become a widow. It didn't mean anything special. She just needed to ride it out and take care of herself so the awareness of all she'd lost and all she couldn't have didn't start her on a downward spiral.

She couldn't drag her own heart and her ticking biological clock through the mud of a doomed attraction. So she'd suggested that Landon meet her in the library for tutoring one day, and in her own kitchen the next.

The tutoring sessions had been okay. It was early times, and she was still assessing his status at the same time she helped him with his immediate issues. She'd sent an email to Dev, copying Ashley and recommending that Landon be tested for dyslexia by a licensed educational psychologist. Meanwhile, she'd worked with him on a test review, and she was pretty confident that Landon had passed the test, so that was something.

On the other hand, he had trouble sitting still and got frustrated easily. She had her hands full trying to keep him on task and engaged after a full day of being in class. So ADHD was something they should also keep in mind, but she wasn't going to dump all that on Dev and Landon at once.

Today's excursion would be good for Landon, a chance to burn off some energy and find out what the Colorado mountains were really like, since she'd guessed from things he'd said that he hadn't had much time out in nature when he'd lived with his mom in Denver.

It was also a chance for him to feel like a part of things, rather than the new kid with the reading problems.

She'd like to see Landon discover the thrill of reaching the top of a mountain under his own steam.

"Have they assigned groups yet?" Hayley rushed over from the kitchen door.

"Not yet. Or rather, they've assigned them, but they haven't told us yet. You get to go?"

"I'd better. I'm grilling the hot dogs. Listen for my name, will you? I have to grab my hiking boots."

"Sure will. Hope we're together."

But it turned out they weren't. Instead, she learned that Landon had begged to be in the same group as Emily and Lady, and whoever had assigned the groups had given in. So he and Dev clustered with Emily and the other members of their group of ten, waiting for further instructions. The other two adults in Emily's group were Stan Davidson, the math teacher, and Maria, from the counseling department, whom Stan seemed intent on impressing.

"To make things fun," Ashley said, "we're going to race to the lake at the top of the trail."

"Yeah, let's go!" one of the boys said. Others pumped arms in the air, and two actually started running for the trailhead.

"Whoa. Stay here, guys. It's not that kind of race—it's a timed race. Each group will take off ten minutes apart, and we'll see who reaches the lake in the least amount of time based on their start."

Emily had participated in these challenges before, but being with the kids in the gorgeous Rockies never got old.

Being with Dev, though, was going to be more of a challenge. She gave him a little smile, but he didn't return it. Maybe it was because he was focused on checking Landon's knapsack.

Or maybe he just wanted to keep his distance.

Which was a good thing, she reminded herself, even though it didn't feel that way.

Their group was second, and the kids rushed ahead. Stan gave a loud whistle. "Remember the rules," he yelled. "Adults in sight all the time."

"And pace yourselves," Emily called out. "If you start too fast, you'll get tired and hit a wall."

The kids waved and yelled their agreement and hurried ahead anyway. But when they started around a bend, they stopped and waited until the rest of the group caught up.

Emily tried to talk to Stan, but he made it obvious her presence was unwelcome as he bragged to the pretty school counselor about his professional successes prior to coming to Bright Tomorrows. Dev was bringing up the rear, so Emily quickened her pace and reached the kids in the front of the group.

After just a few minutes of climbing, it wasn't hard to keep up, because the kids had slowed way down. Everyone was short of breath.

They crossed a rushing, icy stream on a double-plank bridge. Surrounding them were pines and, beyond those, peaks capped and lined with snow. The ground was rough and the trail faint, and when the kids made a wrong turn, Emily called out and reminded them to look for the cairns—little stacks of rocks—that stood in for signs for much of the way.

She took deep breaths of the cool air and listened to the sound of water on rocks, mingled with kids' voices and the caws of bright blue Steller's jays. The path curved onto the edge of a drop-off and then climbed higher.

Some of the kids moved faster, and when they shouted, Emily hurried to find out what was wrong. But the boys were all whooping and jumping around at a spot where the trail opened out onto a wide, nearly flat field covered in white. "It's snow!" one of the newer boys yelled.

It was no surprise to Emily that the snowpack remained in April, but it was a delight to the kids. They ran and slid along the snowfield and then picked up the path again on the other side.

The boys were getting excited as they climbed higher, wanting to be the winning team, and the other adults dawdled behind her, almost out of sight. Emily was thankful for Lady, trotting along beside her. She'd taken off Lady's service dog vest and put her on a long leash so she could sniff and dodge back and forth across the trail like any other dog. Lady still checked in with her frequently, though, looking up, panting, seeming to smile.

She was a good companion. Better than another person. Especially a person like Dev. Sure, he was good-looking—very—and a good guy overall, but the way he ran hot and cold would be tough on any woman he dated.

Did he date anyone? It was hard to imagine he'd already met someone in Little Mesa or at the school, but maybe he'd left a hometown sweetheart behind in Denver.

Deliberately, she pushed thoughts of the handyman out of her mind and focused on the wind in the trees and the sunshine sparkling on the little stream that ran beside the trail. It was so beautiful here, so easy to see God at work, the artistry of His creation. She prayed without words, feeling gratitude for all God's blessings. He'd brought her joy out of pain. No, she'd never forget the awful things that had happened to her, that she'd caused, but with God's help, she'd built a life where she could be of service. She loved her work; she had friends; she lived in a beautiful place. That was a lot to be thankful for.

Most of the group had continued hurrying ahead, waiting impatiently whenever a bend in the trail threatened to put the lagging hikers out of sight. But Landon had fallen behind the other boys, and now he sat on a rock beside the trail, breathing hard. Another boy was with him.

"Taking a rest?" Emily asked as she reached them. She smiled her approval at the two boys. "Good for you, following the rules about how nobody should hike alone."

"This is hard," Landon complained between gasps.

"It's the altitude, dude," the other boy said. "You're not used to it."

"You're right. Hank, can you run up and get the other boys to stop? Landon isn't the only one who's not used to the altitude. We should all take a break, get some water and maybe some trail mix."

The mention of food wiped the protest off the two boys' faces. They wanted to win the challenge, but food was a bigger draw.

Stan and his prospective, way-too-young girlfriend came around the curve, and then Dev behind them.

"Anything wrong?" Dev asked, striding to Landon's side.

"I got tired." Landon's face was flushed, and he was still breathing hard.

"It's a good time for a break, anyway," Emily said. "The next section is tougher. We should all drink some water."

"We want to win," one of the boys said, scarfing down trail mix. "C'mon, let's go."

"We'll go ahead with the boys," Stan said, gesturing to himself and Maria, "if you city folks want to stay back and take a slower pace." He glanced at Dev as he said it, then at Maria.

Emily rolled her eyes. Stan was trying to show off his manly hiking skills by putting down Landon and Dev as inferior.

Dev wouldn't be baited, however. "Good idea," he said easily. "This is a big group to keep all together."

"Can we win if they're not with us?" one of the boys asked.

"Yes, if the majority of our group is fast. It's the overall statistics of the thing." They headed off, Stan continuing to explain how the winners would be decided based on average time.

So Emily had to make a choice: she could stay back with Landon and Dev, or she could go forward, listen to a math lecture and get in the way of Stan's planned romance.

"Do you mind if I walk with you guys?" she asked Dev.

"Of course not," he said, his voice neutral.

"Walk with us!" Landon urged, and while she figured that his enthusiasm had more to do with Lady than with her, it still felt good.

They headed across a field of glacial rocks, and it was tough going. Landon even said he wanted to turn back, but Dev wouldn't allow it. "We can go slow, but we need to get to the top. We committed to the hike, and we'll finish it."

Finally, they made it across the field and to a wooden sign, and since Landon was out of breath, they stopped beside it. "Can you read it?" Emily asked. "Look, trace the letters."

Dev frowned at her. "It's a day to be free from school."

But Landon was running his fingers along the carved wooden letters. "Lak-uh," he sounded out.

"Silent *e*," she reminded him.

"Lake!" He looked up at her. "Right?"

"Yep. Good job. Any guesses about what the first word says?" She covered up the second half.

He sounded out the first part easily. "Mag!"

"Exactly." She pulled her hand back from the rest of the word, and he shouted it out before she could offer help. "Magpie! Another silent *e*!"

"Really good job," she said, giving him a quick hug and then glancing up at Dev, afraid she'd been too hands-on with his son. But Dev stood looking at the sign, not at them. He was even running his fingers along the letters, the same way Landon had done.

He looked up, seemed to notice that she was watching him and backed away from the sign. "Might be making some new direction signs for the school," he said, flushing. "This is a nice design. We should get going."

"Sure," she said, wondering why he suddenly seemed uncomfortable. "It's about ten, fifteen minutes more to the top."

"You hear that, Landon? We're almost there."

They hiked quickly now and soon heard the sounds of the rest of the group. They came out of a strand of pines and stopped, all three of them staring at the vista before them.

The mountain peaks, snow-capped and majestic against the deep blue sky, formed a circle around the sparkling lake. Overhead, a couple of eagles swooped and soared. The air smelled crisp and piney, and the buzzy chirp of frogs sounded from a rushing creek that fed into the lake.

"Wow, cool!" Landon said.

Dev was looking around, nodding slowly. "Wow is right."

"Can we go swimming?" Landon asked.

Dev and Emily looked at each other, amused. "That's some cold water," Dev said. "Way too cold to swim in."

"I think you can even see some ice on it," Emily said.

"It's sure beautiful. I'm glad we came." Dev's tension finally seemed to have left him. They headed over and greeted the others, shucked off their backpacks, and then Dev, Emily, Landon and a couple of other boys from their team walked down to the lake. The boys stuck their hands into the water and, indeed, shrieked about how cold it was. The boys gathered ice shards and then, urged by Ashley as she passed by, collected sticks for a fire. Dev and Emily leaned on a large lakeside rock, admiring the scenery.

"We're not in Denver, that's for sure," Dev said. "You've hiked up here before?"

"Yes," she said, "but I still get thrilled every time."

"Wait a minute," Landon said, "did we win?" And the boys went running over to the rest of the group.

Leaving Emily to admire the view and the man beside her.

What would it be like to be a normal, carefree pair of people who were drawn to each other, who'd just taken a hike and now had a few minutes alone in a gorgeous place? What would it be like to let her gaze linger on Dev, rather than looking quickly away at the far mountains? What would it be like if instead of shivering alone, she moved closer to his warmth?

Those were questions she shouldn't be asking, but here, surrounded by God's beauty, she somehow couldn't stop herself.

Dev sucked in mountain air and studied the peaks and the lake. He was trying to keep his focus there instead of on Emily, but it wasn't easy.

There was no one he'd rather be with to see this wonder. He'd really tried to keep his distance, but being here, in God's beautiful creation, he just couldn't do it anymore.

Things like reading ability receded in importance next to all this splendor. Maybe he didn't have to feel so ashamed, didn't have to hide so much.

For sure, things like reading apps and text-to-voice technology seemed to reside in another world.

A breeze blew a strand of hair across Emily's face, and before he could stop himself, he brushed it back behind her ear.

She looked up at him, eyes wide.

Oh, did his hand want to linger, to cup that soft cheek, to drown in those warm, chocolate-colored eyes. He even moved an inch or two closer and noticed that she was shivering. "Are you cold?" he asked, starting to put an arm around her.

"Come and get it!" A loud call from behind them reminded Dev that he was in public. He stepped back.

"Guess we should go get our hot dogs before the boys eat them all," she said. Her voice sounded a little breathless.

"We should." He didn't put a hand on the small of

her back as they headed toward the group, even though he wanted to. Wanted to a lot.

And wanting to touch her was the tip of the iceberg, because his feelings were starting to go deeper.

You can't even read the sign your son figured out. What would she think if she knew?

But maybe it wasn't so awful. Maybe she'd be understanding.

Maybe he could, real quick, learn to read at a decent adult level. He'd looked at those letters, traced them with his finger, and they'd clicked into place. Lake. Magpie Lake.

"Before we eat, we'll have a prayer," Ashley Green said. "Let's all hold hands in a circle and thank the Lord for His blessings."

That led to some grousing among boys who were squeamish about touching one another, but Ashley was firm, and so they all did it. Which meant he got to take Emily's hand in his.

He squeezed it a little, and she squeezed back, and then he scolded himself and tuned into the prayer. Ashley was kind of going on long with it, talking about how God who made everything didn't make mistakes, that everyone here was His perfect creation, accepted just as they were. "And we thank You for that acceptance, and promise to live up to it and be closer to the people You want us to be. Amen."

As the boys rushed to grab hot dogs from Hayley and her helper, and as they all sat around eating, Dev deliberately took a spot apart from Emily. His thoughts were reeling.

Was it true that God accepted everyone as they were—accepted him, even?

God was a father, the father of all. Dev's own father hadn't been there for him, so that connection of human fathers with God had never really jelled for Dev.

But now that he was a father, and an involved one, he was starting to understand the comparison. When Landon made mistakes or struggled, Dev didn't dislike or abandon him; he tried to help him and loved him just the same.

Maybe God loved Dev just the same, too, despite all his flaws and weaknesses.

Maybe— "Hey!" he yelled as something cold exploded against his back.

"Snowball fight!" Stan said. He lobbed another snowball, this one at Emily.

Dev wasn't going to take *that* sitting down. He jumped up and formed a couple of snowballs and beaned Stan good.

Then the boys were all in it, laughing and throwing wildly and acting not like delinquents or struggling students, but like kids.

Lady chased snowballs and then looked confused when they broke and melted in her mouth, making everyone laugh.

"We leave in half an hour," Ashley called. "You may want to rest a little. It's a long trip down."

"Good idea," Emily said, wiping sweat from her forehead and heading toward the backpacks.

Of course, the boys didn't pay the suggestion about resting a lot of attention, but Hayley went over and flopped down beside Emily, who was leaning back against her pack and...yeah. She was actually reading a book, some thick, serious-looking one.

Dev walked around picking up a few scraps of paper the kids had left, keeping an ear open to their discussion.

"What do you think of it so far?" Hayley was asking. "Do you love it as much as I did?"

"It's *so* good," Emily said. "I stayed up way too late last night. I'm at that part where the Nazis are coming into Paris, and they're hiding in that basement..."

They went on chattering about the book, and Dev listened for a couple of minutes and then headed down to the water. Even if he *did* learn to read better than he could now, he wasn't likely to ever get to the point of reading a big thick book like that. Didn't even know if he wanted to. He might prefer to just watch a TV show about World War II.

So did that mean he and Emily were incompatible?

"How are things going, Dev?" It was Ashley, who'd come up alongside him and now perched on a rock, inviting him to join her.

"Good. Great place." He gestured at their surroundings.

"It is." She studied him. "Is something wrong?"

"Well, I..." He hesitated. She looked so understanding. Maybe he could confide in her about his trouble with reading. Maybe she'd know how to help him, the way she knew how to help Landon.

But she was his boss. She might fire him if she realized he couldn't read the warning labels on the cleaning solutions he used, not without scanning them into his phone and using the text-to-voice program. Better to keep it all to himself.

"I'm fine," he said instead of talking to her about himself. "Did you know we got Emily to do some extra tutoring with Landon?"

"I heard. She had to clear it with me, since she's kind of moonlighting." She smiled at him. "I'm sure Landon will catch up. It's just a matter of persistence and confidence, which I'm sure you can help him with. Anyone can learn."

"Yeah. Thanks." He watched her thoughtfully while she went off whistling for the kids to gather their things and start their downhill trek.

Anyone can learn. He knew that to be the case in many areas of life, but he just wasn't sure it was true about something so unnatural to him as reading.

Eight

"You didn't have to do this." Dev leaned back in his chair the next Tuesday evening and gave a satisfied sigh. "But I'm glad you did. The beef stew was great."

"Yeah, thanks, Ms. Carver. Dad never makes stuff like that."

"You gotta love the Crock-pot," she said, waving away the compliments. And it *had* been easy, but she'd gone to a little extra trouble, browning the meat and onions first, making biscuits to go with the hearty stew. She was the first to admit she wasn't much of a cook, but she'd wanted to do something nice for Dev and Landon, wanted to please them.

Food was always pleasing to men, she knew that. Especially after a long day of work or school. And meat and potatoes, comfort food, were high on most males' lists.

"I wanted to thank you," she said. "You did me a big favor driving me to see Mom again on Sunday."

"We'll go every week if I can go to the arcade!" Landon was kneeling beside Lady, rubbing her belly. "Can we, Dad?"

"Oh, no, I wouldn't—" Emily started.

"Maybe not *every* Sunday—" Dev said at the same time.

They both laughed, and Emily hurried to get her comment in. "The mechanic thinks he'll have my car done this week, or next week at the latest." And thanks to the generous wage Dev had offered, she was able to put the repair on her credit card, knowing she'd be able to pay it off.

"It was fun," he said. And it had been. They'd turned up the radio and discovered that all three of them liked to sing along to country music. They'd stopped for pizza again on the way home.

It had felt like a family outing, and even though Emily's mom hadn't been very responsive, Emily had felt good when she'd gotten back home.

"Landon and I will do the dishes," Dev said.

Landon made a face.

"I have an idea," Emily said. "I have a new audiobook of a mystery story, and the book, too. If Landon would want to listen to it, maybe he could do it while we clean up."

"Could I watch TV instead?" Landon asked.

"Good try, buddy, but no," Dev said. "It's reading or dishes."

"You can keep Lady company while you listen to the story." Emily smiled at Landon, glad she'd figured out the way to his heart—or, at least, to his cooperation.

"Okay," Landon said instantly, proving her right.

"But you do have to follow along. There are good pictures." Emily got Landon set up and then returned to the kitchen, where Dev was clearing dishes off the table. "I think he'll like this book," she said. "And this is a terrific way for him to improve his reading. I can let you borrow the materials."

"Good," he said. "I, uh, I sometimes listen to audiobooks myself. Nothing deep," he added, waving a hand. "Want me to wrap up these biscuits?"

"Sure." Emily indicated the drawer that held plastic bags and wrap, then pushed up her sleeves and turned on the water to fill the sink.

Dev bagged up the biscuits, then came to stand beside her. He touched her arm. "What are the scars from?"

She pulled away. Dev had been around her more now, had seen the scars multiple times, and she'd forgotten to be self-conscious around him, until now.

He looked contrite. "Sorry. It's definitely not my business."

"No, it's okay. I… I was in a fire."

"Rough. Same fire as your mom?"

Emily drew in a breath and let it out, slowly, and nodded.

He nudged her aside and dunked dishes into the water. "Let me wash. You can dry. And you don't have to tell me, but I'm interested if you would want to. And I'm here if you just need to talk." He glanced at her, his eyes warm, his kindness obviously sincere.

"Ah, I… Thanks." How did he *do* that? How did he make her feel so very good and cared for? "It was just…" She swallowed and couldn't go on. Of course she couldn't. She couldn't tell him how awful she'd been or what she'd done.

He leaned a little closer, his arm touching hers. "Life stinks sometimes," he said. "Is the fire what made you need a service dog?"

She cleared her throat. “Yeah. I… I wasn’t getting over it. Lady helps.”

He moved behind her, put his hands on the backs of her shoulders and rubbed, gently. It felt like the perfect amount of warmth and pressure. She let the pan she was drying slip to the counter and closed her eyes.

How had he guessed that she held her tension in her shoulders? And when was the last time anyone had touched her so sweetly, with the intent of comforting her?

All too soon he dropped his hands, stepping away.

Emily turned to him, her shoulders tingling where he’d rubbed them. Her face felt hot.

“Don’t worry.” He’d taken a couple of steps back. For the first time, she noticed how big he seemed in her little kitchen, and how masculine among the frilly curtains and flower centerpiece. “I won’t make a habit of that. Just… I don’t know how to make it better. I thought—” He broke off. “I don’t want to stress you out more.”

“Thanks.” Emily walked over and peeked into the living room, saw that Landon had dozed off, using Lady as a pillow, the book open on his chest. The sight made her smile, made her feel tender inside.

But in the kitchen, there was still Dev to deal with, and her feelings for him were far more complicated. She couldn’t think of anything to say to him. Because she couldn’t blurt out that she liked the way he’d touched her, that no one else touched her so gently and kindly, could she?

“You’ve gotten past it.” He leaned over the trash can and pulled the bag out, tied the drawstring, and over and above the fact that she still felt warm from his touch, she marveled at a man who would take the trash out without being nagged to do so.

"I'll take this out when we go." He walked over to the sink and washed his hands.

The kitchen felt so small. She was hyper-aware of him moving through it. He turned toward her, and everything in her yearned for him to take her in his arms, to hold her, make her feel that warmth and safety, that gentle tenderness, again and more.

Lady barked in the front room, probably at someone walking by on the road. Landon stirred.

"I should get Landon home," Dev said. "He's tired. He'll go right to bed." And then he put a hand on Emily's arm. "Come with me."

"What?"

He didn't look away. His eyes were on her, warm brown eyes, intense. His hand seemed to burn her shoulder. "I just want to be with you."

Her heart seemed to reach out of her chest toward him, so great was her yearning. She wanted to be with him, too. Only what did that mean?

He was still studying her, and she couldn't quite recognize the look in his eyes. It was still kind, but there was an intensity there that she hadn't seen in him before, and it scared her.

Emily stepped back, confused. She wanted to be with Dev, too, longed for it. But she was pretty sure he didn't mean the same thing she did. "I've given you the wrong idea. I don't do that." It came out sounding prudish, and maybe he'd think she meant she wouldn't put herself into a potentially intimate situation with a man.

Which was true.

But what she'd really meant was, she didn't get to

be close with a man like Dev, hadn't earned it, didn't deserve it. The scars on her arms were a daily witness to her failure.

Connecting with Dev was too enticing, making her long for things she couldn't have. "I'll see you at work," she said, and she deliberately moved away from him, starting to scrub her stove, which didn't need scrubbing.

He stood behind her for a minute, without speaking. She could hear his breathing, a little quickened, just like her own was.

"Right. Sorry. Landon, come on." He walked into the living room, and she heard him waking Landon, helping the sleepy boy gather his things. Then he gave her an impersonal wave, and they were gone.

Emily dropped the sponge and sank down onto a kitchen chair, wrapping her arms around herself.

This was getting too dangerous. She was at risk of getting her heart entangled, and maybe Dev's, too. Worst of all, Landon's, if he was starting to think of her as a mother figure.

Her decision to stay away from relationships had seemed relatively easy up until now. Meeting Dev and Landon, though, had opened up a vista to her, as wide and free and beautiful as the view at Magpie Lake. It was a vista of a new life, a new family, motherhood, the love of a good man.

For the first time, she realized what she was throwing away when she turned her back on Dev and Landon. Her life seemed to stretch in front of her, lonely and empty and sad.

And she had absolutely no right to feel that way. She'd brought her situation on herself. Moreover, she had much to be grateful for. She ticked the positives in her life off on her fingers: her job, the kids, her friends, the natural beauty around her, her faith most of all. It was something she did regularly, at the suggestion of one of her counselors: focus on the positive. Think about all there was to be grateful for.

And she *was* grateful, truly. It was just that Dev and Landon were so special. She'd never meet anyone like them again.

She stood and walked over to her dish rack. Best to stay busy.

She reached for the clean plates and stopped. Her hand dropped back to her side.

She *liked* the look of that full dish rack, so different from her usual solo plate, cup and fork. Liked the look of having had people here. Almost like a family.

Her lower lip trembled, just a little. Lady stood, shook herself and walked over to her side.

Emily sighed and then started pulling dishes out of the rack and putting them away, trying not to think about Dev and Landon. About the fact that Dev had asked her to come over, had said he wanted to be with her.

That couldn't happen.

She needed to back off and create a distance, but it was getting harder and harder to make herself do that.

Emily's shocked "no" still rang in Dev's ears the next day as he swept the floor outside the library, cleaning up a mess of popcorn someone had spilled.

And why wouldn't she have sounded shocked? For one thing, she didn't think of Dev that way, he was pretty sure. For another, she must have thought he was asking for more than just her company.

He hadn't been…had he? He'd just spoken from his heart; he hadn't wanted the evening, their connection and warmth and new openness, to come to an end.

It was all for the best, though. He couldn't have someone like Emily, and he shouldn't be getting so close to her.

"Dev?" He turned, and she was there. Behind her in the library, a small group of students labored over notebooks. "About last night. I'm sorry. I didn't mean to push you out. I just… I'm not up for…whatever it was you were looking for."

He leaned his broom against the cleaning cart and wiped his hands with a clean towel. "I'm the one who should apologize. When I asked you to come over, I was out of line. I didn't mean…you know. I wouldn't ask that. I was just enjoying being with you, and I didn't want it to stop."

It was all true. He wouldn't ask anything inappropriate of her, but he did long for her company.

She was staring at the ground, face red.

"I can keep more of a distance," he said. "I don't want to push, but I felt for you last night, for what you told me. If you need a friend, I'm here."

She raised her head slowly and met his eyes, and Dev seemed to see a spark, bright and dazzling, arc between them.

"Thanks," she said. "I could use a friend."

"Me, too." He felt like something more needed to be said. "And in the spirit of being a friend, I won't try anything. No touching, no nothing."

Her cheeks flushed pink. "Okay."

"So, friends?" He held out a hand.

"Friends."

And he could control the part of his heart that wanted more than friendship from Emily Carver.

After that awkward conversation, things got easier between them. They fell into friend-like patterns, eating meals together, hanging out with Landon together, talking about things. It was good. It was friendly.

And if it made Dev want more, want what he couldn't have, well, so be it. He could handle it.

Nine

Normally, Emily loved going to the Miners' Diner. The homey atmosphere and real local food were just right, and it was right for her budget, too.

And normally, she loved going out to eat with her best friend. Hayley was fun and funny and wise, and even if Emily had had a bad day at work, Hayley usually joked her into a better mood.

Today, though, Hayley had a gleam in her eye that told Emily something was going on. And when Hayley asked for a table in the back corner, she got even more curious. What was on Hayley's mind?

They walked past Doc Harper, who was still the county's main physician at seventy-two. He was having dinner with his younger brother, the area's premier veterinarian, a young-looking, vital seventy-year-old.

Jennie, a longtime waitress, came over as soon as they'd sat down at the directed table. "Good to see you ladies. How's life up at the school? Can I bring you drinks? Or a Cinco de Mayo appetizer?"

"Iced tea for me, thanks," Hayley said.

"Just water." Economizing was one of Emily's superpowers. Someone had once told her how much money the average person spent on beverages in a year, and she'd decided on the spot to never order anything but water at a restaurant again.

Then again, she had a little extra money now. She could afford to treat her friend. "We'll celebrate Cinco de Mayo with an order of nachos to share while we look at the menu."

"Coming right up."

As soon as Jennie was out of earshot, Hayley put down her menu and leaned forward. "So tell me everything."

"About what?"

"You and Dev!"

"What about us?" Emily studied her menu for another minute before looking up at her friend.

Hayley pulled it out of her hands. "You're together every day! Stan says you eat dinner at each other's places almost every night."

Emily could have strangled Stan and his nosy ways. "Not *every* night. It's just… Sometimes it's easier, since we're together for Landon's tutoring after school. And we're friends."

"*Close* friends?" Hayley waggled her eyebrows.

Emily sighed. Clearly, Hayley wasn't going to take the hint that Emily didn't want to talk about it. "No. Not close. We, well, we agreed to be just friends."

Hayley stared. "It was *discussed*?"

"Uh-huh. And that's what we agreed."

The nachos arrived, and Jennie took their order and stuck around for a minute to share the local gossip. Then the Harper brothers came over to say hello and discuss a fundraiser they were helping with at the school. Lady bucked her training and jumped up to put her front paws onto her vet's lap, earning an ear rub instead of a scolding. Country music played on the old-fashioned jukebox. By the time the men had headed out, Emily's trout and Hayley's elk burger had arrived, and they dug in.

"Mmm, there's nothing like the Miners' Diner," Hayley said. "I'm not going to eat again for a week."

Emily laughed. "I'm taking the rest of these nachos to Dev and Landon. There's no way we can..." She trailed off, seeing Hayley's expression.

"See? See that? You're talking about them like they're your family. There's more than a convenient friendship going on here." She held up a hand. "Which is fine! Totally fine. I'm happy for you. You deserve to settle down and be happy."

"It's not like that. It isn't." Emily looked down at her plate, but her appetite was suddenly gone. "We're friends, and that's all, and that's that."

Hayley tilted her head to one side. "Still punishing yourself, are you?"

"Not sure what you mean." She so did not want to go into this, but she knew Hayley. The woman was relentless and wouldn't give up until she'd wrung every secret out of Emily. It would have made Emily mad, except that she knew Hayley cared and had her best interests at heart.

"Well, for example," Hayley said, "you organize that 5-K race in memory of Mitch, because his parents want you to, even though it's a miserable experience and doesn't even raise much money."

"Don't remind me," Emily groaned. "I'm expecting a call from them any day now. We said last year was the final one, but I just know they'll want to keep it going."

"Yeah, as long as you do all the work. If they call, you should say you won't do it."

"Well..." The thought was undeniably tempting, but it also made her stomach churn with anxiety.

"You're always looking for ways to deny yourself happiness to make up for your so-called mistakes," Hayley said. "Isn't it time to stop? Give yourself a break and look for some happiness?"

"I'm happy," Emily said. "Pretty happy. And being around Dev and Landon is nice. Fun." She looked through her lashes to see if Hayley was buying it.

"Nope. I've seen how you look at each other, and it doesn't spell fun. It spells wanting and caring and romance."

"It does not— Wait. Does he look at *me* that way?"

Hayley made her thumb and forefinger into a gun shape and pointed it at Emily. "Bang, you've got it. He does. But why would you care, if all you want is to be friends?"

Emily stuffed down the happiness that wanted to rise in her at the thought of Dev looking at her in some kind of special way.

It didn't matter. Maybe he had a lack of prospects so far here in Little Mesa, but that wouldn't last. He was too good, too kind, too attractive to stay single for long.

And even if he *did* have more than a passing interest in Emily, she wasn't going to let him act on it. There was a reason she had lived through the fire when she wanted to die, and it wasn't to enjoy herself. It was to help others. To teach.

Not to be a wife and mother. She'd already had her chance at that, and she'd failed.

"What's going through your head right now?" Hayley asked.

Emily shrugged. "Just the fact that I'm not going to be anything more than friends with Dev or anyone. Reminding myself of that."

"Because you're a horrible human being who doesn't deserve happiness?" Haley raised an eyebrow and took another bite of her burger.

"Well…it sounds stupid when you say it like that, but yes."

Hayley gestured with her burger, swallowed her bite and glared. "It *sounds* stupid because it *is* stupid! Do you know how many Christians the apostle Paul persecuted before his conversion? And yet he was forgiven and went on to evangelize the world and practically write the New Testament!"

Emily fought back a smile at her friend's dramatic version of the story. "He didn't get married, though."

"That's debatable, and anyway, how did we get on the apostle Paul? We're talking about you and your ridiculous plan to deny yourself happiness because you think you were at fault in the deaths of your family. But tragic as that whole thing was, I don't think anyone but you would lay all the blame about that at your feet. What about your husband? What about your mom?"

Emily leaned back and slid down a little on the booth's bench. She looked up at the rough-hewn rafters, wagon wheels hanging down from them, wired with lights. "We've gone over all this before. Mom wasn't able to think straight—"

"But you didn't *know* that," Hayley interrupted. "Her dementia wasn't diagnosed."

"I was her daughter. I should have seen it. And I for

sure knew Mitch had a drinking problem. I was the competent adult. The *only* competent adult, as it turned out, and I failed."

"We all fail at things!" Hayley sounded positively fierce. "Do you think I've never done anything wrong in my life, never made any mistakes?"

That startled Emily. "Yeah, I do think that," she admitted. "Nothing serious, anyway."

"Well, you're wrong. And yet here I am, putting myself out there, embracing life. Because that's what God wants us to do."

Emily studied her friend, eyes narrowed. "I want to hear about these mistakes in your past."

"That's for another time. We're talking about you. How you need to let Dev and Landon in."

Emily opened her mouth to make another reasonable, logical argument, but her feelings rebelled. Why was Hayley pushing her like this rather than being her usual supportive self? "Don't you think I want to let them in? Do you think it's easy to keep them at a distance? You have no idea how much I want to give Landon all the hugs he needs and, and explore things with Dev, but I can't. I can't. Do you understand that?"

Hayley shook her head. "No, I really don't."

"Then don't criticize what you don't understand."

Hayley bit her lip and looked off to the side, toward the now-crowded restaurant. But it was obvious she wasn't seeing the people there.

After a minute, she looked back at Emily, leaned forward and gripped her hands. "I'm only going to say this once," she said. "You're making a huge mistake, and you're fooling yourself if you think it's going to work out for you to keep all your feelings squashed down. Not to mention that you're insulting God."

"Insulting *God*?"

"That's what I said. Because God has the power to do anything. Any. Thing. That's what Scripture tells us. If you don't believe Jesus can wash you clean, are you really even a Christian?"

"Hayley!" Emily slid out of the booth and stood, snapping her fingers for Lady to come to attention. "I love you, my friend, but I'm not going to sit here and let you question my faith. Come on, or I'll find another ride home."

Inside, she was reeling. Hayley had thrown her for a loop. Was her best friend right, that she was insulting God by not accepting His forgiveness?

But God knew her inside and out, and He knew that every time she got close to a date, or a man, or any kind of happiness, she locked up inside. She had to assume He was making that happen because she didn't deserve to have whatever was on offer.

Their ride back to school was quiet. Emily expected Hayley to apologize, or take back what she'd said, but she didn't. She just pulled up to Emily's cabin and stopped.

"Thanks for the ride," Emily said stiffly. "Come on, Lady."

The shaggy poodle mix jumped out of Hayley's back seat and trotted into the little yard.

"Guess I'll see you later," Emily said.

"Think about what I said," Hayley said. "Think about what you're missing. You could have things the rest of us only dream about. Don't throw them away."

She wasn't throwing them away, Emily thought as

she let herself into the cabin. She was seeing them on the other side of a fine sheet of gauze, but they simply weren't accessible to her.

On Friday, Dev was headed back to his cabin when Stan flagged him down. "Need your help with something," the white-haired math teacher said.

"Sure." Dev was bone tired, but Stan was a neighbor.

Stan led him over to the side of his cabin and indicated a square of ground that was marked off with stakes and twine. "I need to dig this up and work in some compost," he said. "Hoping you'll help. I got an extra shovel."

Dev blew out a breath. Maybe the teacher had been sitting at a desk all day, but Dev had been lifting and hauling, doing physical work. The last thing he wanted was more of that.

But Landon was over at the boys' cabins, having a supervised playdate—only Dev wasn't allowed to call it that, of course, because Landon was *way* too old—with a couple of the other boys. Dev had no plans, and he'd already learned that Friday nights could be lonely up here in the mountains with little else than the stars for company.

A hawk swung its solitary way across the sky as the sun sank toward the mountains, lighting them up with a rose-gold glow. Around him, in the trees beside the cabin, chickadees fluttered and dived, calling out cheery greetings to one another. Sage and pine scents blew in on a cool breeze.

Even though Dev had done physical work all day, he'd been stuck inside. "Sure, I'll help." He took the shovel Stan offered and started digging. "Planning a vegetable garden, are you?"

"Sure am. It's tough up here, a short growing season, but working with the earth keeps me sane." Stan grinned. "Plus, the new horticulture therapist is a real beauty. I'll consult with her."

So I'm digging your garden to help your love life?

The work wasn't easy. The ground was dry and hard. And it seemed to Dev that he was digging at twice the pace that Stan was. Oh, well. The guy was probably twenty years older than Dev. Dev was grateful he had the health to work hard.

He doubled down to it, figuring he'd get the job done as soon as possible and then head home to a shower and the hockey game.

"Noticed you've been spending quite a bit of time with Emily," Stan said out of nowhere, leaning on his shovel.

Dev's senses went on alert. He kept shoveling but studied the white-haired man from the corner of his eye. "Yeah?"

"We're a little protective of our own," Stan said. "We—or I, rather, I shouldn't speak for anyone else—I'm a little concerned."

The *we* and *our own* language made Dev feel like the outsider, but he supposed that was only right: he *was* the newcomer and the outsider. And Stan had the right to be protective. "It's just fallen out that way since she's tutoring Landon," he explained. "We're friends, or getting to be. That's all."

"Uh-huh." Stan started digging again, not responding further, as if waiting for Dev to go on.

But there was nothing more to say. He wasn't the

type of man a smart, educated woman like Emily would go for. He'd known that, but she'd made it even clearer last week when she'd backed off his invitation to continue their conversation at his place.

Rubbing the tension from her shoulders had felt wonderful. But it wouldn't happen again. He'd given his word that he wouldn't touch her, and he didn't go back on his word.

"She's been through a lot, you know. Had a hard time." Stan was digging steadily now.

"I gathered that, from her burns."

"Right. And I'm pretty sure there's more to that fire story."

Dev frowned. "More than what?"

"Pretty sure she lost more than her looks."

Dev stared at the man. "She didn't lose her looks. She has some scars, that's all."

"Uh-huh." Stan's eyes were steady on him. "Ask her about it sometime. If you're her *friend*."

He was curious enough that he would. But Stan's words rang another bell. "Are you telling me to stay away because you're interested in her yourself?" Stan was way too old, but to some guys, that didn't matter. Stan seemed to like younger ladies.

"Me? No. Not my type."

"Uh-huh." Dev thrust his shovel into the hard soil, irritated for reasons he didn't fully understand.

"But if you're not serious about her, then you *should* stay away," Stan said, his voice gruff. "She's a good gal."

"I'm not serious about her. She's not for me."

It was true; she wasn't. She was way too smart for him. Way too professionally advanced.

"Good. I think that's best."

Stan's words were nothing more than what Dev had thought himself, but he still didn't like hearing them from the older man. "I can finish this myself," Dev said, waving his hand at the half-dug garden. He'd do it all if he could get this irritating man out of his way.

Not paying attention to whether Stan stayed or left, Dev went back to digging the garden, hard.

He was angry about all of it. Angry that he couldn't learn and that his lack of intelligence ruled out a woman of the sort he actually liked. A woman like Emily.

Why hadn't God given him a good brain?

But Landon would have the advantages and would improve his ability to learn. That was the important thing.

He kept digging, trying to lose himself in the work, to shut out thoughts of what he couldn't have.

Landon's future and happiness were a lot more important than the ache in Dev's heart.

Ten

Emily walked into the church building the next Sunday, steeled for the pain she knew the day would bring.

At least, she *thought* she was steeled for it. But when she saw Hayley passing out carnations to all the grandmothers and mothers, saw everyone cooing over several new babies, she nearly turned around and walked out.

Mother's Day. For many women, a highlight of the year. But when you'd lost a child and were losing your mother a little at a time to an awful disease, every Mother's Day was painful. She'd had two beautiful, happy Mother's Days and six excruciating ones after that.

Hayley handed her a carnation, her eyes full of sympathy. "These are for all women, of course. We all find ways to nurture others. But you'd be forgiven for staying home today, you know. Watching a service on TV or just reading your Bible and worshipping on your own."

"No, I'm fine." She wasn't, but she hadn't come to church so people would feel sorry for her.

"You sure do love to beat yourself up." Hayley hugged her. "If you want to get together after, I'm here. And…

listen, I'm sorry I was intrusive at the diner. You have to make your own choices and live your own life."

"It's fine. I know you were saying it all out of care. And thanks for the offer, but I'm going to see Mom later today." She didn't want to fuel Hayley's concerns by admitting that her car wasn't fixed yet and that Dev was taking her.

The sun shone through the little sanctuary's stained glass windows, and the organ music played softly, not muffling people's excited conversations. The kids were doing a special music performance today, it seemed.

Landon wouldn't be in the performance, since he was spending the weekend in Denver visiting his mom.

But she thought of him. Thought of how tall he was, and how her own child might have been that tall.

Would James have resembled her side of the family more, or Mitch's? Would he have liked to read?

Would he have made her something special for Mother's Day, or would he consider himself too grown-up for such emotional stuff?

Automatically, she reached for Lady, but the dog wasn't there. Why had she left Lady at home today? Without the comfort and support of her service dog, Emily just might fall apart.

Maybe Hayley was right. Maybe Emily was obsessed with punishing herself.

She tried to control the tears, but they were dripping down. Tried to remind herself that other women suffered, too: some had lost a baby to miscarriage or a child to cancer, others had lost their own mothers, and some were estranged from mother or child. She'd even participated in a focus group the pastor had conducted, as he'd honed his ideas about how to frame the Mother's Day service so it was sensitive to the various ways Mother's Day could cause pain.

She felt for other women, but their circumstances didn't take away her own pain. She dug in her purse for a tissue and wiped her eyes. When she took a deep breath and looked around the congregation, she saw several people looking at her, concerned or curious expressions on their faces.

This might not work, sitting through church. In previous years, she'd avoided it.

This year she'd decided to try, but she might not be able to do it. And if she was going to be an emotional mess, she'd bring others down, others who were even now oohing and aahing as the little children came in to sing a special song.

She watched as the children finished their song and ran to their mothers, seated in the congregation. As women picked up their beautiful, healthy children, sat them on their laps, praised them, Emily felt as jealous as a child at a birthday party, watching the birthday girl get a pony.

Which was wrong and mean and ridiculous. She should be happy for all those women. Should remember that, however sweet everything looked on Mother's Day at church, they all could be struggling—to support their children, to handle a difficult relationship with the father, to deal with a child's illness or behavior problems.

But it didn't help. She'd have welcomed those motherly struggles compared to the sheer emptiness and hollowness she felt now.

She wiped her face as best she could, looking around at the banners on the church wall. One caught her eye, bright green lettering on a white background. "And be ye kind one to another, tenderhearted, forgiving one another, even as God for Christ's sake hath forgiven you."

Had she forgiven her mother, and Mitch, for their part in the fire and the loss of lives therein?

And then the second part of the verse seemed to blink at her like a neon sign: *even as God for Christ's sake hath forgiven you.*

God had forgiven her.

Had He, though? Had He really?

She clutched her carnation and watched the little children file out. Prayed along with the pastor and his sensitive thoughtful prayer.

Tried to tell herself, over and over, that she could do this, had to do this, had to learn to live in the world with all its celebrations and holidays. If it hurt, she deserved it.

At least, she'd always thought she deserved it, but was Hayley right? Was she flagellating herself, throwing away God's gift of forgiveness?

When the congregation stood to sing the opening hymn, the pain grew too sharp. She slipped out, weaving apologetically past the family that had filled in her pew, keeping her head down to avoid showing her makeup-streaked, wet-with-tears face.

She'd tried, she really had. But she couldn't do it. So she'd go home and wrap Mom's gift.

She'd pretend to sleep on the way to the care home, maybe. That way, she wouldn't have to make happy conversation with the man she was developing way too many feelings for but couldn't have.

At seven thirty that evening, on the way home from driving Emily to visit her mother, Dev slowed his truck on the mountain road, squinting.

Emily had been dozing. "What's going on?" she asked sleepily.

He liked her sleepy voice, a little too much, so he focused on the road. "There it is." He saw a small sign, then a pull-off.

She sat up straighter, reaching back to touch Lady in the back seat, as Dev pulled the truck over a rutted parking area and stopped.

Sure enough, there was a bench. And an amazing vista before them.

The setting sun emerged from behind a purple cloud, shining golden onto the closer foothills, making them glow. More distant were the dark peaks behind which the sun would settle in just a short time.

He'd really, really wanted to help Emily feel better ever since he'd seen her so broken up in church. He assumed it was because of her mom being sick, which had to make Mother's Day difficult. And indeed, she'd had a rough visit today.

Dev had gone into the care home with her for half an hour, but he'd soon discerned that his presence wasn't helping to calm the older woman, was maybe making her worse. So he'd gone out to wait in the truck. He'd sat there using the phone app he'd recently found, a learn-to-read app for adults. He was working on decoding and comprehension, and it wasn't awful, especially if he took breaks every twenty minutes or so. He felt like a dork working on such simple stuff, but he found himself really wanting to improve his skills. Maybe, just maybe, if he could make enough progress, he'd keep up with his son and feel more on a level with Emily.

Finally, she'd come out of the care home, her face

pale and drawn. But when he'd asked her about it, she'd shrugged. "Mom's Mom, and she wasn't having a great day. At least they're not hassling me about paying my bill now. I have you to thank for that."

He was floored by her ability to focus on the positive. He was also starving, they both were, so they'd stopped at a taco truck and grabbed a couple of tacos each. Conscious of Stan's protective warnings about Emily, he'd kept it light, not a sit-down restaurant where things could be romantic, but a quick stop for tacos.

Only she'd gotten into a conversation with the family operating the food truck, and he'd joined in. They'd sat down at the picnic table outside the truck to eat and ended up talking to two of the kids in the family. They both liked kids and spoke Spanish, so it had turned into a fun experience.

In certain ways, he and Emily were really compatible.

But at the end of the impromptu visit, the little girl had hugged her mother and talked about Mother's Day, and they'd argued about the date, which was different in Mexico than in the US this year. And Emily had gotten sad again.

Now, she climbed out of the truck at his urging, but her movements were mechanical. Clearly, she wasn't her usual upbeat self.

And then she saw the view and her face lit up. She had a really, really pretty smile, and when she smiled, her cheeks flushed a little under that fair white skin. Like a pink rose just blooming, and when did he ever get poetic? But she inspired him.

He came around to her side of the truck. "Let's sit

for a few," he said. "Landon won't be home until late tonight, so I'm not in a big hurry. Are you?"

She shook her head. "No. Not since Lady's here with us. Come on, girl."

The big dog jumped out of the truck and started sniffing.

They walked over and sat down on the bench, Lady on a long lead and sniffing around the area.

"How'd you find this place?" she asked as she looked around. "I've lived around here for a long time, but I never knew there was such a cool viewing spot here."

"Stan told me about it, actually."

"I didn't know you and Stan were getting to be friends."

He held out a flat hand, tilted it from side to side. "Kinda. More like he's taken it on himself to give me advice."

"Yeah? Like what?" She sounded amused. "He's a big-time mansplainer, but I didn't know he'd do it to another man."

Should he tell her? But they seemed alone in the world, alone except for the dog and the little vole she was chasing after, and the eagle soaring overhead. It made him want to be as open as the landscape before them, and while he couldn't do that, he could at least share some of what Stan had said. "For one thing, he told me to stay away from you."

"What?" She jerked around to face him, staring. "What do you mean?"

Dev lifted his hands, palms up. "He noticed we were spending a lot of time together. Let me know it wasn't a good idea."

Her eyes narrowed. "Since when does he have a say over how I spend my time? Or how you do?"

He shrugged. "I explained that we were just friends, but he didn't believe it."

She stared at him for a moment longer, then looked out toward the distant mountain range. The anger seemed to seep out of her. "Yeah. Hayley noticed, too."

He wanted to know whether Hayley had warned her off him, but he was too afraid of the answer to ask. "People keep matching us up because we spend so much time together," he said instead. "But we're neighbors, and you're tutoring Landon. Can't a man and a woman be friends?"

"Right?" She looked back at him.

Once their gazes tangled, he couldn't look away. Her eyes darkened as he looked at her, and his heart rate sped up.

Which pretty much negated his point. "I'm not going to say it's easy," he said slowly.

Her forehead creased, and she bit her lip.

"Don't worry," he said. He wanted to reach for her, put a reassuring hand on her shoulder. Holding back almost killed him, but he did it. "I made you a promise not to touch you. I'll stick to that."

She nodded quickly, looked away off over the mountains.

The sun was sinking behind them, sending out light-filled rays, tinting the sky pink and gold. "Wow," she said softly.

"Yeah." The need to pull her close was palpable, a living thing.

A bird swooped past them and to the ground, then back up. Gray wings, brown-and-black-patterned back.

A gray head with black-and-white cheeks. Lady went alert, watching it.

"It's a kestrel!" Emily exclaimed.

"Sparrow hawk!" he said at the same time.

They both laughed. "I think it's the same thing," he said, relieved—kind of—that the romantic moment had passed.

"Really?" She pulled out her phone, tapped something into it. "You're right. Look." She held out her phone, and the sudden movement made the small hawk fly up, calling *Klee! Klee!* Lady barked sharply, straining at the leash Emily had tightened.

Dev didn't expect the creature to come back, but it did, flying down, then up again.

"That's a mating ritual," she said, reading from her phone. "There must be a female nearby. That's so cool!"

He loved her ability to get excited about things, to forget her problems. It made her fun to be with.

They sat for a little while then, watching the sunset. The breeze got cool and she shivered a minute, then scooted over close. "It's silly to stick to a rule for a rule's sake," she said. "It's cold, but so pretty. I don't want to leave just yet. And friends are allowed to keep each other warm, right?"

He found an extra jacket in his truck and wrapped it around her, but she still snuggled close and rested her head on his arm. "You know, Mother's Day is hard for me for a particular reason," she said. "I really appreciate your company."

"Want to talk about it?"

"I'm just going to tell you quick. I don't want to dig into all the feelings." She sucked in a breath. "Okay.

That fire, where Mom and I got burned? I… I lost my husband. And my two-year-old son."

All the breath whooshed out of him, and he pulled her close and wrapped his arms around her, because a hug was the only way to react to such horror. "That's… I don't even know what to say."

"That's just it. There's nothing to say." Her voice sounded a little ragged. "Not gonna pretend I'm fine now, but I'm functioning. I just wanted you to know, but I don't really want to talk about it."

He cuddled her close then, head spinning as his view of her broke and resettled. He'd known she had experienced trouble in her life, but he hadn't had an inkling of how bad it had been. She'd had awful problems, and for all that, she kept making her way through.

Admiration for her surged, and with it, tender compassion. "I'm so sorry," he said.

"Thanks." She turned her face up to look at him. "Friends help. And…and Landon helps. Sometimes being around him is hard, because James would have been just Landon's age. But I think he's helping me heal."

"Just Landon's… Oh, wow." He touched her cheek, wanting to show his sympathy.

"Thanks," she said. "But Landon's a great kid. I think it's healing me to know him, and to see that life goes on."

A strand of hair blew across her face, and he brushed it back, and another emotion blended smoothly in with the sympathy he felt for her. "You're something else, you know?"

She met his eyes for a moment and then looked away, her cheeks going pink. "I'm not. I've made so many mistakes. You have no idea."

"Maybe not," he said, "but I can see your heart." Emotions surged in him, mixed, conflicting, intense.

And then, because he wanted to blot away the pain in her eyes, and because he was only human, he lowered his head and pressed his lips to hers.

Eleven

Dev's kiss felt perfect. Gentle and respectful, but not hesitant. He wanted to kiss her, *really* wanted to kiss her, and he let her know that with energy.

Emily relaxed into his arms, warmth spreading through her. How long had it been since someone had held her? She was used to being the caretaker, the teacher, the one responsible. She'd stopped thinking someone might take care of her, but that was what Dev's embrace felt like, and she loved it.

Lady settled at their feet with a gusty sigh.

He cupped her face as he kissed her, treating her as if she were precious and fragile. His hands were rough with work, yet so gentle as he brushed one over her hair and let his finger trace her jawline.

The kiss, the embrace, felt so new and so special that it chased rational thought from her mind. She hadn't been kissed for a long time, and she tried to remember the reason for it. There was a reason for it. She wasn't supposed to be kissing Dev.

But she couldn't think—she could only feel. His touch, so tender, swept her worries straight out of her mind.

He lifted his lips from hers and looked at her, his brown eyes warm. "Is this okay?"

In some part of her mind she knew that the answer was *no*. It wasn't okay, but instead of focusing on that, she let her own fingers tangle in his hair. Springy, short, coarser than hers.

She felt so good being close to Dev like this. He was so tender, so caring. So much what she didn't deserve.

But she didn't want to think about that. Instead, she turned her head and rested her cheek against his chest and let him hold her, felt the breeze on her face, opened her eyes to drink in the beauty of their surroundings. He had brought her here. He had cared enough to want to show her this special place, to make her feel better, and it was good of him. *He* was good.

And then all the old feelings forced their way back into her heart. He might be good, but she wasn't. She wasn't supposed to feel this good, wasn't allowed to, wouldn't let herself. The small worries built up steam until she tugged away.

He let her go, but only after the slightest tightening of his hands told her he didn't want to let her go.

She didn't deserve a man who didn't want to let her go. The moment she left his arms, the rest of the old, bad feelings rushed back in.

She didn't deserve any of this.

She stood, and it felt like tearing herself away from the best thing that had ever happened to her, but she had to do it. "I have to go. We have to go. Right away."

He stood and shook his head the way Lady shook off water. "Wait. Can you slow down? Just a little?"

His voice magnetized her, and she knew if she didn't

break away now, she wouldn't be able to, and that would be wrong. "No, I can't slow down," she said. "Let's go."

She walked over to the truck and gripped the cold door handle. Cold. Hard. That was what she needed to focus on. Not beautiful, tender warmth.

"Emily?" He came to stand behind her, very close. "Are you okay?"

She stared at that cold, hard silver door handle and shook her head.

"Can we talk about it?"

Again, she shook her head without looking at him.

The ride back to the school was quiet. Twice, Dev tried to open a conversation, but Emily didn't respond.

She was churning inside. Why had she let him kiss her? Why had she practically initiated it herself? Why had he gone along, after he promised not to touch her?

She knew it wasn't fair to blame him, knew the kiss had been mutual, but she had to find a way to push away this appealing, magnetic man, this man who was much too good for her.

So when he pulled up into the driveway, she got out and paced back and forth. "Dev, that can't happen again. I don't want it."

"I'm sorry, Emily," he said. "I thought… Never mind."

Lady was nudging at her, clearly sensing Emily's agitation. In fact, her heart was pounding; she was on the verge of a panic attack. How had she… Why had she… "I have to go inside," she said.

"Emily, wait," Dev said. He picked up something inside the truck and handed it to her, her bag. The bag that had held her Mother's Day present—the gift that she'd taken to her mother, who hadn't known what it was and had pushed it away.

Dealing with her mother was a trial, and it grieved her every time she went. These last two weeks, when Dev had taken her, she'd looked forward to it, but not because of Mom. Because she got to spend time with Dev—Dev and sometimes Landon.

She'd let herself get attached to them. Let expectations and hopes build that shouldn't have been there.

"Look, I'll keep teaching Landon, but I need to stay away from you. That was unacceptable." She hated the harsh words coming out of her mouth, but it was the only way she could do what was right.

Dev's expression hardened. He opened his mouth as if to say something and then shut it again and studied her. "I see," he said finally, and she could read the hurt in his eyes.

No, you don't see, she wanted to scream at him. She wanted to pull him back into her arms, to explain that it wasn't something about him, that it was about her. She wasn't good enough for him.

But none of that would make sense to him. Better to hurt him a little now than a lot later.

So she spun on her heel, snapped her fingers for Lady to follow and marched into her cold, lonely cabin.

By the end of the school day on Monday, Dev was beat. He hadn't slept well after that disastrous kiss with Emily. And then he'd stressed out all day trying, and failing, to avoid her. There was a broken window in the library he had to fix. He'd passed her in the hall three times. And though he'd gone to the staff lunchroom at a different time than either of them usually did, she'd been there. Probably trying to avoid him the same way he was trying to avoid her.

Never had the Bright Tomorrows school seemed so small.

When Landon rushed out the doors of the school and ran to him, practically bursting with excitement, Dev immediately felt better. Back in Denver, and in the early days here, Landon had trudged out of school with a frown on his face. In just five weeks, Landon's attitude toward his classes had undergone a complete turnaround. He wasn't making As, but he was passing, keeping up. That was worth any amount of embarrassment on Dev's part.

"Dad! Can I join the drama club? Will you help build the set? I already said you would."

"Drama club?" Dev smiled to see his son's excitement.

"Yeah! They do a performance at the end of the year, and they need more people, and they're doing a play about superheroes! Not the exact same ones as in movies, 'cause of copy, copy something—"

"Copyright?" They walked slowly down the lane toward the cabin, the sounds of shouting, glad-to-be-done-with-school boys diminishing behind them. The sun shone down on them, warm like summer. The snow-capped mountains in the distance seemed far away.

"Yeah! And I can be, like, one of the helper heroes, if I can remember lines. Or maybe someone who gets hurt, and then I could have fake blood all over me!"

Not for the first time, Dev was impressed with Bright Tomorrows and the way the school engaged the boys. He'd never have expected a school for troubled boys to have an enthusiastic drama club, but if they put on superhero plays, it made sense. "Wait, how come they're only starting the spring play now?" School here went on longer than ordinary schools, well into June, but classes would end in just six weeks.

"They do a lot of plays and they're starting a new one, and I have to decide this week." Finally, Landon was running out of breath. "Sometimes they don't have a fancy set, but if you help, they could, and all the guys want you to."

"It sounds pretty good." Dev was learning not to say yes right away, though. "Let's think it through." They were approaching their cabin now, and from the other direction, Emily was approaching hers.

Dev's stomach plunged. She'd taken the long way around. Trying to avoid him, most likely.

For the thousandth time, he kicked himself mentally for kissing her. Why hadn't he stuck to his no-touching plan?

But he knew why. When he'd seen Emily's willingness to be close, when he'd felt her snuggling against him in the cool mountain air, all his willpower had blown away on the breeze. He'd given in, and for a few blissful minutes, he'd gotten lost in her sweet perfume and soft hair and tender, hesitant touch.

And then it had all gone wrong. He didn't quite understand why she'd abruptly backed away and cooled off and gotten angry, but it had happened and now he had to deal with the fallout.

He dearly wished they weren't neighbors. He wished she wasn't Landon's tutor. But wishes weren't reality.

"Please, Dad? I really want to."

Thinking about Emily, and tutoring, reminded him of the major obstacle to Landon joining the drama club. "You have tutoring after school."

"Yeah, but… Hey, Ms. Carver! Ms. Carver!" Landon

waved frantically and then ran ahead to meet Emily. "You gotta talk to Dad about the drama club!"

She smiled—obviously fake and forced—and let Landon grab her hand and tug her toward Dev. They met on the road in front of their two cabins.

Dev couldn't force a smile. "Sorry," he said to her. "Landon's excited."

"I can see." She ran an affectionate hand over Landon's hair. "We do need to talk about the drama club."

"Tutoring is the most important thing," Dev said.

"Oh, Dad…"

"You have to pass the achievement tests at the end of the year to go on to fourth grade. That's what we need to focus on." He looked at Emily, forced himself to see her as a professional, not as the soft, warm woman he'd held in his arms. "Is there a way to do both? Would that be a good idea, or too much?"

"It's great Landon wants to participate. I think we can make it work." She stroked Landon's hair again, and Landon leaned against her, and Dev's heart gave a big, painful thump as worry filled his mind.

Landon was getting attached to Emily, and from the looks of things, it went both ways.

Emily was a good person, the type of person he'd want Landon to attach to. Even, if God willed it, the type of person who'd make a good stepmother to Landon.

And a good wife to Dev, except that she didn't want to be anywhere near him. In fact, maybe she was trying to get out of tutoring Landon as a way to avoid Dev. "I still need for you to tutor him," he reminded her. He wished, now, that they'd done a formal contract. "We can make…adjustments, about where it happens. Do it right after school in the library, and I can pick him up afterward."

She glanced quickly at him and then away, but it was enough for him to see that she understood: he was offering to make it so she didn't have to spend time with him. He wasn't going to force himself on her.

"Drama club's right after school," Landon protested.

"Every day?"

"Three days a week," Emily said. "And I can guarantee that after rehearsal, Landon isn't going to be up for tutoring. We might have to work together in the mornings on those days, before school."

A picture flashed before Dev's eyes: Emily in the morning, sleepy, hair mussed, drinking coffee at the same breakfast table as him and Landon. Longing rose up in him, but he pushed it away, forced himself to be a neutral, concerned parent. "As his tutor, what do you think? Would it be a good idea to change his routine like this?"

Landon looked up at her, his eyes wide. "It would be, Ms. Carver! I'd still do all my schoolwork!"

"You don't like getting up early," Dev reminded him.

"I can do it! I can set my own alarm."

Emily smiled at Landon and then looked at Dev with a bland, professional expression. "It's good Landon is so motivated," she said. "It would be good for his confidence and his reading skills."

"And you're willing to change the schedule?"

"Of course. In fact, I'd need to change it anyway, because—"

"Yay! And you'll help with the sets, right?" Landon bounced up and down, his smile wide and confident, like he knew Dev would do it.

And Dev was a sucker. He wanted Landon to be that certain of his father's willingness to help. "Okay. As long as you keep improving in school, you can do it, and I'll help."

"I asked Dad if he could build the sets for us," Landon explained to Emily, holding her hand and swinging on it.

"That's…great," she said without enthusiasm.

Her tone was strange, and he wondered why.

And then he knew. "Who's running the drama club?" he asked.

"Three of us take turns," she said. "And it's my turn."

Their gazes held for the shortest moment as Dev processed just what he'd agreed to.

Instead of spending less time together, they'd be spending more.

Twelve

The school stage was a part of the multipurpose hall that served as the gymnasium, the cafeteria and the assembly room. As such, it always smelled slightly of kids' sneakers and whatever Hayley had served up for lunch. The good news was that the mostly glass wall that looked out to the mountains could be opened to allow the kids to roll tables outside in good weather.

Plus, importantly, it let in fresh air. So Emily pushed it wide-open before she gathered the student actors and stagehands at the long table closest to the stage. To avoid distracting the kids, she'd already taken Lady to a sunny corner of the cafeteria and given her the "stay" command.

"Do we have to memorize a lot of lines?" Chip Peterson, so nicknamed for his love of potato chips, held a bag of his favorite snack. "I want to be in the play, but I'm no good at remembering stuff."

"Memorizing is part of it, but we'll have prompters just like people on TV do." That was thanks to a grant from one of the school's generous benefactors.

A shadow crossed Landon's face, and Emily was

pretty sure she knew why. A teleprompter only worked if you knew how to read. Landon, like some of the other kids who were eager to be involved, wasn't a strong reader. His lessons were helping, and he was improving, but he had miles to go before he could glance at a teleprompter, read what was on it and carry on acting without the audience noticing the extra support.

The flip side of that was that kids who didn't read well were often good memorizers. "Part of what I'll be doing over the next few days is talking through the parts with all of you, figuring out your strengths. We'll make sure that everyone gets a part he likes and that he can succeed at." It was a tall promise, but one Emily felt confident making. She'd chosen the play because of its appeal to young boys and its balanced mixture of parts in a true ensemble cast.

The boys were talking among themselves now, passing around snacks, speculating about what parts they might get but also telling stories about their days and tossing paper wads and shoving and elbowing each other, getting physical. Emily knew she had to put them to work soon or she'd lose them. "One last thing, and I want everyone to listen up," she said and waited until she had their attention. "Being in this play can't take away from your schoolwork. If you have homework to do or a meeting with a teacher, you let me know and we'll work out a way for you to do it while staying in the play. Got it?"

There were murmurs of assent.

"For today, we're all going to take part in set design," she said.

"My dad's going to do that," Landon said.

"He's going to supervise," Emily corrected, "but you boys are going to do all the work."

The question was, where was Dev?

She would never have chosen to get him involved, given how awkward things were between them. But due to Landon's innocent plea for his involvement, there was no choice and no way to graciously refuse his help. The other teachers had been thrilled to know the new janitor was willing to take on this sort of work, and Emily had the feeling that Dev was going to be a set designer for many productions to come.

Which was great, but she had to figure out how to get through the first play while working closely with him.

Without thinking continually about how wonderful it had been to kiss him.

She'd beaten herself up about that since practically the moment after it had happened. She should have known better. What had she been thinking, snuggling up so close with him? What had she expected to take place when she let things get physical?

A part of her was even glad. She'd had that one kiss with a man she admired and cared for, those few minutes of dreaming about being a couple with Dev. That wonderful sense of protection and caring.

She'd have it to cling to, to keep forever.

That was why she had done it, she supposed. After the day of grief about her lost child, and struggling with her mother, she simply hadn't had the willpower left to resist his magnetic pull. She hadn't wanted to. She'd wanted the closeness, the warmth, the caring.

A stronger, better woman would have kept that invisible barrier between them, the barrier of "we're just friends." Dev wouldn't have broken through it without encouragement from her. He was a man of honor; she knew that about him just from their short acquaintance.

But no, she'd cuddled right up against him in that beautiful place, surrounded by God's majestic creation. She'd craved the comfort of his nearness, his strength.

And because she'd given in to that craving, she now had to keep total distance from him. She'd had to be rude and push him away, hurtfully.

It was more kind in the end, she reminded herself.

Dev strode into the multipurpose hall then, tall and muscular, his sleeves rolled up. He looked harassed as he came over to the table of squabbling, chattering boys. "Sorry I'm late," he said to Emily, keeping his voice low. "Vandalism incident in the upstairs restroom."

"Oh, no, is everything okay?"

He flashed a smile. "Caught the perps in time. They're up there scrubbing, supervised by Stan."

"Oh, good." She started to smile at him and then remembered that she had to keep her distance. She cleared her throat. "Are you ready to get the boys started on sets, or do you need a minute?"

He forked a hand through his hair and looked away from her, as if he'd also only just remembered that their friendship held a big dose of awkwardness now. "I, uh, I'm ready. Tell me what you want."

She pulled out her laptop and found photos from other productions. He leaned over her, looking at them. "Yeah. We can do that." He pointed. "But you want to keep it simple, right? So maybe that would work better." He pointed at another example.

"Perfect." She could smell his cologne, something woodsy. She remembered that from when they'd kissed, and it swept her back to that moment. Her skin heated. "Let's go up to the stage."

And she'd better bring the boys along to keep things from getting personal between them.

It worked. Dev scouted the area, thought for a minute and then turned and knelt to talk to the boys, describing what they'd do. "We're going to need older boys to do some sawing and hammering. Younger boys to paint," he finished.

The boys paid attention to what he said. They liked him already, she could tell. The school was small enough that everyone knew everyone, and even though Dev had only been on the job a little over a month, he seemed to have met every kid in the school. She was impressed that he knew all the names already and had even noticed that Camden was good at art and that Chip spent extra time in shop class.

He took three of the strongest boys with him to gather supplies, and Emily worked with the others, showing them clips from a video of another performance of the play. Dev and his crew returned with carts loaded with plywood and paint and tools. More quickly than Emily would have expected, he had all of them occupied with age-appropriate tasks. He was gruff with them, businesslike, but they didn't seem to mind; they rose to the occasion and worked hard to earn his occasional flash of a smile.

Emily was surprised and impressed to see this side of him. He was really good with the kids. Was there anything this man couldn't do?

Since he had them well under control, she was able to pull out one boy at a time. She had the stronger students read for the lead roles and showed those who didn't read well a video sequence to act out. Chip showed a real propensity for slapstick, just as she'd suspected from his clowning around in reading class, so she assigned him a major comic role.

In between kids, she watched Dev work. That was okay, wasn't it? He didn't know. And she liked seeing him kneel beside the younger boys, teaching them to paint properly or hammer a nail. She was impressed at the way he stopped an argument from escalating with a few quiet words.

They listened to him, and part of it was the fact that they needed and benefited from male role models, and that Dev was still new to them. But another man could have easily blown that advantage and chaos would have ensued, because these boys could be difficult.

Dev held their attention without any trouble. Impressive.

When it was almost time to go, she suggested that they clean up and then stood near Dev as the boys worked. Honesty compelled her to compliment him. "You're really good working with these boys. Are you sure you weren't a teacher in another life?"

He snorted. "No way. Not the academic type."

"You work with them well."

He shrugged. "I was like them, growing up. One of the so-called troublemakers, so I don't judge them the way some of the teachers do."

Interested despite her better judgment, she studied him. "Why were you a troublemaker?"

He shrugged. "Moved around a lot, in the system. Didn't do too well in school. The usual reasons." He glanced at her quickly and then away.

"That must have been hard." She wanted to know

more. Wanted to hear about what it had been like to move from home to home, school to school.

Her phone buzzed, and she pulled it out and looked at it. When she saw the number, her heart sank. "I have to take this," she said, "but it'll be quick. Sorry. Can you..." She gestured at the boys.

"I've got them. Go ahead."

She walked away and gathered her patience to speak with her late husband's mother. "Hi, Suzanne."

The woman was already crying. "Did you forget that it's time to start working on the race?"

Emily sat down at a table, her mood plummeting. "We said last year was going to be the final one."

"We talked about that. But I can't stand it." Suzanne was sobbing heavily now. "I can't... I just can't...forget him. I know it's easier for you..."

Don't react. Emily reminded herself to take deep breaths. Lady came and leaned against her. For several minutes, she listened to Suzanne cry and gasp.

When her mother-in-law finally sputtered to near silence, Emily spoke. "Is John there?"

"No," Suzanne said. Audible breaths. "No, he's golfing. Golfing, and me in this state!"

Emily mentally congratulated her former father-in-law for taking care of himself. She put a hand on Lady's curly head and rubbed and scratched the dog behind her ears. Lady slowly sank to the floor, leaning against Emily's hand.

"I w-w-want to do it again, one more time," Suzanne quivered. "Can't we do it one more time?"

One more memorial race for her late husband. Could she manage it?

Of course she could. But last year, the race had only

raised $200 for the charity designated, and the number of participants had been embarrassingly small. John, her father-in-law, had barely found time to announce the race to his work colleagues. It wasn't that he didn't care, or miss his son, but he'd resumed the rest of his life.

Suzanne, although she had always expressed enthusiasm for the race, had done less and less of the actual work each year. Last year it had fallen entirely on Emily to organize, fundraise and execute an event for the husband she'd struggled to stay with.

Naturally, she'd felt horrible about his death, especially when the cause of the fire had been determined to be her mother's leaving food cooking on the stove. The fact that Mitch had fallen asleep drunk, that he'd told her he'd changed the smoke alarm batteries when he'd really just pulled the old ones out—none of that carelessness meant that he deserved to have his life cut short.

She'd missed him, too. Maybe more, because their relationship had been troubled and there hadn't been time to work anything out. No time to talk through her own anger that he hadn't been alert enough to save their child. No time for him to explain. No time to laugh together, to make up.

In the end—and this was what Suzanne and John had jumped on—it was Emily who'd chosen to go out with friends, leaving their grandson and Mitch and Emily's mother alone.

The guilt of it swirled up in her. "I'll think about it, Suzanne, but please don't get your hopes up. Let's also consider just making a donation to the fire department instead."

"But that wouldn't have the same meaning…" Suzanne talked on, and Emily looked at the stage. Dev was still working with the boys, but he kept glancing her way. Probably wondering why she was talking on the phone rather than fulfilling her responsibilities.

"Look, I have to go," she said, cutting off the stream of words. "I'll be in touch within the next few days about the race, but please think about alternatives."

"I guess I'll have to contact some of Mitch's friends," she said, her voice rising toward anger. "I'm sure *they'd* be glad to help."

Not really, Emily wanted to say. Mitch's friends weren't exactly volunteer-of-the-year types, or at least, they hadn't been. Emily had never gotten along with them.

"I'm at work, and I really do have to go," Emily said, and when Suzanne kept talking, she ended the call.

Which would infuriate the woman, and understandably so, but there wasn't much to be done about it. Suzanne didn't understand things like jobs, because she'd never had one. She'd had everything go her way in life—until she'd lost her son and grandson, of course—but those early advantages hadn't made her happy. She'd provided the same environment for her son, and it hadn't served him well, either, though he'd certainly been handsome and charming enough to sweep Emily off her feet.

She shoved her phone in her pocket, gave Lady a final head rub and went up the stairs to the stage. "Thanks for taking over," she said to Dev. "I think we can start them cleaning up."

Dev put two fingers to his mouth and whistled. "Okay, everyone. Lids on paint cans, tools back in their containers. Everything can be stacked against the far wall.

Landon and Chip, you're on sweeping duty. Brooms on the cart."

Emily was stunned at his efficiency. "You're good at that!"

He laughed. "Years of experience telling people what to do. I've headed up teams at a couple of jobs I had. Are you okay?" he added, his face sobering. "Seemed like you had a rough phone call."

"I did," she said. But she didn't want to talk about Mitch to Dev, didn't want to speak ill of him or his parents. "Just a flash from the past. It'll all work out fine."

At least, she hoped so. As soon as she'd ended the call, she'd regretted not just saying a firm no right away. Doing the race again would be a mistake. She made a vow to herself that she'd contribute $200 to the fire department as soon as she'd gotten her car fixed.

It was a way to ease her conscience, and so maybe a little selfish, but it would do some good.

The trouble was, Suzanne had a vindictive side. If Emily didn't fall into line with what she wanted, Suzanne would undoubtedly attempt to make her pay.

But Emily was finally getting stronger. She wasn't going to let a troubled woman guide her life.

She just hoped the retaliation wouldn't be too swift and severe.

When they'd gotten the boys off to their house parents—Landon going along, so he could share dinner with some of his new friends—Dev looked around for Emily, only to see her walking rapidly away, toward their cabins.

She didn't want to spend time with him. That was obvious.

Also obvious was that the phone call she'd received had been upsetting. Was still upsetting, if the slump of her shoulders was any indication.

He thought about following her, pushing her to tell him what was wrong. They were supposed to be friends.

Only the friendship had gotten overcomplicated by the fact that they'd shared that kiss. That they'd pushed it over the line from friendship into something more.

Dev wished it hadn't happened, because it meant that he couldn't be a true friend to Emily now without having it colored with a desire for romance.

He also felt motivated to try and make something work between them.

They'd been good together this afternoon, working with the boys. He'd enjoyed it, had been impressed with the efficient way she'd kept the project moving ahead and sympathetically matched up some of the boys with roles that fit their skills. Never once making anyone feel lacking or bad about it.

And she'd seemed sincere in admiring the work he was doing with the boys, too.

Landon was ecstatic. He loved the idea of being in a play, loved working on the set and, most of all, loved the new friends he was making. Unlike at his old school, here he wasn't ostracized for having trouble with reading. Everyone here had problems of one kind or another, which meant they didn't judge quite so harshly as mainstream kids.

Landon also really, really liked Emily. For the first time, Dev wondered whether Landon's effort to get Dev to work on the show had included an element of junior matchmaking.

If so, maybe the kid had a point. Maybe Dev and Emily would make a good couple.

But Dev had something to overcome first.

He looked back at the school and noticed that Ashley Green's office light was on. Before he could second-guess the idea, he went back inside and tapped on the half-closed door of the principal's office. "Hey, Ashley?"

"Dev." She looked up, smiled and beckoned him in. "How'd the rehearsal go?"

He admired the woman for how she seemed genuinely welcoming to everyone who came into her office, even if they were interrupting her work, and also for how she seemed to know everything that went on in the school. "It went well," he said. "Kids had a good time."

"Good." She studied him. "Sit down and tell me what's up. You're not one to drop in for no reason."

He nodded. "I… I wanted to talk to you about something."

"Landon?" she asked. "I hear he's improving, although we're still keeping it open whether he repeats the year or not. He was pretty far behind."

"I know, and we're working on that." He skimmed his damp hands down the sides of his jeans. "It's not Landon, it's…it's me."

She nodded and waited.

"I, well, I have a problem, and I need your help with it." He sucked in a deep breath, trying without success to calm his racing heart. "I need… I need help with my own reading—" He rushed over the words, not wanting to give her time to react. "And I don't want to distract Emily from Landon. Is there another teacher I could pay to tutor me?"

Underneath the fear and the shame, he felt the slightest flicker of hope.

He shouldn't feel hopeful, because he was telling his boss something that could probably get him fired. A smarter man would've called some anonymous literacy hotline.

But there was something about the Bright Tomorrows school that encouraged optimism. Maybe it was the photos of former students that lined the school office, some wearing suits, some in humbler work clothes, but all of them smiling, looking proud.

It gave you the feeling that maybe you could succeed, make yourself and others proud, too.

She studied him. "I suspected you struggled with reading," she said.

Dev stared at her. "You *did*?"

"I did." She twirled a pencil in her hands. "I'm a reading teacher by background, too, and I noticed the signs. You always forget your glasses, so someone else has to read to you. You talk things through rather than writing them down. And you have a very sharp memory. You've had to, I'm sure, to achieve this level of professional success with weak reading skills."

He blew out a breath and leaned back in his chair. He was embarrassed, but he also felt strangely relieved. There was something tiring about having to hide his situation from everyone. It was good to have a person who knew.

"I think you're right that Emily doesn't have time," she said. "And…my guess is that there are other reasons her tutoring you wouldn't be a good idea."

Dev met her eyes steadily. "If you're worried about us getting to be too close of friends—"

"No," she interrupted, raising a hand like a stop sign. "If I were worried, I'd say so. I have confidence that the two of you are goodhearted, discreet individuals."

He opened his mouth to tell her there was nothing between them and then shut it again. There *was* something between them. Something strange, and probably doomed, but something.

"If I could make a suggestion," she said. "I'd like to work with you on a few tests to find out what you're dealing with. Have you ever been diagnosed with dyslexia?"

"No. No way."

She lifted an eyebrow. "It's not a disgrace, it's a disability. And there's a chance your son may have it. That came up in our meeting about Landon this week."

"It *did*?" Why hadn't Emily told him?

Then again, things hadn't been exactly friendly between them.

"It was in the letter Emily sent home… Oh." She gave a rueful half smile, and he saw the realization hit her: Dev couldn't read the school papers Landon brought home. Of course, he did his best to puzzle out the meaning of the ones that looked important, but inevitably, he missed things. Like that Landon should be tested for dyslexia.

"It tends to run in families," Ashley went on. "If you were never tested yourself—"

"I don't have dyslexia. I'm just…slow. With reading, writing, things like that." As he uttered the words, he flashed back to the boy he'd been. *Slow.* He'd heard the word jostled around as he'd been transferred from school to school, foster home to foster home.

He was just slow.

"I don't think you're *just slow*, Dev," she said. "I've

seen you fix a boiler without directions, mix up cement without measuring, just by feel. You know the name of every kid in the school. You've developed superior coping skills, some of the best I've seen."

He waved off her words and the small surge of pride they engendered in him. "I think, after seeing the way Landon's working, that I could improve. I can read," he emphasized quickly, his face reddening. "Just not well."

"I agree that you can improve," she said. "And if you'll give me, say, three one-hour sessions, I can help you figure out next steps."

"Wow." Could it really be that simple? "Are you sure you have time to work with me?"

She leaned forward. "I do, because I care about my employees. You have a lot of potential, Dev. It would be to the school's benefit for you to reach it."

Dev's face heated.

She waved a hand. "I'm sorry if I sound like I'm speaking to a kid. Career educator. And obviously, I can't continue working with you beyond some initial tests. For one thing, my reading certification is expired. And there's the time factor. But there are some terrific online teachers who could work with you on a regular basis. You're motivated. You'll make fast progress."

Dev blew out a breath and leaned back. "I… Wow. I never really came clean with anyone before, at least not for a while." He'd admitted the truth to Roxy, and it hadn't turned out well. "I don't want to miss work hours, but I notice you're usually here early. Could I come in before the school day starts? Maybe while Landon is getting tutored?"

She pulled out a calendar and they set it up. "I'm glad you came to me, Dev," she said. "This is going to be a big, positive change in your life, and I'm impressed you're ready and willing to make it."

"Thanks." Dev left with a bounce in his step. He hoped Ashley was right. If she was, coming to Bright Tomorrows might turn out to be the best thing for him as well as for Landon.

And if he could get up to par with reading… He looked toward Emily's cottage. Maybe, just maybe, he'd get up the confidence to try to convince Emily to explore a relationship, too.

Thirteen

"You did great today!" Emily hugged Landon on Friday morning after their tutoring session. "Now, pack up your stuff while I make you one of my speedy egg sandwiches." He'd seen her eating one when he'd arrived, doughnut in hand, and had said it looked good. She'd offered to make him one as long as he worked hard in tutoring, and he had.

It was just a simple English muffin topped with an egg and cheese, but she found herself humming as she sizzled butter in a small pan and then cracked an egg into it. Landon, having quickly stuffed his books into his backpack, was on the floor with Lady.

Could she be blamed if she pretended, just for a few minutes, that she was Landon's mom?

Outside was cold enough that her breath had made clouds when she'd gone out on her porch to welcome Landon.

Dev had stood on his porch, too, and had given her a wave, but he hadn't come over. Which was totally fine. Good, even. They'd be spending so much time together between random school day encounters and working on the play. There was no reason they needed to have a conversation first thing in the morning.

The muffin popped up in the toaster. She poured Landon a glass of orange juice and then built the muffin sandwich. "Here you go," she said. "Eat fast. We need to get going."

"I'm gonna get an A on my word problem homework," Landon bragged as they walked to school. He briefly got distracted by a magpie that landed on a fencepost beside them, chattering and scolding. He jumped and yelled until the big bird flew up to land on a bare aspen branch. "Then I'm gonna get an A on the test!" He frowned. "Or a B. Bs are okay."

"They sure are," Emily said, amused by him. They walked into the school lobby, where a few day students waited for the first bell.

"Let's see which signs you can read," Emily suggested. "I'm guessing you can read this one."

Landon looked up and frowned. "That's too long."

"You can sound it out," she encouraged. She covered all but the first two letters. "*R* and long *e*."

"Ree?" he said.

"Yes! Now here's the hard part." She covered both ends of the word. "Remember we talked about blending sounds? There's an *SP* here, like in…"

"Sports!" He'd struggled with that word this morning and figured it out.

"Good. But this has an *e*…" They went on, working through the long word, and she was proud of how Landon stuck with it. He would have kicked the wall or run away just three weeks ago.

Groups of kids were arriving from the residence houses. As the lobby got more crowded, the office door opened, and Ashley emerged to give her daily greeting to the students.

Dev was with her.

They were both laughing. They'd been in her office together.

Ashley was beautiful, tall and blonde and slim, her skin perfect. She had a ready smile and was already well-liked by the teachers.

Apparently, she was well-liked by Dev, too.

A primal *nooooo* formed instantly in her mind, and she actually took a step toward the pair.

And then she stopped herself. What was she thinking? She couldn't have Dev. She couldn't have any relationship; she'd made that decision on a cold night six years ago, so choked with tears and smoke and guilt that she could barely breathe.

"Dad! Look what I can read!" Landon rushed to Dev and tugged him over by the hand. "Look at this long word. It says, 'Ree-spect-ful.' Respectful."

"Wow, that's great," Dev said.

Ashley had followed them. "Good job," she said warmly.

Landon saw Chip and rushed over to him, leaving Dev, Emily and Ashley standing together.

"Early-morning meeting, huh?" Emily could have kicked herself as soon as she blurted it out, but she wanted to know.

Dev chuckled awkwardly. "Something like that."

"Well, I have a school to run," Ashley said. "See you soon."

Did she look at Dev in a special way? Did she mean something specific by *see you soon*? Did the two of them have plans?

She felt like putting an arm around Dev, claiming him in front of everyone, shouting out that he'd kissed *her*, not Ashley.

Although maybe he'd kissed Ashley, too, during their "something like" an early-morning meeting.

"When you get the chance, I'd like to get an update on Landon's progress," Dev said.

"Sure. Of course. He's doing well, but I can give you the details. In fact," she blurted out, "we could go to dinner after tonight's rehearsal."

He studied her for a moment while her face heated.

"Okay," he said slowly, "we can do that. Pretty sure Landon has a movie night at the residence houses tonight."

"Great! Got to go, get set up for the day!" She escaped to the library, her heart pounding.

Why on earth had she just asked Dev out on what amounted to a date?

Why had Emily asked Dev to go to dinner?

Okay, granted, he'd asked her to update him on Landon's progress. And granted, he was more than happy to see her outside work, and that probably showed.

But she'd made it clear she didn't want *that* kind of relationship. Had she changed her mind?

As he held the door for her at Café Aztec in Little Mesa, he couldn't help noticing her pretty dress, different than the practical clothes she usually wore to school. The rose color of it brought out the pink in her cheeks, which looked pinker than usual. Was she wearing makeup or was she blushing?

Once they were seated, she gave him a shy smile. "I didn't realize it would be this formal," she said. "I've never been here before. It was out of my…" She trailed off, her cheeks getting pinker. "Anyway, I wanted to try it, and I'm glad you were game."

"It's not very often that I have an evening without Landon," he said, "or that a pretty lady asks me to dinner." When she blushed harder and looked away, he could have kicked himself.

She didn't mean it like a date. She meant it like a meeting. Maybe. Probably.

"Emily Carver, is that you?" An older lady stopped by their table. She wore some kind of big, long cape, purple and blue, and a lot of jewelry.

"Hi, Mrs. Armstrong." Emily's voice sounded strained, and her smile looked forced. "How are you?"

"I'm well, dear." She looked at Dev appraisingly.

"Mrs. Armstrong, this is Dev McCarthy."

"Nice to meet you." Dev started to stand.

"Likewise, and don't stand up, I'm just saying hello," she said. "Emily, I'm glad to see that you're recovering so well." She gave Dev another glance, then swept off, her jewelry clanking.

Emily watched her go, frowning.

"Not a friend?" he asked.

"No. She's a friend of…my former mother-in-law. And I'm sure she's already on the phone with Suzanne, letting her know I'm out with a man."

He narrowed his eyes. "Your husband's been gone for a while, right?"

She nodded. "Six years. But for Suzanne, it's like yesterday. She'll be furious." She bit her lip. "This isn't good."

Dev studied her. She looked so worried, maybe almost ready to cry, and he didn't get it. "She doesn't have a say in your life, does she? After all this time?"

"She shouldn't, but…it's complicated."

The waiter came over and asked about drinks, and they both ordered iced tea. "We haven't even looked at the menu yet," Emily apologized in Spanish.

"*No hay problema.* Take your time."

And here they were at the most difficult part of any restaurant outing. Some places had pictures on the menu, which helped, but not this one. The words on it seemed to blur together. "What are you having?" he asked.

"I'm not sure. So many choices. What are you thinking about?"

Sweat dripped down his back. "No clue. I'll ask about specials when the waiter comes back."

He hated being this way, having to pretend all the time. And in fact, he and Ashley had spent a little time talking about that today: how he shouldn't be ashamed; how there was a good possibility he had dyslexia, which was a disability; how it was like a person who used a wheelchair or couldn't hear well—you wouldn't blame them for it.

"Yeah," he'd said, "but most adults can read better than I can, right? Even if they're dyslexic?"

After he'd told her about his background, she hadn't sugarcoated it. "Your social workers and teachers and foster parents did you a disservice, not helping you figure out why school was a struggle. Most people have more advantages, frankly."

"But can I learn?" It was a pathetic question, but he had to know.

"Of course!" She'd seemed shocked that he would

doubt it. "You'll learn, and quickly, once we're certain of a diagnosis and get you into a program."

"How quickly?" he'd asked.

She'd lifted her hands, palms up. "Everyone's different, but I would think you'd be reading well in a couple of years, maximum."

He'd covered his reaction, but inside, he'd groaned. In a couple of years, he'd be forty-two years old. Landon would be finishing elementary school, maybe here, maybe somewhere else.

In a couple of years, Emily would probably be married to some guy of equal intelligence and education.

"Have you decided?" the waiter asked, breaking into Dev's thoughts.

"What are your specials?" he asked after Emily had ordered, and the waiter recited them. He heard one that sounded good, and told the man he'd take that, and the difficult moment was over.

But he was thinking. Maybe he didn't have to wait a couple of years. Maybe he could tell Emily the truth, and soon.

"You wanted to talk about Landon," she said now. "He does seem to have a reading disability, probably dyslexia. I think I mentioned that in my note. Does that run in the family?"

And he was sweating again. "Um… I… I don't know. No one ever talked about it."

"It can sometimes go undiagnosed," she said.

"Can he get past it?"

"Of course!" She displayed the same confidence about Landon that Ashley had displayed about him. "It's a matter of showing him strategies to recognize words and sounds. Partly, it's getting him to slow down enough to try to decode words. He's smart, and he's gotten away with guessing so far, I imagine."

Dev liked hearing that Landon was smart. He'd always thought so. "He has a wicked good memory. He can recite the dialogue from any movie he watches. I'll get an earful of *MonsterMan* tomorrow, I'm sure."

She smiled. "That's a strength we can use. I've already ordered him audio versions of his textbooks. Once he hears them, I'm sure his test grades will shoot up."

"Are there audio versions available?"

She nodded. "Yes, and the school has to provide them once his disability is identified."

"Great." He was thrilled to already see a path forward for Landon. "So you think he can pass third grade?"

"I do. He knows a lot of the material just from listening in class. It's a matter of helping him learn to write out answers. And meanwhile, as soon as he has a diagnosis, he can take some tests orally."

"Wow." He wondered what school would have been like for him if he'd had those kind of supports in place.

Their food came then, and they dug in. Dev enjoyed his meal—delicious, authentic Mexican food—but even more, he enjoyed watching Emily enjoy it.

They chatted about the school, and about local hikes they'd both like to do in the summer, and about the Denver Broncos' chances for another good year. She offered him a taste of her *chile rellenos*, and he shared his *posole*, and it all felt natural. Fun. Nice.

He'd half worried that, on a social occasion, he and Emily wouldn't have anything to talk about, or that dinner out would be awkward. But just like at work, or on their car rides to visit her mom, they got along as if they were old friends.

He felt like a kid who was unwrapping a present he hadn't expected to receive. He'd known he was attracted to Emily, but that wasn't enough for a relationship. He'd figured she was out of his league, intellectually, but they actually got pretty deep talking about the pastor's sermon last week, and he held his own.

Plus, according to both Ashley and Emily, reading problems didn't necessarily mean you weren't smart. They could just mean your brain worked differently.

Still, the thought of how Roxy had mocked him about his inability to read well made him shrink from telling Emily the truth. And if he couldn't tell the truth, then they couldn't have a relationship; it was that simple.

So he shouldn't be feeling excited. A better man would put his feelings on hold, keep it friendly and no-touch.

The problem was that Emily looked so sweet and pretty, sweeter and prettier than any woman Dev had ever known. And as pretty as she was, that wasn't the main thing about her; she was a good person inside, too. No wonder he felt that push to get closer.

When the check arrived, he reached for it at the same time she did. "I'll get this," he said.

"No, it's okay, I'll pay my share."

"Your money's no good here." He tried to make a joke of it, but the truth was, he wanted to pay. Treating her would make him happy, and besides, he knew money was short for her.

Paying also made it feel more like a date, for him, at least.

After a little more protesting, she let him pay, and when they walked out together, he touched the small of her back, then took her hand.

The whole time he was yelling at himself. *Don't do it. Don't hold her hand. Don't raise expectations.*

He didn't listen. Not as he held her hand on the way out, and not as he opened the door for her, and not as he drove them home.

When they got there, the air felt pregnant with promise. He wasn't sure she felt the same way, but for him, he could hardly breathe for wanting to pull her into his arms.

She looked at him, her gaze direct. "Thank you for dinner, Dev," she said. "I appreciate it, but I won't ask again."

"Why's that?" He turned off the truck and climbed out, then came around to get her door, giving both of them a chance to think.

He helped her down but dropped her hand immediately. He wasn't going to push himself on her. It was wiser to keep a distance if this wasn't going anywhere.

And until he shared the truth about himself, it *couldn't* go anywhere. His head knew that, but it was having a hard time convincing his heart.

She put her hands on her hips and faced him. "There's something between us. We're both adults, and we know what we're feeling isn't the same as just friends." She blushed, laughed a little. "Well, me, anyway. But I have too many issues to pursue it."

"It's not you, it's me? Is that what you're saying?" He tried to keep it light, but the words came out sounding hurt.

She sighed, and then she did reach for his hand, held it in both of hers. "Oh, Dev, you're such a great guy, and any woman would be blessed to have you as a boyfriend. It's just… I'm not who you think I am." She squeezed his hand and then dropped it, turned, squared her shoulders and walked to the house.

I'm not who you think I am, either, he wanted to say.

He didn't say it. But he did think that maybe, maybe they could wait for each other. Maybe be friends until they were ready to be more.

A little spark of hope lit in him, a kind of pilot light. He'd keep it burning and see what happened.

He went to pick up Landon with a light heart.

Fourteen

Saturday morning, Emily gathered her gardening things and went outside. At this high elevation, it was a little early to plant spring flowers, but she wanted to prepare the ground. Soon enough, the risk of frost would pass, true spring would come and she could plant all the colorful flowers she loved.

She wet the ground with the garden hose and pulled up a few weeds. Though the air was cool, the sun warmed her shoulders. Lady chased squirrels and leaped at butterflies, looking as happy as Emily felt inside.

The date with Dev last night had been wonderful. Of course, it hadn't really been a date, but it had felt like one. He'd insisted on paying for the meal. He'd held her hand and opened doors for her. He'd acted like he cared, and by now, she knew him well enough to know he wouldn't fake that.

He cared for her!

She wrapped her arms around herself, smiling at nobody, feeling breathless. He cared. Dev McCarthy cared for *her.*

And despite the past six years she'd spent saying

she was fine, just fine focusing on work and dodging a social life, she could admit now that she wanted that for herself. She wanted to care and be cared for again.

Like the newly fertile ground she was digging and tilling, springtime was coming inside her, too. She wasn't quite ready yet, but the possibility of new life, new love, was in reach.

Maybe she and Dev could give a relationship a try.

The sound of a car coming up the road this early surprised her. "Lady," she called, and the poodle ran to her side.

She expected the big, dark luxury sedan to drive on past, but it stopped in front of her cottage. She stood and squinted, and her heart sank.

Her former in-laws were inside.

As they climbed out, her good feelings seeped away like air from a slow-leaking tire. Guilt and hurt and anger churned inside her.

She stood as John opened the passenger door for Suzanne.

And then they marched toward her, side by side, not smiling.

"Is it true what I heard," Suzanne asked, "that you were out on a date with some man, practically on the anniversary of Mitchell's death?"

Emily blew out a breath and stripped off her gardening gloves. Lady leaned against her, and she put down a hand to touch the dog's curly head. "Hi, Suzanne. John. I wasn't expecting you this morning."

"Well?" Suzanne's voice rose to a higher pitch. "Is it true?"

Involuntarily, Emily glanced over at Dev's place,

then wished she hadn't. She looked back at her in-laws. "Would you like to come in?"

Suzanne planted her hands on her hips. "I was *going* to talk to you about the memorial 5-K, but now I see why you're not interested. Why you don't care anymore!" Her voice got louder, punching out each word.

Next door, Dev walked out onto his porch, Landon beside him. He didn't even pretend he wasn't paying attention; he actually came to the side of the porch and looked over, arms crossed.

He was so handsome. So thoughtful and kind.

So out of her league…but, she reminded herself, he seemed to care about her anyway.

Landon came partway down the porch steps, stopping at a quiet word from his father. "Hi, Lady," he called.

Lady's tail thumped, but she stayed by Emily's side.

John turned to look at Dev and Landon. "What did your friend say he looked like?" he asked Suzanne. Before she could answer, he glared at Emily. "Is this the man?"

The questions and emotions swirled around her, and she bit her lip and kept a hand on Lady.

"You okay, Emily?" Dev called across the lawns.

"I'm fine," she said, nodding at him. "Everything's okay." Obviously untrue statements, but what she meant was, *don't come over, I'll handle it.*

He seemed to get the message, because he nodded once and went inside.

Which was what she needed to get John and Suzanne to do, if they insisted on staying. She didn't need an audience for their scolding. "Why don't you both come inside? I'll make coffee."

Suzanne ignored the suggestion. "After you caused

our son's death, you dare to go on with your life? I'll never go on with my life!" She wiped tears from under her eyes and held out a hand, and John gave her a clean white handkerchief. He'd always carried one, even before Mitch's death, because Suzanne's meltdowns were frequent and teary.

"We didn't just lose our son," he added, putting an arm around Suzanne. "Our grandson, as well. Our only grandson."

Emily squeezed her eyes shut as waves of guilt crashed over her. They were articulating the worst things she told herself, on her worst days, and it was hard to hear them said aloud. And a shallow part of her worried that Dev would hear them blaming her. Both Suzanne and John had voices that carried.

And she felt deep, deep sympathy for them, she really did. She of all people knew how devastating it was to lose a child.

"We've been talking to some of Mitch's friends, your mutual friends," John said. "They had an interesting perspective."

"We hadn't been in touch with them since the tragedy, but because you didn't seem like you wanted to work on the race, I reached out to them." Suzanne's voice quavered.

Emily felt her shoulders tightening more, which hadn't even seemed possible.

"They think you knew he'd had too much to drink," John said, "and yet you went out anyway."

"I got my mom to come over and help, in case..." Emily trailed off, knowing that to defend herself was fruitless. But it was the truth. She hadn't known Mitch was already drinking that night, didn't think he had been, but she knew his habits. That was why she'd asked her mom to come as backup.

"Your mom has Alzheimer's! She caused the fire!" Suzanne's voice rose at the end, her face a dangerous shade of pink.

John tightened his arm around Suzanne's shoulder. "Criminal negligence, even if the police wouldn't call it that."

Emily sank down onto the steps. Their words felt like physical blows, pounding her head and shoulders, crushing her.

Lady trotted up the steps and sat beside her at the top, leaning hard against her.

Alongside the pain John and Suzanne were causing, a little anger flickered. It had been six years, six painful years, since the horrible incident had occurred, since her own life had been ruined. John and Suzanne had always hinted at these blameful attitudes, but they'd never been this explicit before. Probably because she'd always meekly done everything they'd asked of her. She'd never stepped out of line.

"I don't know how you dare show your face in public, laughing and enjoying yourself with another man." Suzanne looked daggers at her.

"Does *he* know what you did?" John asked, pointing at Dev's house.

She couldn't help looking over there. Dev was nowhere in sight, but Landon knelt on the porch, a couple of forgotten action figures at his side, his expression distressed.

She'd caused that. Here she'd pretended Landon was her son, let herself imagine Dev as her boyfriend. She didn't deserve either.

"You should be ashamed of yourself," Suzanne shouted and then broke down sobbing again.

"Disgusting." John put an arm around Suzanne and guided her back to the car.

As they drove away in a spray of gravel and dust, Emily sat still, arms wrapped around her knees. If she moved, she might shatter like fragile glass.

Lady nudged at her, but even the dog's gentle touch didn't lessen the pain she felt.

It was true, what they'd said. The disaster she'd experienced was her own fault. She needed to go back to focusing solely on her work. Stop trying to have fun like a normal person who hadn't done anything wrong.

The penance for her sin would last a lifetime, and even that wouldn't be enough to make up for it.

There was a sound from next door, and concern for Landon made her look over that way. But it wasn't Landon; it was Dev.

Relief loosened the tension in her body and she turned a little toward him, putting an arm around Lady for strength.

Dev wasn't smiling as he walked toward her. "Is all that true?" he asked, his voice abrupt. "What they said. Is that how it happened?"

"I..." She swallowed, nodded. "Basically, yes."

"You were at fault?"

Shame churned inside her. "I... I don't like to admit it. But yes."

He studied her for a long moment. His face was stiff and still, but his eyes seemed to burn through her. And then he spoke. "Landon doesn't need that kind of influence."

"What?" That was the last thing she'd expected him to say.

"I'm taking Landon out of tutoring."

She stood, distressed. "But he needs consistency to pass his final tests."

"There are other teachers, online teachers," he said. "Maybe even Ashley."

Ashley. Perfect, innocent Ashley.

There was a noise from the bushes surrounding Dev's porch, and then Landon burst out. He'd obviously been eavesdropping. "Dad! I don't want another tutor, I want Ms. Carver!"

"We need to make a change," Dev said, his voice gentling a little as he looked down at his son.

"I don't want a change!" Landon started to cry.

Emily's heart felt like it was reaching out of her chest toward the little boy. She took a step toward him, but Dev held out a quelling hand.

"I want Ms. Carver to teach me." Landon's voice shook with tears.

Lady whined.

"Go," she ordered quietly, gesturing toward Landon. The dog didn't need a second command. She ran to Landon and nudged him, and he knelt down and hugged the dog, still crying.

"Come on, Landon. Let go of the dog." Dev's voice was flat and gruff.

"I don't—"

"Call her off," Dev said to Emily.

"No," Landon sobbed.

"Now," Dev said.

Her throat felt impossibly tight, but she pushed out the words. "Lady. Come."

The dog hesitated a moment, then wiggled out of Landon's grip and trotted back to Emily.

"Come on," Dev said. He put an arm around Landon's shoulders and ushered him inside.

As she listened to Landon's sobs, Emily's own heart seemed to turn to sand.

Dev spent the rest of the weekend trying to manage Landon's emotions and to stifle his own.

He'd built Emily up into something she wasn't, and now both he and Landon were paying the price. Dev was kicking himself for not realizing what was happening: Landon had gotten way too attached to Emily and to Lady. Losing one meant losing both.

But if he let Landon continue to work with Emily—which meant not only getting tutored, but getting hugs and hot breakfasts and a dog to play with—Landon would learn the lesson that it was okay to cover things up, avoid responsibility, lie about what you'd done. That was what had started him down the wrong road before.

Why hadn't he done his due diligence before agreeing to have Emily tutor his son? After his experience with his wife, he should have known better.

Landon fussed and whined and threw things, reverting to the unhappy kid he'd been under his mother's care. Which served Dev right, and he tried to make things better by skipping church and taking Landon fishing, but Landon was too easily frustrated and neither of them caught anything. Dev was almost relieved when an afternoon storm blew in so he could have an excuse to take Landon home early.

Flashes of Emily's devastated face kept intruding into his anger. Of course, she must feel terrible about what she'd done. She wasn't a monster, and what mother wouldn't grieve hard at the fact that she'd caused her child's death?

He felt sorry for her; he did. He just didn't want to be involved with that kind of person. Couldn't risk Landon's safety getting close to someone that careless and thoughtless, that self-absorbed. She'd known her husband had been drinking, and she'd gone out anyway. She'd left her son in the care of someone who couldn't handle the responsibility because she had Alzheimer's.

Criminal negligence. He'd gotten involved with someone who had been criminally negligent toward her own child.

And there was the crux of it: Dev had gotten involved. He'd started to hope that, once he managed some of his own deficits, he'd be able to build something with Emily, or with the woman he'd thought she was.

He'd been stupid, which was his trademark. He'd made another idiotic mistake, and now Landon was miserable because of it.

When Monday morning came, he was relieved, until he realized that Landon was going to miss tutoring, which meant that Dev would miss his session with Ashley. Not only that, but there was a rehearsal tonight, and he was supposed to work with Emily on the play. He committed himself to a major cleaning of an unused third-floor classroom to give himself time to think.

How could he help with the set, how could he talk in a civilized way to Emily, when he was so angry with her?

Maybe Stan would be willing to take over working on the set this time; the man was handy and liked Emily. Probably a little too much.

He was dimly aware that he, himself, was not living up to his responsibilities. What lesson would he give Landon by quitting the show?

His cell rang, and when he looked at it, he saw his boss's name. Of course, he answered right away. "Hey, Ashley. I'm on the third floor. What's up?"

"Is Landon with you?" she asked.

He straightened and gripped the phone tighter. "No, he should be in class."

"He's not," she said. "A couple of the kids said they saw him leave the building."

Dev blew out a sigh. *Cutting school again, Landon? Really?* It was another throwback to his behavior problems back in Denver. "Thanks for letting me know," he said and started putting his supplies away. Deliberately moving slowly, giving himself time to calm down. "I'll find him."

"Hey, Dev…" Ashley said and paused.

"Yeah?" Was there more?

"Just…don't be too hard on him, when you find him. Kids' progress isn't all in one direction. Give him some grace, okay?"

Grace. Not his strongest suit. "I'll try," he said. "Thanks." And he ended the call and started the hunt to find his unhappy, acting-out son.

Fifteen

At ten o'clock Monday morning, Emily headed into her biweekly meeting with Ashley.

She was dragging, puffy-eyed, but work was the best cure. The meeting happened during her free period, and that was good. The last thing she needed was free, unstructured time. She'd never be able to concentrate on lesson plans or test evaluations, not the way she felt right now.

She'd gotten a double blow on Saturday, with her in-laws' accusations and cruelty and then Dev's rejection. The rest of that day, she'd barely held herself together.

But years of working on her anxiety had shown her how to avoid being debilitated by it.

Sunday, she'd gotten up, taken a long run and then gone to church. She'd forced herself to stay for Sunday school afterward and scored an emergency counseling session with the pastor. She'd gone directly home then, not looking toward Dev's place, and had driven her car—repaired, but still old and loud—to see her mom.

Now, she almost wished she hadn't gone forward

with the car repair. She'd lost her tutoring job, and money was again going to be a struggle.

But she'd also lost her ride to visit Mom. How quickly she'd come to depend on Dev's support and Landon's cuteness to get her through her days.

She'd tried to focus on the pastor's words, tried to trust in God. She'd repeated positive Bible verses to herself all the way to and from Mom's care home.

It had helped. She still felt devastated, and she'd still tossed and turned—and cried some—last night. But today she'd gotten up at her regular time, used the hour she should have been tutoring Landon to take another long run with Lady and then gone to work.

She hadn't let herself focus on what her in-laws had said. It was a well-trodden path, although they'd come up with some new twists and turns. She'd think it through sometime, but not now. She knew herself well enough to understand that diving deeply into the past could devastate her, make her unable to do the job she loved, unable to help the children.

Lady stood close as Emily tapped on Ashley's half-open door. "You ready for me?"

"Sure, come on in." Ashley turned from the desktop computer she'd been typing on, smiled and then did a double take. She leaned forward and studied Emily's face, her expression concerned. "Are you okay?"

"I'm fine." She thought about Dev and Ashley coming out of this very office, laughing together.

Ashley didn't have a horrible sin on her conscience, didn't have a tragedy in her past. Ashley was upbeat and professionally successful. And pretty. She'd be a much better match for a man like Dev.

The idea seemed to be at the top of his mind, too.

He'd immediately mentioned Ashley as a possible tutoring substitute for Emily.

"You sure?" Ashley gestured for her to sit down, then leaned forward, her face concerned. "Dev told me you're not going to be tutoring Landon anymore."

The words hit Emily like blows. Dev had already confided in Ashley about what had happened. "Did he say why?" she asked, her voice hoarse.

Lady leaned against her and whined, and Emily rubbed the dog's side.

Ashley shook her head. "He just asked if I could help him find another tutor."

That was a small blessing, at least—he hadn't gone into the whole ugly story of what Emily had done.

"I know you've needed the money for your mom's care," Ashley said, her voice kind. "If I hear about any other tutoring options that fit your skills, I'll get in touch right away. You're such a wonderful teacher."

Emily swallowed and stared at a spot on the worn rug. Ashley's kindness was harder to bear than outright cruelty would have been.

And Ashley was right about one thing: Emily was a good teacher. She'd really been helping Landon. He'd liked her, and that was important. He'd looked forward to her tutoring sessions, and it wasn't just about Lady's fun presence; she'd tried to make the lessons relevant to his interests, and he'd responded well.

To substitute another student for Landon…no. She'd looked forward to seeing him. She'd let it get personal, let herself take care of him. Let herself care for him. He was a great kid.

Of course, she'd have to take any other job that came around, whether tutoring or something else. In a small community, there weren't a lot of options. When she'd seen her mother yesterday, Mom had been having a good day, laughing with the staff, smiling at Emily, recognizing her.

Emily needed to keep her mom where she was, safe and as happy as she could be. She blew out a sigh and met Ashley's eyes.

"I know I'm technically your boss, but I'm here as a friend if you need one," Ashley said. "But I won't push you. I'm a private person myself."

Ashley's eyes were steady and kind. Ashley was actually a little younger than Emily, but something in her demeanor had always suggested to Emily that the woman had a lot of life experience.

"Dev dumped me from tutoring Landon," she blurted out. "It wasn't my choice. I would never have left Landon in the lurch."

Ashley nodded. "I didn't think so."

"My, uh, my former in-laws came over and raked me over the coals, pretty loudly, and Dev heard something he didn't like about my past."

Ashley frowned. "Are you willing to share what it was?"

Was she? Could she tell the perfect Ashley what she'd done?

She couldn't feel any worse, any more a pariah, than she did right now. "You've seen my burns," she said, holding out her arm.

Ashley nodded.

"They're from a fire that happened when I'd gone out with friends." She swallowed. "I left my two-year-old home with my husband. He wasn't that reliable, he drank a lot, so I asked my mom to come over and help."

"But your mom has—" Ashley broke off, studying Emily's face.

"Alzheimer's," Emily said. "We didn't know it at the time. Her symptoms were just starting to show, and I never would have thought a woman in her fifties...and Mom loved her grandson so much... Well." She cleared her tight throat. Among the sadness of losing her husband and child, there was grief about Mom, the constant, ongoing loss of the woman she'd been. And *for* Mom, who'd lost everything.

"Anyway," she went on, "Mitch, my husband, fell asleep with the baby. And Mom put a pan on the stove, and then she fell asleep, too. It was an old place, and we didn't have the working smoke detectors I'd thought we did. The fire started up fast, and..." She had to pause, collect herself. "Mitch and the baby died from smoke inhalation. Mom was downstairs, so I was able to pull her out."

The night came back to her in vivid detail. She'd called 911 the moment she'd realized it was her house that was on fire, of course, and the volunteer fire department had responded quickly. The dispatcher had told her to stay away from the house, that they'd have ladders to get safely upstairs, but she'd gone in anyway to find her mother wandering downstairs, disoriented.

She'd tried to fight her way to the stairs, but she hadn't been able to get through the flames. She'd pulled Mom out just as the fire trucks had arrived, and she'd screamed at them that her baby was upstairs. They'd put a ladder to the window she'd indicated and gone up, and they'd come out carrying James, and she'd sagged with relief.

Until she'd noticed the faces of the firemen, which

hadn't brightened as they'd carried Mitch out. Though they'd rushed James and Mitch to the hospital, there had been nothing they could do. The lung damage was too great, and they'd both died.

She told Ashley the short version of the story, keeping her voice matter-of-fact while her heart screamed at the telling.

After finishing the story, she looked at Ashley, expecting horror. But instead, the woman's mouth twisted in sympathy. "So…is that really all your fault? Objectively?"

"My in-laws think so. And Dev does, too."

She waved an impatient hand. "What does Dev know? He wasn't there. He heard what your in-laws said, and did he hear any other side of the story? Like yours?"

"My side is the same. It was my fault."

"Really, Emily? Deep in your heart, do you believe you're at fault? Think a minute."

Emily opened her mouth to respond and then shut it again. She thought about what had happened. Had she known Mitch was unreliable? Yes, but she'd tried to cover for that. Had she known her mother had the beginnings of Alzheimer's? Definitely not.

"If I hadn't gone out that night," she said slowly, "they'd still be here."

Ashley nodded, looking sympathetic. "Awful things happen," she said. "But do you mean you should never have gone out? That you should have stayed home with your son every single minute? Was that even possible?"

"No, but—"

"You needed to have friends, have a life, keep perspective. What kind of a mother would you have been if you'd never left the house?"

Ashley's words brought Emily a memory she had forgotten. She'd stayed home with two-year-old James almost all the time she wasn't working, and the strain of it had worn on her. Finally, she'd recognized that she was getting irritable with James and downright angry with Mitch. She wasn't being a good mother or a good wife.

She'd realized how much she missed her friends, how much she needed to get together with them. "I shouldn't have needed to go out. I should have been content with what I had. I didn't know it could be ripped away!" Tears pushed at her eyes, and she blinked, rapidly and hard.

Ashley handed her a box of tissues and then picked up a fancy pen, tapped it on the desk, turned it over, tapped again. "Everyone needs an escape sometimes. Even God rested on the seventh day. You had a two-year-old and worked full-time, right? And a husband who drank? That's a lot."

Emily blew out a sigh. "Yeah. It was." She'd spent so much of the past six years rehashing that one awful night and feeling guilty about it. She hadn't given much thought to the way she'd felt before that, but Ashley's questions were bringing it back to her.

"You tried to take care of yourself, and it backfired in the most horrible way imaginable. That's awful. But does it mean you can't ever take care of yourself again?"

"What do you mean? I run, I eat right—"

"I mean fun. Doing things with friends. Falling in love."

Emily lifted a hand. "Stop. I'm not going there."

But Ashley *didn't* stop. "I've seen how hard you work. How your main recreation is volunteering in town or doing extra jobs at the school. You're very hard on yourself, but you know what? Even that won't keep disaster away. And it won't erase the awful thing that happened to you." She held Emily's eyes steadily. "Through no fault of your own. Understand me? Something awful happened to you, and it wasn't your fault."

The strong statement from a woman she respected opened up a chink in the prison walls Emily had created around herself. A tiny ray of light came in.

"What would God think of what happened? Would He condemn you forever?"

Emily's eyes widened. "No, of course not, because Jesus died for our sins."

Ashley smiled as if Emily were a precocious student. "Exactly."

They sat for a moment, and Emily felt the chink in the walls widen, letting in a little more light.

"I'm disappointed in Dev," Ashley said. "I'm disappointed that he believed your in-laws without finding out the whole story from you."

"I'm disappointed, too," Emily said, surprising herself. "I thought—" She broke off, then studied Ashley's face. "Are you and Dev getting together?"

Ashley looked baffled. And then she laughed. "Oh, because you've seen us together? No, not at all. He's not my type, although I do like him as a friend. And as a friend of both of you, I'm a little mad at him for how he's acting toward you."

Ashley's affirmation brought out something positive in Emily, too. She felt good that Ashley considered her a friend. And she felt *really* thankful that Ashley wasn't dating Dev.

"There's something going on between the two of you, isn't there?" Ashley asked shrewdly. "And don't feel you have to answer that. It's not my business. It's just, I do have eyes."

Emily looked around the office, out the window at the sunny mountain morning. Lady had settled down to sleep beside her. "I can tell you about it," she said, "if you have an hour or so."

Dev was hot and annoyed. He'd be tempted to ground Landon for a year when he found him. For Landon to feel cranky and upset was one thing, that happened to everyone, but skipping school because of it was unacceptable.

He'd looked everywhere he could think of at the school and in its surrounding environment. He still hadn't found Landon, and now his annoyance was laced with worry.

He covered the ground to the cabin in record time and marched inside. "Landon!"

No answer.

"Landon!" His heart pounded as he strode from room to room.

No sign of his son, but there was a sheet of paper on Landon's bed. Big, angry crayon letters covered the page.

Dev studied it, turned it sideways, tried to decipher it. Clearly, it was a note, an effort at communication. But whether it was because of his worry or Landon's poor handwriting—combined with Dev's newly discovered probable dyslexia—the letters just seemed to jump and blur together.

He jammed it into his pocket and took off running. As he sprinted by Emily's cabin, he called out—"Landon! Hey, Landon!"—but there was neither sight nor sound of his son.

He ran back down toward the school, his work boots pounding, swiveling his head from right to left to search. So many places a boy could be.

With no success, he burst into the school office. “I need to see Ashley,” he told Mrs. Henry and strode past her toward the principal’s door.

“But she’s—”

He ignored the mild protest, knocked and then walked in. And saw Emily sitting in front of Ashley’s desk.

Emotions exploded inside him, but there was no time.

“Dev! Emily and I are having a meeting. Is everything okay?”

“I don’t know,” he said, pulling the paper from his pocket and handing it to Ashley. He couldn’t help the feeling of shame that washed over him, but his son was more important than his ego. “Landon’s missing, and he left a note. And I can’t read it.”

Sixteen

"Landon's missing?" Emily jerked herself out of the comforting warmth of her conversation with Ashley. Swept right past Dev's odd declaration that he couldn't read Landon's note. "For how long? Where'd you see him last?"

"Listen." Ashley was studying the note. "It says he wants Ms. Carver to tutor him. He loves her."

Emily's chest warmed. She loved Landon, too. But where was he?

"And he wants to... Let's see. I think it says he wants to help her." She looked up, then passed the note to Emily. "See what you think—you're more familiar with his writing."

Emily studied the crayon letters. Landon had come a long way with writing in just a few weeks. The spelling was phonetic, but that was a stage. It was easily readable. "He, yes, he wants to help me."

"That's it?" Dev sounded stunned. "No clue about where or how?"

Ashley shook her head and moved over to stand beside Emily so they could both study the note. "You saw that he drew a picture of Lady, and books, right? And…is that money?" She pointed at a couple of rectangles on the page.

Emily looked more closely at the drawings. "Yes. I think those are dollar bills. Look, each picture is labeled. *Dog, bok, mune.* Dog, book, money."

"We need to split up," Ashley said. "Where are the most likely places? I'll get Mrs. Henry to help, but we'll give it ten, fifteen minutes before we call the whole staff into action. If he's just hiding, we don't want to bring attention to that, for his sake and to avoid giving the other boys ideas."

"Makes sense." Dev sounded relieved, and Emily felt that way, too. Ashley took the boys' misbehavior in stride. That was why she was a good administrator of a school like Bright Tomorrows.

Underneath Emily's worry about Landon, hope bloomed in her, a fragile flower. Could Landon's shenanigans repair the rift between her and Dev?

But she shouldn't hope for that. A stronger woman would brush her hands together and move on from a man who'd misjudged her so severely, disappointed her so deeply.

Not Emily, though. Yes, she was strong emotionally, strong enough to rebuild her life after a horrible tragedy, but she was weak inside when it came to love. Dev and Landon had opened her heart when she hadn't thought that could ever happen again.

"I need to stay in the school, so I'll take the library and his classrooms. Because he drew books." Ashley was already turning toward the door. "Dev, I hate to say it, but check anywhere Landon knows there's money. Including the petty cash, if he's ever heard you talk about it, and the cash register we use for guests in the cafeteria."

"And the teachers' lounge, in case people have their wallets there," Dev said grimly. "He's never stolen before, that I know of. But if he took the trouble to write and draw money, that could be what he's up to."

"That covers books and money. Emily, figure out what places he associates with Lady and check those out."

"My cabin and yard, I guess," she said, and turned to Dev. "Did you look there?"

"I went through my cabin, but not yours. I didn't see him when I ran past, though." His eyes were dark, hooded, but she knew him well enough to see the emotion underneath. Worry about his son, something more complicated about her. And of course, like a man, he was holding it all inside.

"We'll stay in touch by cell and meet back here in fifteen minutes," he said curtly. "Let's go."

Emily read the fear in his eyes. "We'll find him," she said, but he just gave her an unreadable look and didn't speak. Then they all headed in their separate directions.

Emily was glad she'd been running so much as she jogged toward her cabin, pushing her pace as fast as she could in her work shoes, Lady trotting beside her. Her stomach churned with worry about Landon. Surely he was just hiding, though. It had happened with several other boys at the school—efforts to escape punishment, trouble or their own emotions. Because of the school's open layout, every such case had been resolved in a short time, and successfully.

As she got closer to the cabins she smelled something strange—smoke, but an oily, chemical kind of smoke.

Familiar panic rose in her, and she put her hand down to touch Lady's head. Someone was burning something nearby.

She turned toward her cabin, Lady beside her, and stopped, her heart rate shooting up until her whole chest seemed to rattle, nearly choking her.

Was that fire, shooting from the open door of her car?

Panic rose in her, and she ran faster than she'd ever run in her life. "Landon! Landon!" He couldn't be inside the car, with it on fire. Could he? Was he conscious? Like a nightmare, her past pushed into her mind. Thinking the fire was small, contained; going inside to see that it was actually raging through the house. Hoping her family had fled to the neighbors'; figuring the firefighters could save anyone who hadn't made it out.

And learning just how quickly smoke inhalation could kill a strong man and a healthy toddler. "Landon!" she screamed as she got close enough to feel the heat of the blaze, to nearly choke on the oily fumes.

She heard his voice—from outside, not inside the car, sweet relief—but he sounded panicky. The smoke was thick, heavy, awful-smelling. "Landon, come over here, come toward your house." She coughed as she scanned the area with burning, watery eyes. She couldn't see him. This situation was getting more dangerous every minute the fire burned higher. "Get away from the car! Fast!"

Her phone. She tapped the contact number for Dev. "He's at my house and there's a fire!"

She shoved the phone back in her pocket and ran forward, gagging as the oily smoke seemed to coat her throat and nostrils. Heat surged from the car, and the flames grew higher. "Landon! Where are you? Talk to me, yell to me!"

Lady was beside her, and she heard the dog coughing and choking. "Go back," she ordered, pointing, and then went forward herself. "Landon!"

"I can't put it out!" Landon's voice rose in a wail, and she'd never been gladder to hear anything. She followed the sound, and there he was, by the side of the house where she kept her hose, shooting a weak stream of water at the car.

She pulled him into her arms. "I'm so glad you're safe! You scared me so much!" Lady barked beside her as if to echo her words. "Now, come on, get away from the car!" He was too heavy to pick up, so she pulled at him.

"I hafta put it out or I'll get kicked out of school!"

"No, you don't!" Through her fear and her relief and her memories, the fact that they were still in urgent danger was dawning on her. "Come on, we've got to get away."

"No, I hafta put it out!" He struggled out of her arms.

"The car could blow up and hurt us, Landon!" But the panicky boy wouldn't obey.

Dev burst onto the scene, followed by Ashley and Mrs. Henry. "Landon!" Dev picked up Landon with ease. "Come on, get away from the car! Everybody!"

Ashley was pulling at Mrs. Henry, who'd doubled over, probably sickened by the choking smoke. They ran, stumbling and heaving, away from the flaming car.

For a scary moment, Emily couldn't feel Lady beside her. "Lady!" she called, her voice hoarse and ragged. "Lady!" And then she felt the dog's head beneath her hand, heard Lady gagging and choking. Her instinct to protect hadn't allowed her to run as her animal nature surely wanted to do.

Emily grabbed the leash Lady was dragging and started to run, and then there was an explosion. A huge burst of hot air pushed them forward. Emily stumbled, fell, and Lady stopped beside her, nudging at her. Through her confusion and the pain where she'd landed on her knees, she felt an overwhelming determination: no one else was going to be hurt while she had life and breath. She tried to crawl forward, croaking out commands to Lady to go and run, commands the dog disobeyed.

And then Dev was there, picking her up, carrying her out of range of the now wild inferno while she kept a death grip on Lady's leash.

"Come on, let's go!" They all hustled and encouraged each other, choking, all eyes streaming. Emily turned back to see that the car was completely in flames, and way too close to her cabin. Thankfully, she also heard fire trucks.

They reached Landon, and Dev put her down and went to his son. Emily sat, gasping.

Wild, disconnected thoughts swirled. Another fire. Another child at risk. Another connection to her.

Would bad things always follow her?

But this time, at least, no one had been hurt.

Dev made his way back to his cottage, taking Landon with him, and they returned with bottles of water. The five of them—Dev, Landon, Mrs. Henry, Ashley and Emily—sat on the grassy slope and drank water, caught their breath and watched as the firefighters efficiently put out the small blaze.

The rest of the school had heard, of course. Several

teachers came out, along with Hayley, and then went back to report to the others. They were a community and they cared.

"What were you doing, Landon?" Emily finally asked, since Dev looked too shaken to say anything.

Landon was crying. "I'm sorry."

"I'm sure you are," Ashley said seriously, "but you know setting a fire is a very dangerous thing. You know you're never supposed to do that."

"It was to help Ms. Carver," he protested. "Remember? Mr. Davidson said it would be better if her car burned up so she could get the 'surance money. And she needed money after Dad said she couldn't tutor me anymore." He rubbed his eyes with dirty fists. "I was just trying to help."

All the adults stared at him.

"Well, if that's not the sweetest thing," Mrs. Henry said.

Ashley shook her head. "It's sweet and foolish. Never again, Landon."

Emily's heart melted, and she hugged Landon. "Thank you," she said, her voice breaking. "The way you did it was very, very wrong, but your heart was pure."

Dev looked over at her. "He almost died. Don't encourage him."

Dev was still taking an attitude toward her, which rankled. But Landon and Lady and everyone were safe. Emily wasn't going to focus on one man's negativity, no matter how much she cared for him. She looked up at the sky and whispered her thanks.

"Daddy, I left you a note. I wrote it myself. So you could find it."

"I..."

"Did you read it? Did you?"

He blew out a breath. "I tried. Ms. Carver and Dr. Green helped."

"'Cause you can't read," Landon said, sighing.

Ashley stood and held out a hand to Landon. "Why don't you come with me," she said. "I think the firefighters will want to talk to you."

Landon's lip started to tremble.

"Daddy?"

"He'll be right behind you. He needs a minute with Ms. Carver." She firmly led Landon away.

Emily stared at Dev. "You know," she said, "I'm not going to care what you think, not anymore. You're blaming me for something that's not a sin. Maybe I used bad judgment to thank him for what he did, but I don't think so, because he's already beating himself up and I'm sure there will be consequences. Meanwhile, he needs to know someone loves him."

She stood. "I'm going to go check on my home. Oh, and Dev," she said. "I thought we were friends, at least. So why didn't you tell me you couldn't read?"

On Wednesday, Dev, Landon and Chip pulled into the church parking lot as soon as school was over.

Play rehearsals had been postponed while Emily recovered—she was the only one of them who'd sustained a few burns, and according to Ashley, her PTSD had kicked up enough that her doctor had ordered her to rest. So they'd come to the church. Landon was happy for the chance to skateboard around the church parking lot while Dev met with his cousin.

Dev was mostly just happy Landon was alive and safe.

They'd both had trouble sleeping the night after the

fire. Yesterday had been a day of talking to the fire chief and Ashley, Landon's fearful, shaky apologies, discussions of consequences. They hadn't seen much of Emily; after the school nurse had bandaged her knees and arm, Ashley had driven her to the hospital. She'd been pronounced fine, according to Ashley, just in need of a couple of days off. She seemed to have retreated into her cabin, which thankfully hadn't caught fire nor sustained any water damage.

Dev couldn't think about Emily, not yet. His feelings were too confused. So he focused on Landon. He wanted to figure out what had possessed the boy to take such a radical route to what he wanted, but he also just wanted to keep his son close. Those moments when he'd run toward the burning car, before he'd seen that Emily had Landon and that both were safe, had been the worst of his life.

It kept flooding his mind: how Emily must have felt, losing her child and husband in a fire.

And shame pushed at him because of how he'd judged her. He realized, now, that he himself could be judged just as harshly. He'd upset Landon, hadn't kept on top of his mental state enough to realize how distressed and desperate he was at the notion of losing Emily as a tutor.

He parked the car, and the boys opened the doors and scrambled out. "Landon." Dev used his most serious voice. "Wait a minute. Chip, you can start skateboarding, just here in the parking lot. Landon will join you in a few minutes."

"Aw, Dad..." Landon broke off when he saw Dev's expression.

"This is about getting you some counseling, first

off," he said. "We're going to talk to Uncle Nate about it." That was one part of the agreement that Landon could stay at the school, even after doing something as serious as starting a fire: that he have counseling. And they'd all decided it would be good for him to work with Dev's cousin the pastor, who was trained in doing therapy with young people and who would include a strong spiritual element in the discussions.

"Hey, cousin." Nate came out of the church, his old jeans indicating he was ready to work. Dev had offered to help repair the retaining wall beside the church's outdoor pavilion. "Landon, what's this I hear about you doing something stupid for a very kind reason?"

Landon had to puzzle that one out, but he clearly understood that Nate wasn't angry and wasn't going to take a punishing attitude toward him. He wrinkled his nose and grinned. "I was wrong to set the fire and I know it. And I know I hafta talk to you about it, but do I hafta do it now?"

"Landon," Dev scolded. "Attitude. If Uncle Nate wants to talk to you now, you'll talk to him now."

"But Chip—" Landon glanced longingly toward his friend, who was practicing skateboard passes at the far end of the parking lot. "Yes, sir. Thank you, sir."

Nate smiled. "I think if we set up a half-hour session every Saturday morning, that'll be fine. And we might be able to do it while skateboarding. I'm pretty good at it myself."

Dev laughed. He remembered.

Landon stared. "But you're—" He broke off and looked at Dev.

"I'm old, I know." Nate gave an easy laugh. "I don't take the risks I used to, but I can teach you some tricks.

Now, go practice some ollies with your friend. I've got work to do with your dad."

"Thanks!" Landon ran over to Chip, his board under his arm.

Dev scratched his head. "Really, you still skateboard?"

"Good way to reach the kids. How do you think I sprained my wrist last year?"

"Like Landon started to say, you're old."

"Not as old as you, *primo*." Nate slid easily into using the Spanish word for cousin. "Now, let's get to work and you can tell me the real story about what happened up at the school two days ago."

They went to the shed behind the church and found shovels, trowels, premixed cement and a wheelbarrow. Once they'd carried it all to the site where Nate wanted the wall repaired, they started digging out the broken section.

"Since you said you wanted the real story," Dev said, "I assume that means the rumors are flying."

"They are. Ranging from 'those delinquents tried to burn down the school' to 'that McCarthy boy is a real sweetheart' to 'the new handyman committed a crime of passion to get the attention of the reading teacher.'"

That last one had Dev leaning on his shovel. None of it was true, of course, but the idea of passion toward the reading teacher… "Let me tell you what happened," he said.

So he filled Nate in on the incident, beyond the bare details they'd discussed on the phone. Nate whistled. "You could have lost him, man. Her, too. If that car had blown up any sooner…" He shook his head.

"I know. Thinking about losing Landon has made for some sleepless nights." And was continuing to give him empathy over what Emily had gone through. Empathy that had no outlet, because he hadn't seen her since the fire. He'd texted her a couple of times, had tried to call, but she hadn't answered.

"Well. I'm sure you've talked to him about safety and thinking through decisions, and I'll reinforce that in the counseling sessions," Nate said. "Is he at risk of being expelled from the school?"

"Thankfully, no." Dev pulled out a couple of big rocks, welcoming the effort and the strain on his muscles. The newly uncovered ground sent up an earthy, sage-like smell, unique to this part of Colorado, Dev suspected. "The principal is very understanding. She held a staff meeting and talked about what happened, and everyone got behind giving Landon another chance. Only one, though." He shaded his eyes and looked over to where Landon and Chip played, the picture of happy, carefree boyhood. "I don't think he'll do it again. I think he learned his lesson."

"You thought that last time, correct?"

Dev gave a wry grin and carried more rocks to the wheelbarrow. "Yeah. I did."

"So there's going to be prayer involved as well as counseling and discipline. Because none of us can parent kids without the help of the Lord."

"For sure." Dev didn't often pray with Landon, just reminded him to say his prayers. Maybe that needed to change.

It was Nate's turn to lean on his shovel. "Seems like Landon is pretty fond of Miss Emily Carver. Does that hold for you, too?"

Dev glanced over, realized he couldn't minimize it to his astute cousin and nodded. "Yeah. I care."

"Is it serious?"

Dev shook his head and started laying thick, plaster-like cement over the exposed top of the stones. "No," he said, "because I wrecked it."

"How'd you do that?" Nate carried over a couple of rocks and lined them up where Dev had prepared the wall.

Dev sealed the cracks between the stones and didn't look at his cousin. "I was ashamed because I… I really can't read, much. Tried to hide it, and was a jerk toward her." He'd been judgmental toward her without knowing her whole story, just based on what her in-laws had said. That was his biggest mistake, but he didn't want to go into that with Nate. It was Emily's story to tell or keep private.

His reading problems were part of it, though, and he waited for Nate to express shock about them.

Nate kept bringing over rocks. "Uh-huh."

"Wait a minute." Dev put down his trowel and faced his cousin. "You knew I had problems with reading?"

"I did." Nate glanced over. "Knew you couldn't read, and knew you were ashamed about it."

Huh. Nate knew, and Landon had known, too. Obviously, Dev hadn't kept the big deep secret he'd thought he had.

"You didn't look down on me for it?" He couldn't believe that. Not after being called stupid in several of his foster homes and a couple of schools, not after Roxy's belittling of him.

But Nate just frowned like Dev was being an idiot. "Of course I didn't look down on you. For one thing, you're a child of God no matter what your abilities or disabilities. And for another, you're crazy smart."

"I'm crazy smart." Dev stated it flatly, because the idea was so ridiculous. "Right."

"You are! You've always been able to fix everything in sight—without reading the directions, obviously—and you have a memory like an elephant." He snorted. "Not saying you're smart in every area. You're pretty dumb when it comes to women."

"That's for sure." They went on working, and Dev thought about the conversation.

Nate had turned around Dev's worldview with just a few sentences. Really, he was smart? Dev wouldn't go that far, but he did know Nate was right about his mechanical skills. He could look at an array of disassembled parts—whether of a furnace, a car or a Swedish warehouse bookcase—and see, in his head, how it all fit together. He was always surprised when other people couldn't do the same.

His memory was a product of necessity. He'd had to train himself to recall every word of a lecture in high school, every explanation a teacher had made of how to solve a math problem. Same on the job, and it had just carried over into the rest of his life.

That skills like that bespoke intelligence had never occurred to him.

He knew he wasn't book smart—the total opposite, in fact. But maybe that wasn't the only kind of smart.

For a woman like Emily, though, books and reading were central. And in those areas, Dev was pretty much an imbecile.

Nate had carted off a wheelbarrow load of broken rocks and dirt, and now he came back across the yard with a load of new, rounded stones. As he started laying them atop the cement Dev had troweled on, he spoke.

"Truth is," he said, "I don't think your problems with women—with Emily in particular—have to do with literacy at all."

"What do you mean?" Yeah, he'd been a jerk in other ways, but it all came back to that basic inadequacy in him.

"Reading and writing are important, and I can see why it would be hard to lack skill in those areas," Nate said, starting to sound like the preacher he was. "But those are outward things. I think the real problem is deeper." He turned from his work and tapped his chest. "I think it's your heart."

Here it came, the lecture. Dev spread the last of the cement.

There was something wrong with him, and he'd been told it in so many ways that he'd learned to tune it out.

"In your heart," Nate went on, "you don't believe you're smart and successful enough, *good* enough, to be loved. To have a family. And to be loved by a smart, beautiful woman like Emily—"

Dev went on alert and glared at his cousin. "Wait a minute, you think she's smart and beautiful? What, are you hitting on her?"

"Nope." Nate grinned. "Not that it didn't occur to me, when I first met her. I'm a single guy her age, and she's a great woman. But I could tell she didn't feel a spark. I'm not one to chase after someone who doesn't want me, so I turned my attention elsewhere."

"Good. Keep it there."

"You're creating a distraction from my point," Nate said patiently, as if Dev were a recalcitrant parishioner. "The way you've closed off your heart from love and a family makes sense, given the way you grew up."

"I've gotten over all that." Dev had gone through periods of resentment about the families who'd passed him off to someone else, as an adolescent, but he'd come to peace with it. "I know it's hard for foster parents. Most of them aren't in it to raise a child all the way to adulthood. And I was a handful."

Nate snickered. "You were. But then, so was I. So are most boys." He nodded toward Landon. "Ever think about giving him up? Passing him back off to Roxy? He set a fire, after all."

Dev stared at Nate. "No way!"

"Exactly. And that's how my parents felt when I stole from the corner drugstore and cheated on a math exam. They were angry, they punished me, I learned. But nobody ever thought about giving me away."

Giving him away. No, Nate's parents wouldn't have given him away, any more than Dev would give Landon away.

"You've reconciled what happened in your head, I'm sure," Nate went on. "But your heart knows it wasn't fair, and maybe your heart doesn't want to risk opening up to that kind of hurt again."

This was getting a little too heavy for Dev. "Thanks. I'll think about what you said." He brushed the dirt off his hands and turned away.

"Just don't let it stop here," Nate called after him. "Don't let it define you."

Dev thought about what a jerk he'd been to Emily. He stopped walking, turned back. "I think I already did." Because he'd pushed her away well and hard.

Nate's gaze was steady. "You giving up? He didn't." Nate pointed toward Landon.

Dev looked at his son, still running and playing,

cheeks red, arms and legs pumping, laughter flowing out of his mouth.

Nate was right. Landon had screwed up, both in school and in his behavior. But he wasn't turning into a sullen failure. He'd picked himself up, apologized, worked hard. And he was ready to try again.

Could Dev do any less? "I don't want to give up," he said, "but I really did ruin things with Emily."

"Like I said," Nate said, "you're pretty smart. You can find a way to fix it."

Dev frowned after him, thinking. How did you fix something like what he'd done to Emily?

It couldn't be some quick apology, something that didn't seem sincere. It had to be bigger. And not just six bouquets of roses or a bunch of balloons like you saw on the feel-good shows he and Landon liked to watch in the mornings, while they had breakfast and got ready for the day.

No, for Emily, he needed to do something meaningful.

He stared at the wall they'd repaired, thinking, and it came to him. He knew exactly what he needed to do. "You might have to help me."

"We need water," Chip gasped out in mock drama beside him.

"Help me apologize to Ms. Carver for some things I said and did," Dev admitted.

"Oh, sure, I'll help," Landon said.

Dev wanted to grab his son in his arms and hug him. For being safe, for being helpful, for being an inspiration. But they were guys, so instead, he just pointed at the hose. "Water's over there," he said, and laughed as they ran to soak themselves, not accidentally, while they drank deeply from it.

Seventeen

The Sunday after the fire, Emily sat beside her mother at the little table in her room. An aide had opened a window, and the warm breeze from outside carried with it the smells of pine and sage, the trills and whistles of birds that gathered at the feeders outside. She, Hayley and Ashley had driven here together in Ashley's car, and Emily's friends had gone shopping while she visited her mother. Afterward, they were all going to a concert.

Mom seemed peaceful today. A new exercise routine had done wonders for her mood, according to her caregivers. They'd gotten her to join a group that walked for fifteen to thirty minutes daily, and she'd started doing a gentle strength-training class twice a week. That, combined with an experimental new medication, seemed to be having a good effect. Mom looked almost like she'd used to look, rosy cheeked, her face unlined.

It inspired Emily. "Hey, Mom, I need to talk to you."

"Sure, what's the latest?" It was a phrase Mom had used during their discussions before the diagnosis, and Emily's throat tightened.

She leaned closer to the bed and took her mother's

hand, holding it lightly. "I think I kind of messed up," she said. "I thought I had a, well, a relationship, but it didn't work out."

"The man who comes?" Mom asked.

"Yes."

"I like him," Mom declared. "He has good hair like your father did."

That made Emily smile. Her father had had thick, curly hair. She thought of Dev's hair, how it had felt beneath her hands. "Yes, he does."

"Why are you giving him up?" Mom asked.

"He judged me harshly."

"For the fire?"

Emily tensed. Mom usually got upset when the subject of fire came up. But since she'd gone in that direction mentally, there was no point in trying to turn her back. "Yes. He thinks the fire was my fault."

"It was *my* fault." Mom frowned.

"It was all of our faults." Emily took her hand, her stomach twisting. *Please, Mom, don't freak out now.*

But her mother met her eyes in much the way she'd used to. "I'm sorry," she said simply. "Sometimes, all you can say is I'm sorry. Do you forgive me?"

"Of course I forgive you!" Emily leaned forward and gave her mother a careful hug. "I forgive you for what role you played, if you'll forgive me for what role I played. We both lost so much."

"Ye-es..." Mom looked confused and began to twist her hands. She'd forgotten the subject of their conversation.

Emily went over to the shelf of family picture albums, took one down, and brought it back to her mother's bedside. They'd never looked through it before, because

Emily feared it would upset her mother. In fact, Emily had never looked through it herself; it was an album Mom had made, back when she'd been healthy and into scrapbooking.

But today just might be the day.

She pulled her chair close beside her mother's and opened the album.

The pictures took her rushing back to the past. There was the sonogram, and a photo of herself pregnant. There was James as a newborn, so red-faced and wrinkly.

Oh, how she'd loved him. Loved being a mother.

Mom turned the page and pointed to a photo of herself, holding James, who couldn't have been more than two days old. "Sweet baby," she said.

Emily nodded, blinking back tears. "He was. He really was."

Slowly, they paged forward, looking at the milestones: first smile, first tooth, scooting, sitting up, crawling, walking. Emily was in some of the pictures, Mitch in some, Mom in others. Those had been such good days.

Oh, she hadn't always been happy at those times. She and Mitch had struggled; the partying lifestyle that hadn't bothered her before James's birth had gotten worrisome afterward. She hadn't communicated her feelings well. She was pretty sure she'd nagged him into sneaking around, spending money they didn't have, taking up with a rougher group of friends.

But, as evidenced by the photos, they'd had some good moments. They'd both loved their son.

Mom had, too.

Emily blew her nose and looked at Mom, who was smiling, running a finger over a big studio picture of

James at age one. "He's in Heaven," she said. "I'll see him there, soon."

Emily blinked. "Oh, no, Mom. Not for a long time."

"I'm ready to go."

"No, Mom!" As far as Emily knew, it was possible Mom would live another twenty years. She wasn't even sixty yet. On the other hand, Alzheimer's was a killer. Today, it seemed like Mom knew that.

"When the time comes," she said, "I'll take care of little James for you. And in Heaven, I'll do it perfectly, with no mistakes."

Emily's eyes filled with tears again. "Oh, Mom," she said. "I don't want you to go, but I'm glad you'll take care of him. I know you'll be wonderful at it."

And until that time came, Emily resolved, she'd make sure Mom had all the care and love it was possible for her to have. Today had reminded her that Mom was still here, even behind the curtain of her disease.

Of course, every day wouldn't be this good. Mom was likely to swing back into confusion and distress soon, and Emily knew the proportion of bad days would increase, maybe slowly, maybe quickly.

She could hope that the new regimen would keep Mom with her a little longer. Regardless, Emily would love her and do her best to make sure she could stay here, receiving good care.

Which meant, of course, that she needed to find another job so that she didn't slip back into the money problems she'd had before starting to tutor Landon.

It took most of the concert before Emily had recovered enough from her emotional day with her mother to get into the music.

When she did, she was glad she'd come.

Christine Deschamps was a Christian singer who'd gone back and forth from performing to not performing, whose struggles with a stalker and ultimate happy marriage to her bodyguard had been big in the news. When she sang, it was as if you could hear all that history in her voice and in her music, most of which she'd composed herself. She was beautiful, and talented, and wildly popular…and Ashley happened to know her. So after the concert, they were able to meet her in her dressing room and share girl talk and faith talk, until her husband and bodyguard, Logan Scott, knocked on the door and suggested she finish up so they could get home. She insisted he come in and meet her friends, old and new. They all left a little bit starstruck.

"That bodyguard-slash-husband was seriously hot," Hayley said on the ride home. "Why don't I ever meet somebody like that?"

"Christine went through some very hard times in order to meet him," Ashley said from the driver's seat. She maneuvered the mountain road skillfully, at a slow pace that was appropriate for the darkness.

"Didn't you think so?" Hayley asked Emily, turning around from the passenger seat. Emily had insisted on taking the back seat, because she'd been grateful that they had driven her to her mother's place. And maybe a little so that she could keep it to herself if she got emotional.

She felt scraped raw. The past that had come up today, with Mom, and Mom's up-and-down state generally, was a constant presence in the back of her mind. Landon and Dev were another. They'd seen each other during the past week; Dev had made courteous inquiries about her injuries and how she was doing, and she'd checked on Landon. But it had all stayed at a distant, impersonal level after the huge, heavy emotions of the fire.

The fact that Dev couldn't read, or not well, had shocked her at first. He was so *good* at things, it was hard to imagine he had such a major deficit.

And it was hurtful that he hadn't seen fit to tell her, when they'd talked so much about Landon's literacy needs. You'd think it would have come up. Didn't he trust her?

But in the days since, she'd thought more about it and even gone back to one of her old textbooks that talked about adult illiteracy, something she hadn't studied nearly as much as children's issues with reading. It was a more common problem than most people realized, simply because a lot of adults found ways to work around it. Also, it was embarrassing to many who struggled. Expecting Dev to be open about it was probably asking too much.

That part she could understand. But he'd also put her down, thought the worst of her, blamed her. He'd placed himself squarely in her in-laws' camp, and now she felt like she couldn't trust him.

"Well, didn't you?" Hayley persisted from the front seat.

"Didn't I what?" Emily needed to get out of her own head and pay attention to her friends.

"Didn't you think Christine's husband, Logan, was hot?"

"Truthfully? I barely noticed him. I'm a little distracted." She meant by her day with her mother.

But Hayley narrowed her eyes. "By Dev? I can't

think of any other reason you'd barely notice that amazing specimen of manhood."

"Stop objectifying Logan," Ashley said. "He's a smart guy who walks the talk of his faith. And he treats Christine like a queen."

"Okay, okay, sorry." Hayley raised a hand. "My bad. Emily. Tell us what's distracting you and making you so quiet back there."

"Well, it's a little bit about Dev. Maybe more than a little," she said. "But it's also about my mom. Since I've lost the tutoring job, I'm going to have to find a way to keep paying the bills."

"Are you sure you've lost the tutoring job? Did you talk to Dev about it?" Ashley glanced over her shoulder. "I'm pretty sure he'd rehire you. You were doing so much good with Landon."

"I miss him," she admitted. "But the thing is, I was getting too attached and so was he."

"You're not too attached," Hayley said, "if you and Dev get together. Then, it'll be good if you're attached to his son."

"Yeah." Emily swallowed. "But that's not happening. And the truth is, I have an interview for another job."

Ashley braked and glanced back over her shoulder. "You *what*?"

She sighed. "I might as well tell you. It's an hour in the other direction from Mom's place. It's a private school, and it pays more, enough that I could keep Mom in her care home easily. I don't want to go, don't get me wrong. But…there are reasons it would be good for me to leave in addition to the one we've talked about, Landon getting too close."

"Reasons like what?" Hayley sounded like she was about to cry. "I can't handle it if you go."

"I know. I'm still thinking about it. I value my friends at Bright Tomorrows, so much. But the truth is..." She paused.

To their credit, like the good friends they were, Ashley and Hayley didn't rush her.

"The truth is, I don't think I can stay here and watch Dev and Landon from afar. I care. Too much, and not just as a friendly colleague or a tutor."

"Are you sure it's not about money?" Ashley asked. "Because we could work on a little bit of a raise..."

"And Pastor Nate has a potential job at the church, helping interpret for the Spanish-speaking community. I'm sure you could get it."

She shook her head. "You're both sweet, but it's not about that, as much as the other. That I can't..." Her throat tightened too much to speak as the possible future formulated before her.

Dev waving, unsmiling, as he'd done for the last week. Landon moving on with another tutor.

Dev moving on with another woman.

"It's okay." Hayley reached back and patted her leg, and Ashley turned up the radio, and Emily had the time to collect herself.

When Emily got dropped off at her place, she hurried inside, wanting Lady. She'd gone out on a limb and asked if Landon could feed her and let her out, for pay, checking with Dev first. By impersonal text, and he'd responded equally impersonally that it was fine, the responsibility and the chance to earn a little money would be good for Landon.

That was what she had to look forward to, she thought

as she let Lady out and then ushered her back inside. She sat down on the couch, and Lady jumped up beside her, seeming to know that Emily needed comfort.

She and Dev would be impersonal friends, colleagues. Maybe she'd give Landon a hand from time to time. Maybe she'd refocus on rebuilding her life as a single person. She could go on some of those women's trips Hayley was always asking her to go on. She could go out at night. Go out with someone who wasn't Dev.

She rested her face on Lady's sturdy side. "I just don't want that," she murmured to the dog.

Something brushed against her face. She looked and noticed, for the first time, that there was a plastic bag attached to Lady's collar with twist ties.

She pulled it free and looked inside.

She smiled a little. This looked like Landon's work. She opened the plastic bag and drew out the paper.

A letter. But it wasn't from Landon. She started to read.

Early the next morning, Dev paced in his kitchen, looking over at Emily's house.

Had she gotten the letter? Had she read it?

Had she despised it? Laughed at it?

It was six thirty. In half an hour, Landon would be up and wanting breakfast. And then Landon would have to go to school, and Dev to work. And he wouldn't know how Emily had reacted.

Now or never. He gathered his courage, strode across the two yards and knocked on Emily's door.

She opened it immediately, a cup of coffee in her hand. She didn't say a word, although her eyes were wide with some kind of emotion he couldn't interpret.

And then he saw that the letter was in her other hand.

"Did you—could you—read it?" he asked, stumbling over his words. His heart hammered like a drum.

She nodded. "Of course I did. Of course I could. Thank you."

"You're welcome." He stood then, looking at her. Wasn't she going to react any more than that?

Of course, maybe it wasn't a big deal to her. After all, she wrote letters all the time.

Or maybe she'd been shocked at how rudimentary was his spelling, his handwriting, his style. "I didn't have anyone check it," he stammered. "I just, I didn't want anyone else but you to read it. I warned Landon before he put it on Lady's collar that he wasn't to try to read it." He held his breath.

She came out onto the porch, put her arms around his neck and kissed his cheek. "It was a beautiful letter, Dev. I appreciate the apology, and I would never judge you for what's probably a reading disability, and which is definitely not your fault."

"I should have known that," he said. "I know your kindness. I know you don't make fun of people or look down on them. I should have trusted you more."

She smiled at him. "Yes, you should have."

But she wasn't softening the way he'd hoped she would. Maybe because he hadn't been able to say all he felt in that letter he'd labored over for hours. "Can we sit down a minute?"

She looked back toward her kitchen. "Um, sure." She was dressed for work, in a blue-and-white-striped dress, tied at her slender waist, flowy around her legs. She sat on the top step and tucked her legs under her.

"Look," he said, "I'm not the most articulate guy,

and definitely not on paper. I wanted you to see that I trust you now, but…there's more to say."

"Yeah?" She snapped her fingers, and Lady came to her side and leaned against her.

She needed emotional support to be around Dev. Well, he'd earned that. He'd been awful to her. And while his apology might have helped, she still didn't quite trust him, and understandably so.

He sucked in a breath and prepared to make the speech of his life. "Emily, I just want you to know that I think you're an incredible woman. You're beautiful, but that's not it. You're kind and good." He needed to show her the words weren't just empty, and that was easy to do, because the examples crowded into his mind. "You're wonderful with the kids, and you've helped me and Landon feel at home here. You volunteer at the church and in the community, but you always have time for your friends. And you're smart, smarter than I'll ever be."

Finally, she cracked a smile. "Well, smart at books. I'm not smart at repairing a car or building a stage set."

"But see, that's why we'd make a good team," he said. "You're good at some things, and I'm good at others, and we could help each other become better. Or just do things for each other. I'd fix your car anytime."

Two vertical creases formed between her eyebrows. "What are you suggesting? A business partnership?"

Lord, show me how to do this better. He took her hand and squeezed it, gently. "No. I'm proposing we get to know each other better."

Her eyes widened. "You mean like dating?"

"Like dating. I would love to take you out to the movies, or a nice dinner. Or on a romantic picnic." Yeah, he'd love that a lot. "I'd like to give you the chance to get to know me better, and then maybe, if you did..."

The front door of his cabin opened. Landon came out, spotted them and ran over at top speed. "Did you ask her?"

"Ask her what, son?" He put an arm around Landon, who'd gotten dressed but clearly hadn't washed his face, combed his hair or brushed his teeth yet. The kid was a mess.

"To marry you!"

Dev's jaw nearly dropped. He stole a glance at Emily. She looked shocked, too. Her cheeks were pink.

"Landon, I wasn't—"

"It's okay with me. I want you to marry her, and she could be like my mom..." He frowned, obviously thinking it through, while Dev tried to figure out how to stop this premature, kid-created marriage proposal. "Like my second mom, and Lady could be partly my dog." He ducked out from under Dev's arm and moved over to Lady, putting both arms around her.

Lady licked his face.

Dev's own face felt hot. Should he backtrack, back off, deny what his son had said?

But from somewhere in his heart, he found the courage and strength to seize the opportunity. He turned toward Emily and took her hand. "Look, Landon kind of jumped the gun. I didn't intend to say that today, to propose, but it's what I had in mind."

She looked skeptical. "Really, Dev?"

Tell the truth. You don't have to hide your real self from her. "Really. Hey, Landon, why don't you take Lady over to our yard and run around with her for a few?"

"Yeah!" Landon jumped up, then looked at Emily. "Is that okay?"

"Um, I guess?" She brushed her hands through her hair as Landon and Lady took off.

Game time. Dev got on one knee, his heart pounding. "Emily, I do want to marry you. Nothing would make me happier, because you're the best woman I've ever known, and when you smile, it's like the sunrise." He sucked in a breath.

She bit her lip, her mood unreadable.

He'd started, so he needed to finish. "I know this is way too fast and I have a lot to prove. I was so quick to judge you, and I'm not… Well." He looked down, then back into her eyes. "I wasn't going to ask you until I'd gotten better at reading," he said. "Someone like you, so smart, such a book person, I know you couldn't consider—"

"Dev. Wait." Her voice sounded a little shaky, and she squeezed his hand and dropped it. "Please don't tell me all the things that are wrong with you, just tell me if you…if you really mean it, what you're saying about how you feel."

He moved up to sit beside her and wrapped one arm around her, gently. "I've never meant anything more," he said. "I love you, Emily."

"You…" She pressed a hand to her mouth. "You're not just saying that?"

"I'm not just saying it, and I'm not just following Landon's lead. Although it matters a lot, how much he cares for you." He drew in a breath and told her what was true. "I'm sincere in wanting to marry you. When you're ready. If you're ever ready. No pressure."

* * *

Emily looked into Dev's eyes, so anxious, so warm. Emotions rose in her, and she put a hand over her mouth. "You just asked me to marry you."

Somewhere across the yards, she could hear Lady barking and Landon shouting. Here on the porch, there was only Dev. Handsome, nervous, flawed, wonderful Dev.

"Is there any chance you'll say yes? Not now, but if I can prove to you that I'm a man worthy of marrying? Even though I messed up pretty badly, and I'll probably do it again and again?"

"You're forgiven." And it was true. He'd been wrong to judge her, but he was admitting his mistakes. What more could a woman ask?

"Then you'll think about it?"

She touched his cheek. "I will. You're a wonderful father and a caring man, and… I really care about you." She paused, then let herself say the wonderous truth. "I care about you, and I…yeah. I think, no, I know… I love you."

She felt dazed, renewed, joyous. Thankful. So very thankful.

Dev put a hand on either side of her face. "You just made me so happy. I don't have words for it, except… I'll say it again. I love you, Emily." And then he kissed her.

And she melted into his arms, her heart full. This wonderful man wanted to marry her, and as she searched inside herself, she realized that the last bitter chains around her heart had broken, leaving her free. Free to love. Free to allow herself happiness. Free to reach for joy.

He lifted his head. "I'm so glad you didn't turn me

down flat," he said, laughing a little. "Man, when Landon blurted that out… I did plan a better buildup. And I'll do a proper proposal, with a ring, when we've had a chance to really date. I want to show you how well I can treat you, Emily. Not just as a coworker and team player and neighbor, but as a man who's crazy in love with you."

"That sounds wonderful," she said, "and I want you to do it. I *really* want it, so don't think you can get out of it! But Dev." She laid a hand along his clean-shaven cheek. "The truth is, I don't need time. When you pulled me out of that fire, I knew how I felt. So…yes. I love you, and I want to marry you. The sooner, the better."

Dev whooped and picked her up and twirled her in his strong arms. "She said yes!"

And then Landon and Lady were jumping around them both, and Dev kissed her right there in front of them. And then they all hugged, and Stan came out of his cabin to see what all the fuss was about.

And then they went to work, because the world didn't stop just because they'd fallen in love and decided to get married.

It only felt like it had.

Epilogue

Two months later

"I really don't want to do this." Emily sat in the Mountaineer Café, drinking coffee with Ashley and Hayley, Lady dozing on the floor at their feet. Around them, bridal magazines and books on wedding planning were scattered over the table.

She looked longingly over at Dev and Landon, who sat at a table on the other side of the restaurant with Pastor Nate. Landon was fidgeting, playing with an action figure, nearly knocking over a glass of water. Dev looked almost as fidgety.

She wanted to go over there and hug him. Wanted to be with him and Landon. Even though they'd spent nearly every day since getting engaged together, it wasn't enough. She couldn't wait to start being a real family together.

"If you're getting married, you have to start planning your wedding," Ashley insisted. "That's why we're here, because when we're on campus, you always find other things to do."

"It's our version of an intervention," Hayley said. "If you don't start planning now, the campus is going to combust with all the romance swirling between you and Dev." She clapped her hand to her mouth. "I'm sorry. Fire metaphors are so wrong with you."

Emily patted Hayley's arm. "It's okay," she said. And it was. She'd truly resolved her feelings, with the help of Dev and an assist from Pastor Nate, who'd been doing some premarital counseling with them. "There *is* a lot of romance between us. We can't wait to get married. It's just, neither of us is that interested in this stuff." She waved a hand at the books and magazines.

"Maybe you should just run away together," Hayley suggested.

Ashley clapped her hands. "Not a bad idea. We could stop hounding you about wedding planning."

"That sounds wonderful." Emily propped her cheek on her hand. "But it won't work. Landon has to be involved, and we want a church wedding."

She sighed and looked over at Dev, Nate and Landon. Nate had a laptop out and was looking at Dev with an expression of impatience.

Dev caught her eye and mouthed the word *help!*

"You know," Emily said slowly, "maybe we don't have to run away. Maybe we could just sort of elope right here in town."

Hayley's forehead wrinkled.

But Ashley lifted her hands, palms up. "Why not? Hey, Nate! Dev, Landon, c'm'ere!"

Landon ran over, followed more slowly by the two men.

Dev put a hand on Emily's shoulder and squeezed,

and they shared a smile. She felt so much better just being close to him.

"Pull up some chairs," Ashley ordered, showing her leadership skills. "We have a proposition."

Nate raised his eyebrows. "Oh, you do, do you?"

"We do." And quickly Ashley summed up the elopement idea. "I'd suggest doing it today, but I'm sure there are legal details to manage."

Nate looked thoughtful. "Not really. All you have to do is drive over to the county clerk's office. It's pretty relaxed here in Colorado."

"No waiting period?" Dev asked.

Nate shook his head. "No. And no witnesses needed. As a matter of fact, I knew one couple who had their dog sign their marriage license."

Landon's eyes lit up. "Could Lady sign?"

Emily put an arm around him and ruffled his hair. "Only if you sign, too."

"I can do that! I'm good at writing now!"

"You are *so* doing this," Hayley said. "Pastor Nate, I know Mondays are usually your day off, but do you have time to perform a wedding?"

Nate looked at his watch, laughed and nodded. "For my favorite cousin, I think I can fit it in."

"I have a white sundress you can borrow," Ashley said to Emily.

Emily felt breathless in the best possible way. She looked at Dev. "What do you think?"

His forehead wrinkled. "I want you to have the wedding you want. Flowers, bridesmaids, the works."

"The works isn't what I want," she said. "I just want to be married to you. With as little fuss as possible."

His face broke into a huge smile. "I for sure just

want to be married to you. As soon as possible. The less fuss, the better." He turned to Nate. "Could we really do it today?"

"If you get in the car with your fiancée and hit the county clerk's office."

"And we'll stay back here and get things ready," Hayley said. She hugged Emily. "This is perfect!"

Emily couldn't have agreed more.

So it was that on Monday, July 21, in their own church, with a few friends, Landon and Lady all sitting in the front pews, Emily and Dev were married.

Afterward, they had dinner at the only restaurant in the area that was open on a Monday. Emily felt joyous, surrounded by her friends, safe at her new husband's side.

Her only regret was that she hadn't been able to have her mother attend. But it was doubtful Mom could have come to any wedding, and they'd agreed to visit her as soon as they got back from their short, thrown-together honeymoon at a nearby mountain lodge.

After dinner, Emily and Dev walked everyone to their cars. Landon was going back to stay with Hayley for tonight, and then he'd spend a couple of days with his friend Chip, whose family lived nearby.

Lady would go on their honeymoon with them, helping Emily with her bridal jitters.

Although she mostly felt happy, not jittery. They waved to their friends and then turned to each other. The sun set behind the mountains, and Dev pulled her into his arms.

Another kiss, this one just for the two of them. Deeper, lasting longer than the one they'd shared in the church.

"You're sure this was okay?" Dev asked. "You don't feel shortchanged without the big to-do?"

"Not at all. I feel blessed." And as she wrapped her arms around him and laid her head against his strong chest, Emily felt at home.

The sun sent its last rays into the darkening sky, and it felt like a benediction. She couldn't stop the smile from spreading across her face.

There had been darkness, sadness, loss. But it was just as the psalmist said, just as Nate had quoted in their marriage service: *Weeping may endure for a night, but joy cometh in the morning.*

Emily's long time of weeping was past, and she lifted her face to the heavens in thanksgiving.

Now was the season of joy.

* * * * *